Praise for *The Past*

D0204736

Winner of the 2018 Willie Morris Award for Southern Fiction

Winner of the 2019 Mississippi Author Award for Adult Fiction
selected by the Mississippi Library Association

Winner of the 2019 Mississippi Institute of Arts
and Letters Award for Fiction

Winner of the 2018 Janet Heidinger Kafka Prize for Fiction

"Haunting and beautiful, steeped in history and myth, *The Past is Never* unwinds the darkest knots of what binds families together and reveals the marvels and monsters which lie within us all. In lucid, piercing prose, Tiffany Quay Tyson pushes to the raw edge of life, where the real and the unreal almost touch. This is great southern fiction."

—Kent Wascom, award-winning author of
The Blood of Heaven and *Secessia*

"You hold in your hands *Stranger Things* but with a satisfying ending. In the sort of cleanly tuned prose that makes another fiction writer happy, Tyson penetrates your imagination with characters and places so real they feel like your own suppressed memories. I'll never look at the Everglades the same way again."

—Carrie La Seur, award-winning author of *The Home Place*

"Wise, disturbing, and quietly powerful, *The Past Is Never* is an American novel for our time. With rare and unflinching honesty, Tyson shows us the darkness, then reaches into it and extracts light. The discovery is breathtaking."

—Margo Catts, author of *Among the Lesser Gods*

"Tiffany Quay Tyson has written a gripping novel steeped in the Southern gothic tradition, with a compelling mix of contemporary grit. Dark as the quarry that spooks a Mississippi town and twisty as the Florida mangrove tunnels traversed in search of answers to unraveling family mysteries, *The Past is Never* had me turning pages long into the night."

—Kelly J. Ford, author of *Cottonmouths*

"Tyson writes characters so distinct you'll swear you can hear their footsteps outside your reading room, and does so in prose so elegant you have to remember to breathe. *The Past Is Never* is a beautiful, moving, brilliant novel."

—Benjamin Whitmer, author of *Cry, Father* and *Pike*

"Creatures, real and imagined, fact and fable, inhabit Tiffany Quay Tyson's South, a place stranger than life and all too real. *The Past Is Never* will alter your vision, make you see anew things you thought you already knew. It's a flash of lightning in a summer storm."

—William Haywood Henderson, author of *Augusta Locke*

"A sumptuously written novel."

—Theresa Alan, *New York Times* bestselling author

"Tyson offers an intriguing exploration of family and identity alongside the complexities and emotions of life's haunting regrets."

—*Booklist*

"An ode to William Faulkner. . . . As Southern as it gets."

—*Deep South* magazine

"Mesmerizing Southern Gothic. . . . The author's skillful storytelling reaches a high mark with this novel. Nothing is as it first appears in this dark, complex story that draws upon inner strength, extended family ties and personal determination. As with her first novel, Tyson has an award winner on her hands."

—*The Clarion-Ledger*

"Haunting, mysterious, and at times very disturbing, *The Past is Never* is an extraordinary example of Southern Gothic literature . . . one that is certain to keep you up long into the night."

—*The Literary South*

"Tyson's rich prose turns the Everglades into another world, distinct from Mississippi but just as mysterious."

—*The Florida Book Review*

"A notable contribution to Southern gothic fiction. . . . Tyson's stylistic writing and unique voice bring the reader into the heart of the Mississippi Delta and create an eerie atmosphere similar to that of William Faulkner's *Sanctuary* and William Gay's *Twilight*."

—*New Orleans Review of Books*

"Tyson's novel is a profound entry point toward the region's many interconnected caves and deep mysteries."

—*Entropy* magazine

"*The Past is Never* reads like a new kind of southern fiction."

—*bottoddy.com*

the past is NEVER

a novel

TIFFANY QUAY TYSON

Skyhorse Publishing

First Paperback Edition 2019

This is a work of fiction. Names, places, characters, and incidents are either the products of the author's imagination or used fictitiously.

Skyhorse Publishing books may be purchased in bulk at special discounts for sales promotion, corporate gifts, fund-raising, or educational purposes. Special editions can also be created to specifications. For details, contact the Special Sales Department, Skyhorse Publishing, 307 West 36th Street, 11th Floor, New York, NY 10018 or info@skyhorsepublishing.com.

Skyhorse® and Skyhorse Publishing® are registered trademarks of Skyhorse Publishing, Inc.®, a Delaware corporation.

Visit our website at www.skyhorsepublishing.com.

10 9 8 7 6 5 4 3 2

Names: Tyson, Tiffany Quay, author.
Title: The past is never : a novel / Tiffany Quay Tyson.
Description: First edition. | New York : Skyhorse Publishing, Inc., [2018]
Identifiers: LCCN 2017042996 (print) | LCCN 2017046307 (ebook) | ISBN 9781510726833 (ebook) | ISBN 9781510726826 (hardcover : alk. paper) | ISBN 9781510747814 (paperback)
Subjects: LCSH: Magic realism (Literature)--Fiction. | Delta (Miss. : Region)--Fiction.
Classification: LCC PS3617.U39 (ebook) | LCC PS3617.U39 P37 2018 (print) | DDC 813/.6--dc23
LC record available at https://lccn.loc.gov/2017042996

Cover design by Erin Seaward-Hiatt
Cover photo courtesy of iStockphoto

Printed in the United States of America

The past is never dead. It's not even past.
—William Faulkner, *Requiem for A Nun*

For John, always

THE CREATURE WATCHED AND *waited. It crouched just beyond the trees or beneath the waterline or over the horizon, just beneath the shifting sugar sand or just above the clouds, up beyond the stars. It waited for me. It will wait for you, too.*

I don't know how long I floated beneath the hot sun, how long I drifted in the land of alligators and crocodiles, where men walk on water, where God and the Devil shake hands, where the dead rise up to live again. At some point my body stopped sending signals to my fevered brain. I stopped wanting water or food. I stopped clawing at the stinging welts from the mosquitoes and black flies. The numbness from my leg spread across my body. Soon, I guessed, I'd feel nothing at all. Thank goodness. Thank God.

My life never flashed before my eyes; instead it unfolded like a child's picture book. And other people's lives, other people's memories, other people's stories came to me, as well. I recognized some of the people, and some were strangers to me, but I knew them all. We were joined together and there was no way to tell me from you or you from me, no way to separate sisters and brothers, mothers and fathers, friends and enemies. There was no past or future. Everything that ever happened existed in a single moment. We were all connected.

A large black bird circled above me, waiting for me to die. I smelled fires burning from one hundred years ago. I smelled the clean sweat of a man swinging a pickax. I smelled cornbread and stewed collard greens. I smelled the sweet scent of brambleberries growing wild in the haunted woods. I smelled stale smoke from my mother's cigarettes. I smelled the damp rotting decay of my father's body. I smelled my sister's hair; it smelled of summer. I smelled the metallic threat of rain. I smelled my grandmother's lemon pound cake. I smelled my brother's clothes after a long night on the water, briny and sharp. I smelled mustard and onions. I smelled the damp clay from the quarry and the sulfur-ripe stench of spent fireworks.

People talk about heaven and hell, about seeing the light or the darkness, but I got no sense of an afterlife. No angels descended to comfort me. No fire-and-brimstone visions. Only a man in a boat. A man both familiar and strange. And as I floated across the water, I wished I could go back. I wished I could return to the day when we first came here, when we first navigated the fresh rivers and the brackish swamps, when we swung beneath the mangrove tunnels, our monkey arms sunburnt and tight, when the swamp chicken called us forward, when the anhinga stretched, stretched, stretched its wings, when we touched pineapple plants sprouting from nothing more than humidity and hope, when we saw the strangling fig choke the bald cypress and I mistook it for a hug.

But no.

I wished to go back even further.

I wished to go back to the beginning. Or I wished to skip forward to the end. It came to me, floating on that small boat in the Gulf of Mexico: the beginning and the end were the same thing.

And monsters were everywhere. And dead men walked on water.

ONE

IT WAS AUGUST AND hotter, somehow, than July, a heavy, smothering heat that left us sticky and restless even in the dark of night. It rained most afternoons in the Mississippi Delta, violent thunderstorms from soft gray skies. The rain should have brought relief but when the clouds parted and the sun came out, steam rose from the dead grass and the cracked asphalt and the brown fields, and it was hotter still. Folks who believed in voodoo or signs from above said the heat was a warning. We didn't believe in superstitions back then, but we were wrong to dismiss things we could not see.

In the summer of the bicentennial, we wore red, white, and blue. The cheap colors faded quickly, like sparklers burning out on a summer evening. We spent the long sweltering days together. We watched bad sitcom reruns on television, ate sugary cold cereal for lunch, read books we pulled from dusty shelves, and complained about the heat and the humidity and the boredom and our lives.

Willet, at sixteen, complained the loudest. *It's hotter'n a bitch in heat*, he'd yell upon waking. Or *I'm sweating like a pimp in Sunday school!* He refused to wear a shirt or shoes. Teenage boys could get away with being crude and half-dressed, but girls had to remain fully clothed and weren't allowed the relief of profanity. Instead of cussing, we whined. Pansy, just six years old, had mastered the skill of prying ice from the plastic tray in the freezer. She'd suck on the cubes while lying still as a corpse in front of the box fan in the living room. The heat left me restless. Like any fourteen-year-old girl, I yearned for something new to happen, something different or interesting or scandalous.

I sat beside Mama on the living room couch, an old, faded, overstuffed floral monstrosity that once belonged to her mother, the grandmother for whom I was named. I lifted a thin blue towel from the plastic basket to fold. You can bet Willet and Pansy never helped with the laundry. "Where is Daddy? What is he doing? When will he come home? Why does he leave?" My questions went on and on.

Our father had been gone for three weeks. He'd disappeared the week after the town's Fourth of July celebration, when I'd eaten myself sick on hot dogs and peanut brittle, when Willet had nearly lost a finger to a Roman candle, when Pansy had fallen asleep under the live oak in front of the courthouse. His absence wasn't unusual. Daddy often disappeared for a stretch—traveling for work, he said—but the details of his work were vague. He wasn't like other fathers. He didn't sit behind a desk all day or wear a tie. He didn't come home at night and sit in front of the television with a stiff drink. He didn't mow the lawn on weekends or putter around in our garage. He wasn't interested in the news of the day. Daddy lived in the past, in the murky netherworld of legend and lore. *Everything that might happen in this world has already occurred*, he would tell us. *There is nothing new.* Daddy showed up and disappeared without warning. We were expected to be glad to see him, and mostly we were. He was charming in the way dishonest men have to be and too handsome for his own good. He bore a striking resemblance to Paul Newman. He said so himself.

That summer, he and Uncle Chester spread counterfeit bills all over the south. They made no secret of it. They bleached five-dollar bills until they turned a soft pale gray, and then printed them as fifties and hundreds. Daddy was proud of their work. The five-dollar bills were the perfect canvas, not so soft as one-dollar bills. Folks might get suspicious if a hundred-dollar bill was too soft, he said. They laundered the cash by spending it. A few hundred dollars' worth of merchandise could be bought and returned. The refund cash was real. Cashiers couldn't detect the fake bills. Some cashiers swiped larger bills with a pen from the bank, but the pen only outed bills on bad paper; Daddy's canvas was legit.

Sometimes Daddy and Uncle Chester sold their bills. Men in trouble with the law or unable to find steady work would show up at our front door and ask to invest in some art. Daddy would sell them a fifty-dollar bill for twenty-five dollars, or a hundred-dollar bill for forty. Mama hated when these men showed up, hated the desperation in their eyes and the dirt on their hands. They had a way of shuffling and mumbling that drove her near crazy, and she begged Daddy to find another line of work or at least keep the counterfeiting away from our house. *We have children*, she reminded him, as if he might forget. It did seem possible he might forget about us on one of his long trips. I didn't like it when Daddy went away.

I often pestered Mama about Daddy's absences, asked her when he would come home. Willet would scold me, tell me not to ask questions when there ain't no answer. He protected Mama, even before things got real bad.

Mama snatched the towel out of my hand. She hated it when I went on and on about Daddy. She didn't have any answers for me. "For God's sake, Roberta Lynn."

Mama was the only one who called me by my whole name. I hated it. It was old-fashioned and sounded like the name of someone destined for a career in country music or who would someday have too many children. I couldn't carry a tune and I had no dreams of motherhood. I greatly preferred being called Bert. I was a tomboy, always trying to keep up with my brother. At a time when prairie skirts and gingham blouses were the style, I wore overalls and faded T-shirts. Willet said I was a roughneck. I wasn't a hundred percent sure I understood what he meant, but I got the gist. It was an insult, but I didn't mind.

When Mama got fed up, when she got sick of our whining and my persistent questions, she kicked us out. "I don't want to see one freckle on your faces until suppertime, you hear me?"

She got like that, especially when Daddy was gone for too long. We grabbed a few things and fled, letting the screen door shut hard behind us, because the slamming sound drove Mama crazy.

Once exiled, we always went to the same place, the forbidden and abandoned rock quarry, a two-mile journey across blistering asphalt and through choking dust. The sun shimmered like an oil slick. It had a way of making folks see things that weren't there or maybe things that weren't there anymore. On that hot August day, Pansy swore a wild dog was bounding toward her from the bottomland hardwoods. Willet tried to hitch a ride on a phantom farm truck. Something dry and cool slid across my bare foot, a water moccasin seeking moisture. When we reached the quarry, we kept right on walking until we stepped over the edge and sank hard into the cold, dark water, the first plunge a small death.

Daddy said the quarry was a mile deep. Sometimes he told us stories about how the quarry was dug and how the men who unearthed those stones suffered and died. He warned us away from the quarry and from the woods surrounding it. "It's an evil place," he told us. "The Devil will find you there."

We ignored his warnings, desperate to immerse ourselves in cool water.

Earlier that summer, Willet had strung up an old rope on a live oak tree. We took turns swinging out over the water and dropping in, plunging deeper each time.

The country club in town had a swimming pool full of cool, clean, chlorinated water, but we were not members of the country club and never would be. Daddy said it was evil for different reasons. It was a place where white men played golf and smoked cigars, where white women ate cold chicken salad for lunch, where white children swam and ate ice cream sandwiches. We were white but not that kind of white. Daddy said it was wrong to swim in a place where so many people were excluded.

There used to be a public pool, but men had tossed broken bottles into it at night as a protest against integration. We wore shoes to swim there, but even so we came away with cuts on our legs and arms. Strands of red floated in the chlorinated water. Eventually, the city decided it was better for no one to swim than for black children and white children to swim together. So they drained it and turned it over to a used car dealer. The quarry was our only option.

We dove into the forbidden waters. We tried to reach the bottom. Diving left us dizzy and strung out. Pansy didn't care how deep it was. Only the cool water mattered.

She was the smart one, the lucky one. She was supposed to start school in a few weeks and she wasn't happy about it. She'd spent no time in day care or with babysitters. Mama had enrolled her in kindergarten the year before, but Pansy threw a fit about it. Daddy said she was already smarter than half the kids in town and she didn't need an extra year of sitting in a classroom. Mama had let her stay home. It was like that with Pansy. She got what she wanted. There was no way Mama would have kept Willet or me home for an extra year, let me tell you. But Pansy would have to leave Mama's constant care soon. Kindergarten was optional; first grade was mandatory. Pansy would have to sit in a classroom like the rest of us, no matter how many fits she threw.

Mama called Pansy her little miracle, because she'd shown up unexpectedly when Mama and Daddy thought they were done with all that. She wasn't saddled with the names of the dead the way Willet and I were, but she was brought into the world the same way.

We were not born in hospitals. Daddy didn't trust the cold, sterile instruments. He didn't trust the doctors and nurses. He didn't trust the drugs. It was unnatural, he said. We were born onto a soft quilt. And the same hands that stitched the quilt pulled us from our mother's womb. We were brought to life by the hands of our Granny Clem. We were not the only ones.

Granny Clem had a way with pregnant women. She knew which herbs would dull pain and what to do to bring on contractions. She knew how to get a breach baby to flip by massaging a woman's back and placing a warm hand inside her. She knew other things too, darker things. Sometimes women came to her with pregnancies they hadn't planned, pregnancies they didn't want. Granny Clem would send the women home with a week's worth of strong tea made from pennyroyal, tansy, cotton root bark, and who knew what else. Most of the time, the tea brought on the women's bleeding and emptied their wombs, but when the tea failed, Granny Clem took stronger measures. She knew how to push a long steel wand into a woman's cervix to eliminate a pregnancy. For many women, Granny Clem was their last hope.

Abortion was legal by then, but the clinics were hours away by car and often overrun with protest groups and news cameras. Wealthy women went to private doctors or flew to areas of the country where clinics were not so scarce and where they could recover in a nice hotel with room service. Poor women and high school girls made do with the clinics when they could reach them, or took matters into their own hands, or sought out the services of people like Granny Clem. Mama didn't approve of Granny Clem's abortion business, but Daddy said his mother was doing God's work. Daddy said no child should be brought into a world that doesn't want it.

Even though Mama and Daddy hadn't planned for Pansy, they wanted her very much. It was a difficult pregnancy. Mama gained more weight with Pansy than she had with either Willet or me. Her feet swelled and a dark rash crawled across her face. We found long strands of her hair in the sofa cushions and the breadbox. When she went into labor, she howled like a wounded animal. Daddy told Willet to keep an eye on me and he dragged Mama to his truck. She could barely walk; her knees buckled and her feet dragged across the ground.

Willet put an arm around me as they drove away. "It's all gonna be fine, Bert." He couldn't have known that and he must have been scared, too. At ten years old, he'd taken seriously his responsibility to keep me calm. It was the middle of the night and we knew we wouldn't sleep. We ate peanut butter on saltine crackers and drank root beer over ice. Willet taught me how to play gin rummy.

Mama labored for nearly twenty hours. Granny Clem had her suck on peyote to make the experience less painful and to wash away bad associations. It was under the influence of the peyote that Mama blurted out the name of her favorite flower in a fit of giggles after finally giving birth. The name stuck. When I asked what Pansy would be named if Mama hadn't been all dopey, Mama said Pansy was Pansy and could never be anyone else.

Pansy was strange from birth, different from us in so many ways. She was born with a head full of coarse black hair and a blotchy tan. A large purple birthmark spread across her left thigh. Willet and I were bald and pale as ice cream in our baby photos. Pansy's almond-shaped eyes were sage green and wide-set, where ours were round and the color of milk chocolate. Pansy was born with teeth, four of them jutting out of her bottom gum. Granny Clem said it meant Pansy was special, powerful; she certainly seemed to hold power over our father. He held her and stroked his thumb across her birthmark as if that purple blemish were some sort of sign from God.

During her first months at home, Pansy cried and cried. She seemed angry. She rarely slept. When Mama tried to breastfeed her, she refused to eat or clamped down hard with her grotesque teeth until Mama cried out in pain. Mama switched to bottle-feeding, but only the most expensive brand of formula would satisfy Pansy. Daddy said she'd eat us into the poorhouse before her first birthday but he didn't seem mad about it. In fact, he sounded kind of proud. Starting her on solid food didn't help. As a toddler, she was so picky Mama worried she'd be malnourished. While we ate mushy vegetables and cornbread, Pansy got peanut butter on toast. While we choked down greasy cabbage rolls with ground beef and onion,

Pansy got chicken fingers and French fries. If anyone tried to insist she eat whatever the rest of us were having, she threw a tantrum so violent her whole face turned purple. Mama rubbed her back while she gasped and hiccuped.

It was obvious to anyone that Mama and Daddy loved Pansy best. Willet and I were ordinary children, but Pansy was charmed. When Daddy was home, he sang soft songs we'd never heard before and carried her around like a precious object. Every single morning, Mama brought Pansy a glass of chocolate milk in bed. Pansy wouldn't get up without her special treat, and Mama indulged her—though Willet and I weren't allowed food in our beds. I did small chores even as a toddler, but Pansy never helped out around the house. I won't pretend it didn't hurt, to see Mama and Daddy dote on Pansy, to feel second best though I was there first. There were times I wished Pansy would go away, times I wished she'd never been born. Shameful thoughts from a petty child, but still.

There was no explaining why our parents chose to give in to Pansy's demands so often and so willingly. At first, I thought they felt sorry for Pansy because she was so ugly, with her old man hair, splotchy skin, and bizarre infant teeth. But the coarse hair fell away, and in its place wild and silky dark curls appeared. She lost her natal teeth, and her complexion smoothed and softened until it was something people wanted to touch. Even I could see it. I loved her as much as I resented her. She was a beautiful child. Who doesn't love a beautiful child more than an ordinary one?

Pansy floated on her back, still as a log on the surface of the deep water. Her skin was tanned, as it was by the end of every summer. Willet and I burned and peeled and freckled, but Pansy's skin soaked in the sun. Everyone wanted to be tan back then and I envied how easily it came to her. Everything seemed to come easy for Pansy. She could float for hours. Sometimes she fell asleep. I couldn't float for ten seconds without lifting my head and looking around, worried I might miss something important. Willet would not be tamed. He hurled himself into the water again and again, all banshee cannon-balls and Tarzan yells. Only Pansy seemed at peace on the water. She had faith the world would hold her up.

We splashed around for hours, and by midafternoon I was half starved.

"I could eat a gator," Willet said.

Pansy didn't open her eyes. "I'm fine."

"We ought to call you Dandelion instead of Pansy," Willet said. "Someday you'll just up and blow away."

"Oh, shut up." Pansy's voice was as calm as the water.

"There's wild berries across the road," Willet said.

"What if they're poison?" I was a worrier from birth.

"They're just brambleberries, no different than the ones in the store."

We told Pansy we'd be right back. We didn't think twice about leaving our six-year-old sister alone in a deep pool in the middle of nowhere. She was a stronger swimmer than either of us would ever be. We figured she was charmed and, like most children—hell, like most people—we thought primarily of ourselves.

Willet led the way to the leggy bushes, which grew in a clearing a little further into the woods than I cared to travel, but my hunger was stronger than my fear. The black raspberries were plump and sweet, and we ate them as fast as we could pick them.

Willet wiped his hands on his shorts and looked over his shoulder. "I'll be back in a sec," he said.

"Don't leave me here!"

"I'll be right back."

I followed him until he turned and told me I was acting like a baby. I hung back and waited. The sound of branches popping beneath Willet's footsteps faded. The scent of smoke, sweet and smoldering, drifted through the air and I figured it for the lingering aroma of a fire built by Boy Scouts or some family avoiding campsite fees at the state park. The berries grew large and angry in my stomach. I rubbed my aching belly and wished for Willet to reappear. I closed my eyes and counted, telling myself Willet would be there when I reached ten, then twenty, then fifty, then one hundred. My too-small swimsuit dried and wedged in my butt. I tugged at it, angry with Mama for not buying me a new suit that summer. Clouds rolled in, sending the clearing into shadow. A swarm of gnats gathered around my face and I waved my hands to keep from inhaling the pesky creatures. The sky, which had been blue and clear all morning, turned gray and menacing. I'd had enough.

"Willet!" I shouted. "Willet, this isn't funny!"

The tall trees swallowed up my voice. It was like one of those bad dreams where you scream for help but don't make a sound. A hot wind traveled through the woods; the leaves on the trees quivered and quaked. Dark gray clouds blocked out the sun. The first fat drop of rain hit my bare shoulder. I called for Willet once more, then walked in the direction he'd disappeared. The sky let loose a roll of thunder. The rain swept through in heavy, blinding sheets and the dust beneath my feet turned to mud. It was an angry storm.

Up ahead, something moved. It was a person, darting among the trees.

"Willet!" I chased after the darting figure, already thinking about what I'd tell Mama when we got home. "You are in so much trouble!" I hollered.

The storm grew darker. My feet slipped on mud and slick fallen leaves. I put my hands out to avoid crashing into the trees surrounding the clearing. They seemed to pop up out of nothing. Thunder cracked and the ground shook. I'd been caught in bad weather before, but this was worse than anything I'd ever seen. The rain was so thick it looked like something you could grab by the handful. Clouds obliterated the daylight. It was dark as night until a bolt of lightning lit up the sky. In that flash of light I saw a dark creature lurch across the clearing. It hunched forward. It wore tattered, ill-fitting clothes, and in the lightning glow, the creature's skin seemed to be the same color as the clay from the quarry—a slick greenish gray. It reminded me of the trolls from children's storybooks. It carried something in its arms, something too large to be lugged through the woods in a storm. I stood very still, hoping to escape the creature's notice. I barely breathed. At the next bolt of lightning, I tried to spot the creature again, but it was gone. I stood frozen in the downpour, afraid to move forward or go back. What had I seen? Was it a monster or a vagrant? Was it the Devil himself? Was Daddy right about this being Satan's sanctuary?

Anything seemed possible in the midst of that dark storm. I thought of Margaret Halsey, a classmate who'd told her mother she was having a sleepover with a girlfriend but instead spent the weekend with her boyfriend at his family's deer lease, not far from these woods. Margaret wouldn't talk about what happened, but she'd come back changed and not for the better. Some people said a gang of rough boys had violated her with the barrel of a hunting rifle. Others said she got drunk and let her boyfriend and his friends do what they wished, and she enjoyed every minute of it. People avoided her, as if whatever had happened might be contagious. If it happened to her, it could happen to me. She'd been touched by evil, and I wanted no part of it. If I stood very still and remained silent, maybe the evil would pass me by.

The rain slowed. The violent stinging sheets became soft drops. Clouds rolled apart and soft fingers of light began to creep across the sky. Steam rose off the trees, the mist clearing away irrational fears. I told myself I was being silly, imagining things.

"Willet!" I called out.

When he didn't appear, I turned back on the path to the quarry. Willet would be there, probably wondering where I was. Maybe I missed him in the storm or maybe he'd circled around and gone back a different way. I shook like a dog, water flying off my hair and skin. My hands were stained purple from the berries. Leaving the woods, the sun hit me with a blinding brightness. Any coolness from the rain disappeared, melted into sticky sweat between my thighs. The quarry water lay still and peaceful. I circled the lip of the quarry, looking for Willet to pop out of the woods or waiting for him to rise up from the deep water, gasping from holding his breath. Out of the rising heat, Bubba Speck appeared. I couldn't figure where he'd come from; suddenly he was just there. Bubba was shirtless, and even at sixteen it was clear he would be a fat man someday. His pudgy belly sagged over the waistband of his shorts and his breasts were larger than mine, which had barely begun to announce themselves to the world.

When we were younger, Bubba and Willet were good friends. They shared a fascination with building things, mostly explosive devices fashioned from old car parts and match tips and household cleansers. In seventh grade, they set off a small bomb in the girls' bathroom at the junior high school. The principal had told the sheriff and the woman from the local news that it was only by the grace of God no one was hurt. The grace of God was something a lot of folks believed in back then.

"What are you doing, Bubba?" I hollered.

Bubba tossed a rock into the still water of the quarry.

"Have you seen Willet?"

Bubba tossed another rock. It was like he couldn't hear me, like I wasn't even there.

"You got no right to ignore me, Bubba Speck!"

Bubba looked up at the sky, pointed a finger to some spot above his head. I looked where he was pointing, but all I saw were dissolving clouds and the bright, white sun. My vision filled with fiery spots that flared and went dark. By the time I could see again, Bubba was gone.

Between Willet and Bubba, I didn't know what to think. Why were they treating me so mean? I couldn't think of anything I'd done to deserve such treatment. I resolved to ignore Willet for the next week at least and to tell Mama how he'd abandoned me in the woods and hid when I called him. I was running down the long list of things Willet had done to make me mad when I realized something was wrong.

Pansy was not floating on her back in the quarry where we'd left her. Pansy was not sitting on the edge of the quarry with her feet dangling in the water as she sometimes did. Pansy was not walking on the path into the woods. Pansy was not climbing the oak tree with the swing. Pansy was not anywhere at all. The berries I'd eaten expanded and rose into my throat. I spewed out a hot mess of the sweet fruit, splashing my bare feet.

I yelled for Pansy. It seemed I'd spent the whole afternoon shouting for people who wouldn't answer.

"Willet! Bubba! Pansy!"

I called their names over and over, but no one called back. I held on to the idea they were playing a joke on me. Any minute they'd burst from behind a tree and laugh at me for getting all worked up. But they didn't come out, and even the birds seemed to have gone silent. The sun, bright and hot and unforgiving, dipped in the sky.

It was getting on toward suppertime, and I thought about Mama at home making cornbread or stirring a pot of purple hull peas. Maybe Willet and Pansy were on their way home without me. Maybe they were teaching me a lesson. I played the last week in my head and tried to figure out what I'd done to make them angry. Instead, I devised a long list of slights I'd suffered. Someone ate the biscuit I was saving for breakfast. Pansy kicked me hard enough to leave a bruise when I asked her to get her laundry sorted. Willet called me an "idget." Ordinary sibling grievances, but there I was, alone, abandoned for some reason I couldn't fathom. My chest felt heavy and tight. I was lightheaded and ashamed. I didn't know why. My face burned, but my arms prickled with chilly goose pimples. With no option but to stand there or walk on, I set off down the road toward home. I was halfway there, on that stretch of hot, shadeless road, when I heard Willet call my name. Any anger I held against him fell away. I'd about convinced myself the whole world had disappeared during that storm and I would walk in the door of our house to find Mama vanished and no supper on the stove. When Willet caught up with me, I threw myself around him like a spider monkey. His skin smelled sharp and sweet, something unrecognizable rising from his sweat.

"Where were you?"

"Jesus, Bert, I'm right here."

I started to tell him about the storm and the creature in the woods and Bubba, but he interrupted me.

"Where's Pansy?"

"I thought she was with you."

"Why in the hell would she be with me? She was in the quarry." Willet's face shimmered with sweat. His eyes were all pupil.

My chest got real tight then, and I felt starved for air. Everything went woozy and dark until the world was the size of a knothole. I grasped Willet's arm to keep from keeling over. "Maybe she went home without us."

Pansy had never walked home alone.

Willet shook me so hard I bit my tongue. The metallic taste of blood crept through my mouth. "How could you leave her?" Spit flew from Willet's lips.

"I thought she was with you. I thought you were playing a trick on me."

"We have to go back."

"But it's nearly suppertime," I said. "Mama will be worried."

"Worried? She'll be damn near crazy if we come home without Pansy. Goddammit, Bert, make some sense."

My head felt fuzzy. Normally, I was the sensible one. Pansy was young and still prone to fanciful thoughts, imaginary friends, bursts of sudden temper. Willet was unpredictable, wild and untamed in the way boys brought up with too much freedom tend to be. I followed the rules. It drove Willet crazy. He warned me I was on a path to spinsterhood. *Men hate that shit*, was how he put it. He had a way of drilling down to the heart of things, but now he seemed unable to focus. The world spun in the wrong direction, and I wondered if the berries we'd eaten were poisonous, if this was all a sick fever dream. We stood there arguing far too long. The sun dipped closer to the horizon. Finally Willet told me to go home. He turned to go back to the woods, back to the quarry where we'd last seen Pansy. I shivered as a vision of the creature from the woods came to me, but Willet was already a good piece down the road. I didn't call him back. I didn't warn him. I didn't trust what I'd seen and, anyhow, I knew Willet wouldn't believe a crazy story about some monster in the woods.

"Be careful," I whispered, though I knew he couldn't hear me.

A HOLE IN THE ground, a depression in the earth, a gaping wound, an open mouth. That's what it was—a greedy open mouth drinking in rainwater and sucking sunshine into darkness. At night when the stars hid behind clouds and the moon was reduced to a sliver, people brought offerings to feed the mouth. They tossed their sins into the muddy water and hoped to be cut free from guilt or shame. Sacks of bones, mostly canine, lockboxes with love notes from someone else's husband, the sticky remains of an unformed child, a bloody knife, a hunting rifle, a broken mirror, a single leather glove—these things sank into the deep water and lodged among the gray stones left unearthed. Of course it was an evil place. It held too many secrets to be anything else.

The things he knows can't be found in books or newspapers or in the scrawled notes of local historians. The things he knows, he knows deep beneath his skin. He gathers the stories of the ghosts and combines them with his own. They melt together like candle wax. Lately he's begun writing everything down in a small notebook, everything he can remember and all the things that are deeper than memory.

—

The quarry was dug by slaves in the earliest years of the nineteenth century. The slaves had fled the nearby cotton fields and were caught by the brutal man who owned the land. The man promised to break them with labor a cotton picker could never know. He chained them to one another and forced them to dig with pickaxes and shovels and bare hands. The men worked from first light until dark without resting. If a man grew thirsty, he drank muddy water from the ground. If a man needed to urinate or move his bowels, he did so while continuing to work his tools and his hands through the earth. Each evening, the plantation owner brought meager rations of cornmeal mush and cold beans. The men pulled the slop up with their filthy hands from a communal bucket. Soon enough, the weakest of the men fell ill and died. The plantation owner left the man's corpse chained to the workers as a reminder of what might happen.

"This man's soul now toils in hell," he told the men. "You'll join him soon enough, but until that day you'll toil for me."

The men talked about the bad feeling they got when they dug. One said they were digging in the mouth of hell. One lost his mind and used a small shovel to hack off his leg and free himself from the shackles. He bled to death, and the work went on around him. All of the men gave their lives to the quarry.

The plantation owner who'd ordered the work gave his life, as well, though not as quickly. He used the first stones unearthed from the site to lay the foundation for a house for his daughter. His slaves, the ones still working in his fields, carried the stones in slings around their necks from the quarry to the home site nearly a mile away. They dug a level trench in the earth and lay stones in like a puzzle until they'd made a foundation so stable only God himself could move it. The plantation owner worked beside his slaves to build the house. He wanted it done right, and he imagined showing it to his daughter and her fiancé with a sense of pride, telling them he'd built it himself. He used the best pine logs available and put in windows to capture the morning light. He put in a fireplace and a woodstove.

He constructed walls for three bedrooms and imagined his future grandchildren sleeping peacefully there.

But when the house was finished, it didn't please him. Something about it looked askew, though he'd measured every angle himself. The house was as square and level as any house could be, but it sat wrong on the plot of land. He knew this and it made him angry. The house was constructed from his plans and his vision, so there was no one to blame but himself. Nonetheless, he found reasons to whip the men who'd worked on the house. He accused them of sabotage.

At his daughter's wedding, he could think of nothing but the disappointment she would feel when she spent her first night in the new home. His wife told him he was being silly. She said the house was fine. She said the daughter was lucky to have a father who would provide such a generous wedding gift.

But the house was never right. His daughter said she was always cold inside its walls. She kept the fireplace burning even during the hottest days of summer. Every meal that was cooked in the woodstove came out ruined. She slept too often, even in the middle of the day. She produced no children. She told her husband her womb was too cold to carry a child. Nothing went right. On a warm summer night while they slept, an errant spark escaped the fireplace and settled on the woven rug covering the wood floors. The spark smoldered and gathered strength. Flames leapt through the main room, catching the curtains and a pile of quilting scraps. By the time the woman and her husband woke, the house was filled with smoke. They made it out and watched as the house burned to the ground. After the ashes were cleared, the only thing that remained was the bed of stones from the quarry. The woman came down with a persistent cough and spent the next year trying to catch her breath. Her lungs failed. She died exactly one year from the date of the fire. She was twenty years old. Her husband moved on, married another woman, but the plantation owner lived out his life in mourning. He felt responsible for his daughter's death. He blamed the house.

His slaves knew better. They held their children close and told them stories about how the land could turn evil. They warned the children not to play with the gray polished rocks from the quarry.

"Those are Satan's stones," they said. "Don't you steal from the Devil."

TWO

WHEN I GOT HOME from the quarry, I could smell the ordinary odors of supper being cooked. In the kitchen, a pot of butterbeans simmered low and slow on the stovetop. Cornbread, golden and fresh from the oven, sat in a cast-iron skillet on the counter. A bowl filled with sliced okra tossed in flour and cornmeal waited beside the stove, ready for frying. Mama came in the back door holding a jar of pepper jelly she'd fetched from the garage.

"I was starting to fret." Mama pressed the glass jar into my hands.

I twisted the jelly lid, part of a batch we'd put up last summer. Mama turned up the heat on the skillet for the okra. A cigarette dangled from the corner of her mouth. She talked around it, smoke seeping forth with each word.

"Y'all get washed up for supper."

"But, Mama . . ." The lid popped loose.

"Stand back, Roberta Lynn. This oil might splatter."

I moved away from the stove, listened to the oil hiss and spit. I didn't want to tell her about Pansy. I didn't want to set all that worry in motion. I wanted to fill my plate with good food and watch something silly on television. Maybe if I stalled, Willet would come through the door with Pansy. Maybe everything would be okay.

I pulled plates from the cabinet and stacked them on the dining table along with a pile of forks and a spoon for the jelly. I looked out the window, hoping to see Willet and Pansy walking toward the house, but the street was empty. Back in the kitchen, Mama tucked fat pats of butter into warm slices of cornbread.

I wished Daddy were home.

In the bathroom, I ran my hands under the faucet until Mama called out and said to hurry up because the food was getting cold. Time seemed to slow down, but everything happened too fast. I turned off the faucet and wiped the drops from the porcelain basin with a bit of tissue. I sat on the toilet without any plans to use it, elbows resting on my knees, head propped in my hands. My heartbeat seemed to echo against the dingy tile floor. My chest felt tight and hollow. I flushed the unused toilet, watched the clean water swirl in the bowl, then ran my hands under the faucet again.

No amount of stalling would keep me from facing Mama. The bathroom door creaked when I pushed it open. The hallway seemed to expand into a long tunnel. I moved slowly, hoping Willet would come through the front door with Pansy and everything would go back to normal. Mama gave me a strange look. She seemed young and vulnerable. Her old shorts and faded blouse were dusted with flour and spotted with grease. She never did bother to put on an apron when she cooked. Her feet were bare. She wore no makeup and her hair was pushed back off her face with a cheap plastic headband. A moist line of sweat beaded across her upper lip.

I couldn't tell Mama Pansy was missing. I couldn't say it. Bad news about Pansy would be the worst news of all. It would be better if I disappeared, or Willet. Mama would trade us both for Pansy, I suspected. I couldn't say the words. She knew, though. She read my face and knew something was very wrong.

"Where are they?" she asked, her voice soft, without a hint of tremor. "Where?" Mama sank onto the living room couch with a thud.

The cold knowledge of how we'd failed Mama by leaving Pansy in the quarry became all too clear. We were older and should know better. She'd trusted us. We were supposed to watch our sister, to keep her safe. Pansy was still a baby. Pansy was Mama's baby. Willet would find her, I thought. Willet could do anything. I remembered the time he killed a snake with a pellet gun, the time he swung himself onto the roof to fetch a stray ball and how he'd dropped from that great height with the gracefulness of a cat. When I came down with the chicken pox, Willet colored with me in the cheap paper books brought over by the church ladies, even though he'd outgrown such things. Willet had never let me down. He was brave and strong and fearless. He would bring Pansy home. He had to.

But when Willet came through the front door, he was alone. Mama and I were still staring at one another, both of us working up the courage to speak. I don't know if we'd been like that for an hour or for five minutes. The timeline of that day is all wonky in my mind. Willet said some things I can't remember. What I do remember is how he looked. All of a sudden, my brother looked like a man. When Mama went to stand, he reached out and held her arm, steadying her in a gentle way. At some point, he put on a shirt, as if walking around half-naked was too casual for our current situation. He stood with Mama while she called the police and spun the dial for her when her hands shook. He put on a pot of coffee and turned off all the burners on the stove. How did he know what to do? Had he been preparing himself for tragedy? Had he rehearsed this moment in his mind?

Meanwhile, I remained useless and clumsy. I dropped a water glass in the kitchen and gashed my thumb trying to clean up the shards. Blood crept across my palm like a lazy river. Willet thrust my injured hand under a stream of cold water and wrapped it in a kitchen towel. He could see I was feeling woozy. He held my shoulders and looked straight into my face. It was like looking in a mirror. We had the same brown eyes, the same freckles across our pale cheeks, the same dishwater hair. His face was sharper and wider than mine, but no one could ever doubt we were related.

"We need to help Mama," he said. "Do you understand?"

Help her do what, I wondered. What could we possibly do to make this mess right? We could find Pansy and bring her home. Nothing else would be any help at all.

A car pulled into our driveway. It was a police cruiser, but there were no flashing lights or sirens, just two uniformed officers with notebooks. Mama brought them right inside our house. Daddy wouldn't like that, I thought. Even from where I stood I could smell the bleach from the laundry room where Daddy worked. He had a cardboard box full of bleached bills stashed behind the washing machine. It's not like you could stumble over it but it wasn't exactly locked up tight. Mama didn't seem worried about any of that. She cared about Pansy, of course, and nothing else.

The officers, one fat and balding, one thin with a thick afro, talked to Mama. They wrote down information about Pansy's height and weight and age and hair color. They questioned Willet and me, together at first, then separately. We answered whatever they asked until the questions ran together like wet paint.

What time did you leave Pansy to eat berries? What time did you leave the quarry? Neither of us wore a watch. *Why didn't Pansy stay with you?* She wasn't hungry. She'd rather swim. *When did you last see your father?* A few weeks ago. *Was anyone else with you?* No. Bubba Speck was there but just for a minute. *What time was that?* I don't know. *Would Pansy leave on her own?* I don't think so. *Would Pansy leave with Bubba?* I don't know. *Was she angry with you for any reason?* No. I don't know. *Where is your father?* I don't know. I don't know. I don't know.

The skinny officer asked Mama for a list of Pansy's friends or neighbors she might visit. Mama looked at him like he'd lost his mind. "We're her whole world."

Oh, God.

I sat with the fat officer and answered more questions, one hopeless response after another. It was hot and I wanted to reach out and wipe away the stream of sweat from his bulging jaw. The scent of vegetable oil gone cold and slightly rancid settled around us. My stomach growled, though I couldn't imagine eating anything.

I answered the officer's questions, but I didn't offer any additional details. I didn't tell him about the creature from the woods; it was too fantastic and it seemed like a bad dream. I told him I'd returned to the quarry just after the storm. That's when I'd seen Bubba and realized Pansy was missing. The officer had a lot of questions about Bubba, but I couldn't answer anything in a way that seemed to satisfy him. "Bubba wouldn't hurt Pansy," I told him.

Sweat trickled from the officer's forehead to his neck. He wheezed a bit whenever he took a deep breath. The buttons of his uniform strained against his bulging belly. He had the look of a man about to burst. He asked me what Bubba and I talked about at the quarry.

"We didn't," I said.

He grunted and scribbled in his notebook, thanked me for my time, and said he might want to ask me more questions later.

By the time they finished with us, I thought that day was the only day there ever was. It was impossible to imagine we would eat or brush our teeth or put on pajamas or go to sleep. It didn't seem possible we'd ever wake up to a different day. The options narrowed to nothing. It seemed I would sit and nod or shake my head for an eternity.

While we had answered questions, two men in scuba gear dove deep into the quarry to search for Pansy. Here is what they found: a 1969 Volkswagen bug, a Japanese motorbike turned to pure rust, two identical refrigerators, three hunting rifles and one pistol, a machete, enough dog bones to make a pack, hundreds of amber beer bottles, an old guitar, coins of every denomination, a burlap sack filled with the carcasses of a litter of kittens, five ladder-back dining chairs, three barstools, a plastic box containing syringe plungers, a backpack filled with swollen school books. Here is what they did not find: Pansy.

After the officers left, Lorna Speaks came over from across the street. She was a religious woman, who was always trying to get us to go to the Baptist church. We went occasionally, on Easter or near Christmas, but Mama never made us go on an ordinary Sunday. Neither she nor Daddy were particularly religious. It was one more thing that set us apart from other families. Most of the folks we knew were devout; even the terrible people made it to church every week.

I knew Lorna must have been watching from her living room window, curious to the point of shaking about the cops at our house. Mama always said she was the nosiest woman on the face of the earth, but Mama didn't turn her away. She told her about Pansy and let Lorna pull her in for a long hug. When Lorna started praying, Mama bowed her head and clasped Lorna's hands.

"Dear Lord," Lorna said, "lift up this family in their time of trouble. We pray for you to return Pansy safely to her home, to keep her from harm, to fold her up in your love and protection. In your name, we pray. Amen."

"Amen," Mama said.

I had never heard Mama pray before.

Willet offered Lorna a cup of coffee. His manners were suddenly impeccable. He called her ma'am. It was like everyone in our family had transformed in some terrible way. I didn't want a brother with good manners. I didn't want a mother who prayed. All I wanted was for everything to go back to normal. I wanted Pansy to wander home and tell us some fantastic story about where she'd been and what she'd done. Most of all, I wanted my Daddy. He would know what to do, and he would not be dazzled by nosy neighbors and probing police officers. Daddy would fix things the way he always did, without bringing in a bunch of outsiders.

Mama sat with Lorna at the dinner table, both of them letting mugs of coffee go cold between their hands. Willet and I cleaned up the uneaten supper. I took a bite of the cornbread and it swelled like wet sand in my mouth. We scraped everything into the garbage and piled the dishes into a pail of soapy water in the sink. Willet told Mama we'd wash the dishes in the morning. He asked if she needed anything.

Mama shook her head and I realized she wasn't making eye contact with Willet. She was mad at him, mad at both of us for leaving Pansy. This whole mess was our fault and no amount of polite helpfulness was going to fix anything.

It was late by then, but there was no question of trying to sleep. I couldn't stand being alone in the bedroom I shared with Pansy, so I huddled with Willet in his room. I couldn't stop talking. How could this have happened? How could we fix it? Maybe if we'd done this or that, things would be different. I poked at the day from every angle, trying to find a path that led somewhere other than where we were. Willet let me ramble. He interjected occasionally to tell me it wasn't my fault. He was the oldest. He should have been more responsible. He spoke in a sad, flat tone that scared me. One of the things I loved most about my brother was the way everything sounded more interesting coming from his mouth. He cussed to great effect. He used bad grammar even though he knew better, and it made everything he said sound rough and exciting. I admired his talent for getting at the truth through exaggeration. He had nothing clever to say about Pansy, though, which told me how dire things were.

I droned on and on, scared to let the cold silence fall around us, but I didn't mention what I'd seen in the woods. If I told Willet about the creature he would say I was making stuff up, letting my imagination go wild. He said we needed to find our father. I couldn't disagree with that. Mama would surely feel better with Daddy home, but Willet's aim was not to provide comfort for our mother. Willet thought Daddy had something to do with Pansy's disappearance. I couldn't understand the logic. If Daddy were going to take someone on one of his adventures, it should have been me.

"He wouldn't do that to Mama," I said.

Willet sat quiet for a long time. When he spoke, he sounded serious and sad. He said our father was not a good man. He said he wouldn't care about Mama's feelings. He said Daddy would take anything he wanted, including our sister, and he wouldn't care who got hurt in the process.

I couldn't believe it. Willet's relationship with our father was a hard one, but it was because Willet was a boy and the oldest. Daddy had to be harder on him than he was on me and Pansy. The idea that our father would snatch our sister up and take her away with him didn't seem right. But nothing seemed right.

"At least," I said, "if Daddy took her, she's safe."

Willet said I shouldn't be too sure about that.

I knew Willet felt responsible for Pansy. We both did. We'd left her alone in the quarry while we fed our hungry bellies. We'd turned away when we should have been watching, both of us selfish and thoughtless and weak. Maybe Pansy got up out of that quarry and walked away on her own. Maybe the creature from the woods carried her away. Maybe she sank into the deep water, her flesh turned liquid. None of it seemed possible and yet she was gone.

HE HAD SEEN MEN come home from war. He'd seen their dead eyes, but the wars fought overseas didn't haunt him in the same way as the wars fought at home. He'd read about the battles, the ones that took place nearby and the ones farther away where whole towns burned to the ground. The war had so many names: the War of Northern Aggression, the War Between the States, the War for Southern Independence, and, of course, the Civil War, which seemed the least accurate name of all. The old people of White Forest referred to it simply as *our recent unpleasantness*, and it did seem recent. More than a hundred years gone by, but he could hear the crack of the muskets and smell the sulfurous gunpowder smoke. He could feel the creep of gangrene in every scrape of his legs. He heard the shouts and whispers of the men as they led their horses across the rivers. Mostly he heard the voices of those who stayed home: the elderly, the women, the children, the slaves. The voices of the powerless were the loudest voices of all.

In 1862 Confederate soldiers needed something more stable than conviction and mud to march upon. Slaves moved from the cotton fields to the quarry and from the quarry to the roads. They spread the stones with a mixture of clay and silt across roads prone to wash-out from nearby rivers.

While the men worked on the roads and in the fields and at the quarry, their wives and daughters and sisters worked in the kitchens of stately plantation homes and modest houses. The women were invisible, or so it seemed, because the people in those houses talked about things as if they weren't standing there listening. This was how the women heard news of slaves rising up and taking freedom by force. This was how they learned about a community of former slaves settled deep in the Florida Everglades where no white man would trespass, and if he dared, he would be shot on sight.

Ungrateful, said the white women. *Disgraceful*, said the old men.

The house slaves took news back to the field slaves. Over meager meals of grits or cornbread, they talked about the war and whether its end would mean anything to them. One man, neither field slave nor house servant, heard everything. Moses Fortune distinguished himself by learning to read and write as a young boy. No one knew how he'd acquired these skills. Neither of his parents was literate and the only book he ever saw was the Bible. Even the ugliest landowners would permit their slaves a Bible, though they considered them beyond redemption. It was the Christian thing to do. Moses stared at the Bible as a child of seven and eight and nine years old. His mother teased him about it, told him he'd go cross-eyed if he didn't stop squinting at the squiggles on the page. When he was ten years old, he stood up after supper one evening and began to read aloud from the book.

"Stand fast therefore in the liberty," he said, in a deep voice his own mother barely recognized. "Wherewith Christ hath made us free, and be not entangled with the yoke of bondage."

It was Paul speaking to the Galatians, but those who heard Moses read that night swore Christ himself had descended from heaven to deliver a message to them all.

"Stand fast in the liberty," Moses said. "Stand fast."

By the time Moses turned fifteen, he was preaching regular sermons to the slaves. His master encouraged it.

"I keep my slaves happy," the old man said. "They'd rather be here with me than out in the wide world on their own."

The old man walked with a severe limp and used a cane to steady himself. Despite the slow gait, he walked his land daily. He liked to keep an eye on things and make his slaves aware of his presence. He spoke with them and not only to give them orders.

"Ain't you happy here, Moses," he called out one afternoon. "Ain't it a beautiful day?"

"Oh, yessir."

"Ain't you content with your place in the world?"

"I want nothing but what I've got."

"Ain't you glad you don't got to scrape and claw to find food or a place to sleep at night?"

"You give me all that and more."

"And I ask again, Moses, ain't you happy?"

"Happy as Adam before the apple."

The men mining quarry stone worked through the Sunday morning hours set aside for worship and family, so Moses was allowed to preach to them as they worked. The master thought it would inspire the men to work harder, and he was proud of his generosity. He bragged about it to owners of nearby plantations and they asked if Moses would come preach to their slaves. It could only be a good thing to bring the word of God to the godless, they said.

Moses preached to the men from Jeremiah. "Woe unto him that buildeth his house by unrighteousness, and his chambers by wrong; that useth his neighbor's service without wages, and giveth him not for his work." And he preached from Proverbs: "Righteousness exalteth a nation!"

The master often stopped by to listen to the sermons. He was impressed by the strong, singsong quality of Moses's preaching. "I don't know where the boy learnt it," he told his wife. "But he speaks better than most white men."

His wife warned him not to encourage so much speaking and thinking among the slaves. "You don't want them getting ideas," she said.

He waved her off. "They love me," he told her. "They wouldn't leave me if Jesus himself descended to offer them freedom. Where would they go? What would they do without me?"

Moses dropped news into his quarry sermons. Always aware the master might be nearby, he chose his words carefully. He tucked the news between Bible verses and kept his intonation steady. The timbre of his voice lulled the careless, but anyone who knew how to listen would hear plenty. This was how they learned about the free blacks living in Virginia. This was how they first heard of the town sixty miles northwest, where the brother of the Confederate president provided slaves with dental care and education, where black men worked as merchants earning a wage. The world changed around them, but their days remained the same. They dug and hauled stone and pumped away the spring water bubbling up from the ground of the quarry. Or they picked three hundred pounds of cotton each day and submitted to the whip when they failed to meet the quota. They'd worked this way forever. It kept them exhausted and dulled their minds, but something awoke in them when Moses spoke. Rebellion blossomed.

Fall came and went and with it the cotton harvest. The men picked and baled until their hands bled. The women joined them in the fields when the harvest became too much. That year the younger children of the slaves, the ones who were too little to work the fields, tended a garden near the slave quarters. They planted seeds and cuttings pilfered from the woods near the quarry. Moses led the project, telling the parents and the slave owners it was good for children to be busy.

"Idle hands are the Devil's workshop," he said.

The children watered the garden with spring runoff from the quarry. Foxglove, lily of the valley, and water hemlock grew and flowered. Moses praised the children for their work. He called them his sharp arrows, a reference to the book of Psalms.

"As arrows are in the hands of a mighty man, so are children of the youth."

White men, young and old, joined the army. Even the men who were once deemed too old or frail to serve marched off to lend their hands to the efforts. Soon, there were hardly any white men left. The plantation owner with the limp remained. A few of the oldest landowners remained, but their sons and grandsons marched off to join the war.

In spring of 1863, General Grant ordered his troops across the Tallahatchie River on the way to Vicksburg. Confederate soldiers marched in to defend the area, mostly quiet through the fighting until that point. They enlisted the strongest slaves to build a fort. They lugged the cotton bales they'd put away in the fall to the spot where the Tallahatchie meets the Yazoo. People think cotton is a soft substance, wispy and insubstantial, but pack it tight and it's stronger than wood or steel. They covered the bales with dirt and stood ready.

Union soldiers surged into the river, but the Confederates held them back with Colt revolvers and light Congreve rockets. The Confederate soldiers were outnumbered, but the advancing troops were exposed and vulnerable. The Union soldiers retreated. They would go on to take Vicksburg, but White Forest would be spared.

After the battle, some of the Confederate soldiers requested a meal and a bed in nearby homes. The old plantation owner with the limp was happy to oblige. His wife instructed the slaves to cook a feast for the soldiers. Neighbors gathered and brought supplies. Moses told the children to harvest the plants. "This is what we've been working for," he told them. "Let them eat from the labor of your hands." The children delivered baskets of freshly dug plants to their mothers and aunts working in the kitchen. The women chopped and stirred and baked for the jubilant, but tired, soldiers. They stirred hemlock into the vegetable stew and sweetened the tea with foxglove. They ground stalks from the lily of the valley into the cornmeal from which they baked bread. They served it up to the soldiers and the old men and the women and the children. It was an evening of celebration. Someone pulled a bottle of bourbon from a cellar. The men shared pipe tobacco.

By morning, illness swept through the plantation. Everyone who'd gathered for the feast was suffering or dead. Soldiers vomited and lost control of their bowels. The stench was terrible. Feverish and panicked, the women went to check on their children. The littlest ones were already dead. The older ones were close. Over the next two days, forty-eight people died from the poisoned supper.

One of the few survivors was the old plantation owner with the limp. His wife had succumbed to the poison in the final wave of the illness and he thought he would surely die alongside her. He spent a week in bed, drenched in sweat and plagued by hallucinations, but he kept his grip on life. When he gained the strength to walk again, he made his way across the fields to the slave quarters. He found them empty. He would later learn most of his men had joined the Union army. The women and children had traveled north in search of free communities. No one could say for sure what happened to Moses, but rumors came from Georgia and Alabama and Florida about a fiery preacher making the rounds at black churches.

The old plantation owner was angry about the revolt, of course. Hadn't Moses said he was as happy as Adam before the apple? What more could any man want? The answer was scrawled on a wooden cross planted in the children's poison garden. In bold letters scratched deep with a knife blade, it read: THE TRUTH SHALL MAKE YOU FREE.

A mound of quarry stones anchored the cross. The old plantation owner ran his hands over the letters. They meant nothing to him. He could sign his name to purchase land or buy slaves, but he'd never learned to read. It was one of his only regrets. His wife used to read to him in the evenings. She read Bible stories and passages from the few books they owned. She read him the day's news if he traveled to get a newspaper. But his wife was gone now and his sons were off fighting losing battles. All the evenings of his life stretched out before him, long and lonely. He unearthed the cross and carried it back to his home, where he planted it at the head of his wife's grave.

THREE

— ◆ —

THE DAYS FOLLOWING PANSY'S disappearance run together in my mind. Was it Sunday when everyone lined up to search the woods? I think so. I believe the local churches let out early and encouraged the members of their congregations to join in the search for Pansy. I believe the women went home and changed from skirts and dresses into blue jeans and T-shirts. I believe the men set aside their ties and starched shirts and made uncomfortable jokes about the blessings of a short sermon, no matter the reason. When things go wrong, people want to feel useful. And they are curious. Everyone is so curious about a tragedy. No one wants to miss out on the morbid discovery. If, years later, someone brings up the time that girl went missing, people want to say: *I was there. I was there when they found her. I was there when they found her body. You can't imagine what it was like. Let me tell you.*

A hundred people, maybe more, lined up at arm's length and walked for miles. Willet wanted to go, but the police said no. They didn't want him stumbling upon our sister's corpse. Or they thought he knew something and might compromise the search. I don't know. No one told us anything. We didn't line up and march through the woods with our gaze to the ground, searching for any bit of evidence that might lead us to Pansy. We didn't find the blue hair ribbon or the plush alligator or the soggy book of nursery rhymes, all of which were retrieved and bagged and handed over to police officers with careful solemnity.

We were there when the police brought the items to our mother, held them out with a reverence reserved for sacred objects. Mama shook her head, pursed her lips. "No," she said. She turned away, as if the sight of some other child's lost items were an affront. Nothing they uncovered belonged to Pansy. Nothing brought them closer to finding our sister.

"She ain't out there," Willet said to me.

"But where is she?"

"Somewhere else."

Willet had an old motorbike he'd restored from junkyard parts. It was unregistered and illegal, and Mama hated it. She was convinced he would kill himself on it someday. I was forbidden to ride on it, but sometimes, if I begged, Willet took me out for a spin. On that day we weren't riding for fun; Willet had a clear destination in mind. I loved sitting behind him, my arms twined around his torso, my face pressed into his back. The wind pushed against us, and it was like flying. With everything going wrong at home, it seemed shameful to take pleasure in anything. I tucked my face against Willet's shoulder and closed my eyes against incidental joy.

I believe it was Monday, a busy day when people would be at work in offices or on construction sites. A peroxide-blonde reporter from the local news asked Mama to pull together some recent photos of Pansy. The pictures Mama pulled were posed and careful. They were taken at holidays when Pansy wore a starched dress and an impatient smile. They looked nothing like Pansy, if you asked me. Pansy in real life had a headful of untamable curls. She didn't smile often, but when she did it was with a wild grin. She never smiled the way she did in those pictures, with her mouth barely stretched over her tiny teeth. Well, nobody asked me.

Willet and I were in the way. You might think Mama wouldn't want us out of her sight, what with one child gone missing. You might imagine she'd pull us close and pour her energies into protecting the children who were still at home, but you'd be wrong. She was annoyed with us, angry with us for our role in losing Pansy. That morning, as Willet made a second pot of coffee and I straightened up the living room for the reporter with the video camera, Mama swatted at us.

"Are you trying to kill me?" she asked when she tripped over the vacuum cleaner cord.

"But, Mama . . ." There was no use saying I was trying to help. I knew she'd hate it if the television reporter showed us living in the midst of dirt and clutter.

"Put that thing away and get scarce. I don't want you lurking around here today."

When Willet grabbed my arm and pulled me out the back door an hour later, I didn't ask where we were headed. Any place, I figured, would be better than home.

When we pulled up to Uncle Chester's trailer, I reconsidered. Daddy's brother was a hard man. He lived out in the country in a doublewide trailer a few yards from the perfectly good brick house where his mother lived. I don't know if Granny Clem kicked him out or if he preferred to live alone. I wasn't sure it was a good idea to see him, but if anyone knew how to find our father, it would be Chester. I wasn't sure if he even knew about Pansy's disappearance. I'd overheard Mama talking with Granny Clem on the phone, but we hadn't heard a thing from Chester.

Willet was convinced Daddy and Uncle Chester's shady business deals were connected to Pansy's disappearance. If Daddy didn't take Pansy, Willet reasoned, someone connected to Daddy must have snatched her.

"All those men showing up to buy bills? They're desperate, Bert. They don't have a thing to lose."

I wasn't convinced. If someone took Pansy for a ransom, even a counterfeit ransom, wouldn't we have heard from them by now?

Granny Clem was outside when we pulled up. She shaded her eyes against the morning sun and the dust from the motorbike. Willet set the kickstand. He seemed to be taking a long time and I couldn't figure why he was stalling. Now I think he was nervous. It was brazen of us to come out uninvited.

"Does your mother know you're here?" Granny Clem stood on her front porch, hands on hips, sun in her face. I couldn't tell if she was angry or curious.

"No, ma'am," Willet answered. He was polite when it suited him. "We're looking for Uncle Chester. Is he around?"

"I don't rightly know," she said. "You'll have to knock on his trailer. I don't keep track of his goings."

Willet nodded.

"When you're done," Granny Clem called, "you two come in here and see me. I've got pound cake."

Granny Clem was famous for two things: dealing with pregnant women and babies, and her lemon pound cake. A slice of that cake was often the first thing a woman tasted after giving birth and some women swore their children carried the scent of lemon and butter in the folds of their skin throughout adolescence. Later, when I worked for Granny Clem, women would sometimes stop by with children they'd birthed or adopted from her and would encourage me to sniff their toddlers for the lingering lemon odor.

Granny Clem disappeared inside her house. Willet gave me a look. "You ready?"

"No," I said.

"Me neither."

Even so, he walked toward Uncle Chester's trailer. He took long strides and puffed out his chest. He looked like a grown man. He looked like Daddy. There wasn't room on the trailer steps for both of us, so I waited at the bottom while Willet knocked on the door. It was a pretty high-end trailer, but the whole thing seemed to bend a little under Willet's fist. Right away, we heard movement from inside. Chester peeked out from behind a curtain on the far end. I lifted a hand and tried to smile. We heard him rambling around.

The sun baked the back of my neck. A crow let out a menacing caw. The sharp scent of fertilizer filled my nose, though I couldn't see anything growing nearby. It seemed Uncle Chester would leave us standing there for hours, but finally the aluminum door creaked open and he stepped back to let us in. As I eased across the threshold, a skinny white cat darted past me.

Dust motes floated thick in the dim interior. Chester lit a cigarette and sat at a small dining table. He used an old beer can for an ashtray. The trailer smelled like it hadn't been aired out in years. Stale smoke, greasy cooking odors, and the raw scent of Chester himself mingled together in a terrible stench. The salty chemical fumes from the ink he and Daddy used to print bills hovered beneath the bad smells, and I realized Uncle Chester was only living in this tiny section of the trailer. The back half was blocked off for the business.

I gagged, and Willet reached back to smack me. He was right, of course; we couldn't afford to be rude.

Chester didn't seem to notice the smell or my reaction. He wore a stained T-shirt rotted through where he'd splashed it with bleach. His hair was gray and coarse. The sight of him, hunched and filthy, terrified me. I couldn't remember the last time I'd actually seen him. He never came to holiday gatherings or family dinners. Whatever he and Daddy did together, they did it away from our family. Daddy was careful that way. He didn't hide his business from us, but he didn't let it infiltrate our lives on a daily basis. Daddy didn't look like a criminal. Uncle Chester looked like nothing else.

Willet and I remained standing. We had no choice. The furniture in the trailer was buried underneath a layer of junk: old newspapers, crushed aluminum cans, half-empty bags of dry cat food, cracked melamine plates with crusty bits of old beans or canned stew.

"What do you think you're doing?" he asked.

"We're looking for our father," Willet said. "We thought you might have an idea where we could find him."

Chester laughed and the laugh dissolved into a prolonged hacking cough. It sounded as if his lungs were working their way out through his throat. He wiped his mouth with the tail of his T-shirt, leaving a smear of yellow phlegm across the cotton fabric. He grinned. His teeth were a disturbing shade of brown. He took a drag off his cigarette and dropped the butt into the old beer can, where it smoldered.

"You kids know better than to poke around like this. I can't do nothing for you."

It was a mistake to come. Even if Uncle Chester knew Daddy's whereabouts, he wasn't likely to share any information. He and Daddy had a way of doing things that didn't take other people into account. That was why Daddy felt justified in coming and going without ever considering our feelings. I hated them both for a moment. I figured we'd leave, head over to Granny Clem's and have a piece of lemon pound cake, but Willet wasn't so easily deterred.

"Maybe you heard about Pansy," he said. "She's gone missing."

"I heard you two lost her." Chester sounded amused.

"Someone took her," Willet said. "Do you have any idea who might want to take her?"

Chester lit another cigarette. My eyes stung from the smoke. It was everything I could do to stand there and keep breathing.

"You two were mighty careless with that little girl." He took a long drag off the cigarette. Willet tensed up, and I thought he might throw a punch.

"Our mother is a mess," I said. "She's worried half to death. We need to find Pansy."

Chester leaned forward, snorted, and wiped his mouth again with the dirty T-shirt. "That woman was always soft," he said. "I warned Earl not to marry her."

Uncle Chester didn't care for most people. He didn't seem to care much for himself, and his views on marriage and family were anything but generous. Still, it seemed a hard slight to warn our father against marrying our mother. After all, we were standing in front of him, his niece and his nephew, the products of that marriage. And Mama and Daddy loved each other.

They did.

Daddy spent too much time away, it's true, but Mama was always happy to see him when he came home. Now I realize her happiness might have been relief. What would we do if Daddy never came home? How would we live? For all Daddy's criminal activity and lack of steadiness, he provided for our family. Whatever else he was doing on the road, he was earning money and he brought the cash home to Mama. That's a kind of love.

"You sonofabitch," Willet said. "You know something, don't you?"

Chester grinned again; his stained teeth glowed. "What could I know? What could I possibly know about a goddamned thing?"

"Please," I said. "Just tell us how to find Daddy. Or call him and ask him to come home. Can't you do that much?" I was begging and I wasn't proud of it. Desperate times. "If he knew about Pansy he'd come right home. I know he would."

Chester leaned toward me in a menacing way. "What makes you think so?" He sounded genuinely curious. "What makes you think Earl doesn't already know everything? What makes you think that little girl ain't better off wherever she is now? What makes you think your Daddy gives a damn about any of this?"

"Maybe he'll give a damn when the police track him down," Willet said. "Maybe you'll be a little more cooperative when the police question *you*."

Chester stood and grabbed Willet around the neck with both hands. The cigarette dangled from between his lips, and he exhaled smoke into Willet's face. "Boy, I know you got better sense than to threaten me with the law."

"Let him go," I said. "We won't say anything."

"Sure we will." Willet's voice strained. He squinted against the cloud of smoke swirling from Chester's rotten mouth but he kept talking. "The police are at our house every day, and you are a damn fool if you think they won't make their way here. They're already asking questions about our father. They're already looking for him. How long do you think it'll take before they uncover your little counterfeiting business?"

Chester kept a strong grip on Willet's throat and both were enveloped in a thick cloud of smoke, so I don't know how my brother was able to make such a speech, but it seemed nothing would stop him. I noticed a hunting rifle propped behind a pile of old papers. It was out of Chester's reach, but barely. What would we do if he went for it? Was it the only gun? Unlikely. Who knew how many weapons were concealed in the mess of the trailer?

"Look at this place. You think they won't find your printing supplies? You figure they won't uncover your phony bills?"

"You're just as sorry as your Daddy said." Chester squeezed Willet's throat. "A coward who won't never be a man." My brother wheezed and struggled. My stomach hurt and my pulse thumped too fast. Somehow in my panic, though, my brain was clear. I sidestepped toward the hunting rifle. Chester didn't seem to notice I'd moved.

"I got no interest in becoming a man like you," Willet squeaked. His face turned purple.

I took a half step to my left, a half step closer to the rifle. It was possible the rifle wasn't loaded, but not likely. Chester was not the type of man who'd be cautious about gun safety.

"I'd be doing Earl a favor if I slit your throat right now."

I noticed the knife on his belt. It wasn't particularly large, but I figured he knew how to use it. I couldn't stand there and watch my uncle kill my brother. I lunged for the rifle, grabbing it at the barrel from behind a stack of trash. I managed to slide my grip down and get it propped against my shoulder. I pointed it at Chester, but my arms shook. It was heavier than I expected and longer. I put my finger on the trigger. One thing Daddy taught me early was to never aim a gun I wasn't prepared to shoot. He'd said it in the context of hunting deer and squirrel, but I could see how it applied to this situation. If I showed any hesitation, Chester would have the advantage.

"Bert," Willet croaked. "Don't."

"Let him go," I said.

Chester released his grip on Willet's neck. He laughed. "That gun ain't hardly worth holding, little sister. It don't fire but every third pull. Only reason it's out is I was trying to fix it."

"Maybe it'll fire, maybe it won't." I worked to sound steady, though my arms and shoulders ached and my heart drummed heavy in my chest. "Should we find out?"

Chester took a step back from Willet, who rubbed his throat with his hands. "All right. We're done here," Chester said. "No one needs killing today."

"Bert," Willet said. "Put the gun down. It's okay."

I wanted to put it down but I couldn't seem to release the cold steel. My hands became claws. I leaned back to counter the weight of the rifle. If I loosened my grip, I knew I'd fall right over.

Willet came to my rescue. He put his hands under mine and lifted the rifle just enough to take all the weight. I relaxed and stepped away.

"That little girl's got twice the balls you do," Chester said. He wheezed out a thin laugh, lit another cigarette. "Y'all get on out of here now."

"We're not done," Willet said.

"No," Chester said, "I reckon you ain't done, but you done all you can today. Next time I speak with Earl, I'll tell him you came in for a visit. How's that?"

We left Chester there in the hazy blue stench of his trailer. When the flimsy door shut behind us, and we were standing again on natural ground, Willet reached out and pulled me in tight. "You okay?"

I couldn't let myself cry, though I knew it would be a relief. "I'm all right."

He let me go and my legs gave out. I sat down on the hard ground with a thump.

Willet crouched down beside me. "Get up, Bert."

"You know, I don't think I can," I told him. "My legs quit working."

Willet lugged me to standing. He kept a strong grip on me and pretty much dragged me toward the brick house. My legs felt useless as a rag doll's, but I made a show of trying to step steady.

Inside the house, Granny Clem brought me a glass of cold lemonade and a thick slice of yellow cake. Her house was neat as a pin and laundry fresh. Granny Clem wore long sacklike cotton dresses and pulled her gray hair into a tight bun on the back of her head. Coarse hairs sprouted from a mole on her upper lip and a web of fine lines snaked out around her eyes and lips, but anyone could see how beautiful she'd once been. She didn't hunch over like some old people. She never hesitated to step on a ladder. She was small, but not fragile.

"You kids ought not bother Chester," she said. "He's not quite right."

"What makes him that way?" I asked.

Willet shushed me.

Granny Clem patted my shoulder. "He was born that way, baby. Born in violent times and in violent circumstances. Some men overcome that and others sink into it."

She sat across from us in a polished wood rocking chair.

"Have you heard from *him?*" Willet set his plate on the coffee table.

Granny Clem clasped her hands in her lap and shook her head. "I'm sorry. I wish I had."

"He has Pansy," Willet said. "Or he knows who does."

Granny Clem rocked forward and locked eyes with Willet. "I know Earl would never hurt your sister. He loves her. He loves you all."

"Then why won't he come home?" I asked. "Mama needs him."

"I can't say why your father does what he does, but I know he believes he is doing the right thing by you."

"The right thing?" Willet's voice rose. "He ain't hardly ever home. How is that the right thing?"

"Not everything in this world is simple," Granny Clem said. "In fact, almost nothing is. You might not understand your father's ways, but you shouldn't doubt his intentions. He is doing the best he can for you and your mother." Granny Clem paused and rocked hard for a few seconds. She looked at Willet and then at me. "How was that cake, baby?"

"Perfect," I said.

"We didn't come here for cake," Willet said.

"I know that," Granny Clem said. "I wish I had some answers for you. I wish I knew where to find your father. I wish I could tell you what happened to your sister. But you all knew better than to swim in that quarry. I know your Daddy taught you better than that."

"Daddy says the quarry is cursed," I said.

Granny Clem closed her eyes, like she couldn't bear to look at me. "Terrible things have happened there. Ungodly things. Your father knows."

"That's ridiculous," Willet said. "Curses ain't real. They're just some nonsense made up to scare people. And I don't believe in the Devil. I know men can be evil, but it ain't some plot of land that makes 'em so."

Granny Clem opened her eyes. "What you believe or don't believe won't change the facts. Your father warned you to stay away from the quarry and for good reason. Look what happened."

"It's all our fault." My hands shook and I felt lightheaded from the guilt or from too much sugar.

"No," Granny Clem said. "I'm not blaming you, but you need to see that there are things in this world beyond your understanding. You can't dismiss something just because you can't see it."

"Like God," I said.

"Like the Devil," Granny Clem said.

"There's no Devil," Willet said. "I ain't convinced God is real, but I know there's no Devil."

I wasn't sure what I believed, but I'd seen something in those woods and I thought it might have been the Devil. I couldn't talk about such things with my brother, because he only trusted something if he could see it with his eyes or hold it in his hands.

Granny Clem said, "The Devil is real, all right. You just have to learn how to recognize him. He's not some horned beast with glowing eyes. He looks like you and like me and like anyone he chooses."

"Let's get out of here, Bert," Willet said. "I can't listen to no more of this."

I wasn't sure I wanted to leave. Even with all the talk of curses and the Devil, I liked being in Granny Clem's house. I liked listening to her talk. The things she said made sense to me. It was comforting to be with someone who could believe in so many things.

Granny Clem stood with us at the door. She took my hand. "This was not your fault." she said. "Do you understand?"

I nodded, though I didn't believe her.

"I'll stop by for a visit soon. Tell your mother to call me if she needs anything."

Outside, as we climbed on to the motorbike, I said, "Willet, what if she's right?"

"There ain't no such thing as a curse, Bert. People want to blame something other than themselves when bad shit happens."

I wasn't sure what to believe. All those stories we'd heard from Daddy and from Granny Clem, stories about evil rising up from the quarry; we'd always dismissed those stories as silly rumors, no more real than the fairy tales we read in books. But what if we were wrong? What then?

As a boy he'd liked nothing better than listening to the stories of women. He liked the way their voices spilled out in whispers or in laughter. He liked the way they told the same stories again and again. His mother had told him painful stories, hard to hear and hard to tell but necessary, like draining poison from a wound. Sometimes he eavesdropped, but mostly he paid attention. If he stayed silent and still, there was nothing they wouldn't say in front of him.

When Clementine was fifteen years old, her mother fell ill. She said she was only tired, but Clementine could see it was more than ordinary tiredness. They'd spent the weekend canning hull peas and snap beans and tomatoes. Hot miserable work, but work her mother did every year. If Clementine lived to be a hundred, she couldn't eat all the food her mother stored. Her mother said there could never be enough food. Hunger always comes, she told her daughter. When Clementine's father came home that night, coated as always in the gray dust from his job at the quarry, he fetched the doctor. They could hardly afford the fee, but they remembered the influenza epidemic of a few years earlier. They knew the danger of letting illness fester.

The doctor said he'd heard of similar cases, an illness that affected only women. He called it the "Sleepy Sickness." He said Clementine's mother would either rise up in a week or so, or she would sink deeper into the sickness and would sleep her way to death. He knew of no cure or treatment. Every day Clementine brought her mother clear broths and tea and coaxed her to swallow a few mouthfuls. It was difficult, because her mother kept falling asleep with the warm liquid in her mouth. It would spill out her slack lips and drip over her cheeks and her neck. Clementine wiped her with a damp cloth and begged her to open her eyes, but her mother seemed beyond her reach, like someone in another world.

Clementine's closest friend Ora visited as often as she could manage. Ora was superstitious and said a dark spirit had settled in Clementine's mother. She told Clementine to sweep counterclockwise around her mother's bed and to tuck a sprig of lemon balm under her mother's mattress. Still, her mother slept. Clementine opened the window next to her mother's bed each morning to freshen the stale air in the room. She opened it even when the morning air grew colder and frost covered the ground. A fat robin perched on the tree outside the window. It sang to Clementine and she imagined the bird was exhorting her mother to rise. She put an extra quilt on her mother's bed and opened the window wider. There must be a hint of warmth on the breeze for such a bird to thrive. She read to her mother from the Bible and then from the novels Ora loaned her: *Winesburg, Ohio* and *Sister Carrie* and *My Antonia*. Clementine's mother wouldn't approve of the novels, but she gave no indication she heard anything at all, and Clementine could take only so much of the Bible.

When Clementine told Ora about the visiting robin and his throaty morning song, Ora slapped her across the face. "It's the bird of death," she said. "Come to take your mother's soul. It will take yours, too, if you aren't careful."

Clementine cried, not because she believed a bird could steal someone's soul, but because everything seemed hopeless. Her mother wouldn't wake up, and Clementine could barely get her to swallow a mouthful of water each day. She was starving to death, this woman who'd built a storehouse against the threat of hunger, and no one could explain why. Maybe this was God's way of punishing her for being willful and going against her mother's wishes. In the spring she'd been courted by an older boy from a family of merchants. She'd rejected him, though her mother said she wouldn't be a pretty girl forever and might not do better. Maybe if she'd accepted the boy's proposal, she would have enough money to help her mother now. Maybe her mother fell ill from disappointment.

Ora took her hand and pressed it against her breast, over her heart. She told Clementine what to do; to kill the bird, to shoot it or trap it or break its neck, and then wipe its blood across her heart and her mother's heart. "It may be too late for her," Ora said. "Her soul is weak." Ora told Clementine to light a candle in each corner of her mother's bedroom and sprinkle salt across the threshold of the doorway. She told her to wash her mother's feet with soap made from rosemary and goat fat. Clementine had no idea where she was supposed to find such soap.

The next morning, before the sun rose, Clementine took her father's hunting rifle and stood beneath the maple tree. When the sun stretched its fingers into the dark sky, she waited for the bird to send its first notes out into the morning, but the bird didn't come. It knew she'd be waiting. It smelled her there and stayed away. Or maybe it had already taken her mother's soul. Maybe the shallow breathing body in the bed was nothing but a husk. Even so, Clementine lit candles and sprinkled salt. She sliced into her own hand until blood flowed and rubbed the warm sticky palm across her mother's breast. She washed her mother's feet with plain lye soap. She hoped it would be enough to fool the Devil.

The doctor visited again a few days before Christmas and said he saw no hope for recovery. At least Ora had offered hope. The doctor said her mother would not live to see the new year, but

Clementine was determined to prove him wrong. She forced broth and milk into her mother's mouth and talked to her constantly, but nothing revived her.

Clementine killed and plucked a hen on Christmas Eve. Neither she nor her father had been eating well lately, existing on bland grits and cold beans, but she was determined to cook a decent Christmas dinner. She'd put aside a beautiful squash and would make fresh cornbread in her mother's cast-iron skillet. She planned to make her mother's pound cake, too, and had pulled a jar of preserved lemons from the pantry. It was a summer cake, really, and better with fresh lemons, but Clementine thought it would make her father happy to taste the cake his wife made so often. She hoped the scent of the baking cake might stir something in her mother.

She was trussing the hen when she heard the robin sing. It was back, the songbird of death. It couldn't be the same bird, and yet she knew it was. Clementine marched outside with her father's rifle and shot the bird squarely through its fat, red chest. It fell to the ground with a thump. She picked it up and squeezed its still warm body in her fist. The bird's blood oozed onto her hands and she wiped it across her chest. She marched inside, intending to wipe the blood on her mother. But her father knelt by her mother's bedside, weeping, and she couldn't bear to interrupt his grief. Her mother was dead.

One month later, her father put the barrel of the rifle in his mouth and pulled the trigger. Ora came and helped Clementine scrub her father's brains off the back door of the house. Ora helped her dig the grave. They buried him beside her mother, in a plot on the edge of their land. They lined the double plot with stones from the quarry. Clementine had found a pile of them in her father's tool chest. There was no money for a grave marker. The quarry rocks would have to do.

FOUR

———◆———

IN THE WEEK AFTER she disappeared, Pansy's face was everywhere, on television and in the newspapers, plastered across store windows and utility poles. She squatted at the center of our collective mind and whispered *look at me, look at me, look at me.* We looked. We searched. We begged others to do the same. The police officers who'd come that first day were now regular visitors. The fat one brought me a stuffed bear wearing a deputy's badge. Even though I was much too old for stuffed toys, I thanked him and hugged the bear tight to my chest.

Mama was going to be on the evening news again. We settled in with a plate of pimento cheese and saltine crackers. Our refrigerator bulged with casserole dishes from well meaning neighbors, but we were sick of the food they brought. Everything tasted the same. Chicken spaghetti with a hard crust of salty cheddar, meatloaf surrounded by congealed fat, dumpling stew with too much baking powder, runny Jell-O salad with peaches, lemon pie with sweaty meringue. We couldn't stand one more bite.

Mama didn't eat a thing. She smoked cigarettes and drank sweet tea. She shushed us and turned on the television. We held the cheese and crackers in our cheeks until it went soft enough to chew without making any noise.

The blonde reporter came on the screen alongside a picture of Pansy. She looked like the sort of woman who would wear too much perfume. I swear I got a whiff of Chanel from the television.

"This child, this precious innocent child, has been missing for five days. She has brown hair and green eyes. She stands about three feet tall. She weighs only forty-five pounds. Someone has seen her. Someone knows where she is. Her mother is frantic with worry. We talked with her earlier today."

And Mama came on the screen. She pleaded for Pansy, begged for information. Our mother looked especially tired and small next to the reporter with her crisp suit and aggressive shoulder pads. Mama seemed to fade into the walls against the reporter's brassy hair and swinging gold earrings. "Please," Mama said to the camera. "Please bring my baby home. Please don't hurt her. She's all I have in this world." *All?* I looked at Willet, but he stared at the television and didn't meet my eye. The fat policeman came on and gave a number to call with any information about Pansy.

I looked at Mama. I wanted to know what she was thinking. Her hands clasped against her chest; her eyes never blinked. A cigarette smoldered in an ashtray beside her. After everyone was done talking, the whole screen filled with the image of Pansy's face and a phone number for people to call with information. It was terrifying to see our sister's face so large. Pansy's image hung there for a very long time. The cheese and crackers hardened into a knot in my gut. Finally, when I thought we might spend the rest of our lives staring at a blown-up image of my sister, the blonde woman reappeared. She leaned toward the camera. It seemed like she was talking right to us, like she was making eye contact.

"Someone out there is responsible for this little girl's disappearance. Someone out there knows what happened. Do the right thing and come forward. Give this child's mother some peace. Give this community some peace. And parents, hold your babies a little tighter tonight. Watch them and keep them close. Until we have answers, until we have an arrest, we must assume there is evil on the loose. No child is safe."

With that, the reporter brought summer to an end for all the children in our town. There would be no more unsupervised trips to the snow-cone truck. There would be no more bike rides without a destination. There would be no more hide-and-seek in the woods, no more building bridges across Little Sand Creek, no more catching fireflies in mayonnaise jars and using them for lanterns. The only people under the age of eighteen who'd be allowed any freedom at all were Willet and me. Mama was too distraught or too distracted to keep tabs on the children in her home. She was too busy hunting for the child who wasn't there. She blamed us for Pansy's disappearance. Of course she did. If we'd kept an eye on her baby, if we hadn't gone to the quarry, none of this mess would have happened.

People called our home daily with reports of seeing Pansy at a convenience store in Shreveport or in a mall in Alabama. A man called to say he had Pansy and she was fine, not to worry about her. A child playing a cruel prank called and pretended to be Pansy, shouting through the phone line: "Mama, come and get me. I'm all alone out here!" Willet pulled the receiver from Mama's hand and cussed into the phone until the child on the other end wailed and hung up.

A woman who claimed to be psychic said Pansy was in the grips of an evil man. She said she could find her and release her from his grasp if Mama would send her three hundred and thirty-three dollars within thirty-three hours. Something about the number three was important, but I don't remember the explanation. Mama wanted to send the money, but Willet stopped her. The police praised Willet.

"It's a scam," the thin officer said. "Happens anytime we get a missing persons case."

It was during this time that a strange woman showed up at our house. Her hair was gray and thin, the skin of her face stretched too tight across her bones. She wore all black clothing even in the heat of

August. Mama invited her in, offered her coffee and a cigarette. The woman had driven from Pittsburgh, a place I imagined as ugly and cold. She told us her son had disappeared ten years earlier, snatched from the street as he walked home from school. Mama nodded; she remembered the news reports. They sat in our living room, clutching stale cups of coffee, smoking, and talking about her son. Every few months, the woman said, someone reported seeing him. They saw him at a service station with an older man and another boy outside of New Jersey. They saw him smoking marijuana on the streets of San Francisco. Someone swore he stole food from a restaurant in Boulder, Colorado. A grainy film showed a boy who might have been him, who might have been anyone, doing unspeakable things to older men for money.

"People will tell you these things," the woman said to Mama. "You'll believe every one of them, and it will break your heart, but you should never give up looking. I have never stopped searching. I will never lose hope for my child."

"Of course not," Mama said. "How could you? How could I?"

The woman told Mama how she continued to search for her son even as everyone around her gave up. She prayed. She put her trust in God. Her husband left her. Her friends and family grew distant. The police stopped returning her calls.

The police, she said, would give up soon. "They won't keep looking once the case goes cold. And the reporters will move on to other things. You are the only one who will keep the search for your daughter alive. You must be diligent. You should make a pest of yourself. It isn't easy. I know you want to please everyone, to be pleasant. You cannot be pleasant or polite or quiet. You will have to scream and get angry. People will start to hate you, and you have to learn how to not care. Do you understand?"

Mama nodded. "Thank you," she said. "This is all very helpful."

I wasn't so sure. Who did this woman think she was, coming in and telling us to expect this nightmare to go on and on and on? Telling us it might get worse? Ten years she'd lived with the horror of her missing son, but Pansy had been gone for just over a week. It was too soon to start talking about cold cases. If any child could escape kidnappers, surely Pansy could. She wasn't like other children her age. She didn't act like a little kid; she didn't talk like one. I knew Pansy could escape the grip of the creature from the woods. Pansy wasn't like that woman's son. She wasn't some ordinary child lost on the streets. She was different. She was special.

For one thing, Pansy never babbled nor spoke in the soft, slurred way most children do. For the first three years of her life, she didn't say a word. No "mama" or "dada" or "mine" or anything an ordinary child might say. When she was almost four, she began speaking clearly and in complete sentences, with a vocabulary that stunned us all. The first thing she said was, "Mama, I'm hungry, and Bert won't fix me a snack." Just like that. As if I had been ignoring some request from her, as if we'd been having a discussion.

Mama had stared at her, shocked, and then she'd laughed. "Roberta Lynn," she said. "Go fix your sister a sandwich. She's hungry." I'd protested. Why did I have to get her a snack? I wasn't her servant. I wasn't her mother. But Mama fixed me with a dark look. "We honor a person's first request," Mama said. "And a person's last request. We can negotiate the rest." I fixed the sandwich, tearing the bread as I smeared peanut butter across it in short, angry strokes. If this was what it meant to have Pansy speaking, I would have preferred her mute.

Shortly thereafter, Pansy introduced us to Ivy. Ivy, she insisted, was her sister, her favorite sister, and we were all instructed to be kind to her. That we couldn't see her didn't make her any less of an intrusion in our lives. Ivy spent her days lolling on the couch. She wore long, diaphanous dresses. "Here comes Ivy," Pansy would say. "Can you hear her dress swishing against the floor?" Sometimes I swore I could.

Ivy loved sweet things. She was mad for Mama's coconut cake. She couldn't get her fill of biscuits with jam or honey. Pansy reported this to us, and food did seem to disappear.

Mama made biscuits most mornings and we ate them throughout the day, flaky biscuits with butter, with blueberry jam, with honey and sour cream, or plain and soaked in buttermilk. I liked to hold one biscuit back for the next day, when I would split the stale disk in half, slather both sides with butter and run it under the broiler on a piece of tinfoil. I loved the brown, crispy edges of the toasted biscuit, and the way my teeth snapped through the salty outer crust. I kept my biscuit in a corner of the kitchen counter, wrapped in a square of paper towel. Everyone knew it was mine. During an unseasonably cool week one fall my biscuit began to disappear. I didn't say anything the first day, but when it disappeared three days in a row, I was furious.

"Who is taking my biscuit?"

I'd assembled Mama and Willet and Pansy together in the living room for my interrogation. Daddy was off on one of his trips, so he couldn't be responsible. I'd accused each of them in turn over the past days, and they'd denied stealing from me. I guess I believed by bringing them all together, someone would have to confess. No one did. Willet laughed at me and told me to relax. Mama said I was being ridiculous. Pansy swore it wasn't her, but then she paused and grinned. "I bet it's Ivy!"

I hated Ivy. Pansy and I shared a room, and I was forced to listen to her babbling away with Ivy every morning. Now Pansy said Ivy was stealing my biscuit; it was too much. I lashed out at her. "She's not real! She's not a real person!"

Pansy smiled. "Just because you can't see her doesn't mean she isn't real."

Thankfully, Mama spoke up or I might have throttled Pansy. "I know you like to pretend to have a friend your own age, but Ivy is someone you made up. Ivy isn't real, sweetie."

"She's real," Pansy said. "She's my sister, and you can't make her go away."

Mama gave Pansy a long look. "Now, Pansy, it's nice to imagine things, but we've talked about what a bad thing it is to lie."

"I'm not lying," Pansy said. "And you know it."

Mama stood. She brushed her hands together. "I have work to do. This house is a wreck."

There was nothing wrong with the house. It was no more or less a wreck than it ever was. I stamped my foot like a spoiled child. I was about twelve years old at the time.

"Roberta Lynn, I am sorry you're upset about your biscuit, but you know there are children starving in the world. There are children in Africa who've never so much as tasted a biscuit."

That kind of reasoning drove me nuts. Of course I knew there were children who didn't have enough to eat, who didn't have any clean water. If I could give my biscuit to one of those children, I would gladly do so. I would give up eating biscuits altogether if it meant those poor African children could fill their bellies, but that wasn't an option and Mama knew it.

"That has nothing to do with this," I said. "Those starving children aren't stealing my biscuit! Someone in *this* house is stealing my biscuit!"

"Ivy loves biscuits with honey," Pansy said.

Willet rolled his eyes. "That child is touched in the head. She's a goddamned loon."

"Watch your mouth," Mama said. "The inquisition is over, Roberta Lynn. You'll just have to find a better place to keep your biscuit, somewhere it won't get accidentally eaten."

"How can someone accidentally eat something?" I shouted at Mama.

"I want your rooms cleaned," Mama said. "Top to bottom. Wipe down the baseboards. Pull the books off the shelf and dust every one."

I felt like crying, but I knew it would only prompt Mama to add something else to the chore list. Willet didn't care. He kept his room spotless; there was nothing in it to get dusty. Pansy never pitched in to help in our bedroom. I was being punished and I couldn't understand why. The way I saw it, I was the only one who hadn't done anything wrong.

Now I realize Mama didn't see it that way. I was the one who started an argument over something as trivial as a biscuit. It seemed a silly thing to make such a scene over, but it wasn't silly to me. I shared everything with Pansy and she always managed to get more of everything—more dessert, more attention, more of our mother's love. Even when Mama was upset with Pansy about her imaginary sister, she punished me. The unfairness of it festered and ate at me like a disease.

Some years later, I asked Mama about it. I asked her why she treated Pansy so special. She denied ever doing any such thing, told me I was being stupid, told me she treated all her children exactly the same. She denied ever bringing Pansy chocolate milk in bed or making her special meals. "No," she said. "I would not have done such a thing. Although, with everything that's happened, I wish I had." I didn't press her. After all, memory is a slippery thing, and who's to say mine was any better than hers.

Maybe the woman from Pittsburgh would never find her son, but I believed we'd find Pansy. How could anyone take such a child and not return her? Who would put up with her wild imagination? I'd resigned myself to living with the guilt of losing Pansy, but only when the woman from Pittsburgh showed up did I understand how completely our lives had changed. We were not just *that* family now. We might be *that* family forever. And being *that* family meant people could intrude without invitation. Were we required to let them in? Mama seemed to think so.

Mama and the woman talked for hours. It was midafternoon, the hottest part of the day. The sky was cloudless and bright. Our air conditioning hummed and the box fan whirred, but it was no match for the sun and the thick humid air. My body was covered in a sticky sheen of sweat. Willet paced through the house, as if searching for something he'd lost. A sour scent wafted from the kitchen. We hadn't taken the trash out in days.

My thoughts grew dark. I kept picturing Pansy floating in the quarry, how peaceful she seemed, how content she was to let the water carry her. Her disappearance made no sense. Somehow she'd been swallowed up by the creature from the woods. If I found him, maybe he would spit her out again. I left Mama and the woman without excusing myself. I walked alone down the hot dusty road, the same one we'd traveled before. The heat rose up to meet me. It pushed against me, warning me to turn back, but I kept going. It wasn't the quarry I wanted to see, but the clearing in the woods. If the loathsome creature were there, I would confront him. If evil presented itself to me, I was ready. I'd had enough of waiting for Mama and Willet and the police to find Pansy. I'd had enough of waiting for Daddy to come home.

I'd failed my sister by hiding like a frightened child in the woods on the day she disappeared. I'd failed Mama and Willet, but I thought I could make it right. The creature lived among the shadows and he'd taken Pansy to live there as well. Most people couldn't see into the shadows, but I could. I had. All I needed to do was find the same spot in the clearing, find the shadows, and find the creature. Then, surely, I would find my sister. I could not live for the next decade with the terrible gnawing guilt. The woman from Pittsburgh might be content to get angry and pray, but it was not enough for me.

I thought about a story from the book of fairy tales I read to Pansy most nights. It was an old heavy book, full of dark tales about monsters and bad parents. There was a story about a girl who disguised herself as an animal to hide from the king, her own father, who'd declared his intention to marry her after the death of her mother. She knew it was a godless plan. To escape she became "all fur," wrapping herself in animal pelts and using soot to blacken her face. In this disguise she worked in the royal kitchen. Her father threw boots at her head when she brought him his soup. It was a miserable, dark story, but Pansy liked it. She liked the dark stories best. I liked them, too. Perhaps Pansy was hiding in the woods now, wearing a cloak of pelts, biding her time and waiting for someone to come and find her. Perhaps Ivy was with her. I tell you it seemed as likely as anything.

Mosquitoes buzzed across my face and neck, and I didn't bother to swat them away. Welts rose on my exposed skin. My cheeks and neck grew inflamed and swollen. One step and another step and another and I made it to the edge of the woods. My eyes were burned out from staring too directly into the blazing white sun, but I didn't stop to let them adjust. It seemed important to keep moving forward into the darkness, into the shadows where the creature lived.

The woods thrummed with life, though the birds were silent. The trees beckoned me forward. Fear perched high and tight in my chest. Cool pine needles pressed against my blistered feet. A branch reached out and scraped my face. I found the berry brambles where we'd eaten the sweet fruit. They gave off a sugary fragrance that made my stomach ache, but the berries didn't look the same. I'd remembered them as black raspberries, but these berries were dark purple and smooth. Why were my memories from that day so unreliable? I walked away from the berries, retracing my steps, but I came upon no clearing. I doubled back, found the berries again, and set off in a different direction. Maybe I'd been disoriented in the storm. But no matter which direction I walked, I couldn't find the clearing where I'd seen the creature. I walked in circles, weak and dizzy. When had I last eaten? I couldn't remember. A spoonful of soggy banana pudding in the morning—or was that last night? I'd drunk nothing but coffee for a week. Our milk had soured, so I'd taken to drinking it black with a little sugar. My head ached terribly. My hands shook. My legs grew weak.

I couldn't find the clearing. I couldn't find the creature. I couldn't find my sister. And I didn't have the energy to find my way home. The welts on my face and neck began to itch. My skin burned from too much sun. My brain seemed to waver and fade, leaving me with muddy thoughts and long lapses of nothing. I needed sleep. Before Pansy disappeared, it was so easy to slip into the warm drowsiness of a dark room, but now the darkness seemed filled with danger. Nightmares tore me awake at night, and only a steady intake of caffeine kept me going each day. I stretched out beneath a water oak and closed my eyes. The dirt warmed beneath my body. My heartbeat slowed. My arms and legs grew heavy. The soft chirp of insects chased away the bad thoughts. For the first time in days, I felt calm.

Willet found me hours later, dead asleep underneath the tree. He shook me awake, his voice urgent and worried. "Bert, come on! You have to wake up."

I smiled at him. He seemed so far away, his voice echoing as if he were speaking into a tunnel.

"What the hell are you doing out here?"

I told him he was silly. "This is where I belong."

"I'm taking you home."

It was early evening. I could tell by the softness of the dappled light coming through the trees. I'd never felt more comfortable or more relaxed. My body was limp and warm and heavy. I wanted to feel that way forever.

"Goddammit! I've been worried sick. I thought someone took you, too." Willet's face hovered above mine. "Have you lost your fool mind?"

Everything seemed funny. Pansy was part of some cosmic game of hide-and-seek. We'd find her if we followed the rules. "Count to one hundred," I said.

Willet carried me out of the woods. Orange police tape stretched across a line of trees and I wondered how I'd missed it on my way in.

Willet stumbled, but held on to me. "I don't know if I can carry you the whole way."

Even though I knew I was much too old and heavy to be carried, I didn't offer to walk. It was so nice to be held and cared for by someone. Crickets and bullfrogs chirped and croaked in the twilight. Stars appeared above us. There was still a bit of silver light in the sky, but darkness was taking over. I'd been gone for half a day, at least.

"Was Mama worried?"

Willet didn't say anything, just kept moving forward. He didn't have to tell me. I knew the truth. Mama hadn't noticed I was gone.

HE BELIEVED IN EVIL, not in the abstract but as a living, breathing presence in the world. Men committed loathsome violence and no one held them accountable. Sometimes he dreamed of revenge or of justice, but mostly he wondered what made a person turn bad. Were some men born with a streak of evil? Was he? No matter how many different ways he looked at the stories, he never found an answer.

After her father died, Clementine found work at the hardware store. She was seventeen and she needed the job. The owner added a section for gardening supplies and plants. Clementine told women when to cut back their roses and how to make azalea bushes grow tall and full. As a child, she had resisted helping her mother with her constant chores, but she had absorbed the information.

The women who shopped at the hardware store brought in pictures, glossy ads from *McClure's* or *Colliers*, and asked Clementine to help them recreate a particular bed of flowers. She understood what they wanted and she made substitutions to accommodate for the climate or growing season. While Clementine worked with plants, Ora taught herself medicine. She ordered large books from catalogs, and Clementine lugged the heavy packages home from the post office. Sometimes Ora asked Clementine to bring her a particular plant or herb. Some were readily available, but others she ordered special. Ora made teas for soothing a cough and boiled down the tea herbs with sugar to make hard candy cough drops. She bundled together a mix of herbs and roots for a fever compress.

Sometimes Clementine would notice a woman at the store who suffered from a lingering cold or whose eyes were dark-rimmed with lack of sleep. "Come see Ora," she told them. "Ora can help with that."

And Ora did help. Doctors told the women they were weak or hysterical, that their ailments were all in their mind. Ora took their complaints seriously. So many of the problems, Ora told Clementine, had to do with things the women didn't want to discuss with the male doctors. Their cycles were unpredictable after childbirth or too heavy each month.

"It always comes down to blood," Ora said.

Ora developed remedies for women who bled too much or too often, and for women whose blood didn't come. She treated women for the crushing pain that preceded the blood each month and she helped soothe them after they gave birth, particularly when their husbands were too quick to reenter them. Clementine learned from Ora. She enjoyed the work with the herbs and plants. She enjoyed seeing women healed. Ora abandoned her old dark superstitions for the bright science of medicine.

Though she preferred working with Ora, Clementine continued her work at the hardware store. She liked the promise of a steady paycheck, the feeling of independence it gave her. One evening she was finishing up inventory when a heavy storm rolled in. The sky poured gray rain and thunder rumbled. It was the sort of storm that would continue for hours, possibly until morning. She dreaded the walk home. Normally she rode a bicycle into town, but she'd had a flat on the ride home the day before. The walk was long, about three miles, but not unpleasant when the weather was fine. In the downpour she'd be soaked to the skin within minutes. The creek she usually rode through or waded across would be flooded. She'd have to take the longer route, sticking to roads and bridges rather than cutting through farms and fields.

She decided to have coffee at the diner across the street. Maybe the rain would let up. Ora would be worried, but she would worry no matter what in this weather. They didn't have a phone in the house. There was no way for Clementine to call and let Ora know her plans.

At the diner, she ordered coffee and sat at the counter with an old copy of *Scribner's*. A man she knew from the store appeared next to her. He slid a penny across the counter.

"For your thoughts," he said. Ray's wife was a regular customer.

She laughed. "I'm waiting out the weather."

"Might be waiting all night. It's a gully washer."

She sipped her coffee. "I suppose I should just brave it."

"You on foot?"

"It's all I have," she said. "How far?"

"Oh, it's not too bad. Just a few miles north of here, past Sand Creek."

"That's a hike in this mess."

She shrugged. What was there to say?

"It's dark out."

"All the more reason to get moving, I suppose."

He offered to drive her, said his truck was right outside. He was on his way to work the night shift at the cotton gin. She asked if the drive would make him late for work and he said it wouldn't make him late enough to matter. "Plenty of men will be late in this weather."

She thought she shouldn't accept the ride. It wouldn't look right for her to be climbing into a married man's truck after dark, but the walk home would be treacherous and miserable.

"I'm so grateful," she said.

His pickup truck was a nice automobile, well cared for and clean. He took her arm and held the door for her until she was seated with her skirt tucked underneath her. She told him which roads to take. The rain made the night seem darker than usual. No starlight shone across the cotton fields, but lightning cracked and cast a purple glow on the road.

"You walk this far every day?"

"I have a bike," she said. "It has a flat."

"You think it's safe to travel alone like that all the time? Might be wild animals out here. Or other things."

She couldn't imagine what other things might be lurking but she'd seen plenty of animals, mostly deer and wild turkey. She once rode past a pair of mating raccoons in the early morning. They'd hissed at her and barked with an eerie high-pitched chatter, stared her down with their glowing red eyes. She often heard wild dogs howling in the distance and she was careful to avoid snakes, but she'd never been felt threatened by the animals.

"Hear that?" Ray said.

She didn't hear anything out of the ordinary. The truck slowed to a crawl. "Is something wrong?"

"Seems like it," he said. "Maybe something in the engine." He pulled the truck off the road, parked it behind a large oak tree near the old rock quarry, nothing but a deep watery hole now. No one had mined the stones since a season of flooding two years earlier. Clementine stared out the truck's windshield into the dark rain. She couldn't see the old quarry, but she knew it was right in front of her. She shivered.

The rain hammered, louder without the rumble of the engine.

"It might need oil," Ray said.

She waited for him to get out and check under the hood, but he stayed put.

"No use trying to see in this mess," he said.

"Don't you have a light?" Flashlights were a popular purchase at the hardware store. Most of the men who shopped there kept one of the lights in their vehicles for situations like this.

"Gonna have to wait it out," he said. "How can we pass the time?"

She told him she'd walk the rest of the way. They were less than a mile from her house now.

He reached across the seat and took her hand. "Don't be hasty," he said. "I have some thoughts." He put his hand on her neck before sliding it down to grab her breasts. He could strangle her and no one would hear her scream.

"You have a wife."

"Let's leave her out of this." He pulled her legs apart and pushed her skirt up. She wasn't wearing trousers underneath, as she hadn't ridden her bike that day. Instead she wore an old, ragged pair of wool knickers she'd sewed from her father's long johns. She was embarrassed by the unfashionable gray underpants and tried to hold her skirt down around her knees. Ray pulled her arms away and yanked the ugly things down, exposing her to the cool air. What he was doing was wrong, terribly wrong. She knew she should stop him, but he had such a determined look on his face. She closed her eyes.

It only hurt a little and only at first. The physical part wasn't terrible, a lot of poking and jostling, but the sound of his grunting made her sick. His breath smelled hot and sour. The door handle of the truck wedged hard between her shoulders and she knew she'd be left with a bruise. When he finished, he used her ugly underpants to wipe himself clean and then tossed the sticky wad at her. She cracked open the door and dropped them on the sodden ground.

The rain subsided a bit and he got out of the truck and made a show of checking beneath the hood. She straightened her skirt and sat upright. She knew by then there was nothing wrong with his truck. Ray drove on without looking at her. She spoke only to give him the final directions. When he pulled in front of the house, she thanked him. She hated herself for thanking him.

FIVE

———◆———

SOMETIMES THE STRANGEST THINGS come to me, memories fully formed and sharp as cinema: the precise ingredients and technique for making a towering coconut cake, the "Jabberwocky" poem from *Through the Looking Glass*, dance steps from a number on television. These useless bits of information push out the important stuff, like the timeline surrounding my sister's disappearance.

I don't remember which day we went to see Bubba, but we took Willet's motorbike to the run-down neighborhood on the far side of the railroad tracks. The homes were small and crumbling, the yards overgrown with weeds. Bubba was the youngest of six boys, and he didn't have a mother. She died a few days after giving birth to him. His brothers brought him up. His father welded steel from dawn until nightfall. I suspect his father did everything he could to keep those kids clothed. There wouldn't have been any extra. There wouldn't have been enough.

Some of Bubba's brothers were grown and had moved away, but one or two remained in the childhood home or crashed there between permanent situations. They all looked alike—tall, thin boys with long hair and flat faces. Only Bubba was short and round and different.

The brother who answered the door greeted Willet, but he didn't invite us in. "He don't want to see no one," the brother said. "He's done talked to the police three times, and now that blonde bitch from the news is coming around. They think he did something to your sister. Do you think he did something to your sister?"

"No," I said. "No, we don't."

The brother scratched his belly through his faded T-shirt and looked up and down the street like he was scouting for something. "He ain't going back to school," the brother said. "Not here. Pop's shipping him off to that military academy in Port Gibson. They'll straighten him out."

"When does he leave?" Willet asked.

"Next week. He ain't happy about it."

"No," Willet said. "I reckon not."

The brother crossed his arms and studied us for a few moments. "It ain't all about this thing with your sister. He's always been a weird kid. Pops just don't have the energy."

"But Bubba's smart," I said. "He's always been smart."

The brother pointed at me. His fingernails needed cutting and there were gray half moons beneath each one. "Why did you tell those cops you saw my brother at the quarry?"

My face went hot. "Because I saw him," I said. "But I didn't accuse him of anything. I never would."

The brother peered up and down the street again. He seemed nervous. I wondered if he was expecting someone.

"If you let us in, you don't have stand here on the stoop," Willet said.

The house smelled of cabbage and fried fish. It was a small place for such a large family. I'd expected a mess, but everything was tidy and clean. We sat on a small lumpy sofa. The living room was dark, its furniture old and shabby. The television set in the corner was unplugged and covered with a plastic sheet. Squares of tinfoil blocked out most of the light from the windows. I didn't know if they were trying to keep someone from seeing in or if they didn't want to see out. Either way, it gave me the creeps.

The brother sat in an armchair behind a TV tray filled with rolling papers and a small bag of marijuana. He went to work rolling a joint and then another. He placed the rolled joints in a small metal box.

"You buying?" he asked Willet.

"Not today," Willet said.

It surprised me to see my brother so casual about the weed. I knew boys at school who smoked the stuff, but they were stupid boys, lazy and dull. Willet was nothing like them.

The brother closed his metal box and slipped a fat rubber band around it. "Lemme check on the kid," he said. "Maybe he'll feel like company."

"What are we doing here?" I asked when the brother slipped down the hallway.

Willet said, "I want some answers."

The brother was gone a long time. I heard him talking to Bubba in one of the rooms off the hallway, but I couldn't make out what they were saying. I didn't blame Bubba for not wanting to see us. He didn't owe Willet and me anything. Something the brother said must have convinced him to come out, because Bubba shuffled into the living room. He looked like he'd lost weight since I'd seen him at the quarry. He did not look well.

"Hey, man," Willet said.

Bubba stared at us.

"We just want to talk," Willet said.

"About what?" Bubba stood rigid but for his hands, which he kept balling into tight fists. I wondered if he planned to throw a punch.

Willet's voice was tight and angry. "What do you think, Bubba? You think we want to chat about the weather?"

Bubba glared at Willet. He didn't look at me. "They're sending me away."

It was my fault Bubba was in so much trouble. There was no way I could make it right.

"What were you doing at the quarry?" Willet asked.

"What were *you* doing at the quarry?" Bubba said.

"Come on, man, you know what I mean."

When Bubba spoke, it sounded like the words had trouble making it past his throat. "I don't know why I was there. I just was. I didn't do anything bad. I never saw Pansy." I thought he might cry, but he held it together. "I already told the police."

"Were you drunk?" Willet asked. "Did you smoke some of your brother's stash?"

"No," Bubba said. "I don't remember. I was sleeping and I woke up at the quarry. I know it sounds nuts. I don't remember how I got there. I don't remember why I went." He rubbed his face with his hands, like he was trying to wash something away. "You think I'm crazy."

"I don't expect it's completely sane to wake up in the middle of nowhere," Willet said.

"I'm not crazy!"

"No one thinks you're crazy," I said.

Bubba's brother snorted. "You don't have to live with him."

Bubba ignored his brother. "Bert," he said. "What do you remember? What was I doing when you saw me?"

I humored him. "You were tossing rocks into the water. It had just stopped raining. I was on the other side of the quarry. I hollered at you, but you acted like you didn't hear me. You looked up at the sky. You pointed at the sky. Then you walked into the woods. That's what I remember. That's what happened."

Bubba's jaw clenched. "Bullshit," he said.

"She's just a kid," Willet said. "This ain't on her."

"I'm not some baby," I said. "I saw you, Bubba. I saw you."

"But did you see anything else? Did you see anything in the sky?"

"I saw the sun come out after the rain. I saw you. And you wouldn't speak to me."

Bubba turned to Willet. "Where were you, man?"

Willet swallowed hard and picked at a pimple on his chin. "I was in the woods."

"Doing what exactly?"

"Come on, man . . ."

"You leave your little sister all alone out there, and you have the nerve to accuse me of something?"

"I haven't accused you of anything," Willet said.

"I didn't do anything to Pansy. I never saw Pansy. Now, thanks to you, I have to spend my senior year wearing a uniform and marching around like a Nazi." Bubba's face turned red and his voice rose. "All you had to do was watch her! That's it! If you hadn't looked away, she'd still be here. It's your fault, not mine."

Willet pulled my arm. "Let's go."

"But . . ." We hadn't learned anything, and Bubba was mad at us. I wasn't ready to leave. "I'm sorry," I said to Bubba. "I'm sorry they're sending you away."

"Go home, Bert," Bubba said. To Willet he said, "Try not to lose her on the way."

I thought Willet would punch him. Instead he pushed me too hard toward the door. I stumbled.

We were on the bike outside, ready to drive away, when Bubba's brother came out and stopped us. "Sorry about that, man." He'd grown friendlier since he'd first greeted us at the door. "Can I tell you something?"

Willet revved the engine. "Make it quick."

"He thinks the little green men took your sister."

"Do you think this is a joke?"

"I ain't making a joke," the brother said. "Man, I wish it was a joke. He thinks the aliens come down and take him away. Whole days go black, he tells me. It's fucking crazy." The brother shoved his fists into the pockets of his dirty jeans. "I thought you should know. You can't trust what he says, but I don't think he would hurt anybody. I can't believe he would."

"What did he tell the cops?" Willet asked.

"Pretty much what he told you. He doesn't remember how he got there. He woke up next to the quarry. He won't tell them the aliens left him there, because he knows it makes him sound batshit. But that's what he believes. Honestly, they sweated him a long time. I thought they were going to arrest him, but I guess they need some evidence to do that."

"When did he get home that day?" Willet asked.

"Who knows?" The brother shrugged. "Pops was still at work, so it had to be before dark."

"Were you here?"

"Yeah, man, where else am I going to be? I got a business to run." He laughed. "I tell you, it don't help none to have the police hanging around."

Willet revved the engine again. The brother pulled one of the tight-rolled joints from his pocket and slipped it in the chest pocket of Willet's T-shirt.

"On the house," he said.

Willet plucked the joint out and handed it back to the brother. "From here on out, I intend to keep a clear head."

I thought about what Bubba's brother had said. It seemed crazy to blame aliens for Pansy's disappearance, but no crazier than anything else. No crazier than my creature in the woods. No crazier than Daddy and Granny Clem's curse. Unlike Willet, I couldn't dismiss a theory because it sounded farfetched. I had a shelf full of books containing stories about men turned into toads and children outsmarting witches. The real world wasn't any more logical than those stories.

After we went to see Bubba, Willet confessed he and a few other guys kept a stash of illicit stuff buried in a box in the woods—bottles of liquor and a few joints, a handful of pills stolen from someone's mother. He'd heard something in the woods the day Pansy went missing, and he'd thought it might be one of the guys raiding the stash. When he got to their spot, the box was undisturbed. He'd unearthed it and smoked one of the joints. It was the first time he'd had so much pot at once. Time slowed down and he spaced out or fell asleep. I could see by the way he held his shoulders and wouldn't look me in the eye that he felt miserable about the whole thing. "I'm so sorry, Bert. I never should have left you."

"And we never should have left Pansy," I said. "It's not all your fault."

We sat in Willet's room. We always talked there. My room was too full of Pansy's things. Pansy's bed was made up with pink sheets and a floral quilt. A cloth topsy-turvy doll sprawled on her pillow. Little Red Riding Hood on one end and the Big Bad Wolf disguised as grandma when you flipped the skirt and turned it over. Both faces were exposed where Pansy left it, the skirt bunched around the middle. It used to be my doll, but I never cared for it. Something about the wolf's eyes made me uneasy. Now it stared at me every day, the leering wolf and the innocent girl, the trickster and the victim in one.

GOOD THINGS SOMETIMES CAME from bad acts. And even something done with the best of intentions could turn sour. He figured the only way to keep from doing harm would be to die as quick as you were born, and what would be the point of that? There was no predicting anything in this world. You hoped for the best. It was all you could do.

When Clementine went two months without bleeding, she confessed the whole mess to Ora, who said she would kill Ray. She told Ora she didn't care about Ray. She didn't want him dead and she had no intention of confronting him about the mess. "I want this to go away," she said. "Isn't there something we can do?"

Ora pulled one of the old books from a shelf. She told Clementine what she needed. It was a long list of strange herbs and plants. Clementine said she wasn't sure she could get them all.

"You must," Ora told her. "And soon. It may already be too late."

Clementine ordered the herbs. She had to place a call to Boston for some of the rarer plants and she had to explain the call to her boss. She told him she was ordering the herbs for a wealthy woman in town who was having female problems. He looked embarrassed when she said it and waved his hand to signal he didn't want to hear about it. Her boss knew about Ora's business, everyone did. He didn't mind Clementine placing orders from the store as long as she paid for the deliveries herself.

At home, Ora boiled the herbs twice and watched while Clementine drank the bitter brew three times each day. The drink brought on strong cramps and a dark heaviness in her belly. "I think it's working," she told Ora. But days passed and her blood didn't flow.

She refused to cry about it, though Ora cried freely and often. Something would happen, Clementine thought. Somehow the situation would be made right. She rode her bike recklessly, never swerving to avoid ruts in the road. She lifted heavy sacks at work and climbed ladders without hesitation. She hoped to fall. At night, she pounded her fist against her belly, which was growing in spite of her dark thoughts and careless behavior. The baby in her womb would not be forced out before his time. Her clothes grew tight, and she altered them. She developed a prickly brown rash on her neck, and Ora made a salve to soothe it. Finally, six months after the encounter with Ray, her boss said he thought she'd better quit.

"You're obviously sick," he said. She saw the judgment and disapproval in his face, though he wouldn't look at her. "I can't have someone with such an illness working for me. This is a family business."

Ora said it didn't matter. Her business was booming. They didn't need the income from the hardware store. Clementine was grateful for Ora, for her practicality and her medical knowledge and her compassion, but none of that could change Clementine's feelings for the child growing inside her. She didn't want it. She didn't deserve it. She wished for a miscarriage. She wished for a stillbirth. Sometimes she wished to die.

Even as she wished for such things, she knew what would happen. She would have a baby and she would be disgraced. Women without husbands didn't have children. Women who did were whores. She was a whore. These thoughts ran through her head every day and at night they grew stronger. She had terrible dreams and woke in a cold sweat. When she couldn't get back to sleep, she walked outside under the stars, her bare feet slapping against the damp grass and cold, hard dirt, the baby in her stomach turning and kicking and begging for attention. She wanted to work. She wanted to be useful. She wanted to be independent. All of those wants led to wanting less. Desire was unhappiness.

In the final month, the baby kicked so forcefully Clementine stumbled when she walked. When she sat down to eat, the baby rolled and pushed aggressively against her bulging stomach, which rippled and pulsed like a lake before a storm. Ora told her to stay in bed. She said she didn't want Clementine to hurt herself, but Clementine knew there was more to it. She didn't want the women who came for treatment to see Clementine moping and lurching around the house like some fat drunk cow. It frightened them.

Finally, when she could stand no more of the pregnancy, when she was threatening to slice herself open and yank the baby out, her water broke. Ora brought in warm blankets and a damp cloth to bathe her forehead. She held Clementine's hand and told her when to push and when to rest. The pain was incredible. Clementine ground her teeth so hard she chipped a molar.

Ora gave her a sliver of peyote to chew and hold in her mouth. Clementine swallowed it against Ora's instructions and soon the mist rolled over her. Wild beasts crouched in the corner of the room. She heard them snarling and whining. Their hot breath fogged the air. They smelled of raw blood, like a steak gone rancid in the hot sun. They wanted her baby; they wanted to swallow it whole. She begged Ora to make them go away. She hadn't wanted the child, but she wasn't giving it over to the beasts. Ora told her to push and push some more. Clementine was so tired and thirsty. Her mouth was dry and rough as sandpaper, dry and rough as Ray's jaw against her cheek that night. She touched Ora's cheek, her smooth perfect skin, and said *I'm sorry* over and over again. Ora told her to push. She felt the bed falling away or else she rose up, floating above the messy business of giving birth, above the blood and slick mucous. Her bowels let loose at some point, though she hardly felt it for the ripping pain of the baby's head pushing its way out of her. It seemed monstrous in size. How was she supposed to push something so large through such a small opening? How did any woman do this?

Ora became stern. She told her it was almost over. She said this was the worst it would ever be, and she must push. Ora plunged her hands inside Clementine and guided the baby into the world. Clementine felt herself ripping wide and wider still. She was filled with a burning pain that had no source. It wasn't the baby. It wasn't her body. It was an ancient aching pain, flaming hot and unbearable and she knew she was dying. And she knew she was going to hell. She tried to summon prayers, to ask forgiveness for her dark soul, to beg for mercy and redemption. The pain crested and her thoughts grew fuzzy. Darkness washed over her, but in the distance she saw a pinprick of light. The light expanded. Her fear melted. Her pain crept away like an embarrassed hound. The beasts in the corner turned to dust. Ora placed something warm and wet on her chest and the warm thing howled.

"It's a boy," Ora said. "What are we going to do with a boy?"

Clementine looked at Ora, and they both laughed. Ora wiped sweat from her shining face but also tears. Clementine clutched the slippery, howling creature to her chest.

SIX

———◆———

THE WOMAN FROM PITTSBURGH was right about many things. After a month the police stopped coming by the house, and then they stopped calling. They hadn't found any sign of Pansy and they couldn't locate Daddy. They had asked Mama a hundred questions about where Daddy might have gone and where he might hide, but Mama didn't have any answers. Wherever Daddy was, he was being careful. He hadn't written any checks or pulled cash out from the joint account. Maybe he had enough of his funny money to get by for a while, but Mama couldn't tell the police about that. With nothing new to report, the awful peroxided woman on the evening news moved on to other stories. Even the ladies from the church refocused their energies on food drives and beautification projects.

But then, two months after Pansy's disappearance, there came news of another child gone missing. In October, an eight-year-old girl in Miracle Valley, Arizona disappeared during a short bike ride to the mailbox. She'd been sending a birthday card to her aunt. Her older sister went to check when the girl didn't return right away. The sister found the abandoned bike next to the mailbox, but no trace of the missing girl.

I wondered if the sister felt responsible. I knew she did.

"What is happening to this world?" Mama said when the little girl's photo popped up on the evening news. Mama didn't expect an answer. The child's mother took our mother's place on the newscasts begging for her daughter's safe return. The police in White Forest renewed their focus on Pansy. Perhaps the cases were related, they said. Perhaps someone was taking young girls across America. They delved back into their missing persons files and looked for other cases that might share something with the case from Arizona and the case of our missing sister. Had other girls that same age gone missing so completely? Had they been left alone and unsupervised by parents or siblings? Were people careless with other girls the way we'd been with Pansy?

The police found the child in Arizona. They arrested a man who'd strangled her and left her dead body in the hot, dry Tucson desert. The man confessed when the investigators found blood and a torn piece of the girl's shirt in the back of his truck. He said she'd shot out in front of him on the street. He'd hit her by accident and panicked. On the evening news, they showed a snippet from the girl's funeral. I spotted the woman from Pittsburgh in the second pew.

The way Pansy disappeared—into thin air, some folks said—it was no surprise when rumors began to circulate. The people of the Mississippi Delta love a good story. Some said our father was to blame. Where was he and how could he stay away with his daughter gone missing? Others suspected Bubba had something to do with it. They heard he'd been at the quarry that day and everyone thought he was odd. But superstition and folk tales hold more power than science and logic. The unknown gets elevated with myth and legend. Cracks in the physical world get spackled over with fantasy: ghosts and devils, spirits and gods. People want explanations. People want answers. No one can stand the uncertainty of the unknown. The mother from Arizona didn't get her daughter back, but she got answers. We were stuck with questions and wild legends and tall tales.

People talked of ghosts in those woods, ghosts who survived by sucking the breath of the living. Folks who camped or hunted there reported feeling lightheaded and disoriented. People sometimes fainted. I'd felt it myself on the day Pansy disappeared and on the day the woman from Pittsburgh showed up at our door. *Spirit got your breath,* they'd say, when you told them how your vision narrowed and went dark, how your ears felt full of rushing water, and your feet seemed to float a hair off the ground. Pansy, being so small, might have given all her breath to the spirits, might have become one of them.

Willet dismissed talk of ghosts. I didn't say it, but I thought maybe a spirit had swallowed Pansy. She was such a little thing. Probably she wouldn't even run if a spirit came to kiss her. Probably she'd lean in and kiss him right back. But that kind of thinking didn't get us any closer to finding Pansy.

"Don't be a damned fool, Bert," Willet said. "Pansy wasn't carted away by a ghost. She was taken by some real person and I'd bet my right testicle our dear father had something to do with it. He ain't a ghost, but he may be the Devil."

Sensible people didn't believe in ghosts or evil spirits. Sensible people thought it most likely Pansy had simply drowned. It was a large, deep quarry. The divers who'd searched for our sister in the dark waters might have missed her among the debris dumped there throughout the years. After Pansy's disappearance, people took to visiting the quarry and leaving gifts for her: teddy bears, paper hearts, flowers wrapped with ribbon. A pile of offerings rose on the lip of the quarry. A few people erected wooden crosses, which infuriated Willet.

"Crosses are for the grave," he said.

Lots of people took to scattering pansy petals around the makeshift shrine. Most everyone placed a container of pansies on their front porch. I thought it was a nice gesture, but Willet said it was a signal to Pansy's spirit that the people in the house were friendly and meant no harm. I couldn't walk down our street without seeing planter boxes crammed with the bright flowers. They bloomed year-round, through searing heat and bone-wet damp. At least that's how I remember it.

Traffic to the quarry increased. The old access road, which had grown thick with vines in the years since the quarry stopped producing, became accessible again. The vines and brambles were hacked away, the weeds trampled flat.

Halloween came on a Sunday that year. Pansy had been missing for two months and twenty-one days. The holiday was the one time when children on our street would go door to door and adults would chat with one another. We knew our neighbors, but we weren't overly friendly. The men in our neighborhood worked long hours, some in offices and stores, but many in nearby cotton gins and lumber mills. Some of the women worked as secretaries or pulled shifts at the tractor factory in Star River, but plenty stayed home with their children. Our neighborhood was safe and clean and people took some pride in keeping the houses painted, the yards neat. Families in our neighborhood were self-sufficient and proud. If anyone suffered, we didn't know it.

In years when the weather was clear, the neighborhood women would sit outside on Halloween, on front porches or in folding chairs on their front lawn, sipping sweet tea or something stronger and scooping candy into the pillowcases and paper sacks the children carried. It was easier than answering the door all night, they said. The older children watched the younger children, and no adult ever accompanied the trick-or-treaters.

But that year, the mothers walked with their children from house to house and never let them out of their sight. Willet and I were too old for trick-or-treating, but we got a little bag of hard candies and some peanut butter marshmallows to give away. We shouldn't have bothered. No one came to our door and when I stepped outside to see the children draped in sheets and wearing plastic masks, it was a sad and somber sight. No one ran or shouted or hid behind trees hoping to pop out and scare someone. Instead, children marched from door to door and grimly gathered handfuls of sugar-filled treats. The whole thing was over in less than an hour. The kids were tucked away behind the closed doors of their own houses, plopped in front of the flickering blue light of the television before night could fully take hold.

The next day, we learned about Cindy Bartel. Two boys from our school, basketball players, had driven their girlfriends out to the quarry on Halloween night. They drank beer and whiskey they'd stolen from their fathers. They told ghost stories and made the girls cry when they talked about Pansy, the poor little girl last seen floating in the quarry. Cindy wept and begged to be taken home. She said she could feel the cold presence of evil in the woods and she thought the quarry wanted to swallow her whole. Her boyfriend, a lanky point guard named Timothy, tried to calm her. He told her it was all a joke. He assured her nothing evil lurked in the woods, there were no ghosts, but Cindy grew hysterical. Timothy called for the boy who'd driven them to the quarry, but he was nowhere to be found. The driver and his date were clinched together under a tree in the woods and both swore they never heard a thing. Most people believed the couple ignored the calls because they were too caught up in their teenage passion to help a friend, but I knew how those woods could swallow a plea for help.

Cindy grew more frantic. She told Timothy she was walking home. She said she had to get away. Timothy said it was only about ten o'clock when she started walking through the dark woods. He tried to follow her, but she kept disappearing into the trees.

"I didn't know she could move so fast," he told the police.

The next morning, they found her about a half-mile from the quarry, her clothes torn and tattered as if clawed by some wild animal. Her hair was chopped short and ragged, like she'd been coiffed with pinking shears. Her foot was caught in a coil spring steel trap, the kind someone might set to catch a coyote. It was a small trap and Cindy ought to have been able to get out of it, but she'd panicked and, in pulling at it, had torn her skin and struck a blood vessel near her ankle. She passed out from the loss of blood and said she couldn't remember a thing. The doctor tried to save her foot, but the rusty steel had poisoned her blood so he took the foot to save the leg.

The next week, Cindy's father beat Timothy to a pulp and spent a few nights in the county jail. He said the boy had it coming. Cindy defended Timothy, but it didn't matter. There was no one else to blame and Cindy's father needed to hold someone accountable. Parents forbade their children from visiting the quarry, but some boys still took dates there hoping fear would drive the girls into their arms, so the men who ran the town decided to take action.

"It's only a matter of time before something worse happens," said the chair of the county aldermen. They voted four-to-one to drain the quarry and fill it with dirt to prevent any further tragedies at the site. No one said it to us, but some people talked about how they might find things when it was emptied, things the divers searching for Pansy might have missed. They said finding Pansy's body would put to rest all the nonsense about ghosts and spirits.

The alderman who'd led the campaign to drain the quarry also owned a construction company and he was awarded the contract for the work. Bright yellow trucks with submersible pumps rolled in and diverted the quarry water to the Tallahatchie River. The whole project took twice as long as predicted. Of course it cost twice as much as estimated. The county had to find some way to cover the cost. We learned our high school would go without a new gym or air conditioning for at least two more years. Naturally the students blamed Pansy and, by extension, Willet and me.

Draining the quarry caused all sorts of problems. A sinkhole formed in a nearby field and swallowed up a Labrador retriever named Molly. A man working at the construction site fell to his death when the walls of the quarry collapsed as the water levels sank. The other men on the job didn't realize he couldn't swim until it was too late. They thought he was being funny. Turns out drowning looks an awful lot like joking around to some people. Every day, the pumps had to be cleared of some new debris: old cars and trucks and motorcycles; children's bicycles; guns, including one military-style machine gun, three ordinary revolvers, and a half dozen hunting rifles; and more mysterious items like a lockbox sealed along its seams with wax, which, when opened, contained a child's doll with a noose around its neck, plastic eyes removed from its sockets.

It took nearly a month to drain the quarry. Every day I waited to hear that they'd found Pansy among the debris, but the news never came. They found the bones of a small adult and the bones of an infant trapped beneath one of the submerged cars, but they found no child in the gray muck.

"I knew it," Willet said. "She ain't in there. No way Pansy would drown."

He was happy about it and so was Mama, because it shored up their hope of finding Pansy alive. She must be out there somewhere, living and a part of things. If she were out in the world somewhere, we would find her. I confess, I did not share their optimism. Naturally, I didn't hope for Pansy to be dead, though finding her would have brought an end to things. It seemed to me the longer Pansy was missing, the longer we were stuck in this loop of unknowing. It's a terrible thing to not know something so vital.

Granny Clem invited us to eat Thanksgiving dinner at her house, but Mama said no. Granny Clem brought us a coconut cake on Christmas morning and tried to talk us into coming over for a meal later in the day. Willet and I wanted to go. We'd planned to cook a meal, but our spaghetti would be nothing compared Granny Clem's roast turkey and cornbread dressing. But Mama refused, and we didn't feel right leaving her alone. I suggested Granny Clem bring the feast to our house, but she said Chester wouldn't come and she didn't want to abandon him either. I could understand Chester's reluctance. After the quarry was drained and there was still no answer to the mystery of Pansy's disappearance, Willet became more determined than ever to find our father. He visited Uncle Chester again and came home with a black eye.

I don't know why he continued to seek answers from such an unfriendly source. "Even if he knows where Daddy is," I said, "he isn't about to tell you."

Our family was divided, and no amount of food or forced holiday celebrating would change that. We ate our overcooked Christmas spaghetti smothered with jarred tomato sauce and an iceberg lettuce salad. We didn't put up a tree or exchange gifts. We didn't make Martha Washington candy or peppermint bark. Mama barely ate a thing. She drank sweet tea and smoked at the table. She refused a slice of Granny Clem's cake. Willet and I made ourselves sick eating that cake. It was so beautiful, white fluffy boiled icing covered with flaked coconut and spread over four tall layers of yellow sponge; it seemed a shame to let it go to waste. We polished it off in three days, both of us floating through the week between Christmas and New Year's in a sweaty sugar fog. We were relieved to go back to school when the holiday ended. It felt good to turn the calendar to a new year. The past year had been so awful it was hard to imagine things could get any worse. Maybe 1977 would bring good news.

ALL SORTS OF WOMEN came to see Clementine and Ora: wealthy women, poor women, black women, white women, young women, old women. They all had stories to tell. Clementine and Ora never asked, but the women seemed compelled to spill their secrets. He listened to the stories and collected them. He overheard tales about cruel men and lust and betrayal. The world was not a safe place for women, he learned. It was not a kind world to anyone, but women seemed to suffer more than men.

On a nearby plantation, German prisoners worked the cotton fields. It was 1944. The men joked about Mississippi being hotter than the belly of the crematoria, but the prisoners kept mostly to themselves. They worked when they were told to work. They slept when they were told to sleep. When someone brought them food, they ate. Few spoke fluent English, though many understood more than they let on. A Luftwaffe officer named Manfried Brun spoke perfect English. Each day, the young wife of the plantation owner came out to the field and oversaw servants bringing lunch. She carried pitchers of tea or lemonade and filled copper mugs with the cold, sweet liquid. Her hands were milk white and smooth. One day she stumbled as she brought the pitcher around, and Manfried caught her before she fell. He took the sweaty pitcher from her shaking hands and insisted she rest for a bit.

She smiled at him. "I'm all right. Just a bit clumsy."

"You should not work so hard," he said.

She was surprised to hear him speak so easily in her own language. He told her he needed practice. The guards at the camp weren't interested in conversation and many of them were coarse and unrefined. "I would like to speak as a gentleman speaks," he said.

"You sound like a perfect gentleman to me." She offered him her hand. "My name is Mary Helen." He took her gentle, tiny hand in his own and introduced himself.

After that day, whenever her husband was away from the plantation, Mary Helen invited Manfried into the house after lunch. Mary Helen knew her husband would not approve of her friendship with this man, but her husband was old and gray with ugly tufts of hair sprouting from his ears. Manfried was not much older than she was and he was handsome. His hair was black and neat. Even though he worked each day in the fields, he kept his fingernails clean. He smelled like a saltwater breeze. She felt things for him she'd never felt for her husband. When her husband rolled on top of her at night, she closed her eyes and counted until it was over. She only counted to twenty most nights, but her husband smelled of boiled cabbage and every second with him was misery.

One weekend, while her husband was away negotiating cotton prices in Tennessee, Manfried kissed her. Or maybe she kissed him. Either way, she felt something she hadn't ever felt before. She wanted to be with Manfried, to strip off her clothing and expose her tender body to his. It would be different from what she'd experienced with her husband. She wanted him so much, she began to pull at the cotton shirt he wore. They were in the library at the time, surrounded by bookshelves filled with leather volumes her husband had chosen more for appearance than for content.

Manfried grasped her shoulders. "Not here," he said. "You will regret it. I never want you to regret a moment with me."

He asked her if she had access to one of her husband's vehicles. They made a plan to meet that night at the old quarry. She gave him directions. He said he could get away after the evening meal. The night guard usually fell asleep as soon as the sun went down. "We will run away together," he said. "We will be man and wife."

Mary Helen's husband had taken their nice car to Nashville, but he'd left behind an old work truck. She told the kitchen help to forget about supper. She wasn't hungry. At twilight, she backed the truck out of the storage shed and drove without headlights until she was off the plantation. At the quarry, she sat in the dark and willed herself not to think too far ahead. Her husband would be furious, but he'd find another wife. He was wealthy and powerful. The night grew darker, and she wondered if Manfried would come at all. Maybe the guard hadn't fallen asleep. Maybe Manfried had been caught trying to escape. Maybe he'd changed his mind about running off with a silly woman.

Finally, someone emerged from the woods. She could see nothing but shadowy movement. She opened the truck door, slid out, and called his name in a whisper. No answer. She crept forward, toward the figure. "Manfried?"

The figure grabbed her and shoved a dirty cloth in her mouth before she could scream. Behind her, she heard the truck's engine turn over. The man holding her was strong, much larger than Manfried. She struggled in his grip, felt his warm, moist breath on her neck. He spun her around and she saw Manfried in the driver's seat of the truck, another prisoner beside him. He smiled. He would save her, she thought, but the truck disappeared along the dark road and she was left alone with the large guard. He hadn't sneaked past the man at all. Instead, he'd bribed him with the promise of a pretty young woman alone in a dark, isolated place.

The guard had more stamina than her husband. Just when she thought he was done with her, he would pull away and gaze at some point in the distance. After a brief rest, he'd begin again with a vigor that stunned her. She'd fought him at first, but he seemed excited by her resistance. Better to let him get it over with, she figured. She was bruised and bloodied by the time he finished. Her back bore the markings of the gnarled roots of an oak tree. Rocks wedged into the moist crease of her buttocks. The man pulled the cloth from her mouth and used it to wipe his face. He grinned at her.

"My husband will kill you," she told him.

"I don't expect you'll share this with him. What will he think about your plan to run off with a Nazi? No, you'll tell him someone stole the truck and you don't know anything else."

The man was right, of course. She'd been a fool.

After a few weeks, she learned she was pregnant. She knew the child would not belong to her husband. It would be the offspring of the brutish guard. Every time she looked at the child, she would think of Manfried and how he'd tricked her, how he'd seduced her with his good manners and nice hands. She would think of the violent night at the quarry.

It was too much to imagine, a lifetime of hating her own child. She'd heard stories about the two women who lived together and possessed a remedy for unwanted children. She told the women her story and begged for the bitter potion. They were her only hope, she said. She couldn't carry the child. She would sooner strap an anvil to her waist and plunge into the deep, dark waters of the quarry. Clementine and Ora gave her the potion and told her to come back and see them if it didn't work. The woman never returned.

SEVEN

————◆————

JUST AFTER THE NEW year, during an unseasonable warm spell, a man from Eudora, Arkansas was out shooting mourning doves when Fetch, his redbone coonhound, disappeared into a grove of sweet gum trees on the banks of Bayou Macon. The man figured Fetch was running down a rabbit. The old dog's eyes and hearing were failing, but his sense of smell was sharp as a pup's. The man went after his dog and discovered what Fetch had found: the fly-infested corpse of a rotting body in a torn plastic garbage bag buried only about a foot deep. A recent rainstorm had washed away the dirt. Predators had taken care of the rest.

"Another day or so," the man told the sheriff, "I reckon there wouldn't be nothing left but bones."

The county coroner said the body belonged to a young girl, about Pansy's age. She'd been smothered, possibly with a pillow. The coroner found a goose feather in her windpipe. The discovery of this child's body caused a good deal of excitement for the officers working on Pansy's case. The spot where the body was found was just more than an hour's drive from White Forest.

The fat police officer showed Mama a picture of the corpse as it looked before they'd sliced her open to search for clues. We stared at the image of the child on a metal table, her tiny torso covered over with a white cloth. The child was found naked and the coroner said she'd been beaten in the hours or days before she was killed. Her face seemed bloated and much of the skin had rotted away or been consumed by some forest animal. What remained was waxy and green. A portion of the child's jaw was missing, exposing tiny teeth that shone weirdly white against the rotting gray flesh. But sprigs of curly hair sprang from her scalp, like Pansy's.

Mama's hands were surprisingly steady as she studied the terrible image. "No." She handed the photo back to the fat officer. "This is not my child. This child's hair is too dark."

The fat officer tried to get Mama to look more closely. "The hair color might seem dark," he said, "but it isn't clean, and sometimes the film gets overdeveloped."

"I know what my child's hair looks like, clean or dirty. That is not my child."

"Well, it would be helpful to have your blood type," the officer said. "Might not prove anything, but it could help us rule this child out."

"It isn't necessary," Mama said. "That isn't Pansy. I know my daughter and that isn't her."

Willet agreed with Mama. He said nothing about the body in that photo looked like our sister. Still, I wasn't convinced. "Mama, I know you don't want to believe it, but isn't it better to know for sure?"

"I do know for sure," Mama said. "That isn't Pansy. And anyway I don't know my blood type."

"It's a simple test," the officer told her.

"But you need mine and Earl's both, don't you?"

"It would be best."

"Then there's no sense to it."

Daddy's absence loomed over the conversation in the same way it loomed over our lives. The police suspected him in Pansy's disappearance and they'd searched for him, but found nothing. They'd asked Mama a hundred questions about where he might go and they'd been frustrated by her lack of information. We could not adequately explain our father's prolonged absence, even to ourselves. Six months had passed since we last saw him. All my life he'd come and gone without making any announcements or expecting any fanfare. He could travel for two weeks or a month and still he'd walk through the front door and greet us as if he'd only been out for the day. This time was different. I knew it. Willet knew it. Mama couldn't admit it.

Despite Mama's assurances, the police believed the body was Pansy's. The focus shifted from a search for our sister to a search for her killer. It was full-on winter by then and often a damp chill fell across the day. Willet and I kept going to school, though we agreed it was a waste of time. Nothing we learned seemed valuable and our status as the siblings of the missing girl made us either freaks or objects of fascination.

Most of our classmates thought Bubba had something to do with it. Everyone knew I'd seen him at the quarry that day. All he'd ever been was an odd kid, but since he'd gone off to military school, he became a monster. When they found the body in Arkansas, people said Bubba could have hitched rides through the back roads carrying Pansy's body in a trash bag until he found a spot to bury her. It was ridiculous, and I said so. There were plenty of wide-open remote spaces to bury a body closer to home. Why would Bubba go to the trouble of crossing state lines? And when was he supposed to have made the trip? He'd been home when the police came to question him in the days and weeks after Pansy's disappearance. But logic never trumps gossip. People wanted to believe crazy things and they wouldn't be dissuaded by the facts.

None of the gossip mattered. It turned out Mama was right. The body beneath the sweet gum trees was not Pansy. It was the body of a black child killed by her own mother. At first the mother claimed her daughter had run away, but she later confessed the crime to her pastor, who encouraged her to come forward with the truth.

The woman said the girl had been possessed by evil; she was willful and defiant. The mother hadn't meant to kill her child, only to chase away the Devil. "The Devil was too strong," she told the detectives. "He took her right along."

I felt sorry for that little girl. There were no news reports about her going missing. There were no pleas from the blonde reporters. There were no search parties organized by the police department. There were prayers, sure, but no one gathered to light candles. There was no public outrage, no call for justice. I bet the woman from Pittsburgh never visited that mother. It made me both angry and grateful: angry one child's life would be somehow more precious than another, grateful Pansy might still be out there alive somewhere. Mostly I felt worried. If Pansy were alive, why hadn't we found her? And where was Daddy? I worried most of all about Mama.

Mama did things I couldn't reconcile with the mother she'd been before Pansy's disappearance. She sent money we didn't have to preachers on television, who implored her to send more: *God has miracles in store for you. He asks you to sacrifice in order to receive his blessings.* She sacrificed by raiding the bank accounts and sending thirty or fifty dollars to each appeal. Then she started sending hundreds.

Willet and I intercepted the mail when we could. We pulled cash from the envelopes and used it to buy groceries, to pay bills. We tried to talk to her about the money, but she wouldn't listen.

"I have to do something," she said. "What if this is the seed of the prayer that will bring Pansy home? How can I not send it?"

Willet said we'd be broke soon if she kept it up. With Daddy gone for so long, there was no money coming in the door. "I don't care about money," Mama said. She didn't care about us. She didn't care about herself. She cared about finding Pansy. How could we hold that against her?

Willet got a job working after school and on weekends at the car wash. It was minimum wage work, but some customers tipped. "Better than nothing," he said. "But just barely." He thought he could get work on a construction crew, but it would mean dropping out of school.

"You only have a few months to go," I said. "Don't quit now."

"It's not like I'm going to get a job in an office. I'll end up working construction either way."

I begged him to hang on. I didn't care if Willet got his diploma but I liked knowing he was in school with me. I rarely saw him during the day but I knew he was there. He was in a classroom somewhere in the same building, and I could find him if I needed him. I was already dreading next year, when I'd be on my own. I told him everything would be okay when Daddy got home.

Willet laughed. "Wake up, Bert. He ain't coming home this time."

I couldn't believe he would abandon us forever, especially with Mama in such a bad state. Mama wouldn't listen to any sort of speculation involving Daddy, but there was plenty. The fat police officer said most children who disappear are taken by an estranged parent. Mama insisted she and Daddy weren't estranged, but it was a tough argument to make given his prolonged absence.

Willet said they'd questioned Uncle Chester and Granny Clem. I'm not sure how he knew, but he said they hadn't found anything and Uncle Chester swore he hadn't talked to his brother in months.

Nothing made any sense, and the more I thought about it, the more the answers seemed to float away from me. The nightmarish memories of the creature from the woods, of the rainstorm, of the suspicious berries, began to fade. Everything about that day seemed slippery as an oiled snake. I tried to remember the moment we decided to leave Pansy. I would concentrate on the memory of dirt clinging to my damp feet and the vision of Willet leading me into the woods, but it was like grasping at mercury. Was the sun ahead of us or behind us? Was the sky bright blue or packed with fluffy white clouds? Did Willet walk ahead of me or beside me? If I couldn't call up specific details, how could I be sure about anything?

Willet said we had to start taking better care of ourselves and taking better care of Mama. "We can't be children anymore. We've got to go on and grow up."

I was fifteen by then. I wondered what part of childhood Willet imagined I was holding on to. It wasn't like I played with dolls or threw temper tantrums. I cooked dinner most nights, even if it meant only opening a few cans.

Willet gave me this speech while changing the oil in Mama's car. The old Ford sedan had barely been driven since Pansy disappeared. Mama didn't like to leave the house in case Pansy returned or called. I handed him an old rag to wipe his hands.

Willet had gotten the car tuned up and whenever he had a spare hour, he drove out to the edge of the county and beyond. Sometimes I went along with him. He drove past broken-down shacks with cars in the yard, where dusty children played without joy among rusted farm equipment and mangy dogs. He studied their faces and sometimes spoke with them, showed them pictures of Pansy. "Have you seen this little girl?" They stared up at him, their expressions unresponsive and uncaring. The poverty that existed a short drive from our home made me sick. With Daddy gone and Mama sinking into sadness, we were well on our way to being poor, but this was a different level of need.

"I don't know why you think anyone out here would take Pansy," I said to Willet. "The last thing these people need is another hungry mouth."

Willet said he didn't believe they'd taken her, but maybe she'd ended up there somehow. "Would their parents even notice?" he said. "Where are their parents, anyhow? Do you see any adults?"

I did not see any adults, but I knew they existed. They were out working the fields or inside working over a stove, maybe in some wealthy woman's kitchen. I didn't bother to point out to Willet that the parents of these children were no more or less present than our own parents.

On these back road trips, Willet taught me to drive. I pointed the nose of Mama's gray Ford down the straight dirt roads of the Delta and pressed the gas. It was one of the few good feelings I recall from those days. You can't beat the Delta for driving. You can speed up and brake hard without any concern you'll hit something or someone on the straight, flat, empty roads. The first time you really pick up speed and see the cotton fields go from studded white to a blurred blanket, well, it's like driving through clouds. Occasionally Willet sent me out on my own to pick up groceries or run to the post office. I was careful and I never got pulled over. I think Willet wanted to make sure I could take care of Mama and myself. He knew he'd have to find real work soon and there were not a lot of opportunities in White Forest.

No matter what we did, Mama sank further into sadness. She had a lot of bad days. Even her good days weren't great. On a good day, she might put on clothes she hadn't slept in and wander into the kitchen for a tumbler full of sweet tea and a handful of crackers. She might even take a shower. Most days, though, she never made it any further than the couch, where she sat slumped and bloated in her stained T-shirts and ratty shorts. She slept poorly. She smoked constantly. I tried to get her out of the house to shop for groceries or clothes at the discount store. She refused. Pansy could come home any day, she said, and she couldn't bear the thought of her baby coming back to an empty house. Mama talked like Pansy might return and things would go back to the way they were before. It was wishful thinking. If Pansy managed to make it home, I knew nothing would be the same.

OTHER PEOPLE'S STORIES WERE simpler. His memories were tangled like a knot and unraveling them left him with more questions than answers. If he'd never come to Mississippi, would he be a different sort of man? Maybe, but he figured prying a rock from the earth didn't change the nature of the rock.

He and Fern were eight years old when their father left them by the side of the road. He was called Junior then, the first of many names he would carry through his life. "Take care of your sister," his father told him, before boarding a train heading north. They weren't sorry to see him go. They were still adjusting to the loss of their mother.

Ama Story had stood barely five feet tall and weighed no more than one good net of mullet. As a black Seminole, her marriage to a white man caused a scandal on Chokoloskee Island. The family didn't fit in with either the white men running the trading post and attempting to set up schools and medical care, nor with the Native American families who'd lived there for hundreds of years on the shell mounds and in the chickee huts of their ancestors.

But Chokoloskee was the sort of place where people tried to get along. It was a place where outlaws could hide, where a white man and an Indian chief might taste ice cream together for the first time. It was a place where you could cast a net in the evening and pull up a mess of fish come morning. On Chokoloskee, people lived by the tides and the moon; they pulled together to rebuild after a bad storm and they killed a violent sugar baron without arguing about it because, frankly, the man needed killing.

Junior hadn't wanted to leave the island, but times were hard and his mother's death left his father in a bad way. As a younger man he'd made a decent living smuggling rum into the country through the network of mangrove islands stretching out to the Gulf of Mexico, but the end of Prohibition left him floundering for a way to make money. He'd never intended to have one child, much less two, a fact he was fond of sharing with Junior and Fern. He'd loved their mother, but she was the only person he seemed capable of caring about, and when she was gone, he gave up pretending to be a father. He talked about finding a woman to raise them, but no woman would put up with him, and even though both children were fair-skinned, everyone knew their mother had been black. No woman wanted to take the chance her grandchildren might be Negroes.

So the family headed north by boat and by foot and by train, when they could hop one. Their father believed he might find work in the cotton fields, so they traveled toward the Delta. Jobs were scarce. No one wanted to pay a strange man to pick cotton, particularly when the man came with the very real baggage of twin children. Finally, it was Junior who suggested his father leave them behind. Junior knew how to hunt and fish and trap small game. He could tie more knots than a sailor. He had a knack for knowing which berries were edible and which were poison. He and Fern would be okay, he told their father. He met with no resistance and, in 1939, his father left them in a Mississippi Delta town called White Forest. Other than telling Junior to care for his sister, he offered only one piece of instruction: "Don't ever tell no one around here your mother weren't white. They'll run you out of town if you're lucky. Most likely they'll just kill you."

Junior knew better than to brag about being the son of a failed rum runner and a black Indian and he said so.

"I'll come back for you when I can," his father said, before leaping onto a moving freight train.

"Well," Junior said to his sister, "at least that's the last lie we'll have to hear from him."

Fern giggled and took his hand. Junior needed to find them a safe place to stay. He'd be happy living outdoors most of the year, but it would be better for them both if they had shelter. He made his sister wear a hat and a long dress even in the hottest weather, because her skin would turn brown if she spent too much time in the sun, and people would suspect she might not be pure white.

They walked through town, staying underneath the awnings where they could. Like most of the places they'd traveled through, White Forest was struggling. Empty shelves lined the back wall of the dry goods store and a hand-scrawled sign across the diner said CLOSED FOR GOOD. Junior and Fern stood around the corner from the post office, where a trio of dusty old men sat on a bench. The men complained about the price they were getting for cotton and they complained about Roosevelt. It was the same in every town; only the crops were different. In Florida, men complained about the price for sugar and grapefruit. In Georgia, they said it wasn't hardly worth growing peanuts. Junior kept his ear peeled for some piece of useful gossip, something he could parlay into a beneficial situation, but the men only griped for the pleasure of hearing themselves speak.

They walked from one end of town to the other in the span of time it took most folks to eat lunch. "Well, this ain't no place," Junior said, though the town wasn't any smaller than the towns of the Everglades. Fern bent and plucked something from the dusty ground. She tucked a tiny white feather in her pocket. She was always gathering such things. Later she might weave the feather into a dandelion crown or use it to scratch a picture in the dirt.

Fern had been named for the green plants that grew thick on the cypress trees along the rivers and swamps of the Everglades. During the dry season, when the rain ceased to fall and water evaporated, the bright green fern would wither and turn brown. Anyone seeing the dry clumps would assume the plant was dead. But when the rain fell and the basin filled, the leaves drank in the water and rose up to live again. Resurrection Fern.

She had a way of making ordinary things beautiful. His sister turned weeds into long chains, which she wore around her neck and on her head. She could whittle like nobody's business. She used Junior's knife to turn cabbage palm and cypress wood into works of art. She carved the anhinga with its outspread wings and snakelike neck. She carved a yellow bellied turtle and a swamp chicken. She turned sugarcane bark into replications of the delicate pineapple air plants that clung to the cypress in the big swamp. She was born with the knack of making something out of nothing. Junior loved her fiercely.

He hated his own name and the designation of being second. His mother had called him her "little anhinga." When he and Fern were toddlers, he would stand atop the highest shell mound and hold his arms out to soak in the sun. His father said he looked like Jesus on the cross, but his mother thought he looked like the snakebird perched on the branches of the cypress strands. Their father hadn't approved of the way his wife doted on his son. He said it would make the boy soft. He'd whipped Junior often and for any reason. He didn't like Fern's fanciful creations, nor her tendency to drift and get lost in her own head. He'd whipped her once, just after they crossed into Mississippi. Junior had pulled his father's pistol from the sack he carried and pointed it at his father's head. His father laughed at him, said he wouldn't dare shoot. Something in Junior's eyes must have convinced him otherwise, because he let up on Fern after that. He told Junior he would have to be responsible for his sister and for anything that happened to her. Junior was fine with the arrangement.

They walked on, choosing roads by instinct and whim. The place was so flat he thought it would be damn near impossible to get lost. They came to a point at the edge of town where the road forked and they could choose to continue walking alongside the wide fields of cotton or enter into the woods. Junior chose the woods for shade. He hoped to find food and water and was pleased when they came upon a patch of wild berries. Eventually, the woods thinned and gave way to a large clearing, where there was a deep depression in the earth. He took Fern's hand and they stood on the edge and peered down. It made him dizzy. Was it a hundred feet deep? Two hundred? The hole was filled with water, and he knew there must be a spring nearby.

"They should not have dug this up," Fern said.

"I think it's an old quarry," Junior told her. "See how those rocks are the same as the ones on the roads around here?"

Fern took a few steps back, tugging him along with her. "This is a bad place."

His sister was like that, superstitious and intuitive. Their mother had been the same.

"Let's find fresh water," he said. "I'm thirsty."

In the distance, he heard a rushing river. He followed the sound and found the source of the spring. They drank the cool water and ate berries until their stomachs ached.

The twins fell asleep against the trunk of a white oak. They dozed through the hottest part of the day. Junior was so tired from walking he might have slept through to the next day, but Fern nudged him awake in the fading afternoon. A boy was staring at them from a few away. The boy seemed feral, crouched like a panther ready to spring. His lips were wet and open. His small, sharp teeth gleamed. The boy was not much older than he and Fern, but he was better fed and bigger. Junior braced himself to stand and fight or run.

"What do you want with us?" Junior said.

Fern whispered, "He's alright."

The boy grinned and crawled closer. Junior tensed. Fern put a hand on his shoulder to calm him. "He's alright," she said again.

The boy reached out a dirty hand, and Fern grasped it. Junior wanted to run, but he couldn't leave Fern with this wild boy. She was too trusting.

The boy stood and Fern stood with him. He motioned for them to follow. Fern walked off with the boy like she'd known him her whole life. Junior had no choice but to go along. They walked for a long time, through the hardwood forest and across a small creek. Junior kept his bearings by the sun. He knew they'd walked north and west of the small town with its shuttered stores and cranky old men.

The boy led them to a house off a long dirt road. It was a small, well-built home with a porch on all sides. They'd passed grander homes in their walk through town, homes with stately columns on the outside and many gabled roofs, but Junior thought the modest home in the country looked more welcoming. The boy led them to the porch and tried to take them right through the front door. Junior held back and pulled his sister with him. It was one thing to show up on someone's porch, but quite another to walk uninvited into a stranger's home. The boy might not be dangerous, but they couldn't know about anyone else inside the house.

After a few minutes, a woman stepped onto the porch. She wore a pair of overalls and men's work boots. Her hair was bobbed above her shoulders. Junior thought she was beautiful.

"Well, come on inside," she said. "I expect you're hungry. You can tell us all about it over supper."

Fern grinned and sprinted past the woman into the house. Junior followed. What choice did he have?

There were two women in the house and no evidence of any men. In addition to the wild boy who'd brought them here, there were three other children at the table. The women took in children who had no place else to go, they explained. Some of the children stayed for a short time while their parents worked. Others stayed for years until they could take care of themselves.

"This one," said the woman not dressed like a man, "is all mine." She put her hand on the wild boy's head. She told them her name was Clementine. Junior thought she had one of the nicest faces he'd ever seen. She was pretty, but not in a fussy way. She wore her thick dark hair pulled back into a low bun and her skirt seemed to have been pieced together from old flour sacks. Somehow she wore it without looking poor.

The woman in the overalls was called Ora. She asked them about their travels. Junior told her they'd come from Florida. He kept the details vague, not wanting to give too much of himself to strangers.

"And your folks?"

"Dead," Junior said. It didn't feel like a lie. His father might as well be in the ground with his mother. He wasn't coming back for them. Junior didn't like talking about their parents. He didn't care about losing his father, but he missed his mother in a desperate way. Even when she was ill, she'd kept her children close. She would pull Junior and Fern to her side each night and tell them stories about the island before the white men came. Junior loved those stories. They were all he had of his mother.

His grandfather had been a powerful chief and his grandmother was a runaway slave. She'd run to escape the plantation owner who wanted her to do more than clean his home and cook his meals. She fought him and he beat her. She ran away once and he came after her. He marked her left thigh with a cattle brand to signal his ownership. She ran again and found shelter with the Seminoles. When she became pregnant with Junior's mother, she dug away the brand scar with a sharp shell. Infection took her life soon after she gave birth. Ama was born with a large purple birthmark on her left thigh, and her father said it was the mark of her mother's misery. He told her never to curse the mark or feel ashamed of it. The mark kept her mother's memory alive. Junior had liked to put his hand over the mark. It felt warm even when the winds were cool. He liked knowing he was descended from a woman strong enough to carve out a curse from her own leg.

After a supper of beans and cornbread, the women showed Junior and Fern to a room with the other children. There were quilts lined up against the wall and rows of small striped mattresses on the floor.

"It's not much," the woman in the overalls said, "but I think you'll find it more comfortable than sleeping outdoors."

Junior thought it was more comfortable than any place they'd slept since they left the island. It was a stroke of tremendous luck to find these women. Times were bad and food was scarce. There weren't many folks who could afford to take in a couple of kids. Most nights he dreamed of his mother and of the birds and of the warm water lapping against the mangrove islands, but that night he slept a deep, dreamless sleep.

EIGHT

GRANNY CLEM SHOWED UP just after Easter, another holiday we no longer observed: no sugar-cured ham, no blueberry cake, no eggs hidden in the flowers, no wicker baskets filled with chocolate bunnies and jelly eggs. Without Pansy, what was the point?

Granny Clem did bring one of her pound cakes and a pint of blackberry jam. She placed it in the center of our dusty dining table, put her hands on her hips, and looked around. I was ashamed at how shabby and neglected things had gotten. We'd given up on vacuuming and dusting. Mildew crawled across the bathroom tiles and our countertops felt sticky. The whole place smelled musty and sour, like a picnic left to sweat in the sun.

"I wanted to see how you're getting along," Granny Clem said.

Willet put on a pot of coffee, and I went to fetch Mama from her bedroom. There was a half-smoked cigarette in the ashtray next to her bed, and the room reeked of stale smoke. Pansy had been missing for eight months and Mama sank deeper into depression each day. When I told her Granny Clem was visiting, she squinted at me as if she didn't understand what I was saying. I pulled a clean gingham shirt and a pair of cotton pedal pushers from her closet.

"Why don't you put this on?" The nightgown she wore was stained and so thin I could see right through it.

"What is she doing here?" Mama took the clothes from me and yanked her nightgown over her head. She was so thin, I could count the ribs underneath her small breasts. The pants sagged on her hips.

I picked up Mama's silver-plated boar brush from her dressing table. "Let me brush your hair." Dust motes scattered in the air. Mama used to give her hair a hundred strokes with the brush each night. Her hair had once been thick and shiny and long, but now it barely seemed enough to cover her scalp. She had a bald spot the size of a quarter above her left ear, and I wondered if she'd been pulling it out. I smoothed her hair into a ponytail at the nape of her neck and fastened it with an elastic band. I tied a satin ribbon in a bow to cover the band, surprised she allowed me so much intimacy. It made me feel terrible, really. I couldn't remember the last time I'd touched her. She needed bathing. A sour smell wafted from her skin like eggs gone bad.

"You look pretty, Mama."

She stared into her open palms. "I don't want to see her, Roberta Lynn."

"She brought pound cake."

"I don't trust her."

I fetched a damp washcloth from the bathroom across the hallway. When I returned, Mama was sprawled on the bed again, a lit cigarette in her hand. She smoked and stared at the ceiling. I washed her face with the warm damp cloth. How could Mama distrust the woman who'd delivered all of her children into the world, the woman who'd raised her husband?

"Come out for just a little while."

Mama massaged her forehead with her fingers. I thought she might refuse to get up, but she grunted and swung her legs over the side of the bed. She mashed out the cigarette and sighed. I followed Mama into the living room where Willet and Granny Clem sat on the sofa holding mugs of coffee.

Granny Clem smiled. "Loretta, how are you?"

Mama sank into the hard rocking chair. "How do you think I am, Clementine?"

"Let me get you some coffee, Mama," Willet said.

Mama nodded. I followed Willet into the kitchen. "What is she doing here?" I pulled plates from the cabinet.

Willet shrugged. He sniffed a pint of cream in the fridge and poured a splash into a cup of coffee, stirred it with his finger.

I cut large slices from the cake on the table. The scent made me dizzy. The sugary lemon glaze stuck to my fingers. I licked my thumb and savored the flooding rush of sour and sweet.

When we settled again, Granny Clem told us the reason behind her visit. "I was thinking," she said, "maybe Bert could come work with me this summer."

"Me?"

"You're old enough to help out in the garden and I can teach you how to make medicinal teas, among other things."

"No," Mama said. "I don't like the idea."

I wasn't sure I liked the idea either. I thought of Uncle Chester's trailer just outside Granny Clem's house. Did I really want to spend time in such close proximity to my uncle?

"Hear me out, Loretta."

Granny Clem sounded like a woman who'd already decided things and not like a person engaged in a negotiation. I would come to expect it from her, that sense of certainty and complete lack of second-guessing or compromise. It was who she was.

"I'll pay her, of course. And it would be good for her to learn an occupation." She put her cake plate on the end table next to the sofa and clasped her hands in her lap. "She doesn't look cut out for secretarial school, does she? Or beauty school?"

Willet snorted, and I glared at him. I was wearing a pair of his old jeans cut off above the knee and a T-shirt with a faded rainbow across the chest. My hair was uncombed. I'm pretty sure my face was clean. I never dressed up or thought about my appearance. There were so many other things to worry about. How could I spend time curling my hair or applying blue eyeliner as the other girls in my class did? It seemed silly. Plus, I'd heard the talk about Pansy. People said she was an exceptionally beautiful child. They seemed to think her beauty had something to do with her disappearance. Who wouldn't want to snatch such a pretty girl? I hated people who said such things. Still, I couldn't see any benefit to striving for beauty. Beauty seemed like trouble.

Granny Clem kept talking. "We'll stick to the botanical lessons, and I'll not drag her into the messy stuff. Not yet. Not until she's ready. You have my word."

"I don't like it." Mama hadn't even tasted her cake yet.

"I think she's old enough to have a say, don't you?"

I knew I was supposed to agree with Mama, but I couldn't do it. "I think I should. We need the money." Willet gave a quick nod and I was glad he approved.

"First things first," Granny Clem said. "I'll teach her to drive. She'll need a way to get out to the house and she's old enough."

I grinned. I couldn't help myself. "I already know how!"

Mama narrowed her eyes at me. "Don't tell stories, Roberta Lynn."

Willet said, "I taught her how. I'm sorry, Mama. I should have checked with you first."

Mama stood. The cake plate tumbled off her lap and clattered to the floor.

Willet took her arm, but she jerked away from him. "Please stop coddling me," she said. "I'm not a child." She walked from the room and I heard the bathroom door slam.

Granny Clem sipped her coffee and settled deeper into the sofa. She was a tiny woman, but she had a way of filling up a room.

"Thanks for the offer," I said. "I guess maybe I shouldn't do it."

Granny Clem wrapped both hands around her coffee mug and looked at me. "I have a good feeling about you," she said. "I always have."

No one had ever had a good feeling about me before, at least they'd never said so.

Willet said, "Go on, Bert. It'll be good for you to get out of the house. What else are you going to do all summer?"

We worked out the details while Mama hid in the bathroom. Granny Clem said she'd take me for my driver's license the first week of summer break, and I'd start working for her right after. It felt bad, leaving Mama out of everything, but she'd been out of it for so long there didn't seem to be another way.

The second week of summer vacation, I drove to Granny Clem's house. It was the farthest I'd ever driven on my own. When I pulled into the driveway, I glanced at Chester's trailer. I thought I saw a shadow move across the back window, but it might have been a reflection from the morning sun. I wondered if Uncle Chester ever talked to Daddy anymore or if he was as puzzled as we were about Daddy's prolonged disappearance. I didn't believe Chester could keep the counterfeiting business going without Daddy. Chester didn't have Daddy's discipline. Daddy would never send a wonky bill into circulation, but I suspected Chester wouldn't be much concerned with quality control. Still, he was doing something in that trailer. When the wind shifted, I caught a whiff of something sharp and acrid. It smelled of cat piss and dirty laundry.

Granny Clem welcomed me with a cup of coffee. "Are you hungry?"

"I'm okay," I said, though I hadn't eaten breakfast. I never did.

"Well, let's get started." She placed a wide-brimmed straw hat over her silver hair and pulled on a pair of steel-toed work boots. We stepped out the back door and I squinted into the morning sun. Behind Granny Clem's house stood a vast green field. It was nothing like our puny neglected backyard. Tangled tea rose vines surrounded the wooden porch. I never cared much for the scent of roses, but the peach-colored blooms were pretty. We walked onto the damp grass and Granny Clem pointed at one raised bed and another. Plantings popped out of whiskey barrels and an old cattle trough. Every few feet, she'd erected a raised bed of some sort and each bed sprouted some mysterious plant I couldn't name.

Until I worked with Granny Clem, it hadn't occurred to me plants might be useful beyond eating them or looking at them. I never paid attention when Mama tended her backyard garden and I'd certainly done nothing to keep it alive since she lost interest. Granny Clem showed me where she planted her herbs and pointed out which plants were best used in teas and which could be mashed up and used on the skin. "These," she said, pointing to a long bed of hairy leafed plants, "I grow mostly for the roots. But the comfrey leaves will soothe poison ivy. The ivy is terrible around here." She handed me a pair of garden shears. "Cut me a bouquet of those tulips, Bert. We'll put 'em on the front table. The women I treat like to see something pretty." She showed me how to cut the tulips close to the soil. I tucked the gardening shears into the waistband of my shorts and gathered the thick bunch of tulips in my hands. When I turned around, Granny Clem cackled. "Bert, you look like a redneck bride at a shotgun wedding. And a pretty one, at that."

No one had bothered to look at me in the months after Pansy's disappearance. Neither Mama nor Willet gave any thought to what I was wearing or how I looked when I left the house. All they thought about, day and night, was finding Pansy. And it's not like I blamed them. I thought about Pansy, too. I thought of her all the time, but that moment in the garden with Granny Clem was the first time in a long time I'd thought of myself. It made me feel guilty but also good in a strange way. Granny Clem looked at me in a way that reassured me I was real. I wasn't some wisp in a fairy tale. I wasn't a lost child in the woods. I wasn't an annoying gnat buzzing around and waiting to be swatted. I mattered.

Granny Clem taught me useful things and paid me well. I'd have gone there every day for free, but each Friday she handed me an envelope filled with cash. I never looked at the money in her presence but waited until I was a good piece down the road to peel back the flap and count the bills. Usually it was about eighty dollars, but sometimes as much as a hundred. There was no place else in White Forest where a fifteen-year-old girl with no work experience could pull down such wages in a few hours each week.

Willet didn't like me spending so much time with Granny Clem. He was happy for me to earn some money, but he didn't trust her. He never understood the real nature of her business. He didn't see the way she treated the newborns or how gentle she was to the women who ended pregnancies or who gave away their babies. Granny Clem never tried to persuade a woman to change her mind. No one came to her on a whim. "If they're here, they know what they want," she said. "Or they're slap out of options and they know what they must do. They don't need me preaching at them. One person's sin is another's salvation. It's not for me to decide."

I'd been working with Granny Clem for about a year when a young woman showed up, panting hard and complaining about her swollen belly.

"I feel like a tick on the verge of busting," she said.

Granny Clem got her settled in the spare bedroom she used for births. The woman wasn't much older than I was and she looked familiar to me, like someone I might have passed in the grocery store. She said she lived in Clarksdale and wasn't married. She hadn't told anyone about her pregnancy and she was ready to be done with it. As I boiled my grandmother's forceps and pulled together a pile of clean towels, I said I thought the woman was fooling herself if she imagined she'd hidden her pregnancy from anyone. Granny Clem said she was a fat little thing even before the baby, so she expected most people figured she'd gotten fatter.

"People will believe what you tell them to believe," Granny Clem said. "That's worth remembering, Bert."

The woman's labor dragged on for hours, and Granny Clem asked me to stick around until the baby was born. I had assisted with several births by then and was no longer horrified by the mess of blood and pure shit that poured from a woman's body during a long labor.

This woman kept saying she needed to hurry up. "I got to get home or my father will wonder where I've gone off to."

Granny Clem said she should have left a note, because this was threatening to take a while. Out of the woman's earshot, I asked Granny Clem what the woman was planning to tell her father when she came home toting a baby. Granny Clem said the woman wouldn't keep the baby, she would give it to another couple. This was an aspect of Granny Clem's business I hadn't known about before.

It wasn't legal, but people wanted babies and adoptions took years. Some people adopted from other countries, but most folks wanted a child who looked like them. When women came to her with unwanted pregnancies, she helped them either end the pregnancy or place the baby. She filled out paperwork for birth certificates and listed the adopting families as birth parents. Couples paid ten thousand dollars for a newborn infant with documentation, plus an additional two thousand dollars for the birth mother. It seemed a big pile of money to me but it was cheaper and faster than legal adoption. Granny Clem said the babies were getting a better life. Of course, sometimes things went wrong. On that day, for instance, when the woman finally pushed out the baby boy, Granny Clem took one look at him and shook her head. "Marianne," she said, "that couple is not going to take this black child."

Marianne burst into tears. "He's not so dark." She stroked his slick, newborn skin.

"He's dark enough," Granny Clem said. "And he sure is beautiful, but that snooty woman from Olive Branch isn't about to sashay home with a black child and you know it. We're going to have figure out something else."

"Maybe a black family would take him?"

"Maybe so." Granny Clem looked at me. "Bert, clean up this baby. I'm gonna make some calls."

While she called, I wiped the infant clean. It made me furious. This child, this perfect, healthy boy, was less valuable than some other infant because his skin was a couple of shades darker than expected. It wasn't fair. I never got too attached to the babies but I spent a little extra time cleaning and swaddling that little one. I felt mighty tender toward him. When I handed him back to Marianne, I could see she felt tender toward him, too.

"Can't you keep him?" I asked.

Her eyes welled and tears spilled over her plump cheeks. She shook her head. "I can't support my own self. And I'm supposed to go to junior college this year. Daddy would kill me if he knew I had a baby. And a black baby? Well, he'd kill me twice."

Granny Clem came in and said she had a family who might be interested. She would take him to them the next day. This particular couple had five daughters already and wanted a boy, but the woman was worn out from giving birth. She'd been asking Granny Clem for years to give her something to produce a male child. Granny Clem could do a lot of things with herbs and potions, but she couldn't influence the sex of a child. I couldn't believe anyone with five children would want to take on one more, though maybe they were like cats and once you had two you might as well have twenty. It irked me they only wanted the baby because he was male, but I guessed it was a good thing the child would be valued for something.

"I can't give you any money, Marianne," Granny Clem said, "but I won't charge you anything for the birth today."

"I was sure counting on that money." Marianne handed the baby to me and disappeared into the bathroom for a while. I heard water running and I heard her sobbing, but by the time she emerged, she looked about the same as when she'd come to us earlier in the day. "I've got to get home before Daddy calls the law looking for me."

After she left, Granny Clem held the baby and fed him the formula she kept on hand. He sucked greedily, not like some babies who had to be coaxed to eat. He was extra good, I tell you. Granny Clem looked spent and I hated to leave. I knew she wouldn't get any sleep. I offered to stay over.

"Well, Bert, that sure would be a big help to me."

After I called to let Mama know, I took the little boy and rocked him until he slept. I kept sticking my nose into the soft folds of his neck. He smelled sweeter than anything I'd ever got a whiff of before. We sat up most of the night drinking cup after cup of tea and tending to the baby when he needed something. I told Granny Clem I was worried about Mama. Some days she talked like she expected Pansy to walk through the door any minute. Other days it seemed she'd given up all hope. She had a terrible cough and she struggled to breathe. She hardly ate, but she smoked constantly. Granny Clem said she'd send me home with some herbs to clear the lungs.

"You can't force a person to live, Bert. I learned that when I was about your age."

I nuzzled the baby and he made sweet smacking sounds against my chest. The next morning, Granny Clem would take the boy to meet the couple who would raise him. I wondered if he would miss me and if he would think I'd abandoned him. He'd only known me for one day, but one day was his whole life. I asked Granny Clem where the couple lived, the ones who would raise him as their own. She knew better than to tell me.

"He'll be in a better spot," she said. "A good home with parents who will love him. It's everything you could hope for."

Granny Clem talked through the night. She said talking kept her awake, but I believe she was trying to tell me something about our family. She told me about the death of her parents and how she came to work with mothers and babies. I loved listening to her stories. They seemed to settle deep within me and become my own. She said I was like my father that way. "He couldn't get enough of my stories when he was your age. Some people are born to carry stories forward." I liked knowing I shared something important with Daddy.

THEY HAD STAYED ON with the women and Chester for much longer than he had intended. In their home in the woods near White Forest, Mississippi, he and his sister were well fed and cared for and safe. They were loved. He knew they were, but it wasn't the same as the love of a true mother. The women gave the children everything, including a new surname, which they shared with Chester. They were called Watkins in town and at school. Junior didn't like school. It wasn't difficult but it didn't interest him. The teacher droned on about numbers and history and geography. These were nothing like the lessons he'd learned on the island. His mother had taught him to count and do sums by gathering shells. His history was the story of his ancestors, strong men and women who'd been deceived and debased, but not destroyed. The geography of the island came to him in his dreams. He could navigate the islands the way most people navigated city streets. Even after years away, he knew he'd be able to pilot a boat through the maze of bright green bird-filled mangroves and never lose his way.

The things they taught him in school were useless. His teacher had no patience for questions and didn't appreciate being challenged.

When she talked about the Seminole wars, she called the Indians "savages." She described them as violent creatures bent on destroying the white settlers. The white settlers were bringing progress, she said. The white settlers were bringing culture. He knew it wasn't true and he couldn't figure out whether she was lying or just stupid. She didn't speak much more kindly about the slaves. To hear her talk, you would think it was a gift to be rounded up in Africa and brought to America to work on the plantations. What would she think of a half-Negro, half-Seminole woman with two mixed children? Not much, he suspected. There was nothing to be gained by arguing with the stupid woman. He'd had his knuckles rapped by her wooden ruler and he learned to keep his mouth shut, but on days when she preached about the untamed savages like his mother, rage boiled in his stomach. It poisoned his blood and made him violent. One day, leaving school, he turned and punched another boy square in the stomach. The boy fell to the ground, clutching his belly, crying, "What'd you do that for?"

Junior's eyes had filled with hot tears that would never fall. Only Fern could calm him when the anger came. She sang songs they'd learned from their mother, and he closed his eyes and imagined he could hear wind and waves and the call of the birds.

"When are we going home?" Fern asked him nearly every day.

"Soon," he promised.

Fern fared no better than he did in school. She couldn't sit still for so long. Her hands itched to make something. In their first year, she was punished for tearing out the pages of a textbook and creating delicate birds from the paper. She did it without thinking, he knew that, but there was no explaining it to the teacher. She learned to keep her hands at rest during the long hours of lessons. Every afternoon, though, she gathered leaves and bits of bark and insect husks and worked her magic on them until they were beautiful and worth keeping.

Nothing could make school better, but Ora and Clementine were gentle, and cared for the children as if they belonged to them. Clementine loved Fern best. It was sad, because Chester was

Clementine's true child. Chester wasn't smart or handsome or talented. He was prone to fits of anger and temper tantrums even as a teenager. Clementine said Chester had been born of a violent act and he carried violence around with him. Junior didn't mind Chester's fits. He understood them. Fern calmed both boys with her songs and with the things she made. She gave her creations as gifts to people she loved or anyone who showed her kindness. Chester and Junior filled their pockets with paper birds and wooden turtles and orchid flowers made from bits of cloth and bark. Both boys loved her and would do anything for her. Chester was rough and plenty of people thought he'd never amount to much, but Junior saw the good in him. Chester's one great attribute was loyalty and he was especially loyal to Fern.

When Chester was fifteen and he and Fern were thirteen, the three of them spent a long day fishing on the banks of a nearby river. It was early spring and not too hot yet. A gentle breeze kept the bugs down. They cast their lines and bragged about how they would fry up a mess of fish for Clementine and Ora that evening. They'd caught a half dozen bream by midmorning. Fern tired of fishing and wandered off to gather pecan shells, which she turned into tiny replications of stone crabs. She lined up her creations along the sandy riverbank.

Junior wished he could take her home to the islands. She didn't belong here, but he could think of no way for them to travel so far without hardship. Soon, he thought. He was a man now, or nearly so, and ought to be able to find work. Things were not as dire as they had been when his father left them by the train tracks. There was work to be found building bridges or dams or at the logging camps or the cotton gins. Soon he would be able to support them and they could be on their way. Clementine and Ora would be sad to see them go. He'd heard them talking about how good it was for Chester to have siblings. He wondered if Chester would want to come with them, but he knew it would be too much to take Chester away from his home. The island would be as foreign to Chester as this flat, green land was to him. The only thing these places shared was an abundance of green choking vines and mosquitoes as big as birds.

It was no easy thing to leave a place where food was abundant and there was shelter from the rain, but they should have left that spring. They shouldn't have stayed on for that terrible summer, no matter how comfortable and well fed they were. Back home, the white pelicans abandoned their fledglings before first flight. Only when the fledglings got hungry, got desperate, would they leave the safe warmth of the nest. It made Junior ache to think of those birds. They were brought into the world and fed for nearly three months by their mother. She left the nest each day and returned with minnow or shrimp or small fish. And then, one day, she disappeared. The birds, still small, still cozy and warm and safe in the nest, waited and waited, their bellies growing hungrier by the minute. Were they afraid? Were they sad? Were they angry? He thought they must be. Eventually, the birds left the nest. They flew for the first time out of desperation and hunger. Why couldn't their mother stick around long enough to teach them how to fly? Why couldn't she help them for a little while? He knew why. Birds won't fly if they don't have to fly. Birds, like children, must be desperate to leave a warm nest.

NINE

I worked for Granny Clem all through high school. Her house became my second home and if it weren't for Mama, I'd have spent every minute at Granny Clem's. I was more comfortable there than anywhere else. We marked the passing days and months and years with the only measure that made any sense to us. Most days we didn't speak of it, but on special days—Christmas, the Fourth of July, Pansy's birthday—Granny Clem might shake her head and say, *That poor child.* And I knew she was referring to Pansy. Or Willet, on the anniversary of Pansy's disappearance, would make a point of being extra careful with Mama, bringing her sweet tea before she had a chance to ask for it and curbing his tendency to cuss about everything. The first year was the hardest. By the third year it was routine.

I grew up. I would have grown up whether Pansy disappeared or not, I suppose, but by the time I turned seventeen, I'd attended dozens of births and learned the difference between poison leaves and edible ones. I don't know who I'd have been if things had turned out different—if we'd found Pansy or never lost her in the first place. Maybe I'd have gone to prom or homecoming games. Maybe I'd have taken up with one of the local boys, a farmer's kid with a permanent tan or the pale, preppy son of an alderman. Maybe I'd have joined the science club or been a reporter for the school newspaper. All sorts of things were possible before Pansy went missing, but her disappearance whittled my world to a sharp point.

As it was, I couldn't afford an ordinary adolescence. At Granny Clem's, I dealt with life and death. I spent hours in her garden or her kitchen. I carried the work around with me. My skin smelled of purple and green, lavender and mint, hyacinth and lemon balm, birth and death. Black dirt caked beneath my fingernails. By the time I was a senior in high school, her patients trusted me. I knew so many of them. They were the mothers of my classmates. They were the grocery store clerk and the secretaries on Cotton Row. One of them sat three rows ahead of me in American history class. She'd been particularly shocked to find me when she showed up at Granny Clem's seeking an end to an unplanned pregnancy. I learned how to put the women at ease. I figured out how to make my eyes float past them when I saw them on the streets or in the stores. No flicker of recognition, no narrowing my eyes in judgment, no smirk or pity or warmth. The women who came to Granny Clem didn't want my sympathy; they wanted my silence. I gave them what they wanted and they trusted me.

"That one keeps her mouth shut tight," one woman said.

Granny Clem nodded. "She's a secret-keeper. Runs in the family."

I stayed up many nights with Granny Clem and the newborn babies. I liked being awake when other folks were sleeping. The babies smelled like rising yeast dough and lemon. Our house smelled of mildew and of Mama's stale cigarettes and loneliness. Willet was gone a lot. He worked construction on the coast and in cities across the southeast. He'd bought a used truck and left me with Mama's old Ford. I felt bad when I left Mama alone, but we rarely talked when I was home. As long as I shopped for her, as long as I kept her stocked with cigarettes and diet soda and tea, she didn't miss me. I was not the daughter she wanted or needed.

Some nights when there was no reason for me to stay with Granny Clem, I drove the back roads of the Delta and tried to get lost. Many of the roads had no markers and one dirt-packed stretch looked like the next, especially when the cotton grew high. Sometimes I drove out to the site of the old quarry and watched the stars shine on the spot where we lost Pansy. It gave me the willies, being there alone. It was like Daddy said; the place was evil. We never should have swum there or played in those woods. We were courting trouble.

Mostly I drove in silence but when the sound of my own thoughts got to be too much, I turned on the radio for distraction. I rolled the dial past rock music and gospel preaching. I didn't know what I was listening for until I heard a familiar voice:

"Our phone lines are open, so call now. We're talking to Horace Lawrence, abduction survivor, and author of the book *Into That Dark Sky*. This is simply one of the best, most compelling stories I've ever read about the abduction experience. As most of you know, I was abducted repeatedly as a child. Horace's recollections in this book corroborate everything I remember. And I know there are skeptics among you; there are those of you listening to my voice right now who cannot believe extraterrestrials exist, who will not accept the proof right in front of you that these beings not only exist but they visit, and they take children as subjects to be studied. We are part of their great experiment. The evidence is all around us. All you have to do is look up and believe. I'm Bubba Speck, and I'm here to take your calls."

People called in with stories about being abducted, stories about being probed by aliens. One woman claimed she'd been impregnated and had an abortion to rid herself of an alien fetus. A man talked about his missing son and his certainty the boy had been snatched from his bed and carted away in an alien spacecraft. Bubba listened to these people. He sympathized with them. "No one else believes me," they said. "I can't talk about it, or people think I'm crazy." All of these folks who, by the light of day, could find no one to trust their story, found Bubba's warm voice in the dark night.

Pansy's disappearance was always with me, and hearing Bubba and his callers talk about missing people, missing time, and missing memories made my recollections sharper. Pansy's disappearance stuck with Bubba, too. It stuck with us all. Mama sent money to preachers and prayed for Pansy to return. Willet searched for her wherever he traveled. I kept trying to make sense of the nonsensical, but Bubba looked to the skies. Some things never changed.

One summer when we were still kids and Pansy was an infant, still feeding from Mama's breast and crying on a regular schedule, still ugly and angry and needy, Willet and Bubba dragged an old red wagon to the fireworks stand outside the city limits. They'd pooled their money, a meager amount despite two months spent mowing lawns and pulling weeds for anyone who'd hire them. It was late afternoon on the third of July, and fireworks were marked to sell. They came back with a pile of cheap explosives: firecrackers, boomer rockets, whistlers, zippers, sparklers, smoke canisters, and more. Mama said it was dangerous. Willet was eleven. Daddy said he was plenty old enough and nothing in that wagon was going to kill anyone. We sat on the edge of the yard in shaky aluminum chairs. Mama clutched Pansy to her breast. Willet and Bubba laid out their haul in careful rows. Daddy stood nearby with his best Zippo lighter, which he handed off to Willet with a serious nod that left me yearning for something shiny and silver to hold. Willet wanted to light the best ones first, but Bubba stopped him. It would be more impressive to start small and work up to a finale. They had one repeater that promised a solid minute of star showers and multicolored bursts.

"That ought to be the last one," Bubba said. "We can just sit back and enjoy the show."

Willet went along. Bubba had a persuasive way of talking. If you closed your eyes and listened, it was easy to forget he was a kid. Willet lit a sparkler and brought it to me, told me to wave it in the air.

"It's a magic wand," I said.

"Yeah," said Willet. "It is."

Mama pulled Pansy in tighter and stepped away from my crackling wand. She didn't trust me.

The first few fireworks they lit were duds, and Willet cussed about the wasted money. Mama told him to watch his mouth, but Daddy said he was entitled to cuss about some things. That's what cuss words were for. Finally, Bubba set off a fountain and the air lit up with sparks. Even Mama smiled. I waved my sparkler in the air and cheered. For a half hour, Willet and Bubba sent fireworks sizzling and popping and whistling through the night. Willet ran back and forth from the pile of fireworks to my spot on the edge of the yard, bringing me a new sparkler every time one fizzled. I grinned, happy to see I was still his favorite sister despite Pansy's recent arrival. I inched closer to Willet and Bubba as the show wore on, and Mama was too distracted with Pansy to notice or care. The dark sky became crosshatched with silver light and red explosions and ghostly smoke trails. They lit the final fuse and Willet and Bubba stood on either side of me. We tilted our heads back and stood gaping at the night sky.

"What do you think, Bert?" Bubba asked.

"I think it's the prettiest thing I've ever seen."

On a clear spring night when the stars seemed especially abundant, I listened until Bubba signed off the air. It was well past midnight. I wondered if Willet knew about Bubba's show, if he'd stumbled across it some night when he couldn't sleep or when he drove away from a job site, bone-weary from a long day gone into overtime. I knew what Willet would say—he'd say Bubba was crazy. But was he? Why was Bubba's story crazier than anything else we'd imagined over the years?

I stopped the car in the middle of a deserted road and got out to look at the stars. I thought of all those people who talked about strange lights and visitors from another planet. What would it be like, to be lifted into the dark sky? I wanted to know. I hadn't prayed in many years, having left God behind with other childhood totems like Santa Claus and the Tooth Fairy, but I wished very hard to see some sign of life and wishing felt like prayer. As with all the prayers I'd ever prayed, it came to nothing. The sky didn't shift or change. No bright lights appeared. No craft emerged to take me away. The man in the moon didn't give me so much as a wink. If creatures from another planet were searching for signs of life, I'd fallen short. Still, I thought, if Pansy were abducted by aliens as Bubba claimed, wouldn't that be easier for us? For Willet and for me? How could we be responsible for that?

The next day, I called the radio station. A woman told me the program had originated in Jackson at an affiliate station.

"But you air it live?" I asked.

"Yes. Lot of weirdos out there in the middle of the night." I could tell from the tone of her voice she thought I might be one of the weirdos.

I waited a week before driving to Jackson to find Bubba. It was a two-and-a-half-hour drive, even in the dead of night. I drank cheap truck-stop coffee and pulled over twice to check the map. The radio station was located on the west side of town and a wrong turn landed me in a residential neighborhood with barking dogs and men clustered on concrete stoops, smoking and drinking from cans tucked in paper sacks. The men watched me as I crawled past, the whites of their eyes eerie and stark and full of suspicion.

I found the station, a two-story brick building topped by antennas jutting into the sky. A chain-link fence surrounded the parking lot, but the gate was open. The glass front door of the building was locked. I knocked, hoping someone might hear me. No one came. I returned to the car and listened to Bubba's voice while watching the building. I could picture him in there, talking into a microphone and answering calls.

I wondered which one of the five vehicles in the lot belonged to him. I ruled out the vans with the station call letters on the side.

There was a white Camaro with a spoiler on the back and a mustard-yellow Pinto with a rusted out back panel. I hoped he owned the Camaro, but I could see him in the old Pinto. When Bubba signed off, I kept my eyes on the locked door of the station, expecting him to emerge. I'd about given up when I saw him walking across the lot. He must have come out a back door. He didn't head for either the Camaro or the Pinto, but for a motorcycle I hadn't noticed on the far edge of the lot. He passed under a bank of streetlights. He wore a black T-shirt and a ball cap. His hair was long. Otherwise, he looked like the boy I remembered.

I jumped out of my car and shouted, "Bubba!"

He walked faster, like he wanted to get away from me.

"Bubba, it's me! It's Bert!"

He stopped and turned. I ran to him. I threw my arms around his neck and laughed. "Oh, God, it's been forever."

"It's the middle of the night," he said. "You shouldn't be out here."

I stepped away. "Are you still mad at me?"

"I don't know what you're doing here."

His stomach flopped over the waistband of his faded jeans and he had sweat stains under his armpits, though the night was cool.

"I heard you on the radio," I said. "I wanted to see you."

He sighed, looked at the keys in his hands, and shoved them in his pocket. "I assume you didn't walk here."

I pointed at Mama's old Ford.

"I'm hungry," he said.

I drove us to the Krystal's, where we shared a sack of oniony burgers and fries. He scarfed down a half dozen of the small, square, mustard-soaked burgers before I finished one. He drained his extra-large soda and went back for a refill. I figured I'd driven an awfully long way for the silent treatment and a bunch of terrible food, but eventually he started talking. He hit me with a stream of questions, though he didn't pause long enough for me to answer.

"What the hell were you thinking, Bert? Driving all this way in the middle of the night? What if something happened? What if you had car trouble? Does Willet know where you are? Does your mother? How is Willet? How is your mother?"

I ate a greasy fry and studied him under the harsh fluorescent lights. "Are you done?"

"I'm just getting started."

"First of all," I told him, "I'm not a child and you don't need to worry about where I go or when. Second, I wanted to see you. It's been almost four years and I always felt bad about the way you left. I felt like it was my fault."

He wiped mustard from the corner of his lips with a small square of paper napkin. "So you're here to make yourself feel better?"

"I wanted to see you."

He crammed another burger into his mouth and seemed to swallow it without chewing. "Well, here I am. I'm fat. I'm ugly. I'm crazy. You can report back to the good people of White Forest: Bubba Speck is a lunatic. Same as ever."

"I don't think you're a lunatic."

"Everyone else does."

"Not the people who call in to your show."

Bubba shook the paper sack, searching for stray fries. He wouldn't look at me. I babbled to fill the awkward silence. I told him I was working for Granny Clem and I would graduate in May. I told him Willet was working construction. I told him about Mama's poor health and how we hadn't seen Daddy since before Pansy disappeared.

Bubba leaned his elbows on the cold aluminum table and stared at me. It was weird. He was weird. I'd made a mistake in coming to Jackson. I'd had this idea I mattered to Bubba, that he would want to hear from me, but I was wrong. I'd spent the past four years thinking about Pansy and my father and Bubba, but it did not seem like Bubba had spent any time thinking about me. He thought about his aliens and his abduction theories. I was some kid he once knew, some kid who got him sent away.

I stood to refill my paper cup. Bubba grabbed my arm. "Bert, does anyone know you're here?"

"No."

"Not Willet or your mother or your grandmother?"

"I just drove. I didn't tell anyone." His fingers dug into my fore-arm and he pulled me toward him. The way he looked at me made my stomach hurt.

"No one cares if you disappear in the middle of the night?"

No one did, but I didn't want Bubba feeling sorry for me. "Is anyone looking for you right now?" I asked him. "Does anyone care where you are?"

He let go of my arm. I sat back down, my cup still empty, my stomach still aching. I knew I should be afraid but I couldn't fear Bubba. We were the same. Pansy's disappearance got Bubba sent away from his home and it made me invisible in mine. Neither of us mattered.

He rubbed his face and pushed his fingers through his long, greasy hair. He seemed middle-aged then, though I knew he was only twenty.

"I'm tired," he said. "Will you drive me home? I don't feel like getting my bike."

It was two o'clock in the morning. I had no plan. I'd thought I could drive there and back without any sleep, but I dreaded the dark, empty highway. "Where do you live?"

"Just a couple miles from here," Bubba said. "Come hang out with me."

Bubba was a stranger now, but I was different, too. I wadded up the used napkins on the table and piled them on the plastic tray. It was not clear to me what he was asking. I could not predict what might happen if I stayed. I knew nothing would happen if I ran away. I needed for something to happen.

"Tomorrow's Saturday," Bubba said. "You don't have school."

"You said you never saw Pansy that day, but she was there. She was swimming in the quarry. How could you not see her?"

"You know how."

"No, tell me."

"Come home with me. I'll tell you everything I know."

I picked up my keys and he followed me from the restaurant. "Which way?" I asked.

He directed me to the highway and through a series of turns. I tried to keep track of where we were, but Jackson was so much larger than White Forest and the early morning darkness turned landmarks into shadows. We pulled into the lot of a small, ugly apartment complex. We climbed a steep metal staircase on the outside of the building. I followed Bubba inside and wondered if I'd lost my mind. There was no good reason for me to be here. Willet would be furious if he knew.

Bubba flipped on an overhead light. It wasn't much—a fake leather couch, a beanbag wedged in a corner, a small television on cinder blocks, bare walls, the only window taped over with tinfoil, something I remembered from the visit to his home after Pansy disappeared.

"Why do you do that?" I pointed to the window.

"So they can't see me while I'm sleeping," he said. "I don't like it when they read my dreams." He opened a mini-fridge in the corner and pulled out two cans of beer. I took one and pulled the tab. It was bitter and made my nose tingle.

"How old are you now?"

"Nearly eighteen."

He sat on the couch. The fake leather squeaked and sighed. I chose the beanbag.

He gulped from his beer can. "What are you doing here?"

"You asked me to come hang out."

"But why did you come?"

I couldn't answer him.

He drained the beer and opened the fridge for another. He offered me one, but my first was still full. "I didn't go away. I was sent away. My family wanted to be rid of me and they used the mess with your sister as an excuse." He put a hand to his chest and belched. The sour smell of beer and greasy food filled the room. "My father hated me. He thought I killed my mother. If she hadn't had me, she'd still be alive. That's the kind of monster I am. I'm the kind of monster who kills his own mother."

"You were a baby."

"And then when your sister went missing, he thought I killed her, too. Everyone thought it. People believed I dragged her into the woods and did terrible things to her. People believed I buried her or burned her or hid her body in a passing car. You know what they said. You heard them."

I shook my head, though I knew what they had said.

"People thought I raped her. A child. What kind of person would do such a thing? And what does it mean that people think I'm that kind of person?"

Bubba's face went red and splotchy. His eyes were wet, though he didn't cry. On the radio, he talked about surviving the abductions. He talked about the aliens studying his brain. He believed they wanted to read his dreams. They traveled across galaxies to find him again and again. He was special. It must have been a good feeling, even when it was terrifying. I couldn't bring myself to believe Bubba's stories but I knew he believed them. He might have been crazy but he wasn't lying.

I opened a second beer and we drank in silence for a while. My legs went numb in the valley of the beanbag. I wondered about Bubba's life. What did he do after work when he was alone? Did he come here and drink beer by himself until he was able to sleep? Or did he turn on the television and watch whatever crap was airing at two in the morning?

"What do you dream about?" I asked him. "The things you don't want the aliens to see."

"Things I don't want you to see either." He excused himself and disappeared into the bathroom. Through the thin walls, I heard the stream of urine hitting the side of the bowl. I struggled from the beanbag and shook out my legs. I looked at his books. Most were first-person accounts of alien abductions, but not all. I pulled a book from the shelves: *Among the Missing: An Anecdotal History of Missing Persons*. What was the point of such a book? Were people clamoring for anecdotes about missing people? If so, why? It was terrible enough when you were in the middle of it. Why would you read about it if you didn't have to? I slid the book back onto the shelf.

Bubba came out of the bathroom. "What's your plan?"

"My plan?"

"Tonight, I mean. You're not going to drive home tonight, are you?"

I didn't want to spend hours alone in the dark car. I wouldn't have Bubba's voice to keep me company. The radio would be nothing but obscure rock music and religion. Willet was working on a crew in Mobile. Granny Clem didn't expect me until noon. Unless she ran out of cigarettes, Mama would never know I was gone.

"Stay here," Bubba said. "You can drive when the sun's up."

He gave me his bed, a single mattress on a metal frame with a cotton blanket no thicker than the sheets. He went back to the couch. He said he slept there all the time. I heard the television droning throughout the night. I wondered if Bubba ever slept.

When I woke, the room was dark, though it was nearly nine in the morning. The foil-covered windows blocked the sunlight. I never slept so late at home, even after sitting up with Granny Clem and a newborn. I brushed my teeth with my finger and splashed cold water on my face. I opened Bubba's medicine cabinet, touched his acne cream and his ointments. He had a bottle of aspirin and a prescription for Valium.

In the living room, he sat exactly where he'd been the night before. I got the sense he spent much of his life in that spot, watching television or reading or staring into space.

"Thanks for letting me crash," I said.

"You can't do this sort of thing, you know."

"What sort of thing?"

"Show up at strange men's houses and spend the night."

He poured coffee from a percolator on a hot plate. I took the mug from him. "You're not a strange man."

"Bert, I didn't take Pansy. I never saw her. I don't know what happened to your sister. I don't know what happened to any of us."

"I didn't accuse you."

"You had to wonder. Why else would you come all this way to see someone you barely know?"

I sat beside him on the squeaky couch.

"Just because I didn't take Pansy doesn't mean I'm harmless. You're too trusting."

He was wrong. I didn't trust anyone. I loved my brother. I respected him, but I didn't always trust him. Like everyone else, he had too many secrets. Mama, Granny Clem, Willet; they kept things from me and from each other.

"I want to know the truth," I told him. "That's all."

He kissed me then. He smelled clean and soapy, like he'd showered that morning. He pulled his lips away, wrapped his hands around the sides of my face, and pressed his forehead to mine. Our noses touched. We breathed together. "Bert," he said.

I pressed my lips into his to shut him up. He tasted familiar, the way a boy you grew up with should taste. I pulled him on top of me. His body was a warm blanket. He was tentative, touching me first above my T-shirt and shorts. When he slipped his hands beneath my clothes, he paused as if he expected me to stop him. I pulled him closer and pressed into his touch. He shuddered when I breathed against his ear. He held his breath when I traced my fingers along his neck. He was desperate for me, but I could get up and walk away and he wouldn't chase me. I knew he wouldn't. He kept his shirt on. His legs were pasty white and he had a patch of dark hair above his buttocks.

The couch squeaked and sighed with every move. The cheap cushions stuck to my bare skin. The girls at school said the first time always hurt. They talked about the blood on the sheets and how they ached down there for days after, but I felt no pain. My body stretched and opened as if it had been waiting for this moment. Bubba made soft whimpering noises against my neck. Then he went stiff. He pulled away and finished on my stomach.

"I'm sorry," he whispered. "I'm so sorry."

I didn't know what I was supposed to do next. My body wanted something more, but Bubba made no move to continue. I considered moving his hand against me, but it seemed pushy and desperate. Whatever power I'd had moments ago was gone now. He was limp and unresponsive when I pressed against him. He apologized again and again until I told him to shut up.

"I should go," I said. "They might be wondering where I am by now."

He pushed off me to stand. The couch creaked. He turned his back to me and pulled on his jeans. I used a paper towel to wipe the flaky, sticky substance from my stomach before I slipped my T-shirt over my head and pulled my denim shorts up from where they'd settled around my ankles.

"Do you remember the night you put on the firework show?" I asked.

He pulled a pair of loafers onto his bare feet. "Fireworks?"

"Yeah, you and Willet went and bought a bunch of fireworks and set 'em off in our backyard."

He shook his head. "I don't think so. Maybe it was someone else."

"No, it was you. Pansy was still a baby."

"I don't think so, but there are a lot of things I can't remember. I told you, I lose track of time."

He looked pitiful, standing in the middle of his small, ugly apartment. I should have felt sorry for him, but I was angry. How could he have forgotten the fireworks? That night was important to me. It meant nothing to him.

"Will you remember this?" I asked. "In ten years, will you remember fucking me on your cheap couch?"

"Don't talk like that. Don't make it sound ugly."

"I shouldn't have come here," I said. I found my keys and slipped my feet into my tennis shoes.

"Yeah, well, I told you that."

He was angry, too. It made me like him again. It was better to be angry than to be pitiful. I hugged him for a long time. I wanted to remember the way he smelled and the way his arms felt across my back. I thought I might never see him again.

"I won't forget," he said, his mouth moving against my neck. "I promise."

I drove back to White Forest, the glare of the morning sun behind me. Would Granny Clem or Mama be able to look at me and see what I'd done? If they could, they never said so. Finally, I had a secret all my own.

CLEMENTINE AND ORA TAUGHT Fern the secrets of their business. They taught her about the plants they grew and how to brew strong teas from roots and berries. They taught her to cool an angry wound and to bring heat to a cold infant. The mothers loved Fern. She had a way of calming squalling infants. Junior couldn't believe how his sister had grown. No longer a scrawny child, at fifteen she was beautiful and sharp.

Fern made dolls from the cloth scraps in Clementine's mending basket and gave them as gifts to the newborns. She held the babies when they were first born, before they were wiped clean, and she listened to their first cries. She chose dolls based on what the infants needed. Some infants cried for warmth, others for wisdom or compassion; they all cried for love. Fern listened and gave them what they needed.

Mothers coveted Fern's rag dolls. Children cherished them. It was as if she'd sewed some magic into the dolls, something to soothe an aching heart, something to cure loneliness. In fact, she tucked dried herbs in the heart of each doll: lavender for peace and comfort, spearmint to spark energy, pokeroot for courage, valerian for protection.

In the late afternoons, Fern often wandered across the narrow creek and crossed a set of train tracks to visit Melvin and his family. Melvin was a year older than Junior and Fern, and he looked after his little brothers and sisters while his father worked at the lumber mill and his mother worked in some white woman's kitchen. Fern said she could talk to Melvin better than she could talk to anyone else, even Junior. Junior liked Melvin just fine, but he worried about Fern getting too cozy with a black boy. Lynchings were not unheard of in the woods around White Forest.

Fern showed Melvin's little sisters and brothers how to make dandelion chains. She told them stories about the strangling fig that could choke a cypress tree to death with its slow embrace. With Melvin, Fern shed her hat and pushed up the sleeves of her long dresses. She lay back in the grass and let the sun beat down on her face and arms. Melvin told her she was the most beautiful girl he'd ever seen.

Junior scolded her about the sun. She was darker that summer than she'd ever been. Clementine and Ora both commented on how quickly her skin tanned, though they didn't seem to mind. Junior nagged her about keeping her skin light, but she ignored him. She looked more and more like their mother. For seven years they'd lived in this town, they'd attended the white school, they called Clementine their mother and Chester their brother. No one suspected they weren't white, but how long could that last if Fern let her skin go dark? Clementine said people believed what you told them to believe. Maybe it was true. Maybe Fern could pass for white no matter the color of her skin. Junior tried to be optimistic. Everyone else was. World War II ended and men came home. Everyone seemed to have more money all of a sudden. People smiled in the streets. Even the German prisoners whistled as they chopped cotton, their days in this hot, flat land drawing to a certain close.

Junior had begun spending time with a girl from town. Shirley was the daughter of a carpenter and the youngest child in a family full of boys. Her father drank too much, but when he was sober he made the prettiest furniture in town. Shirley let him kiss her behind the live oak tree near the quarry. When she touched him, it was like a stick of dynamite going off in his stomach. He told her he loved her and he believed what he was saying. What else could it mean, these explosions of longing? It was a time when most children grew up with no information about sex, but it was impossible to remain ignorant while living with Clementine and Ora. He knew how babies were made and how they were born. He hadn't, until Shirley, understood the urgency behind it all. At night, he lay awake in a fever, touching himself again and again until he was raw with desire. He begged Shirley to let him touch her beneath her clothes, but she laughed and pushed him away. "My brothers will kill you." He didn't care. Death would be worth the pleasure.

It didn't occur to him that Fern might feel the same urgency. He thought girls were different. His connection with his sister stretched thin as they spent more time apart. Once they'd been joined so tightly he could hear her thoughts, but no more.

Autumn brought a hint of coolness to the air most mornings, but the heat rolled in each afternoon. There was a movie theater twenty miles west and he and Chester often drove there on Saturday afternoons to watch westerns on the big screen. The theater was air-conditioned. On a hot day it was heaven to sit for two hours in the cool dark and be carried away by a story. Junior loved stories. In October, they decided to see a film about the hunt for a Nazi spy. Fern decided to come along.

He'd tried to get Shirley to join them, but she said she was going shopping with her mother and couldn't get away. He knew Shirley didn't care for Chester. She said he was too rough. Shirley had made some remarks about Fern, as well. She noticed Fern's dark skin and said a lady shouldn't spend so much time in the sun. He said his sister had always tanned easily.

"A little too easily, if you ask me," Shirley had said.

At the theater, the man at the front door stared at Fern. "She'll have to sit upstairs," he said.

"What are you saying?" Chester practically spit at the man.

"Negros upstairs," the man said.

"She ain't no Negro," Chester said. "She's my sister."

"And mine." Junior was embarrassed that Chester had spoken up first.

"Then I reckon you're a pack of niggers and all of you should sit upstairs."

People in the lobby turned to stare. Junior's face burned red. Chester's face was red, too, though it was from anger rather than shame.

Fern laughed. "I don't care where we sit."

Chester punched the man in the face. The man's nose bled and he howled. A security guard appeared and pulled Chester's arms behind his back. Chester struggled and kicked. The guard pushed him out the front door.

"Go on," he said. "And don't ever come back here."

"Let him go!" Fern grabbed onto Chester's shirt. "He won't do anything else."

"He's banned from the theater," the guard said. "All of you are. I don't want to see any of you here again, you understand?"

Junior pulled Fern away. Chester's instinct was to fight and his was to run. What did that say about him? Did it make him smart or did it make him a coward?

Chester broke free from the guard's grasp and stumbled forward. He turned and spat on the guard's shiny black boots. "You ain't nothing," he said. "You ain't good enough to lick her shoe."

They ran to the car. Chester drove. Looking back, Junior saw a crowd of people watching, their faces full of hate and suspicion and rage. When they looked at Fern, they saw someone different. They didn't see his beautiful, sensitive sister. They didn't see a girl who could turn something worthless into a work of art. They saw a black girl running wild with two white boys. For years they'd leveled their hateful gazes at the Nazis across the ocean, but now they turned their sights toward home. Black people were getting uppity, they said. It was time to put them in their place.

TEN

———◆———

WILLET NEVER LET GO of the idea that Pansy was alive, that she'd been taken by our father. If we found Daddy, we would find Pansy, he said. I didn't expect to find Pansy and I'd long given up on Daddy. Both of them seemed bigger, somehow, in their absence than when they were with us. They were fanciful, like characters from the fairy tales, and I wouldn't have been a bit surprised to find they were living as birds or beasts under an evil spell. Maybe they were watching us. Any notion seemed as good as another, but none seemed likely.

Willet didn't care what was likely. He saw Pansy everywhere. He called me from Memphis and Baton Rouge and Gulf Shores to tell me about some girl he'd seen at the mall or at a diner or at a fruit stand on the side of the road.

"It could be her," he said.

"Pansy would be older now." She'd been missing for nearly four years, I reminded him. She wouldn't be the same.

Still, he kept looking.

Working construction left him wrung out and dirty, and he hated the tall buildings. Some of the men never clipped into a safety harness. "They're like goats," he said. "Goddamned fearless goats." Willet never got over the fear of falling. "You can't know what it's like up there. You think these buildings are sturdy and straight, but I'm here to tell you they sway like a playground swing in a strong wind."

I begged him not to tell me about it. What would we do if something happened to Willet? The money I made working with Granny Clem might buy our groceries and pay the phone bill but it wouldn't stretch any further. Willet supported us, but it wasn't his income I worried about losing. I'd lost one sibling. I couldn't lose another.

"Come home," I said. "Quit and do something else."

But nothing else paid as well as working construction. A young man like Willet, with no wife and kids, could work steadily. He could move around and sleep in ugly trailers on the job site or cheap motels nearby. He worked hard and kept his fears hidden. Between jobs, he came home and did what needed doing around the house: he painted the front porch, patched shingles on the roof, yanked out a section of rot from one corner of the garage. I finished high school and worked longer hours with Granny Clem. Willet said I ought to go to college, but we couldn't afford it. Plus, Mama needed me. Who else would keep her stocked with cigarettes and sweet tea? Who else would make sure she ate a little something every day? Who else would shame her into taking a bath once a week? It seemed like nothing would ever change for Willet and me. We'd been set on a path when Pansy disappeared and there were no detours in sight.

Then, in July of 1980, Daddy turned up in a motel room in Everglades City, Florida. His body turned up, I mean. He'd checked into the motel three weeks earlier, paid cash for a month, and told the cleaning lady to skip his room. He wanted privacy. She'd obliged. Cleanliness was not a high priority at the Glades Motel. It was the sort of place where people paid for one night and left after two hours. The whole month might have passed without anyone finding Daddy, but someone complained about the smell.

The police at the scene said it was the worst thing they'd ever come across, worse even than the six-year-old boy who mistook the family pistol for a toy and shot his little sister through the brain, worse than the old woman who lost her left leg to an alligator while gigging for frogs. By the time they found Daddy, he was oozing like soft cheese, bloated and bruised from head to toe.

The fat police officer from Pansy's disappearance broke the news. He asked our mother to come to the sheriff's office and look at some photos from the scene, but Mama said she was too sick to leave the house. I called Willet at the motel where he was staying in Ocean Springs. He drove clear across the state of Mississippi after a long day of work. We went to the sheriff's office the next morning and looked at the grainy photos from Florida. We spoke to a detective there by phone and tried to see Daddy beneath the green and blue bloated flesh. It could have been anyone.

"How can you be sure it's him?" I asked.

"His wallet was on the nightstand," the detective said. "Driver's license was inside it. He signed the registry as Earl Watkins."

"But what about fingerprints? Or dental records?" I watched cop shows on television. I thought detectives were supposed to check these things.

"His hands are too degraded to get a fingerprint," the detective said. "And he's missing half his teeth. Gums are rotted black."

According to the detective, Daddy had been a common drunk who'd likely lived on the streets for a time. His body showed evidence of exposure.

"Did you do an autopsy?" I asked.

"The medical examiner didn't think it necessary. There's no evidence of foul play. He was found on the bed in the motel. We believe he drank himself to sleep and never woke up. We've seen it before. It happens more often than you think."

I'd seen Daddy drink, of course, but I'd never seen him drunk. And he was prideful about his appearance. He kept his hair short and neat, scraped underneath his nails, shaved every morning. It was hard to reconcile the photos and the detective's explanation with anything I'd known about Daddy.

"He's been gone a long time," the detective said. "Nearly four years? People can spiral down quick."

Maybe that's why he hadn't come home. Maybe he was ashamed.

"He was in trouble with the law," the detective told us. "He spread counterfeit bills all over Fort Myers. They were bound to catch him eventually."

The man seemed to think we wouldn't know anything about Daddy's counterfeiting business and we didn't contradict him. There was an outstanding warrant for Daddy in Mobile, Alabama. Daddy and Chester had been arrested for stealing a car in 1975, less than a year before he disappeared for good. Chester had done the time, a few months in county lockup, but Daddy skipped bail. I thought back to the year before Pansy disappeared and tried to remember anything unusual, but couldn't. It was the last ordinary year.

"Sometimes men find a way to die rather than be locked up," the detective said. "I'm sorry for your loss. We need to know what you want to do with the body."

"Did he have anything with him?" Willet asked. "Did you check the closets and drawers?"

"Nothing remarkable. Plaid shirt, pair of boots, an empty bottle of rum. Like I said, we think he'd been living on the streets."

"But he paid for a whole month at the motel," Willet said.

"Hard to say where he came by the money. Somebody tourist could have given him a wad of cash or maybe he stole it."

"Were there pictures in his wallet? Pictures of a girl, maybe?"

The detective said the only thing in his wallet was the expired Mississippi driver's license.

"So you don't think he was traveling with a child?"

The fat policeman who'd brought us to the station interrupted. "We were looking for this man in 1976. His youngest daughter disappeared. Thought he might have something to do with it."

The detective cleared his throat. I heard rustling through the phone lines and imagined him flipping through a stack of papers.

"No sign of a child. Look, if he'd been living on the streets with a little girl, I expect social services would've taken notice. We don't have a big homeless problem in Everglades City. Most of our homeless end up in Fort Lauderdale or Miami. More tourists to panhandle, more bridges to sleep under."

"But our father wasn't homeless," I said. "He had a home. Our home." None of it made a lick of sense.

The fat policeman pulled a box of tissues from a drawer and slid them across the desk, but I didn't cry. I remembered the photo of the little girl they'd found underneath the sweet gum tree in Arkansas and how they'd been sure it was Pansy. They were wrong then. They could be wrong now.

"I hate to push you," the detective continued, "but we need to know if you want the body. If you don't claim it, he'll get a pauper's burial in the local cemetery here. If you want the body, we'll have to arrange for transport. Or you could talk with one of the funeral homes down here about cremating the remains and having those sent. Honestly, you're probably gonna want to do that. The body's in bad shape. It's not like you're gonna want a viewing."

Willet said we wanted the body. I was surprised. It would cost a couple thousand dollars to have our father embalmed in Florida and shipped across state lines. On top of that, we'd have to pay for a funeral. Willet had zero respect for our father when he was alive. I couldn't see why he'd go to any trouble to show respect for him in death, but Willet was adamant about burying the body in White Forest. "It's what Mama will want," he said.

"Can we afford it?"

"I've got some money. And Granny Clem can pitch in. It's her son, after all."

Willet leaned back in the hard wooden office chair and stared at the officer. "Do you ever look for her anymore? Or did you give up?"

"I think about your sister every day," he said. "I wonder what we missed at the time. Did we overlook something? But I tell you,

I don't have any more answers now than I did then. It keeps me awake."

Willet stood and looked down on the fat policeman. "It god-damned well ought to," he said.

We left the sheriff's office and drove to the field where the quarry used to stand. It was one of those late summer nights when the stars seemed especially thick and close. If you let your gaze go soft, you felt like you could reach up and grab a handful of light. We sat in the bed of Willet's truck and passed a flask of whiskey between us. We cursed Daddy while toasting him.

"I guess he didn't have Pansy after all," I said.

"Sorry sonofabitch," Willet said. "I sure thought he did."

"We've got to tell Granny Clem. And Chester, I guess." I didn't look forward to breaking the news.

"Tomorrow," Willet said.

"I don't understand what he was doing in Florida. And if things were so bad he was living on the street, how could pay for a whole month in a motel?" I took a sip from the flask. The whiskey burned my throat. "Why wouldn't he come home to us? We could have helped him."

"Don't it seem like our lives are just a bunch of questions with no answers, Bert?" Willet took a long pull on the flask. "I'm god-damned tired of being all question and no answer."

In the distance, something howled. It might have been an old hound dog or a banshee witch. The nearly full moon hung behind a fuzzy wisp of clouds. I took another swig of whiskey. My thoughts went soft and my body felt warm. The whiskey helped drown the heebie-jeebies I felt whenever I was near the quarry. I drank some more. "I saw something in the woods the day Pansy disappeared."

Willet looked at me. "What do you mean?"

"When you left me alone and the storm came, I saw some sort of creature in the woods. A monster. It was carrying something. I think it might have been carrying Pansy."

"What the hell, Bert?"

"I didn't think you'd believe me. I was ashamed to be seeing monsters at my age. It seemed stupid."

"Goddammit, Bert, why didn't you say something back then?"

Clouds moved over the moon and a star shot across the sky. I made a wish, but nothing happened. The old quarry was nothing more than a pile of dirt even after all those years. It ought to have been overgrown with weeds and vines. Daddy was right about the quarry. If even the kudzu wouldn't crawl over it, it must be poisoned land. I asked Willet why nothing grew there.

"I mean, I can understand why there are no trees," I said. "But no wild grass? No pokeweed? It doesn't make any sense."

Willet grabbed my shoulders and shook me. "What did you see that day? Because I heard something. I heard someone in the woods."

"Maybe you heard Bubba." He shook me again. My head felt heavy as it wobbled on my neck.

"I don't believe it was Bubba. It sounded bigger than Bubba and it was crashing through the trees."

"Why didn't I hear that?" My voice sounded funny, like it was traveling through a tunnel. Willet's face kept floating in and out of focus.

"I went looking. I thought it might be some of the boys from school. We used to hang out in those woods, you know? Stupid kid shit, drinking and smoking and pretending to be big men."

I took Willet's face between my hands to steady my focus. "The monster was big." I was drunk.

"Thing is, I can't figure why Bubba was there at all."

I drank some more whiskey and laughed out loud. Willet thought he knew everything about me, but he didn't know about my trip to see Bubba and I wasn't about to tell him.

Willet lit a cigarette. "Go easy on that whiskey, Bert." His advice came too late. I held onto the lip of the truck bed to keep from sliding to the ground. My body felt good and warm and limp as stewed collard greens. We stared at the pile of dirt marking the spot where we'd last seen Pansy. A pair of purple cotton panties was crumpled atop a mound of beer cans. Liquor bottles littered the area. Spent shotgun shells scattered across the ground among the colorful burnt leftovers from someone's fireworks. A mosquito landed on my arm and sucked my whiskey-soaked blood. Another shooting star sped across the sky. I didn't bother to wish for anything.

Granny Clem seemed mostly befuddled when we told her about Daddy's death. Willet told her about the motel and the things the detective said about how he'd been living.

We sat at her kitchen table, clutching cups of coffee. It was early, not even eight o'clock and my head ached from the previous night's whiskey. Granny Clem was dressed for the day in one of her long floral dresses. Her gray hair was knotted into a tight bun at the base of her neck. She was expecting a morning patient.

"He's gone," Willet said.

Granny Clem turned the coffee mug in her hands and pursed her lips. "You say he was in Florida?"

"Yes, ma'am."

She had the same look she got when she was trying to place an unwanted baby, like she was sorting through an enormous file cabinet of possibilities in her mind. She leaned toward us, her elbows on the table, and let out a soft grunt. She gulped her coffee.

Willet told her about the cost of transporting the body. "I have some money, but I don't reckon it'll be quite enough to cover it. And there's the funeral. Nothing fancy, of course. A little something for Mama." He drummed his fingers on the table. "I hate to ask."

"Oh, I'll take care of it," she said.

"You don't have to carry all of it."

She reached out and took Willet's jittery hand. "I'll take care of it. You save your money."

"Why Florida?" Willet set his coffee mug down too hard and it splashed on the table. I reached for a paper towel to mop it up, but Granny Clem waved me off. She swiped at the spill with her bare hand and stared at her coffee-stained palm.

"A man has a right to his own life," she said. "Even a man with a family."

It was a strange thing to say, but I was used to Granny Clem's odd ways. Willet was not.

"What the hell does that even mean?" he asked as he drove us away from Granny Clem's house that morning. "I tell you what we ought to do. We ought to go to Florida and find somebody who knew the sonofabitch. We ought to get some answers."

"We can't just go to Florida," I said.

"Why the hell not?"

"We can't leave Mama alone."

"What if he did take Pansy? Maybe he had another family. Maybe he took Pansy to live with them."

"That doesn't make any sense. The detective said he was home-less."

Willet drove too fast along a dirt road and a rock flew up and cracked his windshield. He slapped the steering wheel with his palm. "Goddammit!" He stopped the truck in the middle of the road. Gray dust billowed and settled around the vehicle. I rolled up my window in spite of the heat.

"It ain't right," Willet said.

I was frustrated, too. It was terrible to know so little about our own father. It wasn't fair, but I didn't see how chasing his ghost to Florida would bring us any answers.

We held Daddy's funeral on Tuesday. It was a quiet service, just me and Mama and Willet and Granny Clem and Chester. Chester cleaned up real good. He wore a baggy gray suit. He'd slicked his hair back with some sort of oil and shined his shoes. He looked and smelled like he'd showered.

Mama wore her best dress to the funeral. She hadn't bought new clothes since Pansy disappeared. Her best was a faded navy sack dress dotted with pink flowers. She looked like a little girl or a very old woman. She coughed so hard we could barely hear the preacher. Not that it mattered. He was a generic funeral home preacher and he didn't know our father. Of course, at that point, we'd realized we didn't know our father either. The preacher read some verses and talked about the value of a life spent serving the Lord. He said our father was in a better place now. It was a load of horseshit, and Daddy would have hated it. The only thing that stunk worse than the preacher's sermon was Daddy's body. The plain pine casket rested on a table in front of the pastor's pulpit. It was closed, of course, as the body was found in such an advanced state of decay. The funeral director tried to talk Mama into cremation. "In cases like this," he told her, "it's a kinder option."

Mama refused. "We are not cremation people," she told him. I was always learning something new about my family.

It was soon clear why burning Daddy's body might have been a "kinder option." After so many weeks spent decaying in the damp Florida heat, the fluids they used to preserve him barely slowed the process. The soft rotting stench filled the room. The pastor held a white handkerchief over his nose as he delivered the eulogy. Willet and I cupped our hands across our faces and traded horrified glances. I tried breathing through my mouth, but the taste of death was worse than the smell. Granny Clem pretended to have a cold and repeatedly pressed a tissue to her nostrils. Chester pinched his nose with his thumb and forefinger and avoided eye contact with any of us. Only Mama kept her hands folded in her lap. Only Mama couldn't smell how rotten things were.

At the cemetery, rain began to fall. It was a relief, as the day was hot and sticky. Men from the funeral home unpacked two large black umbrellas and held them over us for a brief graveside service. Granny Clem spoke.

"It's a mighty awful thing to bury a son. And it's no easy thing to bury a brother or a husband or a father. But this grave is just a place for a body. It doesn't hold Earl. It never could. We should remember that. Bert and Willet, your father is not buried here. Loretta, your husband won't be resting here. Chester, you know your brother could never be held in a box. And when I think of Earl, I'll think of him as the man with big ideas and big plans, who charmed everyone he met. He could be difficult, but the best people are. He was never simple. Thank God for that. He won't be here."

On the drive home from the funeral, Willet brought up his idea of a trip to Florida. "It would be good for us," he said. "To get away." He didn't talk about finding anyone who knew Daddy or hunting for clues about where our father had been living, but Mama wasn't stupid. She knew he wasn't proposing a vacation. She knew what he was after.

"I just buried my husband," she said. "Show some respect."

"Aren't you a little curious about where he was living all these years?" Willet said. "About why he didn't come home?"

"Willet!" I slapped his shoulder and glared. "It's not the time."

Willet clenched his jaw so tight I worried he'd chip a tooth. He drove for a mile without speaking, but just before we turned onto our street he said, "We don't have to decide right now."

"I've already decided," Mama said. "I'm not going anywhere."

Back home, I fixed Mama a plate of food she wouldn't touch and I passed out dead asleep in my clothes. The creature from the woods came to me, but this time he didn't haul anything through the rain. He chased me through heavy fog. I tried to run, but my legs barely worked. I tried to hide, but the trees kept vanishing. I tried to scream, but could only whisper. The creature moved closer. He enjoyed my panic. He toyed with me. There was no escape. He was stronger and faster and he knew the woods better than I did. I found myself on the edge of a cliff. A tangle of menacing vines seemed to beckon me over the side. I peered into miles of jutting gray rocks and trees growing sideways, roots grabbing the earth. It was the old quarry. The creature faded. This was the real danger, this hole where people drowned their shame. All the secrets of the Devil were here. I knew if I tossed myself over the edge, I would discover the truth.

I would understand my father's life and I would know, finally, what happened to Pansy. All I had to do was jump. Bile rose in my throat. I couldn't breathe. If I jumped I would die, but I would know the truth. Which was more important? Life or truth? I needed to know, even if knowing sent me straight to hell. Behind me, something moved. I turned to face the creature and there, on the edge of the quarry, I looked at the beast's face for the first time. Its eyes were as familiar to me as my own.

"Oh, it's you," I said, as I tumbled into the quarry.

After we buried Daddy, Mama gave up on living. She was constantly coughing and hacking and struggling to get a breath but she refused to see a doctor. "I don't need a doctor to tell me I'm sick," she said.

Granny Clem sent me home with all sorts of teas and rubs meant to loosen Mama's congestion or quiet her cough. The remedies worked for a time, but the horrible wheezing cough always returned. I tried to convince her to stop smoking, but she said smoking was her only vice and her only pleasure and she didn't intend to give it up. There was no point in nagging her. I rubbed her back when she coughed. I ran hot showers and sat with her in the steamy bathroom, both of us sucking in warm moist air. Mama wasn't but fifty years old. A hard life will chip away at youth, and Mama's life was harder than most. A bad cough was the least of it.

Willet came and went, sometimes spending months on a job in Louisiana or Georgia. He sent money home to us and I kept it safe in an account Mama couldn't access. She sent less money to the preachers in those days, but you could never tell when she might decide to make a donation. I worried about Willet. In Jackson, an ironworker fell ten stories onto a piece of hard asphalt. He should have died, but instead he broke his neck and spent the next two years undergoing surgeries he couldn't afford.

"I don't want to end up like that," Willet said. "There's got to be a better way to make a living."

I told him to take some time off and try to find something less dangerous. He promised he would, but then someone would offer him a spot on a crew and he'd be gone again. Most of the jobs made him miserable, but when he got a spot on a crew in Tampa, he was thrilled. "I'm going to ask around about the sonofabitch," he said. "See if I can get some answers." But when he called home from Tampa after the first week, he sounded discouraged.

"Might as well be in another state," he said. "It would take me a half a day to get anywhere near where his body turned up." He said he'd try to make the trip on an off day, but he didn't get many of those and never two back-to-back. He wanted to stay in Florida an extra week after that job ended, but I begged him to come home. Mama was getting worse.

"She needs a doctor," I said. "But she won't go."

Willet came home. He made a doctor's appointment and threatened to carry Mama from the house by force. She complained about the waste of time and money, but she relented. At the appointment, the doctor showed us X-rays of our mother's lungs. It looked like a pen had burst and leaked black ink over the image. Her chest was filled with fluid. She was drowning.

"If you'd brought her in sooner . . ." the doctor said. He wanted to drain the fluid, but Mama refused.

"I'm going home."

"You need to be in a hospital," the doctor told her.

"Why?"

"You're dying."

"I can die at home."

"It will be painful," he said.

"It ought to be," she said.

We did our best to make her comfortable. We propped her up with a dozen pillows. We brought her cup after cup of tea with honey and lemon. Willet coated her feet with mentholatum and made sure she always had clean cotton socks. He stopped talking about Florida. Granny Clem came by most days with fragrant herbs and incense to burn. She cooked for us, though no one had much appetite. She made chicken and dumplings, sausage gumbo, and pots of vegetable soup. She made yeast bread and cornbread. We always had one of her pound cakes on the table. I picked at those cakes, pulling off a bite here and there. The pretty yellow bundt cakes soon looked like they'd been gnawed on by rats.

It was two weeks before Christmas and the early morning air was damp and cold. I pulled a blanket from the hall closet before going in to check on Mama. I hoped she hadn't gotten chilled during the night. I'd slept better than I had in months and thought I'd make a big breakfast. Mama's appetite was gone, but I was hungry and Willet would appreciate the effort. The grocery store would open soon and I could pick up fresh eggs and bacon and grits. I could practically taste the butter on my tongue. I looked forward to pulling out the skillet. I wanted to fill our home with the smell of frying pork. I remember this so clearly—my appetite and the cold snap and the peaceful calm of our home.

When I came into Mama's room, Willet was already there. He crouched next to Mama's bed and stroked her thin, colorless hair. His lips pressed together so hard they looked white. Mama's gray lips hung open. Her eyes were wide like she'd seen something terrifying. Maybe she had. I realized why I'd slept so well. It was the first time in years I hadn't been kept awake by Mama's hacking cough and wheezing. I touched her shoulder; she felt hollow.

"The bastard killed her," Willet said. He meant Daddy.

"She killed herself," I said. "She gave up."

He took a long breath and held it. When he exhaled, the room grew warmer. "I have to know," Willet said. "I can't live with all this mystery."

At first I thought he'd said "misery," which made as much sense. I leaned my head against his shoulder. Of course he wanted answers, but Granny Clem always said questions were more abundant than answers and some mysteries were better left unsolved. Willet didn't see it that way.

After we buried Mama, Willet said there was nothing to keep us in White Forest. I wished it were true, but we were tied to the town no matter where we wandered. Willet couldn't see it like I could. Probably it was because he traveled around for work and felt more at ease on the road. My trip to see Bubba was the farthest I'd ever ventured from our home, the farthest I'd ever let myself travel from Mama and Granny Clem and the old quarry where we'd last seen our sister. Leaving seemed reckless. Suppose Mama was right and Pansy was out there somewhere trying to find her way home. What would happen when she showed up and discovered an empty house? Willet said I was a damn fool. I argued it might not be wise to leave behind everything we knew and rush blindly into a strange land.

"We're not heading to the moon," he said. "It's just Florida. And I'm going whether you come along or not." Leaving scared me, but I couldn't stay alone. I'd spent all those years fetching Mama's smokes and bringing her food she wouldn't eat. For weeks after she died, I woke up and wandered around the house, looking for something to do. I made a big pitcher of sweet tea and had to pour it out. Willet and I couldn't stomach so much sugar.

I asked how long we'd be gone. "As long as it takes," was all he'd say.

Willet shuttered the house and sold Mama's old Ford for a couple hundred dollars in cash. I tossed my T-shirts and blue jeans into a duffel bag and, on a whim, tossed in the book of fairy tales. I knew Willet would give me a hard time for bringing the heavy book; he'd told me to pack light, but my belongings barely filled the small bag and I wanted to carry something with me that felt like a connection to home and to Pansy.

I said goodbye to Granny Clem. "Don't go borrowing trouble," she told me.

The day before we drove away, I went out to the old quarry and walked through the haunted woods. I stood on what used to be the lip of the quarry, the same spot where I'd stood and yelled Pansy's name over and over again, and I looked at the mess of trash people tossed there—used condoms and crumpled cigarette packs, liquor bottles and beer cans, shotgun shells and loose razor blades, syringes with broken needles. It made me feel ashamed, to see the waste from people's sinful secrets strewn across the dirt. At least when the quarry was filled with water, these things could be swallowed up.

In the woods I looked for the clearing where I'd seen the creature, but I couldn't find the right spot. It was a cold, cloudy day and the woods seemed like a different place than where we'd eaten berries on that summer day nearly five years earlier. It smelled different, not as fertile or ripe as I remembered. Whatever I hoped to find, it wasn't there beneath the trees. I circled back. It came to me that I ought to walk across that dirt-filled hole. It was like someone whispered the suggestion in my ear. It scared me. There were all sorts of bottles and books and piles of scrap wood scattered across the dirt. A ten-speed bicycle with no tires lay right in the center. Plenty of folks had walked across it. The evidence was everywhere. So why was I afraid?

Even all those years later, it was easy to tell where the quarry began. The fill dirt was a shade darker than the ground around it and not quite level. It seemed to slope like a shallow bowl. I held my breath and put one foot onto the darker soil. The ground felt colder there, even through the soles of my tennis shoes. I shivered, took another step. The dirt seemed springy and thick and alive, like it might reach up and pull me underground. It was my imagination, and I knew it. I'd gone out there alone looking to get spooked. It was like when I used to read those fairy tales to Pansy and the two of us would shiver while imagining ogres and shape-shifting animals and the dark fog of a magic spell cast under the moon. It was like Granny Clem's hypochondriac patient who broke out in actual hives from her imaginary ailments. The mind could conjure up all sorts of things if you let it. I told myself the ground beneath my feet was no different than the ground where Granny Clem planted her garden or the ground in our front yard. No sense letting my mind go wild. I took a deep breath and sprinted the length of the quarry, jumping over the abandoned bicycle like it was a hurdle on a track. As I did, a gust of wind came through and lifted my hair. For a moment, I thought I might fly. It was no ordinary wind. It was the collective sigh of the quarry ghosts. They couldn't believe I was being so reckless. By the time I made it to the far side of the quarry, I was panting like I'd run a hard mile.

Willet thought we could leave this place behind by driving away. I knew better. The quarry was part of our lives, an important part. We couldn't run away from it. Someone had stacked a pyramid of gray rocks between a matched set of wooden crosses, an altar of some sort. We weren't the only ones who'd left a piece of ourselves at the quarry. I took one of the flat, smooth rocks from the top of the pyramid and slipped it in my pocket. The quarry could be evil, or maybe just dangerous, but it was familiar. I wanted to keep a piece of it with me.

FERN SAID SHE AND Melvin were in love and she was going to have his child. She announced the news to Ora and Clementine as if she were telling them about the weather. But Junior could see she was nervous. She twisted her hands behind her back like gnarled tree roots. Clementine sent the boys from the room.

"We need to talk to your sister alone," she said.

Junior and Chester sat on the floor of their shared bedroom and eavesdropped. Junior felt strange, like he couldn't get enough oxygen. He was grateful to the women for taking over. He wouldn't have known how to talk to his sister about such a thing. He leaned his head against the wall and listened to the conversation.

"What does Melvin say about this?" Ora asked.

"I can't bring myself to tell him."

The women talked with Fern into the night. Chester was furious. "I'll kill him," he said of Melvin.

Junior knew his sister had no business carrying a baby. She was only sixteen. Melvin was smart and he knew better, or he ought to.

Fern said to Clementine and Ora, "My skin gets dark anyhow. Maybe it won't matter."

"The world doesn't work that way," Ora said.

"You treat Negro women. You know they're no different than we are. You said it yourself. 'Blood runs red no matter the skin.'"

"It's not so simple," Clementine said. "It's one thing to have a colored person as a customer, but it's quite another to do what you've done."

"What have I done?" Fern's voice cracked.

"Honey," Ora said. "Don't get me wrong, I like Melvin. He seems like a decent boy, but this could get him killed. It could get you killed. People won't stand for it, particularly the people of White Forest. Don't you remember what happened to Bernice Jackson?"

Everyone knew what happened to Bernice Jackson. Bernice worked as a kitchen maid for a banker and his wife. They had a son a year older than Bernice. The son took a shine to the maid and forced himself on her, or else she took a shine to the son and seduced him—it depended on who was telling the story. What happened next was not in dispute. Bernice was walking home when a group of white men, the banker among them, pulled her off the side of the road and hog-tied her. They dragged her behind their truck for five miles or more before stringing her up from the branches of a live oak near the old quarry, a burlap sack over her head. Her mother begged the sheriff to arrest the men, who didn't even have the good sense to shut up about what they'd done. Everyone in town heard the story from at least one of the braggarts involved. But the sheriff said there wasn't enough evidence and he couldn't ruin the reputation of these good men on one Negro woman's outlandish claims.

Did Ora believe they would do something terrible to Fern? Or did she mean they would lynch Melvin? Either way, it was a terrible mess.

"Let me make you some of my womb-clearing tea. You'll drink it for the next week and it'll make you sick. You'll have terrible cramps, but it'll bring on your blood."

Fern refused. "I want this baby. I hope you'll help me, but I'll have it even if you won't."

The women argued with her. She had plenty of time for babies. A baby born now, out of wedlock and from a black father, would bring nothing but trouble for her and for Melvin.

"Well, I won't put Melvin in danger," she said. "If you think claiming this baby will get him killed, I'll keep him out of it."

"How do you intend to keep him out of it?" Clementine sounded bitter. "He's in it up to his neck. Everyone sees how you go over to his house and hang around those children. If I'd had any thought you were behaving so poorly, I'd have forbid you leaving the house."

Fern laughed. "Don't be silly. You can't stop me from anything."

Clementine made a noise deep in her throat. It sounded like she might be choking.

"Maybe I'll head home to the island," Fern said. "Won't nobody there care about my baby. Maybe Melvin will come along with me."

"You can't think Melvin is going to be happy about this," Clementine said. "You surely are not that stupid."

Ora tried to defuse the situation. "Let's be practical, shall we? This is not the end of the world. We've seen plenty of girls in the same predicament."

"But those girls weren't silly enough to keep their babies!" Clementine said.

Junior couldn't stand it anymore. Fern was his sister and he had a right to weigh in on this discussion. He stepped out of the room where he and Chester stood listening.

"I'll take her away," he said. "We can leave right now, before anyone knows a thing about a baby. We'll ride the train south a ways and figure it out. I can find work cutting sugarcane or fishing. I can take care of us. I reckon we've overstayed our welcome anyhow."

"No!" Clementine said. "You know I think of you as my own children. Chester looks to you as his own brother and sister. You belong here." But Junior wasn't sure they belonged in White Forest. Maybe he and Fern would be better off if they'd never left Florida.

Maybe Fern wouldn't have gotten herself into so much trouble back in the Everglades. There was no way to know.

Fern continued her daily trips to see Melvin and she helped Clementine and Ora with the babies, but her swelling stomach began to attract notice. Melvin's father must have noticed it, because he packed up and moved his entire family in the middle of the night. No one knew where they went.

Fern was distraught when she discovered Melvin was gone. "He didn't even say goodbye."

Ora and Clementine told Fern it was time for her to stop running all over town and flaunting her pregnant belly.

"I'm not ashamed," Fern said.

"I'm not asking you to be ashamed," Clementine told her. "I'm asking you to be careful."

At night, when Junior and Chester and Fern were supposed to be sleeping, Clementine and Ora discussed what to do with the baby when it was born. Junior listened to their soft voices and knew it wouldn't matter what they decided. Fern would keep the baby and raise it. She wouldn't consider another option.

Junior got a job at the lumber mill in Jones City. Clementine said it wasn't necessary. She'd prefer it if he finished school. "There's plenty of work to be done in the garden," she said. She offered to pay him. He refused. It didn't seem right.

"Fern's going to need things," he said. "For the baby."

Clementine said she and Ora were prepared to provide for a baby. "It's what we do."

The women had already given them so much. They shouldn't be expected to do more. Fern told him to stop worrying. She said women had been having and raising babies since the Garden of Eden and she figured she could handle it.

Junior did not doubt Fern could handle a baby. He'd seen her with the babies Ora and Clementine delivered. What worried him was the baby's skin. Fern barely passed for white and with Melvin as the father, her baby was bound to be even darker.

By the week before Christmas, Fern looked like she was smuggling a melon beneath her dress. Fern told Junior she wanted him to take her into town to do some shopping. She wanted to get a little something for Clementine and Ora and Chester. "They've been awful good to me," she said. "Especially considering everything." She gestured at her stomach.

Junior told her he'd be happy to pick up anything she wanted from town, but Fern wanted the pleasure of shopping.

"I don't think it's such a good idea, what with you being so far along."

She told him she was fine. He worried about so many people seeing her swollen belly. They knew she wasn't married. But Fern couldn't be talked out of it. She told Junior she'd get Chester to take her if he wouldn't do it. Finally, he agreed to take her to Murray's Department Store on Saturday morning. He'd rather have gone on a weekday, when it would be less crowded, but his work schedule wouldn't allow it. Chester came with them.

The shopping was uneventful. Fern bought a box of stationery for Ora and a brass picture frame for Clementine. She made Chester and Junior turn away as she selected something for each of them. It was Junior's money she spent, and he refrained from making jokes about buying his own present. Junior and Chester bought a stuffed bear for Fern's unborn baby.

When they finished shopping, they walked down the block and settled into a booth at the diner. Fern ordered a chocolate milkshake. "This baby loves ice cream," she said. They ordered ham sandwiches and vegetable soup.

They'd just received the bill when a group of men burst through the doors of the diner, shouting and frenzied. One of the men pointed at Chester and told him to come along with them. The man wore a flannel jacket with a watch plaid pattern and a red wool hunting cap. All the men were dressed in clothes more suited for farm work than for a day in town. Junior recognized the men, but he didn't know their names. Junior tended to keep to himself.

He turned to Chester. "Who are they?"

"Farmers, most of 'em."

"What do they want?" Fern asked.

Chester shook his head.

The men talked over one another, but Junior finally got the gist of their agitation. One of their wives told her husband a young black boy had winked at her on the street. Brazen, was how she described it. The men planned to find the black child and make him answer for his sins. "We can't give 'em an inch," one of the men said. "They'll take all we got."

Fern clutched Junior's arm. He put his hand over hers. They needed to wait it out. These men would move on soon enough. But Fern had other ideas. She pushed herself up from the booth, her stomach leading the way.

"Stop it," she said, her voice calm and quiet against the raised anger of the men. Junior caught Chester's eye. They both grabbed for Fern, intending to pull her back into the booth and shield her, but Fern pushed forward. "Cut it out right now."

The man in the hunting cap gave her an up-and-down stare. He took in her swollen belly and her wild hair. "Ma'am," he said. "You ought not be out in your condition. Your husband ought to take you home."

Fern put her hands on her hips and laughed. "Well, I don't have a husband," she said. "And I'm not in any kind of condition."

"Fern . . ." Junior said.

"Who's responsible for this girl?" The man looked from Junior to Chester. The pack of men stood behind him. They waited for an answer. Junior wondered if they did everything in a group or if any one of them ever had an independent thought.

"I'm responsible for myself," Fern said.

"We're leaving," Chester announced.

The man stepped forward and blocked Chester's exit from the booth.

"We're not looking for trouble," Junior said.

"It ain't decent," the man said. "This is a family establishment."

Chester stood, despite the man's effort to block him. His nose practically touched the man's mouth. "What ain't decent," Chester said, "is your bad manners." Chester plucked the man's cap from his head. The man's face turned purple, and Junior knew there would be no avoiding trouble now.

The men surged forward as Chester threw a hard punch into the man's gut. The man doubled over and Junior saw the bald spot on the top of his head. He probably wore the hat to hide it. Fern covered her mouth with her hands. Junior pulled her away from the group of men.

The man with the bald spot stepped back and punched Chester in the nose. Chester's mouth and chin flooded with blood. It only made him madder. He came at the man with his fists flying, hitting him along the side of his head and under his jaw. Junior got between them and told Chester it was enough already. One of the other men, Junior never knew which one, socked Junior right in his kidney. The pain washed through him, spreading from his legs to his teeth. Fern yelled for them to stop, but no one listened. It was six men against two and it ought to have been over before it started, but Chester and Junior were better fighters than any of the other men. They ducked quicker and punched harder, and they were still standing long after they should have fallen.

The owner of the diner came out from the kitchen and demanded they leave at once. He said he'd called the police. Most of the customers had left when the fight started, but a crowd had gathered on the sidewalk outside the diner's plate glass window. The men knocked each other down and got back up. Dishes lay broken on the tile floor. Soda mixed with blood in the grout lines.

Junior's fist ached. He'd never known he could throw such a hard punch, much less throw one again and again. His knuckles cracked against teeth and cartilage and bone. He absorbed blow after blow. It wasn't until one of the men pulled a Barlow knife from his pocket that Junior felt at a disadvantage. The knife sliced across

Junior's forearm. Warm blood trickled from the cut. The cold blade was such a contrast to the hot skin-on-skin fighting that he knew they were beat. He tried to warn Chester, but the man with the knife was quick.

Junior lost track of Fern during the fight. He didn't think of her standing and watching the mess unfold. He didn't think of her at all until he saw her step between Chester and the man with the knife. He didn't know if Fern meant to save Chester or if she'd only stepped into danger in a moment of confusion. The knife blade arced up on a trajectory for Chester's gut, but it sank into Fern's gut instead, into the space where she carried Melvin's child. She screamed—not a scream of pain or fear, but a primal scream of rage.

The fighting stopped. Fern collapsed on the cold tile floor. Her face went pale. Junior knelt beside her. The men who'd come into the diner in such a frenzy slipped away. Only Junior and Chester and Fern remained. Even the owner of the diner disappeared. Fern lay on her back. Her breathing grew ragged.

"Get your mother," Junior said. Chester ran.

"Help is coming," Junior said.

"The baby," Fern said. "The baby's coming."

Junior told her to hang on and keep breathing. He pushed her dress up over the hump of her heaving belly. The gash from the knife was deep and jagged. Bits of cloth from the cotton dress clung to the wound. It looked bad, but Junior thought she'd survive it. He tore a section from her dress and used it to stanch the bleeding. Beneath his hand, he felt the warm pulse of her heartbeat low and deep in her belly. Her blood ran thick and sticky. Junior's nose filled with the coppery scent of blood and fear, but there was something else, something salty and fishy. His sister smelled of the Gulf of Mexico, of tropical sunshine and swamp heat, of fresh mullet and stone crab, of sugarcane and cypress bark, of their mother.

Junior felt dizzy. The wound on his arm was superficial, but he'd lost some blood in the fight. It left him lightheaded and confused. Fern breathed in short bursts between clenched teeth. Her eyes squeezed shut. She held his hand, grasped it so hard he lost all feeling in his fingers. She reared up and bore down. Sweat rolled slick across her face and neck. She collapsed and panted, lolling her head from side to side on the filthy floor. Nothing had prepared him for this. He prayed, something he hadn't done in a long time. God or someone answered, because Clementine appeared beside him. She put her hand across his hand, the one holding the cloth to the wound on Fern's belly.

"Let me see," she said. He fell back. Clementine peeled away the scrap of blood-soaked fabric and examined the cut.

"The baby's coming." Fern reared up again and cried out. The wound on her belly ripped a bit wider and fresh blood poured from the cut.

"She needs to relax," Junior said. "She's making it worse."

"She's laboring," Clementine said.

Ora appeared. She hoisted a heavy bag on one of the tables, searched through it, and pulled out an amber vial. Fern's mouth opened and closed as Ora squeezed a few drops of dark liquid on her tongue. Whatever it was, it smelled bitter and potent. Clementine and Ora consulted with one another about the wound and the imminent birth and the best thing for pain. They spread a clean cloth beneath Fern's legs, produced a pillow for her head. Junior relaxed. The women were in charge now. He looked around for Chester but saw only the eyes of strangers gawking through the glass window of the diner. Junior recognized some of the faces staring in, particularly the women. The women stood in a solid line across the doorway of the diner. They wouldn't let anyone enter while Clementine and Ora worked. These women had come to Clementine and Ora for their own births or to prevent a birth. They came for painkillers and sleeping remedies. Junior felt safer, seeing the women gathered. They would not allow Fern to be harmed.

"Here she comes." Ora crouched between Fern's thighs and peered into the space between her legs. Junior looked away. Fern grunted and howled. Clementine held a hand behind her back and helped her push. Junior heard a slick popping sound, then silence, then a long wail. He thought the wail came from Fern, but it was the baby. Ora held the tiny child in one hand and examined it. Junior thought there must be something wrong with the baby. It was so tiny and covered with shiny blobs of pink and gray slime, but Ora smiled and placed the slick bundle on Fern's chest.

"A girl," she said. "Just like you thought."

Fern lifted her head to examine the baby. She ran her fingers across its wriggling body. Junior crawled forward. He wanted to see this. It seemed a kind of miracle, though he knew women gave birth every day. The baby was darker than Fern. Her head was covered with a mass of fine black curls and when she opened her mouth to howl, hungry for milk or angry at being pulled into the cold world, Junior saw a glint of white against her gray gums.

"She's got teeth." Fern laughed. "That's a good sign. She'll be tough."

Junior reached out a finger and touched the baby's dimpled shoulder. "She's too small," he said.

Ora snipped through the veiny gray umbilical cord and gathered the blood and placenta into a jar. Junior knew she would boil them into a strong tea to restore strength to Fern's blood.

"She's perfect." Clementine dressed Fern's wound with fresh cloths and a smear of iodine. "I'll sew you up tight," she told Fern. "Don't you worry."

"I'm not worried," Fern said. She stroked the newborn's delicate shell-like ear and moved the baby to her breast. The child opened and closed her mouth a few times before latching on and sucking. "Oh, she's strong!" Fern sounded delighted despite her bleeding belly and the trauma of giving birth in a strange place. Junior thought she'd make a natural mother. She was right to keep the baby.

The rush of adrenaline from the earlier fight and from the fear surrounding Fern's labor left him feeling almost peaceful, but there would be no peace. The crowd outside the window grew loud. He couldn't understand what they said, but he knew they were angry.

Ora draped a small cloth over the baby at Fern's breast. "I was afraid of this," she said.

Clementine took the child from Fern and helped her to stand, but she doubled over, collapsing to all fours. "Can you carry her?" Clementine asked Junior.

He scooped his sister into his arms, careful to avoid scraping the open cut on her belly. Even so, she moaned with pain.

Outside, the curious crowd grew larger. Some of the faces at the window were twisted and angry. The women at the door wouldn't hold the crowd much longer. Ora led them through the kitchen and out to the alley, where she'd asked Chester to wait for them in the car. Junior tucked Fern into the back seat and slid in beside her. Ora sat on the other side with the baby. Clementine climbed in front with Chester. Fern reached for the baby, who was crying again.

"Take the back roads," Clementine said.

ELEVEN

WILLET DROVE US EAST across Mississippi. We left behind the flat dull roads of the Delta. The Big Black River flowed along south of us, though it often looked like nothing more than a muddy stream. Dense forests lay to our north, interrupted by an occasional stretch of farmland. Hills sprang up from the earth and I could no longer see every blade of grass between Willet's truck and the horizon. The trees grew greener and thicker as we drove.

We crossed into Alabama before lunchtime on that first day. I'd never been outside the state of Mississippi before and I had expected it to feel momentous, but the presence of a state line didn't change the geography in any meaningful way. The roadside gas stations were the same. The people, when we stopped to buy a bag of boiled peanuts, were no different from the people in Mississippi. In Tuscaloosa, we stopped at a squat cinder block restaurant for barbecue sandwiches on white bread. I was still licking the sticky sauce from my fingers when Willet pointed the truck south.

We spent most of that first day driving across Alabama. Willet pointed to an enormous shopping mall off the highway. "I helped build that one," he said. "It ain't been open a year." I wondered how anyone could shop in such a place without getting lost. The parking lot looked bigger than the entire town of White Forest.

"More than a hundred stores in one building," Willet said. "You couldn't pay me to shop there."

We crossed into Florida at nightfall and Willet got us a cheap motel room in Tallahassee. A 24-hour pancake house sat across the highway from the motel. We stuffed ourselves with hash browns and maple sausage before going to bed and we had more of the same before driving away the next morning. Willet's plan was to get to Tampa by lunchtime. We took the Suncoast Parkway. Traffic slowed us down for the first hour, but soon the road cleared and we were able to keep up a decent pace. The towns we passed through had pretty names: Gulf Hammock, Crystal River, Homosassa Springs. Many of the homes that stood along the highway were painted bright colors—white with aqua blue or coral trim. We passed mobile home parks where residents sat on plastic chairs under plastic awnings and watched the traffic pass. Every now and again, I caught a glimpse of water through the neighborhoods or through the trees. "Is that the ocean?"

"That's the Gulf of Mexico," Willet said.

Florida felt different than Alabama or Mississippi. The sun seemed brighter somehow. The air smelled like pickle brine and fresh fish. We'd eaten a good-size breakfast, but the smell of fish made me hungry. I tried to talk Willet into stopping ahead of schedule, but he said we weren't stopping until we'd crossed Tampa Bay.

"What's the hurry? We don't even know what we're looking for."

"We're looking for answers," Willet said. "I'm tired of not knowing anything."

The closer we got to our destination, the more Willet talked about our father. He dredged up memories from before I was old enough to remember anything. He talked about the time Daddy brought home a five-foot-long catfish, and the time he shot a rattlesnake from forty yards away. I liked hearing my brother's stories in the same way I liked hearing stories from Granny Clem. It was strange to realize that Willet's memories were not parallel to my own. He told me things I'd never heard before, like the story about the bees.

Willet was six years old when Daddy and Uncle Chester got the idea to rob a bee tree for honey. He begged Daddy to let him come along. Robbing a bee tree sounded like a big adventure, but Daddy was a sonofabitch. He said no. He said Willet was too young. Willet begged, and Daddy finally agreed as long as he promised to stay in the car with the windows rolled up tight. It pissed Chester off to no end. Chester never did like kids. He didn't make any excuses for it either.

Willet said the bee tree was the coolest damn thing he ever saw. They pulled right up next to it, which was not the smartest move. Daddy and Uncle Chester wore gloves and long-sleeved shirts and had their pants tucked down into their socks. They tied bandannas across their noses and mouths. When the door to the car swung open, the tree was singing. It was more beautiful than a church choir. Willet sat in the closed-up car, sweating like a fat hog and wishing he could get out and touch the singing tree. Daddy went to work with a hacksaw. The bees swarmed out of the hollow trunk in an angry stream. Chester went in with his hands and a long knife to slice out the honeycomb.

Willet felt sorry for the bees. Daddy and Uncle Chester were stealing and it was wrong, as wrong as stealing from a store or some-body's house. The honey belonged to the bees. The tree belonged to the bees. What right did anyone have to barge in and take their life's work?

Willet opened the car door and yelled for them to stop. Daddy damn near fell off the ladder. He hollered, but Willet couldn't under-stand him with the bandanna tied over his mouth. The first bee stung Willet right on his cheek. He said it wasn't too painful, just a pinprick. Then the next bee stung and the next and it became a scalding hot sort of pain. He took off running. Pretty soon, he'd lost all sight of Daddy and Uncle Chester and the car. His face and arms swelled up something awful. He could barely see out of one eye. He fell out on a patch of grass next to a field of young cotton. He lay there hoping Daddy and Uncle Chester had robbed those bees of everything they held dear, because he couldn't see how such mean creatures deserved to have even one minute of happiness. Then he passed out.

I asked Willet what he was trying to tell me.

"Just listen," he said.

Once they got Willet home, Mama wailed and cried and fussed over him. He spent the next week taking pills that made him sleepy and gave him wicked nightmares. It was one of the most traumatic moments of his childhood, he said. Yet, about a year later when he refused to go out on the front porch until somebody did something about the goddamned swarming wasps, Mama said she didn't understand why he'd become fearful of a little sting all of a sudden.

Our father, he said, was like those bees: beautiful until you got too close and then mean as hell. And Mama was never interested in the truth. She iced over the bad parts of our father like she iced over a caramel cake. She couldn't stand to look at anything ugly or painful. How else could she forget about Willet's bee stings, about his suffering? How else could she pretend Daddy didn't have a thing to do with Pansy going missing?

I didn't know the answers and Willet wasn't looking for any. He was telling me he'd figured things out, but I wasn't so sure. I wanted to believe in Daddy's goodness. I knew he wasn't honest. I knew he was a criminal, but I wanted to think he'd had good reason to live the way he did. Maybe I was like Mama. Maybe I was too eager to ice over the truth and make something sweet from the bitterness.

We ate a lunch of greasy fried fish po' boys just outside of Tampa. Willet found the Tamiami Trail on the map and we continued south, following the signs to Fort Myers and then to Naples. Once we left the kitschy sun-soaked opulence of Naples, the scenery changed. There were fewer houses by the side of the road and the scent of the water grew stronger. We drove for miles surrounded by thick trees sprouting from algae-covered swamps. We were a long way from home and nothing looked familiar. At dusk, fog rolled in thick and heavy. Willet squinted over the steering wheel of the pickup truck. He drove slowly, adjusting his headlights from bright to dim and cussing when it made no difference. He'd have pulled over if we weren't already on a desolate stretch with no motels or gas stations for miles. Something brackish and rotten stank up the air and the fog made everything soft and surreal, like the first moments of a nightmare. We'd been listening to a music station on the radio, but there was more static than music by then. I fiddled with the knob, trying to dial in something new, but nothing penetrated that lonely stretch of road. We didn't pass any other cars and I wondered if the traffic was always light or if the fog kept people home. Willet said he didn't know. It was easy to imagine we were the only people in the world, that everyone else had been snatched up by God in an apocalyptic homecoming, our invitations lost in the mail. I pulled the quarry rock from my pocket and held it in my fist—a talisman against strange forces, a small piece of home.

We floated around a curve in the road, a curve Willet must have sensed rather than seen, and something leapt out of the mist into the beam of our headlights. Willet slammed the brakes. I slid forward, slamming my chest against the dashboard.

"Jesus H. Christ!" Willet yelled.

A wild tawny creature turned its head and glared at us with golden, glowing eyes. The panther disappeared so quickly, I wondered if I'd imagined it.

Willet drove deeper into the fog. I pressed the quarry rock to my heart. It felt like it would beat right out of my bruised chest. What else would leap from the shadows to confront us? And how could we be prepared?

We checked into the Glades Motel late that night. Willet asked for room seventeen, the room where they'd found Daddy. The woman behind the counter pushed the registry toward us. Willet signed.

"No dogs. No loud music. No drugs," she said. "Clean your fish outside, not in the sink. If you clog up the sink with scales, you'll pay for the plumber." Her voice was raspy and deep. By the smell, I figured she smoked a few packs a day. It made me think of Mama.

Willet showed the woman a picture of our father. It wasn't a recent photo. We didn't have recent photos. It was a faded Polaroid of Daddy holding up a large catfish and grinning. "Do you remember this man?" Willet asked. "He stayed here back in June for a few weeks."

The woman said, "Nice fish."

Willet pressed her.

The woman shoved a key across the desk. "I've already forgotten what you look like."

Willet said, "He's the man who died here. Surely you ain't forgot that."

"All men die," she said. "It don't jog my memory none."

The motel room was small and dingy and dim: a double bed with paper-thin sheets and a scratchy brown bedspread, a bathroom so small you couldn't open or close the door if you were sitting on the toilet, and, in one corner, a knee-high refrigerator, an aluminum percolator, and a hot plate, all generously billed as a kitchenette. Willet rolled a cot from a small closet and tossed a thin blanket on top. "You can have the bed," he told me.

An image of Daddy in a state of decay came to me and I shook my head.

"It ain't the same bed, Bert," Willet said.

"How do you know?"

"You saw the pictures. No way they were getting that mattress clean."

Still, I couldn't do it. I couldn't lie down in the exact same spot where Daddy died. Willet shrugged. "Have it your way, but that cot won't be none too comfortable."

I listened to Willet snore and wondered why we'd come here. What did we expect to find? Some clue as to how Daddy spent the last years of his life? Some idea of why he left us? Some hint of what happened to Pansy?

In my dreams I sat in Granny Clem's kitchen while she worked over the stove. When she turned to serve me a cup of tea, she had the face of a wolf. I was Little Red Riding Hood and she would gobble me whole. I woke in the early morning, my body sore from the stiff cot and the long drive, my eyes bleary and swollen, my head foggy from restless sleep. Even so, when I stepped outside, I nearly cried for the beauty of the place. Despite the stench of rotting fish, it was a stunning morning. I'd never seen sunlight glitter so bright across the gray surface of the water. I'd never seen so many birds swooping and diving for breakfast or so many men working in the early morning sunlight to unload wooden crates and nets full of fish. It made me feel better about Daddy dying there. The motel room was ugly, but there was beauty outside the door.

Willet made a bitter pot of stale coffee in the percolator, and we drank from chipped mugs. I surveyed the room in the morning light. I couldn't picture Daddy shaving in front of the fogged mirror or dressing in the cramped waterlogged bathroom. I couldn't picture him sleeping on the scratchy sheets or drinking his morning coffee in one of the cracked and stained mugs. Daddy liked things neat and clean. Nothing short of a fire could clean that room.

Willet agreed. "I can't see him spending one night in this shithole. He was a sonofabitch, sure, but he liked nice things. Don't you remember how he liked his shirts ironed stiff? How he shined his shoes?"

I remembered. I remembered the clean sharp scent of his shaving cream and the lingering clovelike odor of his hair oil. I remembered how he trimmed his nails and kept them clean even when he and Chester were printing bills. But what good was my memory, really? I remembered a monster in the woods, but Willet said monsters weren't real. I remembered the way Mama doted on Pansy, but Mama denied giving Pansy special treatment. I remembered the fireworks and the scent of sulfur and the perfect summer evening, but Bubba said he didn't remember a thing. And no matter what I remembered or what I'd imagined, it didn't change the fact of Daddy's body turning up in this filthy motel.

"Let me ask you," Willet said. "Can you remember even one time when the sonofabitch was drunk? Because I sure as hell can't. He was miserable, but he wasn't a drunk."

I poured another cup of the bitter coffee and said I couldn't remember him drunk.

"Hell, I used to steal his whiskey all the time," Willet said. "I watered it down to keep him from realizing the bottle was low, and he never said a thing. That's how little he drank. How could he go from someone who barely took a nip to one of those drunks living on the street? It don't seem possible."

And yet they'd found Daddy's body in this awful motel room. Maybe we hadn't really known our father.

Willet said we ought to lay in some supplies before doing anything else. We made a list: bug spray, bread and peanut butter, fresh coffee. We'd passed a grocery store and bait shop on our drive in the night before. We bought the things we needed and a few extras: a deck of playing cards, a flashlight and pack of batteries, saltine crackers and a tub of smoked fish dip, a sack of oranges, a pint of rum, and a six-pack of Coke.

"Fishing today?" The young woman behind the counter rang up our purchases.

"Something like that," Willet said.

She smiled and tucked a strand of bleached blonde hair behind her ear. She blushed. Willet had that effect on women. His shoulders were broad and strong from years of construction work. His hair flopped over his eyebrows in a boyish way. We had the same brown eyes, the same freckled nose, the same sharp chin, but it came together better on him than it ever did on me.

"I hear the grouper are biting," she said.

Willet slid some bills across the counter and pulled out the creased photo. It was the same photo he'd shown to the motel clerk the night before. It was at least ten years old and surely looked nothing like the man they'd found in the motel room. No one was going to recognize Daddy from that photo.

Still, he asked her if she recognized the man.

She squinted at the out-of-focus image. "Don't think so."

Willet slid the photo back in his wallet. "Is there a place to rent a boat around here?"

She bagged our groceries and told us about a few rental spots. She said we'd have to get moving if we wanted to get on the water today. Most of the boats left early for fishing or bird watching. Then she mentioned the tunnels. "Best way to see those is in a canoe or a pole boat. Iggy will rent you one of those."

"Tunnels?" Willet took the sack from her.

"The mangrove tunnels," she said. "Plenty to see. Cypress knees, air plants, turtles, maybe even an alligator."

Outside, the cool breeze from the morning was gone. Bottle flies buzzed around a dead bird near the trash dumpster. We headed back to our room to put the perishables in the mini-fridge and slather on bug juice. Willet said he wanted to hit the boat rental places.

"Do you know how to drive a boat?" I asked.

"You drive a car, Bert. You pilot a boat." He rubbed his neck with sweet-smelling repellent. "Remember when Daddy borrowed that boat and took us out to Grenada Lake?" I remembered. Daddy loved fishing. Still, the lakes and reservoirs back home were drops of water compared to the Gulf of Mexico and the Atlantic Ocean.

"I don't see how anyone's going to know him from that photo," I said.

"I have a couple more in the duffel." He pulled out a manila envelope and spread the photographs across the bed. There was Daddy leaning against his brand-new truck, smoking a cigarette and grinning. There was Daddy standing next to Mama, both of them peering down at the baby in Mama's arms. "You?" I asked. Willet nodded. And there was Daddy, young and smiling, with Uncle Chester and a girl I didn't know. They were teenagers. It was a terrible old photo, indistinct shades of soft gray and white. "Where did you get this?"

"I took it from Granny Clem's house."

"I've never seen it."

"I took it years ago, just after we lost Pansy."

"Who's the girl?"

"Look at her real close, Bert. Tell me if you notice anything."

The girl's hair flew out in a mess of frizzy curls. Her skin was darker than the boys' skin, though it might have been a bad exposure. Her lips were closed in a tight smile, like she was holding back a secret. Her eyes were almond shaped and sat wide on her face.

"She looks like Pansy," I said.

Willet lit a cigarette, took a long drag, and exhaled through his nose. "You see it, then."

"I see it."

"She's got to be a relative or something. Why ain't we ever heard of her? I asked Granny Clem about her and she clammed up, tried to snatch this photo from me. Said her memory wasn't what it used to be, which we both know is bullshit. Her mind is sharp as a boning knife."

Willet shoved the picture in my face, holding it so close it made me cross-eyed. "Look at her hands, Bert. She's holding something. What is that?"

I took the photo and held it so my eyes could focus. The girl balanced something on her palm, something delicate and winged, maybe a butterfly or a small bird, but it was hard to tell from the faded gray photograph. Willet brought out a cardboard box and pulled a small figure from it. He placed the delicate thing between us. It was featherlight, but not fragile: a bird carved from bark or nut husk or something I didn't recognize. Its wings were outstretched in a T shape. Its beak tilted upward.

"That's sugarcane husk, Bert."

I admired its small details. "Where'd you find it?"

"Don't you think that's what she's holding in the photo?"

I set the picture next to the carving and agreed it could be the same object. Willet pulled another figure from the box—a turtle, as finely crafted as the bird. Finally, he pulled out an alligator and lined up the figures side by side.

I'd underestimated Willet. The way he'd thrown himself into work, the way he paid bills and took care of things; it seemed he wouldn't have had time for much else, but he'd been gathering evidence. Evidence of what, I didn't know. He didn't know either.

"Bert, do you know where they grow sugarcane? Here. They grow it right here. I want to know who she was and where these came from." He pointed to the turtle and the alligator. "These didn't come from Granny Clem's house. These were mailed to Mama about a year after Pansy disappeared. They showed up in the mailbox with no return address. The postmark, though, was right here in Everglades City."

"What did Mama say?"

"I never showed them to her. We were getting all those fake sightings at the time. And the psychics were calling. She was sending money to the damned TV preachers. I intercepted the mail, took suspicious stuff to the sheriff's deputies. They thought it was some sort of prank."

All those years I'd thought Willet and I were in this thing together. *We* were looking for our father. *We* were looking for our sister, but no. I understood why he'd keep things from Mama, but I couldn't understand why he'd keep things from me.

"You could have told me."

"You were just a kid," he said. "You can't believe some of the shit people sent. Nasty letters calling Mama a bad parent. Fake ransom notes smeared with real blood. A suicide note that looked to be written by a child. The sheriff's deputies said the world was full of sickos, people who want to be a part of any tragedy."

"Maybe that's true."

"Maybe, but look at these animals. They were all done by the same person, don't you think?"

The carvings were similar, but I couldn't tell if the same person had made all three. It was like the macramé owl I made at day camp when I was a kid. Mine was similar to those woven by the other children, but not exactly the same. Maybe these carvings were someone's camp creations. "Even if they were made by the same person, what does it mean?"

"It means we've been too willing to believe what we're told. I'm sick of it, Bert. I want the truth."

I remembered what Granny Clem said on the day Marianne gave birth to the sweet baby boy: *People will believe what you tell them to believe*. Granny Clem bent the truth to her will every time she filled out one of those fake birth certificates or erased all evidence of a pregnancy. Maybe Willet was right. We'd believed what we were told to believe. We wouldn't uncover the truth until we poked holes in the lies. "You think the truth is here?"

"I know for damn sure it ain't back in White Forest."

CHESTER DROVE THEM AWAY from the diner. Some of the Main Street crowd gathered at the mouth of the alley, but Chester didn't slow down, and they scattered to avoid being hit. He drove fast, but he avoided the roughest sections of road and slowed down where holes pocked the street. Fern dozed. Ora rubbed Fern's shoulders and talked to her in a calm voice.

"Stay with us," Ora said. "Now is no time for sleeping."

Ora told Junior to keep Fern conscious. "She's lost too much blood. If she sleeps, I can't be certain I'll revive her."

Junior talked. He talked about their mother and how much she'd have wanted to see this baby. He talked about the birds in the rookery and how they fed their hungry chicks before teaching them how to fly. He reminded Fern about the source of her own name. "The Resurrection Fern doesn't die," he said. "It grows green and lives again."

Clementine sat in the front seat and raged. She said she never intended to set foot in that diner again. She said it held bad memories for her, too. Ora nodded and alternately tried to soothe Clementine and Fern.

Back home, Junior lifted his sister and carried her to bed. Ora took the baby and Clementine began work on Fern's injuries. She cleaned Fern with a damp cloth and a bit of soap. The blood from the stomach wound was bright and crusted over. The blood from the birth was dark and fresh. Fern burned with fever and seemed to be dreaming, though she did not sleep. Junior knelt beside his sister and held her hand. Clementine pulled a long piece of thread through Fern's stomach, clinching the jagged gash closed in a crooked line.

"It won't heal pretty," Clementine said. "But it'll hold."

Clementine turned her attention to the blood seeping between Fern's legs. "She ought not be bleeding still." Clementine packed a large wad of cotton cloth between Fern's thighs. She propped Fern's feet on a pile of pillows and a folded quilt. She called for Ora.

The women consulted. Ora brought Fern a lukewarm cup of tea with herbs to slow the flow of blood. Fern took the tea by small spoonfuls. Junior cradled the baby, her warm heartbeat fluttering against his. He put his nose to the baby's neck and inhaled the fresh milky scent. Flesh and bone and blood. He'd never been so terrified and happy all at once. Fern slept. Junior wondered if they'd made it home with their packages from the morning shopping trip. He thought about the stuffed bear they'd bought for the baby. He wanted to give it to her now. No sense waiting for Christmas morning.

Junior dozed while sitting on the floor beside Fern's bed. He dreamed of water, deep and wide. He dreamed of the birds and the noisy clatter of their wings at sunset. The clatter came from outside his dream, though it took him some time to realize it. The clatter came from the yard and front porch. It was not birds descending on the trees, but men descending on their home. Chester shouted. Ora rushed into the room where Junior and Fern and the baby slept.

"We have to hide," she said. "They've come for her."

Junior didn't know if Ora meant they'd come for Fern or for her daughter. Maybe both. Ora took the child and Junior scooped up his sleeping sister. She felt limp as a sack of flour in his arms. They slipped out the back door as the men pushed past Chester at the front door. Ora led Junior through the winter-dormant gardens and into the woods. They crouched in the shadow of a large oak. Junior propped Fern at the base of the tree. She opened her eyes but didn't seem to see anything. The men came around the back of the house. They tore through the empty plant beds, their boots kicking up mounds of soil. They were the same men from the diner. Junior saw the man with the red cap. He saw the man with the Barlow knife. Chester ran after them, shouting and cursing. Junior wanted to recede deeper into the woods, but feared any movement might give them away.

"They ain't here!" Chester yelled. "And you're trespassing, you sons of bitches!" Chester carried a rifle. Junior hoped he'd have the good sense not to fire it at anyone.

The baby woke. Maybe the shouting woke her or maybe she was hungry. She cried, a soft, hiccupping mewl that built to a throaty howl. Fern reached for the baby and pulled her to her breast, but it was too late. The men heard the cries and rushed toward them. Junior tried to hoist his sister and the nursing baby, but he was too slow. The man in the red cap grabbed for the baby. Fern, still groggy from the loss of blood and the medicine Ora gave her, was not strong enough to stop him. Junior threw himself at the man. He knocked him off balance, but the man was swift and determined. He ran, holding the baby underneath one arm. Chester and the group of men ran after him. Ora followed.

"Stay with your sister," she told Junior.

Fern told him to take her to the baby. "Ama," she said. "Her name is Ama."

It seemed right she would name her baby after their mother. Junior carried his sister yet again. His arms ached from lifting her over and over. His legs felt weak and heavy. In the distance, he heard a gunshot and he knew it had come from Chester's rifle. Junior struggled to keep up with the men and Ora, but he knew where they were headed.

At the quarry, the man in the cap held the baby above his head. The other men stood watching. They were not as bold as the man in the cap, but they wouldn't stop him from whatever he was planning.

Ora ran at the man holding Fern's baby. She kicked him in the groin and slapped him. The man spit in her face. "Bastard child! Nigger child!" He kept chanting the terrible words.

Fern told Junior to set her down. She stood, unsteady but upright. "Her name is Ama," she said, her voice cutting through the man's ugly chant. "She is my daughter and you've got no right to her. She is named for her grandmother. She is descended from royalty. Any harm you do to her will come back to your family a hundred times, a thousand. Your children will be slow-witted and lazy. Your wife will be unfaithful. You will never prosper. Your crops will wither. You'll see rain on top of floods. You'll see drought when the ground is cracked. You'll be thirsty in the middle of an ocean. You will live a long time in ill health. You will die alone and lonely. And every time you suffer, you will think of me and of Ama and of the dark, ugly nature of your soul."

Fern's speech seemed to cast a spell. The men at the edge of the woods went quiet. She pointed a talonlike finger. The man continued to hold the baby over his head, but he stopped chanting. Ora and Junior waited to see if Fern would say more. They stood on the lip of the water-filled quarry, frozen in suspense. Fern coughed and crumpled to the ground.

For a moment it seemed as if the whole mess might be over, as if the man in the cap might hand the baby to Ora, as if the rest of the men might just walk away. Calm before storm. But Junior saw the man's eyes harden. He took a step away from Ora and tossed the baby into the quarry as if he were tossing trash onto a heap. Ora dove in after the child. She didn't come up. Clementine stood at the edge of the quarry and screamed. "What have you done? She can't swim!"

Chester appeared next to Fern. "Don't leave her," Junior said to him. He ran to the quarry and flung himself over the side. His boots weighed heavy on his feet, threatened to drag him down. The water swirled around him, impossibly cold and dark. He swam in circles, dove as deep as his breath would allow. He found no sign of Ora or the baby, but he knew he was not alone in the water. Evil lived there, a beast beneath the water's surface. Junior felt it pulling him deeper, urging him to open his mouth and lungs. He resisted, but he knew Ora and Fern's baby had not been strong enough to fight this beast. He kept diving well past the point when he knew it was futile. He couldn't stand the thought of facing Fern and Clementine and Chester. As long as he dove, he figured, they had hope. By the time he pulled himself over the lip of the quarry, his hands were puckered and his lips had turned blue with cold.

The men were gone. While Junior dove, Chester had shot the man in the red cap, sending a bullet into his left arm. One of the other men threatened to bring the law. Chester told them to go ahead. He said he figured he was justified in shooting every one of them. The man in the red cap told Chester the law would never be on the side of nigger lovers and white trash. "We've done what we came here to do," the man said. He held his bloody arm against his chest as he walked into the woods. The other men followed him.

"I should have killed him," Chester said. "I should have killed them all."

Junior knew the man in the red cap was right. The law didn't exist to protect people like him and Chester, like Fern and her baby, like Clementine and Ora. The law would always take the side of men with power and money.

Chester and Junior carried Fern through the woods and back to the house. Clementine walked behind them. His boots squished and felt heavy with quarry water. Soaked and cold and shivering with fear and rage, he tried to think of what he could do to make things better for Fern, but he knew there was nothing to be done.

TWELVE

WE TOOK WILLET'S STACK of photos and headed out for the day. Just as the woman at the grocery warned, the boat rental places were unmanned. There were signs on the door about booking tours or boats for the next day. We took our photos to City Hall, where the woman in the records department would barely look at us. Willet asked if we could find out about a former resident named Earl Watkins.

"Name doesn't ring a bell," the woman said. "What do you want to know?"

"I'm not sure," Willet said. "Any addresses under that name? Arrests?"

"You gotta be more specific than that," she said. "And there's a fee to search public records."

"How much?"

"Depends on the record."

Willet asked if the fee applied even if she didn't find anything.

"Yes, and in that case it ought to be doubled," the woman said. "For wasting my time."

We left without any information. We made our way across the town, stopping at every open business.

No one recognized Daddy. No one wanted to recognize him. At the Tote-Sum store, we showed our photos to the clerk, a skinny man with a beer gut and a dirty ponytail who flipped through the latest edition of *Penthouse* with one hand and ate a bag of pork rinds with the other. The man gave us the stink eye and told us he was too busy to help anyone who wasn't a paying customer. Willet bought a soda and a pack of cigarettes. The clerk glanced at the photos, but barely.

"Nope," he said. "Can't say I know him."

"Come on," Willet said. "You hardly even looked."

The clerk slapped the pack of cigarettes on top of the photos and settled back with his magazine and pork rinds. "Can't help you," he said.

We got the same treatment wherever we went. At the end of the day, Willet caught one of the boat captains coming off the water. We followed him to his office next to the marina. He told us we ought not be snooping around.

"But he's our father," I said.

"Maybe he is," the man said. "But I can't know that for sure. I don't know you." The man shuffled through a pile of paperwork and refused to look at the photos. He hardly looked at us.

Willet shoved the photo of Daddy with the fish on top of the man's paperwork. "Jesus Christ! The man's dead. We can't hurt him. We just want to know what he was doing here."

The man pushed the photo off his pile of paperwork and said, "I'm not a real religious man, but if I remember correctly, even Jesus Christ was allowed to go missing for a few years."

The next day at the alligator park a beet-faced man refused to look at the photos but tried to sell us tickets for the afternoon tour. "You'll hold a live alligator in your arms, little lady! Where else can you cradle a fearsome beast?"

Maybe people with no tragedy in their lives longed to cuddle with fearsome beasts, but I did not. Anyhow, there was a wall of photos with visitors holding the small alligator. Nothing about it struck me as fearsome. It was pitiful. The gator's mouth was taped shut, its skin a sickly pale gray. The tourists who held the gator grinned wide or pulled faces of horror, but I saw shame in their eyes. It is one thing to trap something wild for the sake of survival, and quite another to breed and keep a living thing for the sake of entertainment.

At the Wild Catch Cafe we showed our photos to a waitress who was friendlier, but no more helpful. She served us strong coffee and took time to look at the photos. She didn't recognize Daddy. I told her about the men who'd turned us away and she laughed. "What you're getting there is an Everglades welcome," she said. "They don't trust strangers and they sure don't trust strangers asking questions. People like to keep to themselves around here."

I couldn't understand why a whole community would be suspicious and secretive, but I was used to dealing with secrets. The women of White Forest kept plenty of secrets from their husbands and their fathers, and I wondered how friendly they'd be if a couple of strangers showed up and started poking holes in their lives. Daddy could turn five-dollar bills into hundred-dollar bills, so he could surely turn himself into someone new. He could dye his hair or grow a beard or shave his head. There might be a hundred reasons why no one recognized our father from those photos. And there might be a hundred reasons why someone wouldn't admit to recognizing him. We couldn't know how Daddy lived during those years when he was missing, but we knew how he lived when he was with us. Daddy was a con artist, a criminal, and a thief. When I was younger, I didn't question the things Daddy did. He provided for us and I didn't care how. As I got older, I wondered what would set a man off on such a dishonest life. Was it one terrible thing or a series of small injustices? What if we uncovered something terrible? What if we found something we'd rather not know?

After three days of traipsing all over town asking questions, we'd learned nothing new about our father. We were frustrated and I figured it was time to head home. Willet wasn't ready to give up just yet. "Let's go check out that canoe rental spot," he said. "The one the grocery clerk told us about."

We took a few wrong turns before finding the gray wooden building with canoes stacked up outside. An old man snoozed on a rocking chair on the front porch. He wore a pale blue baseball cap pulled low over his forehead. He opened his eyes as we tromped up the porch steps.

"Tour's just left." He rubbed his gray beard with a hand marked by red scars and swollen with arthritis.

"We're just looking for some information," Willet said.

The man spat a long stream of tobacco into an old coffee can. "Name's Iggy." He leaned forward in the chair. "What kind of information you need?"

Willet showed him our stack of photos and Iggy flipped through them. He didn't tell us to stop snooping around or to mind our own business.

"I can't say I ever seen him," he said. "Who is he now?"

"He's our father," I said. "We think he lived around here."

Iggy shook his head, spat into the can again. "He don't seem familiar, but that don't mean much. Lot of people come here and work pretty hard to disappear."

"What does that mean?" Willet asked.

Iggy stood and gestured for us to follow him inside. The store was small, but packed with books and camping gear. He pulled a map from a wooden display case and spread it across the counter. "We're right about here." He put a fat finger on the map. "Now most folks figure this is about it. You could head out to the Keys, of course, do some fishing, but we're pretty well situated at the edge of things. But you see all this here?" He dragged his finger lower on the map and pointed to a cluster of dots. "Well, you'd be surprised at how many men manage to pass a season or two on one of these little islands. Most of 'em aren't even on the map."

"You mean people live out there?" I said. "Without food or shelter?"

"Plenty of both if you're smart about it and know your way around." Iggy dug the tobacco from his lower lip and deposited the plug in his spit can. "Calusa Indians lived on these islands for generations. Some of these places wouldn't exist if it weren't for the Calusa shell mounds. We got more than one hermit living out there. They come in every now and then for supplies, but they're pretty self-sufficient. Plenty to hunt and there's no better fishing in the world."

"How would you find someone living out there?" Willet leaned over the map and scanned the area where Iggy had pointed.

"You won't find no one if they don't want to be found," Iggy said. "That's what makes it such a great place to hide."

"Could someone live out there with a child?" Willet asked.

"*Could* they?" Iggy scratched his beard and looked toward the ceiling. "I guess so. But I never heard of anyone doing it. Can't imagine why anyone would. It's not an easy way to live."

"There's no way," I said to Willet. "Daddy wouldn't do that." I didn't want to go into too much detail in front of Iggy, but I didn't believe Daddy would take Pansy out to some remote island. He might have reason to hide, but what reason could he have to take Pansy with him?

"There's not but about five hundred people in this town," Iggy said. "With Chokoloskee, maybe it's six hundred. Everyone knows everyone else. Tourists come and go, but if your father lived here for any time someone is bound to know him."

We'd made the rounds of every business in town and not one of the people we spoke to recognized our father either by his photographs or by his name. I wondered if Daddy came to Everglades City to die rather than to live. Maybe he'd lived elsewhere. Maybe he'd lived on one of the no-name islands as Iggy suggested. But if so, why come to this town to die in a crappy motel room? What could be the reason for that?

Willet shook Iggy's hand. "Thank you for taking the time to talk with us."

"Wish I could have been more help," Iggy said.

"So do I," Willet said. "But you've been a damn sight more helpful than anyone else in this town."

Iggy laughed. "It isn't a real friendly place at first. I promise it gets friendlier."

Iggy folded his map and we turned to leave. We were almost out the door when Iggy said, "You know, if you want to get a real sense of this place, you ought to get on the water. You'll see what I mean about how easy it is to disappear."

Willet looked at his watch. It was nearly noon and we didn't have much planned for the day. Iggy's shop was about the last place we'd left to visit. "Can you take us out?"

"I can set you up with a canoe and tell you where to paddle," Iggy said.

"I don't want to get lost," I said.

"No, you don't," Iggy said. "But you'll be okay if you stick to the river."

Iggy led us to the boats stacked beside the store. He put his hand on a short gray canoe. "This one ought to work for you."

Willet helped him pull the canoe from the stack. "First day here a girl at the grocery said something about the mangrove tunnels."

"Oh you'll go through plenty of those," Iggy said. "Launch is just across the road. Water's pretty shallow at the mouth. Dig in and get past it. Go ahead and use your paddles like push poles in the shallowest sections. If you get stuck, hop out and pull until you're floating. There's an old gator who suns himself at the launch spot. He ain't gonna hurt you. Just swing wide around him. You'll get to a fork with a bridge to your right and a strand of cedars to your left. If you head toward the cedars, you'll hit the bay soon enough. I'd head under the bridge and stick to the river. And don't be afraid to use your monkey arms." Iggy held his arms overhead and mimed pulling himself forward. "Grab onto the branches and pull. It was good enough for your ancestors. It's good enough for you."

We paddled through the shadowy tunnels and shallow, murky water of the Turner River. A large turtle perched on a stump. It pulled its head in when our paddles came too close. Cypress knees jutted out of the brown water and plants seemed to grow right out of the air.

Birds landed in the trees around us, squawking and flapping. I later learned to identify the swamp chicken, the osprey, and my favorite, the anhinga. I liked the way it perched on a branch with its wings extended, like Jesus on the cross.

We took Iggy's advice and used our monkey arms to pull the boat through the low canopy of branches. The mangrove trees grew sideways as much as they grew tall and in places where the water was shallow, I could see the roots were a tangled, vinelike mass. We floated for a moment in a still pool surrounded by grass. It was hot for the middle of January. Mosquitoes buzzed. A fish splashed up from the water. A bird called out from the trees. A spider spun a golden web across a fallen stump. Everywhere I looked, the air was thick and heavy and full of life. We floated through a swarm of gnats and I nearly dropped my paddle to swat them away. Leaves and branches and bits of hanging moss seemed to reach out and caress us as we paddled by. Tree trunks crawled with fluorescent patches of green moss. We were a few paddle strokes from the Gulf of Mexico, where the brackish waters swam with blacktip sharks, stingrays, barracuda, and jellyfish. There were alligators in the river and snakes along the bank. The water smelled ripe and alive. The way forward and the way back seemed familiar and brand new at the same time. With nothing more than a shift of light and shadow, everything became transformed. Was that the same strand of cedars we'd passed on our way in or had the trees sprouted up in response to some strange prayer? I reached out to touch a jutting cypress knee and when I pulled my hand back, the tip of my finger swelled with a bead of blood. I didn't know if I'd scraped against a thorn or been stung by one of the hundreds of swarming, buzzing insects. Iggy was right. It would be easy to disappear into the swamps or into the Gulf. Who would search for you out here, where everything was beautiful and dangerous and strange?

By the time we returned the canoe, my shoulders were sunburnt and sore from paddling. Iggy told us to come by anytime we needed a boat or had any questions. He said he hoped we found what we were looking for.

That night Willet said we should get out of the motel and eat something decent. We'd been living off cold fish dip and crackers in the motel room and it would be a treat to go out. The motel never felt like any place we wanted to be with its gritty floors and mildew in the corners and thin scratchy sheets. The lamps flickered at odd times. A large papery spider and a pop-eyed lizard lived in the shower. I was happy to leave it behind for a few hours.

We ended up at a local bar. There weren't a lot of options for eating out in the evenings. The crab shacks stopped selling when they ran out of crab around midafternoon. The local gun club dining room served up fancy plates for a price we couldn't afford. That left the bar, which was attached to a family restaurant called the Crab House. The bar offered cheap beer and generous plates of fried food. We ordered the local sampler to share.

In the corner of the bar a small band set up instruments and tested the sound system. A screech of feedback echoed through the room. The wooden plank walls of the bar were studded with fishing poles and lures and photos of men hauling bulging nets into boats. It was early and there weren't more than a few customers in the bar. Willet and I sat facing each other in a vinyl booth against the wall. An old woman with orange hair chain-smoked Pall Malls and studied a pile of papers she'd spread across her table. At the bar a bald man hunched on a stool and slammed back rum-and-cokes. When the waitress brought our food, Willet ordered another round of beers. We dug into the strips of grouper, the crab fritters, the alligator, and the hush puppies. Daddy used to make hush puppies whenever he came back from fishing and the fried cornmeal and onion melted like a memory against my tongue.

Soon the bar began to do a business. Most of the customers streaming in were young and seemed to be there for the band. A few older folks settled at the bar and greeted the rum-and-coke man with a nod or a slap on the back. The clerk we'd met at the grocery store on our first morning walked in wearing a turquoise tube top and a pair of tight white jeans. Her tanned shoulders sparkled with some sort of glitter and she'd rimmed her eyes with blue shadow. She spotted Willet and came over.

"I wondered if you guys were still here. Did you get on a boat?" She gestured to a guy standing behind her. "This is my big brother, Audie. I'm Cheryl." She scooted in next to Willet, her white-blonde hair swinging across her shoulders. I suddenly felt mighty plain in my blue jeans and T-shirt.

Willet shook Audie's hand and introduced me as his little sister. Cheryl said, "I knew y'all were brother and sister. You look alike. Me and Audie don't favor so much."

It was true. Audie's dark brown hair curled around his neck and ears, and his eyes were nearly black where his sister's were blue. When he smiled, his lips barely revealed his teeth. Cheryl was all smile, all flash and sparkle. Audie was dark and serious. He slid into the booth next to me and ordered iced tea and a basket of clam strips.

"Have a beer, man," Willet said.

Audie shook his head. "Working tonight."

Cheryl said Audie was one of the best fishermen in the Everglades. "He just bought me a new Camaro. And you should see his truck. It's beautiful."

"Don't do that, sis." His voice was low and rough.

"Do what?"

"Brag."

Cheryl fake pouted, pushing her high gloss lips out in a pretty way. Willet liked her, I could tell. He had a weak spot for overdone women. The band played a decent cover of "Fat Bottomed Girls" and Cheryl tugged on Willet's arm. "Come dance with me."

Willet left me with Audie, who sipped his tea and examined his hands. During the years when girls in my class were ironing their hair and putting on mascara, I'd been living under the shadow of my missing sister. My trip to see Bubba was my only experience with a man. Thanks to my work with Granny Clem, I knew plenty about childbirth, but I knew nothing about how to talk to strange men. I resented Willet for leaving me alone with Audie. I sipped my beer and shoved another hush puppy in my mouth. It felt strange to sit next to someone and not say a word. When I couldn't stand it anymore, I asked the only thing I could think to ask.

"Do you like fishing?"

He coughed and looked at me. "You ever fished?"

"A little," I said. "Daddy used to take us pole fishing."

"Where was that?"

"Mississippi."

"I've never been."

"You're not missing much."

"What brings you here?"

I told him we were looking for anyone who might have known our father. "I don't think we're going to find anything."

"You never know," he said. "You might turn something up. But be careful. Curiosity ain't too highly prized around here."

I said we'd figured that out already. Audie laughed and asked how long we planned to stick around. I couldn't imagine we'd stay much longer. We couldn't chase our father's ghost forever. "I'm sure we'll head home soon," I said.

Audie said he and Cheryl lived with their father even though Audie paid rent on an apartment. "I hate to leave Cheryl alone with Pop," he said. "His mind is slipping." Their mother had left them years earlier, though not in the same way Daddy left us. She moved to Miami with a man and started a new family. Still, I knew what it meant to be abandoned by one parent and left to care for the other.

Audie looked at the shiny gold Rolex on his wrist and tossed a hundred-dollar bill on the table. "Well, if you decide to stick around for a while, I'll take you and your brother out on the boat. You ought to see the islands while you're here." He left without saying goodbye to his sister.

I hoped we'd get to see the islands before we left the Everglades. I was curious after Iggy's talk about the men who lived on the old Calusa mounds. If Daddy lived here, even for a little while, maybe he hadn't lived in town or on the streets. Maybe he'd been one of the men who tried to disappear in the islands. Willet returned and ordered another round of beers. "Where's Audie?"

"He said he was running late."

Willet picked up the hundred-dollar bill. "Where did this come from?"

"Audie left it," I said. "For the tab."

"He must be the most successful fisherman that ever lived," Willet said. "Who leaves a hundred bucks for one glass of tea and a basket of clams?"

Cheryl came back to the table with a fresh coat of lip gloss and took a long swig of beer. She sat so close to Willet their shoulders touched. "Please stick around for a while," she said. "We never get any new people around here."

I said we'd already showed the photos all over town and we hadn't learned a thing.

"If your father lived around here, someone's bound to remember him," Cheryl said. "Unless he was just passing through. Tourists don't stay. Hardly anyone bothers to remember them unless they do something worth remembering."

"What's worth remembering?" I asked.

She told us about the man who took out his son's eye with a fishing hook, and about the woman who got drunk and fell off the boat on a sunset cruise, and about the kid who climbed a poison-wood tree on a dare.

"Swole up like a balloon," Cheryl said. "Went blind for a solid week."

Daddy always said the quarry was cursed, but bad things happened everywhere. Maybe Willet was right; there was no such thing as a curse, just evil people doing evil things or stupid people doing stupid things. I touched my pocket where I carried the quarry rock.

I'd brought it with me because it seemed like a link to the spot where all our troubles began, a reminder of what we were searching for, a talisman or a key. Maybe it was foolish to assume any one place in the world was more evil than another. Maybe the whole world was a dangerous place.

THE ISLAND WAS NOT quite as he remembered it. People were less friendly. No one remembered him or Fern. One man claimed to remember his mother, called her "the old nigger Indian." It took all of Junior's will not to punch the man. Ora had liked to say all people were the same. No matter where they lived or how they supported themselves or what language they spoke, they were the same beneath their skin. Junior never believed her until he returned to Chokoloskee, but now he saw she was right. Good people like his mother and Clementine and Ora would be good people no matter where they lived. And people like the men who'd killed Fern's baby and caused Ora's death—those people were everywhere. He wondered what sort of person he was, beneath his skin. He was too angry to be good.

Fern settled into a home for wayward girls run by a trio of nuns. She was the least wayward girl he'd ever known, but at least she had a roof over her head. Fern told him to go. "Clementine needs you," she said. "I can't go back to that place, but you have to." He didn't leave right away. He camped for a few days and watched the birds fly out over the water, but he knew Fern was right. He promised her he'd visit often and said she should call him if she ever needed anything. "Everything I needed is gone," she said. She watched him drive away, but did not lift her hand to wave.

He drove straight through and arrived back in White Forest sleep deprived and half crazy with grief.

"I wasn't sure you'd come back," Clementine said.

"Neither was I," he told her.

He said he would stay for a while but he didn't want to be called Junior anymore. Junior was a child's name, he said. It implied a relationship with his father and he knew he'd never see his father again. Clementine offered to give him a brand-new name, a new identity. She showed him her stash of birth certificates and explained the process. She could make him reborn. He thanked her but said she should just call him by his first name: Earl. Later, though, when Clementine slept and Chester went out to hunt squirrel, Earl helped himself to a birth certificate and all the tools to create a new identity just in case. It seemed like a handy thing to have. He suspected he would need it someday.

Chester took to stalking the men who'd sent Ama and Ora to their deaths. He told Earl they met late at night at the quarry. He told them about their white cloaks and the terrible things they said. He told him about the man he'd shot and how his life was turning bad just as Fern had predicted.

"You ought to stay away from that place," Earl told him. "You'll get yourself killed."

Shortly after Earl returned, Clementine took in a girl named Loretta. Her parents had been killed when the car they were driving got stuck on a set of train tracks. Earl couldn't understand why the couple hadn't abandoned the car to the train. Loretta was a few years younger than Earl and Chester. It had been years since Clementine took in a child. After the Depression, fewer children were left behind, but Loretta was an exception, orphaned so suddenly at the age of thirteen.

Earl's grief over his sister settled deep. It lent him an intensity that mingled with his natural charm. Loretta, with her own fresh grief, fell hard for him and wasn't the least bit unhappy when she got pregnant at sixteen. They married and she miscarried. She blamed Clementine, said something in the salves or teas must have caused the baby to let go of her womb. She said she'd get a proper doctor for any future babies. Earl told her Clementine would deliver any child of his and would treat them for any ailments in the same way she'd treated Earl and Chester. He wouldn't trust a doctor or a hospital. If she couldn't accept that, she couldn't have him. For years it seemed she'd never conceive again. Earl thought it was for the best. They were hard years. A group of students from some northern university came down to register black people to vote. Two of them were found drowned in a nearby river, tractor parts lashed to their legs to keep them underwater. One, a black man, was discovered swinging from the live oak tree near the quarry. Crosses burned on the front lawns of anyone who dared speak out for the cause of civil rights. Rocks were hurled through windows. Churches burned to the ground. White people spat on black people in the street. No one was held accountable.

When Loretta became pregnant again in 1960, Earl worried. He knew enough about genetics to understand any baby he produced would carry the blood of his mother. The black blood, the Seminole blood, might bring a dark-skinned baby even though he and Loretta seemed white as lilies. He was relieved when Willet came out with pink skin. Loretta named him for her dead father. When their daughter came along two years later, just as pink, she named her for her dead mother. Loretta wanted a whole brood of children, but they didn't come easy. She and Earl were both surprised to discover she was pregnant again, ten years after Willet was born. When Pansy came out with tanned skin and the purple birthmark, Earl died a little. Things were changing in the world, but they didn't change so quickly in White Forest. A dark baby, even one as light as this, would raise suspicions.

THIRTEEN

————◆————

AFTER OUR FIRST WEEK in Florida we'd learned nothing new, but we'd met a few people who were friendly enough to help us look. Cheryl and Audie and Iggy seemed to understand why we were searching for information about our father. Cheryl suggested we head to Chokoloskee, the island fishing community just south of Everglades City. "You can't leave without showing your photos there," she said. Cheryl didn't want us to go back to White Forest. She was smitten with Willet and determined to talk us into staying longer.

At the end of our first week in the Everglades, Audie took us out on his boat. I'd wanted to see some of the more remote islands, the ones Iggy had told us about. The maps labeled the area as the Ten Thousand Islands, but Audie said no one really knew how many islands there were. "Less than ten thousand," he said. "But more than anyone feels like counting."

Audie took us through the mangroves and out into the Gulf. Along the rivers and in the swampy areas, the mangrove trees grew close together and I thought we'd get stuck as Audie threaded the boat through the thick trees and alongside the massive roots that jutted up from the water. I could see what Iggy meant about how easy it would be to disappear. A man could be standing a few feet from the boat and we'd never see him in the thick foliage. Audie picked up speed when we reached wider waters, but even then the green islands seemed to rise up out of nothing. He sped around them without slowing and without consulting a map.

I asked him how he knew where to turn. He said he'd lived his whole life on these waters and he didn't need any map. He pointed out landmarks—a jut of sandbar, a patch of mud flat, a river of sea grass, a clump of mangrove—and said it was no different from navigating on land. But it was different. On land the buildings and roads and signs didn't shift with the winds and the tide. We idled for a bit near a large mangrove cluster and I wondered how anyone could access such an island. It looked impenetrable. Tangled roots jutted up from the water and thick green leaves made it impossible to see past the rim. Audie steered us to the other side of the island and pointed out a small strip of sand and shells, barely visible unless you knew where to look.

The water around the islands was the color of strong tea, but it swirled and cleared and turned a bright turquoise green when we reached the open waters of the Gulf. Audie killed the engine as a flock of white pelicans rose into the air, wings slapping against the water's surface. I stared at the sky until my neck ached. The day was warm, but a cool breeze blew across the water. My hair was damp from the salt spray and my T-shirt stuck to my skin.

"There'll be lots more to see at sunset," Audie said.

"Man," Willet said. "This is where you work? Sure as hell beats a construction site."

"It beats most jobs," Audie admitted. "Gets cold out here in the middle of the night, though." He asked Willet if he'd ever done any fishing.

"Caught a few catfish in my life," Willet said. "That's about it."

"If you want to earn some cash, I could use some help. I've been thinking about hiring someone, but most of the men around here have their own thing going. It's a different sort of fishing, but you might take to it."

"We're not going to be here long enough for you to get a job," I said.

Willet ignored me. He had his arm wrapped around Cheryl's shoulders. She leaned against him in such an easy, casual way that anyone would think they'd been a couple for years. I'd never seen him with a girl before. There were plenty of girls in our high school who flirted with him, but Willet never paid them any attention. He was always too busy working to have any sort of normal relationship, but now that Mama was gone he no longer had to work so hard. I didn't want Willet getting too attached to Cheryl. It would make it that much harder for him to leave and I believed we would leave soon. We'd encountered too many dead ends to stay.

At sunset, Audie steered the boat toward the rookery. A pair of dolphins leapt from the water behind the boat and danced in our wake. The slick gray creatures were like children tumbling across a field. Cheryl was delighted. "It's good luck when they swim with you, Bert."

I hoped she was right. I figured we could use some good luck.

Audie stopped the boat beside a long span of mangroves situated in the middle of a vast area of water. It looked like the leaves on the trees had turned white, but the white clusters were birds—thousands of them, large and small. The birds descended to the trees in a racket. Their wings slapped against the air and they called to one another as they flew. It was raucous and thrilling. Audie pointed at one clump and then another. He identified the birds for us: snowy egrets, brown pelicans, roseate spoonbills, white ibis, blue heron. "They fly in every night," he said.

"Why do they come here?" I asked.

"This is their home," Audie said. "Where else would they go?"

Flock after noisy flock descended on the trees. I touched the quarry rock in my pocket and felt its cold, smooth surface. White Forest seemed a long way away from these bright waters and squawking birds. Willet looked happier than I'd ever seen him. He grinned at Cheryl and she smiled back and the two of them seemed surrounded by light.

When Audie docked the boat, I found a pay phone and fed a handful of dimes into the metal slot. Granny Clem's voice sounded tinny and far away. I could picture her, standing at the kitchen sink with the phone pinched between her ear and shoulder, the cord stretched long over the table where I'd spent so many mornings drinking coffee and picking at a slice of lemon cake.

I asked how she was doing. She told me Mollie Jordan was ready to pop. Mollie was a fourteen-year-old girl who denied ever being with any man. When asked how she happened to become pregnant, she'd looked at Granny Clem with wide eyes and said, "The Lord works in mysterious ways." Granny Clem called Mollie's unborn child Jesus, the second. Mollie's father insisted the child be sold and any record of Mollie giving birth erased. Granny Clem suspected he was the father of Mollie's child, but the girl wouldn't accuse him of anything no matter how many ways Granny Clem asked.

"I'm sorry I'm not there to help you," I said.

"Oh, don't worry about it. It'll be an easy birth. She's healthy as a horse. I hope we don't see her again in a year or so."

I knew Mollie would show up again. Granny Clem would lecture her about birth control and she'd continue to insist she wasn't having sex, so she didn't need to worry about it. And, anyhow, birth control was a sin. If God wanted a baby in the world, who was she to go against his will? Granny Clem tried to persuade the young girls who came to her that preventing a pregnancy was easier than ending one, but the girls couldn't bring themselves to take the pill and the boys never bought condoms. It was sinful to have sex outside marriage, sure, but it was even worse to plan for it. "Religious logic is no logic at all," Granny Clem said. We'd had the same conversation a dozen times.

"Are you learning anything about your father?"

I told her no one seemed to know him.

"Well," she said. "I wouldn't worry too much about it. You know everything you need to know."

I thought of all the things I knew about Daddy and I came up with very little. I knew he liked stale cornbread soaked in buttermilk at night and fresh biscuits with fig preserves in the morning. I knew he wore soft cotton shirts and crisp denim jeans almost every day. I knew he hated going to church, not because the sermons were dry and boring, but because the folks in the pews were self-righteous hypocrites. I knew he didn't allow us to eat at the all-white supper club or swim in the all-white pool. The knowledge wasn't enough. I wanted more.

"He loved you," Granny Clem said. "That's the most important thing."

She was wrong. I wanted something better than love, something bigger and more valuable. I wanted truth.

The next morning Willet and I drove across the causeway to Chokoloskee. It had rained overnight and dark brown water swirled on both sides of the road. Debris blew across the causeway—leaves and branches, beer cans and cigarette butts. Yesterday's blue skies had faded to gray. The trash and the gray sky and the water reminded me of the quarry. It seemed we were always searching for something in the midst of dark water. Willet drove slowly. I sat with my feet on the dashboard, though I knew it made him crazy. He told me I'd end up with my knees in my mouth if we wrecked the truck. I told him not to wreck the truck.

Soon the morning sun burned away the clouds and dried out the road. I breathed in the thick, clean, rain-washed air. I palmed the rock I carried with me everywhere. That morning it was like a chunk of ice in my hand, smooth and cold and slick. Sometimes it pulsed warm and gentle, and sometimes it felt lifeless and ordinary. I didn't know what made the quarry rock go hot and cold but I imagined the rock carried the memories of all the people who'd held it or stepped over it or dug it from the dirt. If it were true, maybe it carried Pansy's memories. Maybe it would lead us to her.

On Chokoloskee Island, most of the houses sat on stilts. Even the doublewide trailers were elevated, and I wondered how a strong wind didn't blow them over. Cars and boats were parked beneath the wind-washed homes, which seemed practical. Why build a driveway or a garage when you could pull your car right beneath your house? The whole island was elevated thanks to the shell mounds left by the Calusa Indians more than two hundred years earlier. It was an odd feeling, to be driving across the discarded bits of someone's long-forgotten supper.

It was Cheryl's idea to show the photos around the general store at Chokoloskee. She'd wanted to come along with us, but her father was having one of his bad days and she couldn't leave him. I was glad. This was our quest, Willet's and mine. It didn't seem right to bring along a stranger.

Willet drove the length of the small island, turning only twice, and we ended up at the far southern tip where Smallwood's Store perched over the water. I'd thought Everglades City was the edge of the world, but I was wrong. It was Saturday, and kids begged for ice cream while their mothers shopped for canned goods and sacks of flour. On the southern edge of the store, a half dozen men sat talking on a gray wooden porch. They stared at the horizon, spinning stories for God and for themselves. I believe men sit side by side on bar stools and stand shoulder to shoulder when they fish because it makes the lies flow easier. Women are different, something I'd learned working with Granny Clem. Women like to look you in the eye when they lie to you.

We approached the men and asked if they would take a look at Willet's photos. I figured we'd have no more luck with these men than we'd had with the store clerks and waitresses in Everglades City, but one man held up the photo of Daddy with the fish. "Well, it's been a few years, but I believe this could be the man who bought my old skiff." He slapped his leg and turned to the man beside him. "Remember that fellow? Paid me with a wad of funny money. Disappeared into the wind."

"Oh, sure," the second man said. "I remember you threatening to shoot him if you ever saw him again. Smart of him to disappear, I'd say."

"When was this?" Willet asked.

"Oh, it must have been near about five years ago. Maybe more." He laughed and shook his head. "Truth is, that funny money spent real easy. My mistake was letting my wife try to put a chunk of it in the bank. They raised a flag, but the bills worked just fine as walking around money."

I could feel the excitement coming off Willet. "Did you get any idea where he might be living?" Willet sounded like he'd been running.

The man pulled a pack of cigarettes from his front pocket and Willet helped him block the breeze to get one lit. He took a long drag. Smoke trailed out of his mouth when he spoke. "I didn't ask. He struck me as a man who kept to himself. I respect that."

"But you must have signed over the boat title," Willet said. "There had to be some paperwork."

"Ah, hell," the man said. "It was a little old rowing skiff. Wasn't worth what he paid for it, to tell the truth. It was a handshake deal. No paperwork."

Willet was breathless, and I felt weak. The deck seemed to sway with the lapping water. I put my hand on the wooden railing to steady myself. The whole trip had felt like nothing more than chasing ghosts up until that moment.

The screen door to the porch opened and two boys ran out to the man in the rocking chair. "Grandpop," the younger boy hollered. "Can we have all the change in your pockets?"

The old man frowned, but his eyes twitched with amusement. "Well, let's see." He patted his pockets with liver-spotted hands. "I wonder if I've got even a penny to spare for such bad boys."

"We're not bad, Grandpop! We've been minding Mama like crazy."

He pulled a few dimes from his shirt pocket and set them on top of the pile of photos in his lap. "Reckon that'll be enough?"

The older boy snatched the dimes and said, "Oh, come on, Grandpop, you can do better than that."

He dug into the pockets of his pants and pulled out a few more dimes, a nickel, and a dollar's worth of quarters. "That ought to be enough for a couple of chocolate bars," he told the boys.

The younger boy threw his arms around the old man and thanked him for the pocket change. "Mama says we're leaving in ten minutes. That was five minutes ago."

The old man said he'd be ready. The boy ran back inside with his brother to spend the money they'd begged.

"Hang on," Willet said. "You must have talked to the man when you sold him the boat. What did he say? Did he mention his family? Did he talk about a daughter?"

The old man stood from the soft gray rocking chair and told Willet to be careful about nosing around too much. "It ain't a good idea to ask so many questions." He handed Willet the stack of photos.

"What is that supposed to mean?"

"Means just what it means. Don't pry."

He disappeared into the store.

We walked to the far edge of the porch, away from the men in the chairs. Willet kept balling his hands into fists and shaking them out. "I don't know why everybody's got to be so cagey," he said. "It ain't like we're searching for buried treasure."

I looked toward the horizon. Soft waves lapped against the deck pilings. A warm breeze blew my hair back. "What exactly are we searching for?"

Willet didn't say anything for a long time. We stood there, the two of us, staring out over the Gulf and listening to the cry of the gulls. Finally, Willet turned away and walked fast across the wooden porch. I had to jog to keep up with him.

"I wish like hell I knew," he said.

We drove around the island and showed the photos to anyone who would look at them. At the park, a group of kids played baseball while their mothers watched. None of the women on the sidelines seemed interested in helping us. They shook their heads when we showed them our photos. The women wore heavy gold chains around their necks. Their rings and earrings were studded with large, expensive-looking stones. Soft leather purses hung over their arms. The island was crawling with nice vehicles—vintage muscle cars and brand-new pickup trucks with chrome rims and shiny hood ornaments. We passed a trailer with a hot tub installed in the porch. There was fresh paint on the Baptist church. We talked about how strange it was to see mobile homes with fancy cars parked underneath. If someone lived in a trailer in White Forest, it meant they were poor or, like Uncle Chester, they didn't give a damn. These people were not poor and they obviously gave a damn.

"What do people do here for work?" I asked.

"Fish, mostly," Willet said. "Hell, I guess fishing pays better than I thought it did. Look at Audie, leaving hundred-dollar bills for ten-dollar tabs."

We drove back to the motel in the late afternoon. The sky was sunshine white and the day was as warm as summer. Driving past the canals, I saw three large alligators stretched out on the side of the road. Back in White Forest, Granny Clem would be washing up from a patient or mixing a potion of dried herbs. If I were there, I'd be stripping the bed for laundry or sterilizing her instruments or fixing us a pot of tea. Granny Clem would be telling me one of her stories. I supposed she worked in silence when I was gone, though it was hard to imagine. I'd gotten used to hearing her voice every day. What would she think of this place, I wondered. What would she think of the people with their fancy cars and expensive jewelry, of alligators by the side of the road, of the constant call of the shore birds?

I missed Granny Clem, but I knew I wouldn't see her anytime soon. The man on the porch had recognized our father. Now we knew our father had spent time on this island. We knew he'd bought a boat. We didn't know anything beyond that. It seemed a paltry amount of knowledge, but even a drop of water brings hope to a dying man.

EARL STOPPED BY CHESTER'S trailer on his way home from a trip during which he'd successfully swapped out more than five thousand dollars worth of counterfeit bills for real currency. Chester took his share of the cash and told Earl he ought to get a handle on his kids. Chester rarely left his trailer but when he did it was to visit the quarry, the site where all of Earl's nightmares seemed to originate. "They're swimming out there," Chester said. "It ain't gonna end well."

Chester had become obsessed with the quarry after they lost Ora and Fern's baby to its waters. In the days and months after Earl returned from delivering Fern to Florida, Chester visited the quarry most nights. He told Earl the man who'd killed Fern's baby met the other men there and they talked about what they'd done and what they planned to do next. Sometimes the men wore white robes. When a cross was set ablaze in the front yard of the home of the NAACP chair, Chester said it was the men who did it. When a young black man who'd been canvassing the county to register black voters disappeared, Chester swore the men were responsible. As the years went by, the men abandoned their robes and stopped meeting in the dark. The men formed a branch of the White Citizens Council and anyone who cared to could read about their plans in the local newspaper. They talked about heritage and pride and they quoted the Bible.

Earl took some comfort in Chester's reports about the man who'd cruelly flung Fern's baby into the dark waters. He didn't know if it was his sister's curse at work or divine justice, but the man suffered: his cotton crops turned brown with bacterial blight, his daughter ran away to Chicago and married a civil rights worker, his wife left him for a man half his age as his joints swelled with arthritis. It wasn't enough for Earl. No matter how much the man suffered, it would never make up for his horrible acts.

For twenty years Chester had fed Earl stories about the things he saw at the quarry and in the woods. Earl's mind was full of the evil of the place. Nothing good could happen there. He'd warned his children to stay away. He'd told his wife to keep them home, but she said Earl was superstitious and overly cautious. She humored him; they all did. He spent too much time on the road to have any real authority in his home. It couldn't be helped; he had to spread the bills around and he had to check on Fern, though she rarely seemed happy to see him. Two decades gone since that terrible day at the quarry and Earl knew she still lived with it every minute. He lived with it, too, with the guilt and the grief. He'd failed to rescue Fern's daughter from the dark waters of the quarry. Every time she looked at him, his guilt grew heavier.

Fern now lived alone in a small, elevated rental house in Chokoloskee, where she spent most days carving animals out of sugarcane bark and cypress wood. He gave her money to supplement the meager income she earned from selling her crafts and the occasional temp jobs she took on, but he couldn't give her the thing she really needed. He couldn't give her back the daughter she'd lost. That Earl had managed to father three children, that he had two daughters of his own, seemed unfair though Fern never said so. None of them could ever get over that day at the quarry. It was the reason Chester kept visiting the miserable hole in the ground and probably the reason he lived alone in a filthy trailer and trusted no one.

Now Chester was telling him his own children were swimming in that evil place, tempting the Devil and ignoring Earl's warnings. Chester was right. It wouldn't end well.

"I'll talk to them," Earl said.

"They're out there now." Chester lit a cigarette and blew smoke into Earl's face. "Or anyhow they were out there an hour ago. I saw 'em."

Earl left without stopping to see Clementine. He pulled his truck under a tree at the edge of the woods leading to the quarry and sat in the dappled light. His heart thrummed. He smoked a cigarette to calm himself. The midday heat turned his truck into an oven. Sweat rolled across his face and body, leaving him drenched and fevered. He imagined the worst: steel-clawed traps, wild animals, poison plants, evil spirits. These woods were no place for children. The longer he sat in the oppressive heat, the darker his thoughts became. He kept seeing the moment when Baby Ama and Ora disappeared into the dark quarry water. He kept hearing Fern scream.

He climbed from the truck and made his way through the trees. A crow cawed. Branches cracked beneath his feet. His eyes flooded with sweat. He wiped his face with the back of his hand and pushed his hair back with his fingers. Time moved backward. He felt like a child again, and he half-expected to hear Clementine and Ora calling him home for supper. The sky shifted and faded above the trees and blue turned to gray. The air seemed charged with electricity. His hair stood on end.

His hands trembled as he approached the quarry. It hadn't changed. He walked among the ghosts of Chickasaw and Choctaw, of Confederate soldiers and African slaves, of German prisoners and greedy landowners. They gathered around him, the sinners and the saints, and pressed close when he spotted the girl floating in the middle of the deep, dark water. Alone.

FOURTEEN

W ILLET TOOK THE JOB with Audie, which meant he worked most nights and slept through large portions of the day. His hours made things difficult. "How can we search for information while you're sleeping all day?"

"I'm not sleeping all day," he said. "And we need money if we're going to stay here for a while."

"I don't know why we're staying here at all if we don't have time to look for clues."

"Jesus," he said. "We'll look. I don't understand why you're so fired up to go back to White Forest. There's nothing back there. Relax. Try to have a little fun."

We hadn't come to the Everglades for fun and I resented Willet's harsh words about the only home I'd ever known. "Granny Clem is back there," I reminded him.

"Granny Clem doesn't need us. She'll get along just fine without your help."

"How long?" I asked.

"I don't know. Let's give it a month or two and see what happens."

We moved from the motel into Audie's vacant apartment. He'd offered it to us, saying it was a shame to let it sit empty.

"Well, this is a hell of a step up," Willet said.

He gave me the larger bedroom. The kitchen was nothing but linoleum floors and basic brown appliances, but it was a luxury to be able to scramble an egg without hunching over a hot plate. The first week we were there, I made one of Granny Clem's lemon pound cakes and took it to Cheryl and Audie as a way of saying thanks. I baked a second one for Iggy. I had more questions about the birds we'd seen at the rookery and about the islands. If there were answers to be found about what Daddy was doing here, maybe I could find them there. He'd bought a boat, after all. He must have been going somewhere on the water.

Iggy said there was only way to learn more about the islands. He took me out on a pole boat. We traveled through the shallow marsh, past tall grasslands and through cypress strands. It was different from being on Audie's boat. We were closer to the water, closer to the creatures that swam and crawled through the mud. We glided along in near silence. Iggy said motorized tours were killing the Everglades. He especially hated the airboats speeding through the waters, injuring the manatees, spewing the scent of gasoline, and filling the air with noise. I'd seen the airboats zipping around, the tour operators showboating and shouting to be heard above the loud buzzing motors. It didn't look like much fun to me. I preferred the peaceful isolation of the canoe or the pole boat.

"But what about seeing the rookery?" I asked. "You couldn't see that without a motor."

"Course you could," Iggy said. "It ain't a far piece. You could row it."

"But what about the sharks? Or the tides? Isn't it dangerous?"

He told me stories about fishing and camping with his father. They traveled for days by canoe and often paddled well past the rookery. They camped on islands stretching out into the Gulf. I said it seemed like it would be easy to get lost, but Iggy said getting lost was half the fun.

Over the next month, Iggy taught me as much as he could about paddling through the Everglades. He let me take out his smallest canoe whenever I wanted. I grew brave about exploring the rivers and I paddled out past the spot where the rivers dumped into the Gulf. I learned how to push myself free when I got stuck.

Willet spent more and more time working with Audie or hanging out with Cheryl, but we searched for clues about Daddy when we could. If Daddy did take Pansy, Willet figured she might be in the area. We looked for Pansy anyplace children gathered—the park, the ball field, the school. We spent several afternoons watching children board the local school bus, but we never saw anyone who looked like Pansy, though we didn't know what our sister would look like after nearly five years gone. It was too much to imagine we might find Pansy after all those years. What would we do if we saw our sister? She'd be eleven by then and not the same child we'd left in the quarry. Whatever her life might be, it wouldn't be the same as her life in White Forest. She might have forgotten all about us. She might not want to be found. Still we looked.

At night, I slept with the quarry rock under my pillow. I read from the book of fairy tales. Often I read aloud, as if Pansy were there with me. Willet spent most nights on the boat or with Cheryl. I went days without seeing him. Some nights I dreamed of the quarry and the creature from the woods, but most nights I dreamed of nothing. Our connection to White Forest stretched thin as we settled into our new life. I spent more and more time alone, wandering through the streets and alongside the canals of the small town.

Weeks passed, then months, and every time I spoke with Granny Clem she sounded farther away. I called less often. The calls were expensive. Willet never complained, but I felt bad running up bills I couldn't pay. I got tired of hearing Granny Clem's reports about the babies and the women who had them. I didn't want stories about people I hardly knew; I wanted answers about Daddy and Pansy. I talked about it with Willet, but his focus shifted to Cheryl and his work with Audie. He didn't seem to care about why we'd come to Florida in the first place. He definitely didn't want to leave.

That spring, we got a stretch of rainy days that kept me inside the apartment long enough to start going crazy. The driving gray rains turned the streets into shallow rivers. Alligators came up with the water and I saw one of the gray beasts lumbering across the parking lot of our apartment building. It was the start of the wet season. Iggy warned me it would come. I spent one whole day watching soap operas and daytime talk shows until my brain went soft. I ate grape jelly on saltine crackers for lunch and dinner. I drank coffee all day long. It reminded me of the days following Pansy's disappearance, when we lived off caffeine and mush.

Willet kept the photos and the animal carvings on the dresser in his bedroom. I spent hours moving them around like puzzle pieces and willed them to give up their secrets. At night, the rain fell so hard it sounded like gunshots hitting the windows. The thunder came in waves, booming for minutes at a time. When we heard thunder back home, people said it was the Devil beating his wife. I figured the Devil's wife couldn't take much more. One morning I woke to a strange silence inside the apartment. Rain fell outside, but something was missing inside. I half sleepwalked to the kitchen to make a pot of coffee and nearly cried when I realized I couldn't. I flipped the kitchen light switch, but the overhead fixture didn't hum. I put my ear to the phone and was relieved to hear a dial tone. I called Cheryl's house to talk to Willet. He told me the electricity was down there, too.

"It's out everywhere," he said. "Look outside. You won't see the first light."

He offered to come get me, but I didn't want to be stuck at Cheryl and Audie's house any more than I wanted to be alone in the apartment.

"Can't you come home?" I asked.

Willet said he couldn't abandon Cheryl with the electricity out. He said her father was more confused than ever.

"What about me?" I asked. "Why don't you worry about abandoning me?"

"Goddamn, Bert, you're a grown woman. No one's abandoned you. If you were in trouble, I'd be there and you know it. I ain't gonna come running because you're bored. Audie says the electricity'll be back soon. Just sit tight."

I slammed the phone down and stared at the cold coffeepot. I peeled mold off a loaf of bread and ate the stale bits with butter and cinnamon sugar. I hoped it would make me sick. I fetched the photos and the animal carvings and spread them out on the kitchen table. It was the room with the most windows and the only place in the apartment where I could see more than shadows on a day with no sunlight. I found a half-burnt taper and a chipped candleholder in the junk drawer. I lit the candle and stared at the collection for a long while, moving the pieces around and trying to make sense of things. I wished I had magic powers like the witches in the fairy tales. I wished for the gift of prophecy. I fetched the quarry rock from beneath my pillow and brought it to the table. I found the old book of fairy tales, the one I used to read with Pansy, and brought it in, too, even though I knew those stories by heart. I looked at all the things I'd assembled. It seemed like the answers should be there somewhere. I picked up the book of fairy tales and it flopped open to "The Devil and His Grandmother." I never liked the story much. I couldn't understand why the Devil's grandmother would betray her own flesh to save the souls of a few strangers. I didn't like it when she tricked the Devil into handing over the answer to the riddle. Even the Devil, I figured, ought to be able to trust his own grandmother.

I read the story aloud, squinting to make out the words in the dim, shaky candlelight. The story was just as I remembered and I knew when I condemned the grandmother I was siding with the Devil, but I didn't care. I held the quarry rock against my chest. The warmth grew and spread like kudzu during a warm, wet summer.

That's when it came to me. Alone in the cold gray kitchen, surrounded by the bits and pieces of my own riddle, I knew. Granny Clem was no better than the Devil's grandmother when it came to tricks and secrets. I wondered if she knew more than she let on. But if Granny Clem had the answers, whose soul did she hope to save?

I laid the photo of Daddy and Uncle Chester and the girl on top of the book of fairy tales and moved the candle closer so I could study the image. I squeezed the quarry rock in my fist. It warmed and turned hot. My palm burned red. The candle flickered as if a breeze were blowing through the kitchen.

I'd never get any answers if I didn't ask the right questions. I pulled the phone cord across the kitchen table and sat with my shrine of photos and carvings. Granny Clem answered on the second ring. She asked me about Willet and about Florida. She told me about a woman who'd lost her baby to miscarriage in the twenty-first week of pregnancy. Granny Clem buried the stillborns in a special corner of her garden and fed the unfulfilled mothers bitter herbs she grew from the soil covering the gravesite. The herbs were supposed to prepare the women's bodies to give birth in the future, but I suspected the ritual was more psychological than physical. Anyway, I didn't care about Granny Clem's business or some strange woman's lost baby. I had no space for sympathy. I needed answers.

"Tell me about Daddy," I said. The gray rain seemed to soften everything. Even my voice sounded faint. "Tell me about Daddy and Uncle Chester and the girl in the photo." I heard Granny Clem breathing, but she didn't say anything. "Why won't you tell us about the girl? She looks just like Pansy. You know she does."

"Oh, Bert, it was such a long time ago."

I twisted the phone cord around my index finger until the tip turned white and cold. "You've told me older stories," I said. "Why won't you tell me this one?"

"Your brother had no right to take that photo from me."

"What difference does it make? Daddy's dead. Mama's dead. There's no one else to ask. It isn't fair." I pulled my finger from the cord and watched blood flood the tip. It turned bright red, faded to pink.

"This phone call must be costing a fortune," she said.

I laughed. "Have we ever asked you for money?"

"I've given you plenty of money through the years."

"You paid me for working." Spit flew from my mouth and landed on the pages of the fairy tale book. "I earned that money. You came to us and asked for me. You said you needed me." As soon as I said it, I knew it wasn't true. Granny Clem didn't need anyone. So why did she come for me the year after Pansy went missing? Did she feel guilty about what she knew? Or did she want to keep me close and keep me busy so I wouldn't go snooping around?

Granny Clem let out a long breath. I could almost feel the warmth of it in my ear. "I knew your mother wouldn't take money from me. I gave you work because it was the best way I could think of to help your family out after Earl left."

"So you lied about needing me? Just like you lie about everything else."

"I loved having you work with me."

"Just like you lie to all those children growing up with the wrong parents. What do you think they'll do when they realize they don't look like anyone else in their family? How do you think they'd feel if they knew some old woman sold them to the highest bidder?"

"That is not how I work." She sounded angry. "I don't take bids."

"You might as well," I said. "All those babies in the wrong homes—"

"In *better* homes," she said. "With better lives."

"That's not why you do it."

"What do you know about why I do anything? I expect more of you."

Thunder boomed and the lights flickered, but didn't come on. It seemed right that I'd be left in the dark. My conversation with Granny Clem wasn't shedding any light on our family mysteries.

The way she danced around the truth was infuriating. "I know what you expect," I said. "You expect me to keep my mouth shut and not ask questions."

"I expect you to understand that plenty of children are born to the wrong mothers and all I'm trying to do is set things right."

"You're not God," I said. "You don't get to decide what's right."

She laughed. "Do you see any evidence God cares about the babies born in the Mississippi Delta? Or in Florida, for that matter? Maybe he gives a damn about children born in New York City or Los Angeles, but I don't believe he spares a thought for the children I deal with. I don't believe he thinks of me and I don't believe he ever spared a moment for you."

The truth of her words hit me hard. Of course I'd side with the Devil. Siding with God was never an option. Either he didn't exist or he didn't care about us.

"Someday," she said, her voice softer and less angry, "when you have children of your own, you'll understand."

"I won't." I stood and paced the small kitchen. "I won't bring a child into this world. I won't risk it."

"You're young. You'll change your mind," Granny Clem said.

The phone cord wrapped around me as I paced. "You don't know me."

"For heaven's sake, I know you better than you know yourself."

I spun to untangle myself from the twisted cord and felt a rush of dizziness. I leaned against the table. The carving of the alligator slid and tumbled to the linoleum.

"Bert?" Granny Clem's voice came to me from nearly a thousand miles away. "Bert?"

If she wouldn't tell me what she knew about Daddy and Pansy and the girl from the photo, then what did we have to say to each other? Every piece of our relationship was a lie and if I could go back and undo the hours I'd spent working with her, I would. I hated her for being right about God and for pointing out one more way in which I didn't matter.

"I know you're upset . . ." Granny Clem kept talking, but I was done listening.

I set the receiver on the table alongside the book, the photos, and the carvings. Her voice sounded no louder than a mouse's squeak. I walked out of the apartment and into the pouring rain. The parking lot was empty but for a half dozen cars and an alligator who seemed to be camping there until he could reclaim his usual spot near some river.

I was barefoot and I wore nothing but one of Willet's old white T-shirts, the same thing I slept in most nights. Within seconds, the shirt was plastered to my body and I was as good as naked if anyone cared to look. No one did. Or, if they did, they didn't think it worth braving the storm to confront me. I stared at the long gray alligator and dared him to come and get me, but he never moved. He must have figured I wasn't worth the effort. Or maybe he knew, just by looking at me, he was no match for the beasts in my own family.

When Willet came home, I was sleeping facedown on the couch, still wearing the soaked T-shirt. I'd left the door to the apartment standing open and the cheap living room carpet was soaked from the rain blowing in. The phone beeped incessantly where I'd left it off the hook on the kitchen table. I had no idea how long Granny Clem stayed on the line after I walked away and I didn't care. The photos and the carvings and the book were still scattered across the table, but at some point I must have grabbed the quarry rock. I had no memory of it. When Willet shook me awake and I opened my eyes to the light and hum of restored electricity, I felt the painful tenderness of a bruise beginning between my breasts. I'd been sleeping with the quarry rock pressed against my flesh. The bruise was twice as large as the rock, as if I'd slammed it against my chest in wide, violent strokes.

"Jesus Christ!" Willet stood over me looking both angry and confused. "I've been trying to call you for the past hour."

I rolled onto my back and peeled the wet cloth of the T-shirt away from my skin. It was cold in the apartment. The air conditioning had kicked on when the electricity came back. I shivered. Willet's face wavered in and out of focus. He pulled me from the sofa and ran a hot bath. "You're going to make yourself sick."

I sank into the warm water and breathed in the clean, hot steam. I pressed my fingers to the bruise on my chest and wondered at the force required to make such a mark. I had no memory of the past four hours. I couldn't say how long I'd stood in the rain in the parking lot or whether I walked any further. I couldn't say if I'd approached the alligator or if I'd backed away from the beast, but I swear I could feel his scaly skin against my palm. Maybe I'd imagined him or he lived in my dreams along with the creature from the haunted woods and Bubba's alien visitors. I'd spent the past five years swallowing Granny Clem's stories and lies. I couldn't tell the difference anymore between what was real and what was a fable. Fairy tales seemed every bit as plausible as Granny Clem's stories and I felt like Snow White, awake after a long, drugged sleep.

HIS DAUGHTER SWAM TO the edge of the quarry and hoisted herself from the water. Dark clay caked across her thighs. Her arms circled his waist. He lifted her and cradled her soaked body. The sky rumbled and cracked. Rain fell, but not an ordinary rain. This was an angry rain. The thing in the water wanted his child. It took Fern's baby and it took Ora and now it wanted Pansy. He ran, holding her tight. He hunched over her body, as if he could hide her from God or the Devil. The woods swallowed him up and he took a few wrong turns, though he knew every inch of these dirt paths. Lightning cracked. The sky turned glass bottle green then dipped to black. Something hummed and pulsed in the sky. Someone watched him. He felt the eyes following him through the woods. The ghosts ran alongside him until he found his way and burst from the trees just a few yards from his parked truck. The ghosts receded.

He tucked the child into his truck and drove. He was a hundred miles down the road before he came back to himself and realized what he'd done. His daughter sat beside him asking question after question. *What's wrong, Daddy? Where are we going? Why can't Bert and Willet come along? What about Mama? What about supper?*

He considered turning around. He could take her back to Loretta and everything would be like normal, but there was no normal for him or for this child who looked so much like his sister. He should have done this when she was born, when he first saw the birthmark on her leg and those odd teeth, when he saw how her skin wasn't pale and pink. Pansy looked nothing like her brother and sister. In fact, she was Fern made over. Whenever he looked at Pansy, he saw his sister as a child. Earl knew that if Ama had lived, she would have grown into a child just like Pansy. It was as if, somehow, Fern's baby had been reborn. He'd failed to bring Fern's baby back from the waters of the quarry. He wasn't about to let another child be swallowed into the evil pit. He did what he should have done six years earlier—he took the child to Fern.

FIFTEEN

THE WET SEASON SETTLED from early days of deluge to weeks of on-again, off-again rain. Rivers swallowed their banks and when Iggy took me out on the water, we rushed in spots where we used to float. We no longer used our paddles to dig out of the shallow spots. Some of the mangrove tunnels hung so low across the rising water we couldn't float beneath them.

Summertime heat combined with the rain to create a breeding ground for mosquitoes. I slathered on bug juice whenever I stepped outside. Even so, my arms and legs were dotted with swollen, itchy bumps. When I complained, Iggy said the plants and animals of the Everglades needed the extra moisture to sustain them through the dry season.

"This rain ain't for you and me, Bert. God sends this rain for better creatures than us."

I told Iggy I wasn't sure I believed in God. He said God existed whether I believed in him or not.

Iggy saved me that first summer. Without him, I'd have been too lonely to live. Willet was happier than I'd ever seen him. He liked working with Audie, and he made more money than he'd ever made working construction. He was crazy about Cheryl. He never talked about searching for clues about Daddy anymore.

I borrowed his truck a few times and drove to Chokoloskee on my own. I cruised through the streets of the island, searching the face of every child I saw. The store where we'd met the old man and his grandsons closed that year. The owner fell ill and no one else in the family stepped up to run the family business. There were more lucrative ways to make a living in the Everglades.

In June, I turned nineteen. We had dinner at the Crab House to celebrate. Willet gave me a silver bracelet with a dangling canoe charm and gave me the keys to his truck. He'd bought a new car for himself, a brand-new silver Mustang.

"I might need the truck every now and then," he told me. "But it's yours to drive."

Audie and Cheryl gave me charms for the bracelet, an alligator and a dolphin. Iggy gave me a tiny magnifying glass charm.

"Cause you're always searching for something," he said.

After dinner, they took me to the marina and Willet pulled a tarp off a pair of bright blue kayaks.

"This one's yours," Willet said, rocking one of the boats with his foot.

I couldn't believe he'd bought me a boat. I'd never received anything but a slice of cake and a few cards on my birthday. "Who is the other boat for?"

"Me," Willet said. "But Iggy can use it or Cheryl might want to take it out."

I couldn't picture Cheryl paddling the rivers. "How can you afford this?"

Willet grinned and Audie said, "It's been a good year."

I didn't understand how Willet could be doing so well. We'd been in Florida for six months. Already he was permanently tan and the mosquitoes didn't feast on him the way they feasted on me.

"Take it out whenever you want, Bert," Willet said. "Pay some mind to the weather and be careful, but she's all yours."

With my own kayak, I wouldn't need help from Willet or Iggy or anyone to get on the water. It was one more thing I could do all by myself.

"I thought you'd like it," Willet said.

"I do," I told him. "I love it."

I didn't want to seem ungrateful, but I wanted more. I wanted my brother back. I missed how we used to be. I missed the wild days when Willet and I would roam the woods and swim in the quarry without any sense of time or obligation, back before both turned sinister. Everything was different now.

Granny Clem sent me a package in the mail. I opened the box late at night, when Willet was on the water and the apartment was quiet. It was a packet of dried herbs for tea—nothing medicinal, just a blend I liked. She included a salve for my mosquito bites and a tiny hourglass charm. I hadn't spoken with Granny Clem since that rainy day nearly four months earlier, but she'd obviously stayed in touch with Willet. I made myself a cup of tea with the herbs and opened the envelope she'd enclosed with the gifts.

Dear Bert,

I know you are angry with me and I understand. It is a hard thing to want answers and not get them. I want you to know I am not angry with you. You asked me why I came for you when you were fifteen. This is why: I looked at you and I saw myself. When I was your age, my life was hard. You get used to hardship when you don't know anything else. I didn't want you to get used to it. After your sister and your father disappeared, I wanted you to know something other than sadness and loss. I came for you because I thought I could help you escape from grief.

I was wrong.

One person cannot save another person from grieving. It was wrong for me to try. Time is the only thing that makes grief bearable, not because it makes you forget but because you learn to live with your loss. It becomes a part of you. The hourglass charm is filled with wildflower seeds rather than sand. If you scattered them in a patch of dirt, they would grow. Something from nothing.

When I was young, I wanted to travel and see the world. You've already traveled farther than I ever could. But I have seen an awful lot of the world from this little spot in White Forest. Everything the world has to offer is here.

I'm not sorry I came for you. Most of the young women I deal with are weak and desperate. You have never been weak or desperate. Neither have I. Not even when my parents died. Not even when I was giving birth. Not even when I believed I'd lost everything. Not even when I pulled you into the world.

We are more alike than we have any right to be, Bert.

Happy birthday. I love you.

Clementine

P.S. The story of your father's childhood isn't mine to tell.

I didn't call Granny Clem or write her back right away, but I kept the folded letter with me nearly all the time. I put it in my pocket each morning alongside the quarry rock and the anhinga carving and the photo of Daddy and Uncle Chester and the girl. I kept everything in a sealed plastic bag so I wouldn't destroy it when I went out on the water. Willet never asked about any of it. He'd turned over the clues, just as he'd turned over the keys to his truck. Somehow Willet had managed to move on with his life, but I couldn't. Not yet.

I felt like the answers were right in front of me, like I was staring into a blind spot. If I could soften my gaze or shift my vision, the shadows and ghosts would come together as something solid and true. The mysteries of the Everglades were no easier to solve than the mysteries of the quarry and the haunted woods. The trees had shifted from oak and pecan and water ash to mangrove and cypress and gumbo-limbo, but the shadows were the same. The creature from my childhood, any creature, could hide in these trees just as easily as it hid in the trees back home.

Over the next few months I spent every clear morning on the water in my kayak. I explored islands and inlets and bays. Iggy taught me how to read a map and a compass. He taught me how to read the sky. I paddled farther from shore, leaving behind the rivers and venturing fully into the wider waters of the Gulf. I imagined Daddy taking the same routes in the rowing skiff he bought from the old man in Chokoloskee. My charm bracelet clacked against my paddle and I began to feel a new strength in my shoulders. The water calmed my mind. I remembered how comfortable Pansy had been on the water, how she swam and floated without fear. I never felt so brave about swimming. I needed the security of my kayak, something to separate me from the swirling, menacing water, but I understood, finally, how Pansy must have felt when we left her in the quarry. I understood why she wouldn't give up such a peaceful feeling to tromp the woods and search for berries. We were wrong to leave her, and she was right to stay. I wished I could tell her so.

Whenever I got off the water, I spent a few hours with Iggy. He taught me how to paddle more efficiently and how to seek shelter in a storm. "Soon," he said, "I'll have you leading tourists through the tunnels."

It sounded better than selling cheap souvenirs to sunburnt families, which was the only other job I seemed qualified to land. It was clear that we weren't going back to White Forest anytime soon, though I supposed I could go on my own. I no longer felt the strong pull to go home. I'd begun to feel as if I had no place of my own in the world. I had no idea what I was supposed to do with my life. I couldn't picture going back and working with Granny Clem. Cheryl said she'd let me know about any openings at the grocery store, but I didn't foresee much joy in the prospect of ringing up fish dip and live bait. Willet told me not to worry about working. He made enough money for both of us, but I knew I couldn't rely on him forever. I was old enough to earn my own way. Iggy employed a few seasonal tour guides, mostly students taking time off from studying botany or marine biology. I didn't have their expertise, but Iggy said he could teach me enough to keep the tourists satisfied.

"Most of them want wild stories more than anything," Iggy said. "I can fill your head with wild stories."

Iggy told me about the Calusa and Seminole Indians who'd settled the area. He said he was part Seminole on his maternal grandmother's side. "I don't claim it official, though. I don't like being pinned to one group or another. If you claim it, you gotta live by their ways." I understood.

Iggy told me about the sugar baron from Arkansas who'd been shot to death in the middle of town. The man bragged he'd killed fifty men and the Queen of the Outlaws. The residents of the Everglades believed in second chances. They believed a man with a bad past should have a chance to start new, but this man wasn't interested in starting new. He stole their land and one of their wives. "He needed killing," Iggy said. "When a man needs killing that bad, you can't sit around and wait for the law to handle it."

Iggy taught me to recognize the poisonous snakes and the harmless ones. He taught me the difference between alligators and crocodiles. He showed me how to pull meat from the claws of the stone crab without shredding it. He gave me advice about navigating the maze of islands and mangrove tunnels. He taught me to pay heed to the tides and the wind. Sometimes I got lost, but I always found my way back.

"WHAT HAVE YOU DONE?" Fern asked him, when Earl showed up with Pansy at her house late the next day. Fern bathed Pansy and made her a sandwich, but she wouldn't eat. Earl sat at the kitchen table, his head in his hands. He felt like a man waking up from a long, deep sleep.

"She's sick," Fern said. "Feverish."

Fern tucked the girl into her own bed with one of the rag dolls from White Forest. The doll contained a pouch of dried lavender, she told Earl. A soothing scent. At its heart was an empty cradle, no bigger than her pinkie toe, carved from a bit of soft gray driftwood.

"They'll be searching for you," she said. "For both of you."

"I can't send her back there." He told Fern how he'd found her floating in the quarry.

Fern was incensed. "What kind of mother allows such a thing?"

"She doesn't understand," he said of Loretta. "She doesn't have the same history we do."

Fern told him there could be no excuse for such carelessness. "You understand you can never go back," she said. "Not for any reason."

He thought about the birth certificate he'd taken from Clementine so long ago. He'd known he would need it someday. He could become someone new.

"Can you leave your wife?" Fern asked. "Can you leave your children? Can you leave Clementine and Chester? Forever?"

He swore he could. It was a terrible thing they were planning, but no more terrible than the things done to them.

They sat up with her for three days, pressing cool cloths to her forehead and replacing the bedding when her fever broke. Fern sent her brother to Naples to purchase clothes for the girl. He came back with T-shirts and cotton shorts and a pair of plastic sandals.

He called Chester, who told him the police were searching for him. He knew Chester would never betray him, but he didn't admit to having Pansy. He said he'd be gone for a while and he didn't want anyone coming after him. Chester said he understood. Pansy slept while he and Fern talked about what to do next. Earl said they had to tell the child something to explain why she'd been uprooted from her home.

"We'll tell her there was an accident," Fern said. "She's young. Her memories will fade."

Earl thought back to the years before his mother died, when he was as young as Pansy. His memories of those years were fragmented and fuzzy, but not gone. Fern knew what he was thinking. "Clementine always said people believe what you tell them to believe," Fern said. "Your daughter will believe what you tell her."

On the fourth day, Pansy woke with an appetite and Fern brought her a bowl of barely warm broth and a sleeve of saltine crackers. Fern looked happy. He couldn't take Pansy back now. Too much time had passed and the detectives were searching for him and his wife would never forgive him, just as he couldn't forgive her for letting his children swim in the quarry and play in the woods. Things had gone too far. He couldn't unspool the mess he'd made. And as he watched Fern care for Pansy, he believed he'd done the right thing. His sister needed a child to love.

SIXTEEN

IT WAS LATE JULY when I pulled the kayak onto an island on the south edge of Chokoloskee Bay. We'd been in the Everglades for nearly seven months and the one thing I'd come to expect were the unpredictable storms that seemed to churn up out of nothing and pass just as quickly.

That morning, wind swept over the water in a sudden gust. The sky turned from bright blue to slate gray. Thunder rumbled. Rain blew in from the Atlantic. I dragged the kayak to a high spot on the sandbar. The morning had been a scorcher and I'd been paddling for hours. I welcomed a bit of cooling rain. From the looks of the sky, I figured it would be at least an hour before I could head back. The island where I landed was an old Calusa shell mound and I thought I heard children laughing as I pushed past the rim of mangroves, but it was only birds calling or maybe the ghosts of an ancient family.

Rain came down dark and sideways. At the island's high point, I found a small fisher's cabin on concrete blocks. Even in town people rarely locked their doors and I wasn't surprised to find the cabin open. I ducked inside. A jar of peanut butter and a sleeve of unopened crackers sat on the counter. A half dozen cans of potted meat and generic label soup were stacked next to an aluminum pot and a pile of newspapers. A camp stove and a container of propane sat beside a small sink. I found a stash of paper towels, a roll of plastic wrap, and a tube of tinfoil. Three fishing poles and a good-size net leaned against one wall. A tackle box was tucked behind a rolled sleeping bag. I wondered how often someone slept in the small cabin and why. Did they come here to escape something or because they wanted to be alone? Iggy had told me about the hermits who lived on some of these islands, but I could tell no one lived in that cabin year-round. It smelled musty and stale. The countertops were furred over with a thin layer of dust. I lit one of the propane lanterns, figuring no one would mind if I used a bit of fuel. I pulled a newspaper from a stack near the sink and settled into one of the folding chairs. *The Gulf Breeze* published tide tables and big fish stories alongside classifieds for swap meets and boat sales. It wasn't exactly riveting reading, but it was all I had.

I flipped through the February edition from 1980 and wondered why someone would keep a newspaper for more than a year. Most of the stories were about the price of stone crabs and the high school baseball season. But on the fourth page, below the fold, I found this article:

Fisherman Reports Close Encounter with Skunk Ape
by Letitia Duplass, staff reporter

Grandin Bell was setting crab traps near Dead Man's Key just after midnight when he spotted unusual movement among the mangroves.

"I heard something strange," Bell said. "My first thought was a big alligator, but then I saw yellow glowing eyes coming from a spot about eight feet high. It was bigger than any man or bear I've ever seen and the smell would just about knock you out."

Bell said a smell "like rotting flesh" filled the air in the moments before he spotted the creature, which he described as "a great ape in need of a haircut."

Reported sightings of the large apelike creature date back more than a hundred years. More common are reports of the terrible smell associated with the creature. Known as the Southern Bigfoot, the Swamp Ape, the Skunk Monkey, and various other names, the Skunk Ape is part of the folklore of the Florida Everglades and widely considered a myth.

J. L. Stinson, wildlife biologist from the University of Florida, says Bell may have seen a large black bear. Stinson says the strong smell reported by Bell could be attributed to a number of things, including a dead animal along the banks of the river.

Bell disputes Stinson's assertion that the Skunk Ape is a myth. "I know what I saw and I won't rest until I prove it," he said. Bell has been making nightly excursions into the swamp to hunt for the Skunk Ape. "I don't intend to harm him," Bell said. "I'm just looking for proof."

Bell takes out tours most nights, weather permitting. The cost is 50 dollars per passenger. He says the money he collects is used to offset his cost for fuel and to invest in night vision goggles and photography equipment.

Interested persons should meet Bell at sunset at the northeast launch off Sweet Nectar Road. He accepts passengers on a first come, first-served basis.

The man in the picture wore a full beard and his hair was dark black. He smiled. He was heavier than I remembered or his beard made his face seem fuller, but I knew him. I'd know him anywhere. The man who called himself Grandin Bell was my father.

I pressed my face close to the newsprint photo and then held it at arm's length. I ran my fingers over it, softly, so as not to smudge the ink. I imagined I could feel the contours of his cheekbones. The article and photo were dated four months before we got the call about Daddy's body. The detective told us Daddy's teeth were rotted and his body was destroyed by alcohol and years of living on the streets, but in this photo Daddy looked healthy and strong. His teeth were straight and white. I worked to make sense of things, but I kept coming back to the most sensible idea: we'd buried some stranger's rotting corpse. The stench at the funeral was the stench of deception, the stench of lies and secrets left too long to fester. But why? I wanted to launch the kayak in the middle of the storm to find Willet, but rain pounded against the roof of the cabin and wind wailed through the trees. Getting on the water would be suicide. I waited.

I laid the contents of my plastic bag alongside the article: the quarry rock, Granny Clem's letter, the anhinga carving, and the photo of Daddy as a teenager. I compared the face from the photo to the face of the man in the newspaper. You had to want to see the resemblance, but I saw it. The smile, the eyes, the bare tilt of the head; there it was. There he was.

"Daddy," I said.

I put my hand on the quarry rock. It was warm and growing warmer. The wind, the rain, the choppy waters beneath my kayak had delivered me to the cabin and to the newspaper as surely as the oppressive heat had delivered us to the quarry on the day Pansy disappeared. Willet said monsters weren't real, but I knew better. Superstition was my birthright. Ignoring the signs never led me any closer to the truth. No matter what Willet said, the creature from the woods was real, the quarry was cursed, the ghosts took my breath away, and no amount of explaining made any of it less terrifying. But even though it scared me, I closed my eyes and begged for more.

In August it would be five years since Pansy disappeared, even longer since Daddy left us. Mama had tried to wait and hope and pray for them to come back to her, but waiting and hoping and praying didn't do a damn bit of good. She'd died with nothing. Willet played amateur detective by gathering bits of evidence and showing it to strangers. His way got us no closer to the truth. Granny Clem distracted us with lies and secrets. Uncle Chester hid away in his fetid trailer like a hermit without an island. Bubba, poor Bubba who wandered into our family tragedy, could only point at the sky and blame others. And I kept right on denying I believed in anything unbelievable. All of us had spent years averting our gaze from any hint of the ugly truth, but I was done looking away.

I launched the kayak as soon as the rain slowed to a drizzle. Waves slopped over the side of the boat, soaking my legs and my seat. My charm bracelet clacked against my paddle. I'd folded the newspaper article in the plastic bag where I kept my growing collection of clues.

It was early afternoon when I pulled back into shore. Sunshine pushed the clouds apart and burned off any coolness left from the rain. The Osprey was tethered to the dock, which meant Willet and Audie were off the water. I hoped Willet would be at the apartment. He rarely spent a night there anymore, but some days he stopped by to shower and nap while Cheryl worked. I worried about his reaction to my discovery. What if Willet didn't see what I saw in the photo? I stood in the parking lot and pulled the article from the plastic. The face in the photo was Daddy's face, familiar beneath the beard. He would see it as I saw it. I'd make him see the truth.

But when I went inside, Willet was sitting on the sofa with Cheryl. He was always with Cheryl and I was sick of it. She'd changed Willet in ways I didn't like. And now, when I had something important to tell my brother, she was there, taking up his attention and crying like a fool.

"Hi, Bert," she said, her voice thick. "I'm an idiot."

"Why aren't you at work?" I asked.

"You're not an idiot," Willet said to Cheryl. "Give us a minute," he said to me.

"But, Willet . . ." I held the paper out to him.

"Not now."

I should have listened to the tone of his voice. I should have waited and talked to him when I could get him alone, but I wasn't thinking about what I should do. I was only thinking about what I'd learned and how it changed everything. We'd come to this place searching for information about our father. I had real information.

How could anything Cheryl said be more important? I pushed the paper between Willet and Cheryl.

"Just look," I said.

Willet slapped my hand away, leaving a tear across the image of Daddy's face. "Goddammit, Bert!"

I pulled the paper to my chest, protecting it from further injury. I kept my voice level, though it was a struggle. "This is important." If he would look at me, I knew he would understand, but he kept right on staring at Cheryl.

"Not now," he said.

I knew then that Willet was no better than anyone else in our family. He was afraid of the truth. I was on my own, all alone in my search for answers. I shut myself in my bedroom and examined the rip in the paper. It wasn't too bad. When I pushed the edges together, I could barely see the tear. All I needed was some tape. But I wouldn't be able to tape over the rift with Willet.

I tried to remember the last time he'd mentioned Daddy or Pansy. He'd given up on them. He'd given up on me. The newspaper rattled in my hands. My whole body shook and I felt cold, the sort of bone-deep cold that settles in on a damp winter's day. My arms ached from paddling the kayak through choppy waters. My clothes were damp and salt-stained. I pushed my fingers through my grimy, knotted hair, and shuddered. I was alone. Willet cared more about Cheryl than he cared about me. I stripped off my damp clothes. My teeth chattered and my legs cramped. The room was warm, but I couldn't shake off the chill. I curled up under a pile of blankets and closed my eyes.

Through the thin walls of the apartment, I listened to my brother and Cheryl murmuring. I heard Cheryl's sobs and her garbled, tear-choked voice. The conversation on the other side of the wall was mostly impossible to make out, but one word came through: *pregnant*. Cheryl was pregnant. She was pregnant and mystified like all the girls who came to see Granny Clem. And I knew what it meant. Cheryl would take my brother from me completely. I'd already lost him.

They talked for more than an hour. Cheryl's sobbing dried up. Their voices became softer and harder to make out. The cold in my body evaporated and gave way to a seething fury. This grocery clerk at the edge of the world had trapped my brother and would destroy his life. It was all so unnecessary. Willet knew it. I knew it. We'd grown up in the shadow of Granny Clem's business. No one needed to have a baby she didn't want. I waited until I heard them leave the apartment, then I pulled myself out of bed and took a long shower. They would be at Cheryl's house, I guessed, or at the bar. Willet would be full of guilt. I could picture him waiting on her, bringing her tissues and toast. I thought about how good he was with Mama when Pansy disappeared, how he remembered to keep the coffee going and how he offered mugs of it to anyone who came through the door. Offering up coffee and good manners was the only thing he could do when Pansy went missing, but now he had other options.

I called Granny Clem. The phone rang a half dozen times and I wondered if she was delivering a baby or working outside. When she finally picked up, her voice sounded thin and weak.

"Oh, hello, Bert. It's you." She sounded disappointed.

"Are you busy?"

"No more than usual." She sneezed, then coughed.

Granny Clem was never ill. She ate well and took her own medicinal teas as a preventative measure during the flu season.

"Are you okay?"

"I turned over a few of those raised beds and brought in some fresh soil. It's a lot of work. I overdid it."

A few years earlier I'd helped her turn the garden beds and rotate the plants. It was hard and filthy work. My shoulders and back had ached for days and I thought my fingernails would never come clean. Granny Clem was seventy years old and I couldn't imagine many seventy-year-old women who would take on such a task, but Granny Clem wasn't like other women.

"You should get Chester to help you with that kind of thing," I said.

"Easier to do it myself."

She coughed again. It sounded painful.

"Maybe you should see a doctor," I said.

"What do you want?" She sounded impatient.

"It's Willet," I said. "He's got his girlfriend pregnant and I need you to send us the herbs."

"How far along is the girl?" Granny Clem asked.

"I don't know," I said. "Not far."

"You know it won't work if she's too far along. Why don't you let me talk to her?"

"She's not here."

"Let me talk to Willet, then."

"He's not here either." She went quiet. I thought the phone might have gone dead.

"Did they ask you to call me?"

I admitted they hadn't, but said I knew Willet wasn't ready to be a father. Granny Clem emitted a noise that might have been a suppressed sneeze or might have been a snort of disgust.

"If Willet wants my help, you tell him to call me," she said. "Or tell him to drive his girlfriend to me and I'll do whatever I can to help them both. But you know better than this."

"But—"

I heard a loud clatter. Our apartment smelled of burnt toast and mildew, but for a moment I smelled lemons, strong and warm and sweet. "Granny Clem?"

She didn't answer.

I had a vision of her sprawled on the kitchen floor, a trickle of blood running from the corner of her mouth. She was wearing her leather work boots and one of her long, faded skirts. Her hair was loose and it flowed across the white tile like water. I was so used to people dying or leaving. It was easy to imagine her gone.

"Granny Clem?" I said again.

"I dropped the cake."

I was relieved to hear her speak.

"I was pulling a cake from the oven and I lost my grasp."

Was it possible to smell a cake across a phone line or had I heard the sounds of her baking so often it triggered some sort of sense memory? Or was I losing my mind?

"I found a picture of Daddy," I told her.

"Which one?"

I could hear her scraping the mess off the floor. She breathed hard and wheezed with the exertion of sweeping or stooping. She sounded worn out.

"In the newspaper," I said. "He had a beard. He called himself Grandin Bell."

I heard a thump and pictured her sitting at the kitchen table. I sat at our own table and imagined I was looking across at Granny Clem. I wished I had a mug of tea. I wished I had a slice of the ruined cake.

"Grandin Bell?"

"That's right."

"Are you sure?"

I read the article aloud to her and described the photo as best I could. "It's him," I said. "I'm sure of it."

Granny Clem coughed and I listened while she blew her nose.

"I don't think we buried Daddy in White Forest," I told her. "I think Daddy is still alive." I waited for her to tell me I was being ridiculous.

"If your father is alive," she said, "he's gone to a good bit of trouble to hide that fact. You ought to be careful."

She believed me.

"Daddy wouldn't hurt me," I said.

"A desperate man will do most anything to protect himself."

How much did she know? I asked her and I tried to keep my voice from sounding like I was accusing her of anything. I didn't want her to get defensive. I didn't want to fight with her. She coughed again and I waited for her to finish. I heard the sound of running water. She was filling a kettle or soaking a sponge to clean up the mess of cake. Granny Clem never could sit still during a phone call.

"Bert, did you get my letter?"

"Don't change the subject."

"The last time we talked was more than three months ago. And now you call as if no time has passed, begging favors you've got no right to beg."

"But—"

"You were spitting mad at me for giving babies away."

"No," I said. "I was mad at you for lying about it. I think those babies have the right to know the truth."

"The truth about how their mothers didn't want them?"

"The truth about who they really are. The truth about their families."

"But what good comes of that knowledge? What if you were to discover that we didn't share a drop of true family blood; how would you feel?"

It was inconceivable. Granny Clem and I were alike in so many ways. If we weren't family, what would I owe her and what would she owe me? Granny Clem had brought me into the world with her own two hands and she'd come for me when I needed saving. Why would she go to so much trouble if we weren't a true family? I said as much and she laughed.

"But that's my point. We *are* family. No matter what. Sometimes people are born to the wrong mother. I'm not lying to those children. I'm making them a family. I made a family for your father and for you and your brother and your sister. It isn't about blood or a particular name, none of that matters. You are my family. You belong to me and I belong to you. You can throw a fit and not speak to me for a year or two years or for the rest of your life, but it won't change a thing. You're mine. Do you understand?"

I didn't understand, not then. I thought she was speaking in hypotheticals. I thought she was trying to avoid talking about Daddy. I thought she was working to distract me from the news of Cheryl's pregnancy.

"I'm tired," she said. "I'm glad to talk to you, but I need some rest. If Willet and that girl want my help, you tell them to give me a call. And if you go searching after your father, be careful. Don't spook him." She hung up before I could ask anything else.

Willet didn't come home that night or the next. I called Cheryl's house and asked to speak with him. "He's out with Audie," Cheryl said. "But we have some news. We were going to call you. Will you meet us at the Crab House for dinner?"

I didn't want to have dinner with Cheryl and Audie. I already knew Cheryl's news. I wanted to talk to Willet, but I agreed to meet them. I figured I could get Willet alone and show him the photo of Daddy.

When I got to the Crab House, the three of them were already there. They sat in the dining room instead of the bar and there was a pitcher of sweet tea on the table instead of a pitcher of beer. Cheryl grinned and stood to hug me. She was full of some sort of manic energy and I didn't like it.

"Willet," I said. "I need to talk to you. Alone."

"Sit down," he said.

"But, Willet . . ."

"We want to tell you something. Please."

I didn't sit. I already knew about Cheryl's pregnancy and I wasn't going to pretend to be surprised. "I know she's pregnant." I didn't look at Cheryl or Audie. I kept my focus on Willet. "Granny Clem said you should call her and she'll help you handle it, but I have something to show you. It's important."

Willet stood so quickly the table shook. He grabbed my arm and steered me out the front door. It was a warm night and the smell of fried fish wafted from the restaurant. I heard rock music playing in the bar.

"What the hell is the matter with you?"

"What's the matter with you?" I said. "You know you don't have to do this."

"I love Cheryl."

"You hardly know her and you don't know what you're getting yourself into." I told him about the nights I'd sat up with the newborns, all the nights I listened to them cry. Willet didn't have any idea how difficult babies could be.

"I'm not letting Granny Clem kill my child."

"It's not a child. It's tissue," I said. "It's smaller than a squash seed, and anyhow we didn't come here so you could knock some girl up and ruin your life. We came here for Daddy and Pansy. Why can't you remember that?"

A man pulled open the door of the restaurant and we were hit by a blast from the air-conditioning.

"My life isn't ruined," Willet said. "I'm sick of living in the past. I can't keep doing it. I can't keep reliving the same goddamned story every day of my life. Our father left us. Our sister disappeared. It's a crying shame, but I can't do a goddamned thing about it. Neither can you. We've got to move on. Can't you see that?"

"No," I told him. "And you've got no business having a child. Pansy didn't disappear. We left her. You left her. You were the oldest. You were supposed to take care of us. If you can't keep track of your little sister, how can you possibly be responsible for a baby?"

He looked at me like I was a stranger, like I was someone he didn't recognize. "Go home," he said. "Go to the apartment or go home to Granny Clem, but I don't want you here tonight."

"You can't make me leave."

"I asked Cheryl to marry me. She said yes. We're happy. That was the news."

I left him standing outside the restaurant and pushed my way past a large family in the parking lot. There must have been a dozen of them, three generations at least, and I walked right through them. I hated them without knowing who they were. I hated them for seeming whole and complete and happy. Back at the apartment, I ate canned tuna on crackers and drank a lukewarm beer. I hoped Willet would call to apologize, but the phone didn't ring. I knew what I needed to do. I would have to do it alone.

EARL WAS FISHING WHEN he saw something odd moving
through the trees on a nearby island, something large and dark. For
more than three years he'd been living like a ghost. He didn't use
the name Earl anymore, even with Fern. For the most part, he used
no name at all. He didn't speak to anyone unless it was absolutely
necessary. Sometimes he crashed at Fern's house, but mostly he slept
on the boat he'd bought in Chokoloskee or camped on one of the
islands. He'd stashed his counterfeit bills among the mangroves.
Every few months he made a trip to Naples or to Miami where he
could spend the cash in anonymity and then return the items for
real money. Most of the cash went to Fern and to Pansy, though
Pansy wasn't Pansy anymore. Fern called her Hope. She'd been right
about the child's memory. As time passed, she seemed to remember
less and less about the time before he'd taken her from the quarry.
During the first year she sometimes asked about her mother and her
brother and sister, but not anymore. The girl was nine years old and
smarter than any child he'd ever known. Fern homeschooled her for
the first two years, not wanting to let the girl out of her sight, but in

third grade she enrolled her in the public school. Fern couldn't keep the girl hidden forever.

Isolation suited Earl, but sometimes nightmares rolled in swift as the Gulf Stream and then he wished for the distraction of people. When the night terrors left him sweat soaked, panicked, and sleepless, he poured the dark stories from his mind into the notebook he carried with him everywhere. Somehow it helped to write things down and he was always surprised by the details that came to him— bits of conversation, the chill in the air from a hundred years ago, the ache of an ancient wound. Sometimes he felt sorrow for what he'd done, for taking a child from her mother, for running away, for abandoning his family back in White Forest, but he was not a man who dwelled on regret. He'd lost his own mother at a young age and his own father had abandoned him. It brought him to Clementine and Ora and Chester. What would his life be like if he'd never met them? Life unfolded in strange and wonderful and tragic ways. His youngest daughter would be fine.

When Earl spotted the odd thing in the trees, he rowed his boat to the island to investigate. He didn't use his trolling motor, afraid the noise might spook the creature. There were tales of a Southern Bigfoot, a Skunk Monkey, a Swamp Ape. Every community had its legends. What Earl saw, though, was no fabled creature; it was a man in a costume. Earl knew it by the way the creature moved, too upright to be an ape of any kind. In the past years Earl had dyed his hair, grown a beard, put on weight, and gone into hiding. He knew there were all sorts of reasons a man might put on a disguise.

On that November day in 1979, Earl tried to talk to the man in the ape suit, but the man disappeared into a small shelter and Earl knew better than to push his way into anyone's home uninvited. Still, he was curious and the man in the costume gave him an idea. He missed working, even if the only work he'd ever known was counterfeiting bills and laundering money. There was an art to deception and Earl was naturally gifted. Seeing the man in the ape suit got him thinking about a new scheme. The fake cash wouldn't hold out forever. Eventually he'd have to find a way to earn new money. And he needed to try out his new identity, to make sure it would hold up in the world. He couldn't live like a ghost forever. Over the next few weeks, Earl brought bottles of rum and fresh propane and cartons of cigarettes and left them near the man's shelter. After a few trips, the man emerged to ask him what the hell he thought he was doing. The man's voice sounded scratchy and raw, like he didn't use it too often. He told Earl he didn't need any do-gooders trying to save him. Earl assured the man he was no do-gooder.

"Talk to me about the ape suit," Earl said.

The man didn't answer right away. He lit a cigarette and stared past Earl. He looked embarrassed. "I found it," he said. "In a Goodwill bin after Halloween. I thought I could use it to scare people off."

"You get a lot of visitors out here?"

The man shrugged. "Sometimes the tourists bring their boats out. I don't want them camping on my land."

Earl knew the island didn't belong to the man. No one owned the land in these waters, though the government was trying to lay claim to it and regulate it to death. But Earl knew what he meant. The man had staked this place out as his home and he didn't feel like sharing it.

"I'm Grandin Bell," Earl said. He held out his hand. "I have a proposition for you. If you don't like it, I'll go away and you'll never see me again. That's a promise."

The man looked him in the eye for the first time, seemed to consider his trustworthiness. Finally he shook Earl's outstretched hand. "Jonathan Biggums," he said. "I'm listening."

Earl poured them both a drink and laid out his plans for the Skunk Ape tours. "The legend already exists. People want to believe it." Earl said he would split the earnings with Jonathan, but Jonathan pointed out he didn't have many places to spend money. "I can bring you what you need," Earl said. "Booze, smokes, gas, fresh water, books. You could live more comfortably."

As they worked out the details, Earl learned how Jonathan came to be living at Dead Man's Key. When he'd returned from his tour in Vietnam, he'd camped on the island and planned to stay for a few weeks. But he liked the peace of it and as the years rolled by he could think of no good reason to leave. "I can stand anything but people," he often said. Jonathan came to stand Earl, though. They became friends.

The tours were popular. Tourists were willing to pay good money for a cheap thrill. He nearly abandoned the scheme when the reporter contacted him. The girl wasn't much older than twenty and she didn't identify herself as a reporter until they were on the water. He'd thought she was just a tourist with a lot of questions. She'd taken his picture without his permission while he chatted with a man from Arizona. He'd been smiling and the snapshot looked like something posed. When the article came out, he feared someone might recognize him from before. For weeks, he looked at the people on the boat and wondered if one of them might be a local detective or an FBI agent. He thought he might need to disappear again, but no one came for him.

Earl liked working with Jonathan, but Jonathan liked his liquor. For years, the isolation and lack of resources had kept his cravings in check. He'd go on a bender twice a year, when he traveled inland to cash his benefits checks and stock up on supplies, but he didn't have the resources to be a drunk. With the tours, though, he had more money than he'd seen in years. When he sent Earl for supplies, he requested more liquor than food.

In June of 1980, Earl found Jonathan sprawled facedown on the floor of his cabin. His pants were stained with dried urine and his face was caked with vomit. He clutched an empty pint of rum in his right hand. His feet were bare and the left toes were purple and swollen from an infected cut along the sole. Earl hated to see his friend in such a state, but it gave him an idea. The men were roughly the same height and weight. Jonathan was a good bit younger, but he didn't look it. All those years of hiding and lying and hoping no one recognized him; Earl could put an end to it. No one was looking for Jonathan and no one would miss him.

Earl wrapped Jonathan's body in a tarp and loaded it into his boat. He rowed through the shallow, mangrove-tangled inlets. It was early evening when he reached the dock where he kept his truck. Light began to leak from the sky. He caught his foot on a tree root while carrying the body from the boat to the bed of his truck. He pulled on a wide-brimmed hat and a pair of sunglasses despite the falling dusk. At the Glades Motel, he paid cash—real cash, not the fake stuff. The trickiest part was getting the body into the room without being seen. Anyone might peep out of one of the motel windows and wonder what was being hauled through the door of room seventeen. He relied on the innate discretion of the sort of men who stayed in such motels.

Inside, he removed the man's boots and socks, gagging at the rotten odor wafting from his feet. He placed a few empty bottles of rum around the room, hung a couple of shirts in the closet. The idea was to make it look like the man had spent at least a couple of days there before dying. He wasn't sure how accurately the police could figure time of death, but he knew it wasn't an exact science. Everything would be tougher to calculate once the body decayed, and, by the smell of things, that process had begun. He placed the wallet on the bedside table. It contained his expired driver's license from Mississippi. He double-checked the man's pockets for anything that might identify him. He found nothing. When they found this body, they would believe it belonged to Earl Watkins and if Earl Watkins was dead, he could stop running and worrying. No one would search for a dead man.

SEVENTEEN

—◆—

DEAD MAN'S KEY LAY about seventeen miles southwest of Everglades City, according to Iggy's map. I loaded up with supplies including a plastic tarp for shelter, granola bars, and beef jerky. I filled empty milk and soda bottles with fresh water. August wasn't the best time to make such a trip. It was when the weather was most unpredictable and the waters were high, but I couldn't wait. I'd been waiting for five years. I needed answers. Maybe I wouldn't find anything at Dead Man's Key, but the newspaper article said my father had traveled there. Maybe by following in his wake I would uncover something important.

I didn't tell anyone about my plans. Iggy would have tried to talk me out of it. Willet and I weren't speaking. I left a note at the apartment for Willet, though he rarely came by anymore. It didn't say much: "On the water for a few days. Back soon. Don't worry."

I waited until the weather forecasters announced a string of clear days. Maybe an afternoon thunderstorm, they said, but it would be mostly clear and dry. Hot, as always. Good weather for barbecues and picnics and swimming. I filled the dry bag on the kayak with my supplies. I figured I could be gone for two days, maybe three, before anyone started to worry.

I launched the kayak at the Barron River just after sunrise. The early morning sun spilled white light across lapping waves and the breeze smelled salty and fresh. I dipped my paddle into the warm sepia-colored water near the river mouth and propelled my boat toward the deep green expanse of Chokoloskee Bay. A large piece of sun-bleached driftwood jutted from the water like a giant arm reaching toward the sky. I stepped out to pull the kayak across a narrow sandbar and my bare feet sucked against the soft damp surface. Soon I reached deeper water. As the sun rose higher, I pushed south, paddling with the current, though I knew I'd have to turn west at some point. I'd been nervous about venturing out so far alone, but it was a beautiful morning and the tides were in my favor. I avoided high-traffic channels where fishing boats sped across the bay, bringing in the evening's catch. I wondered if Willet and Audie were on the water. I paddled through the rookery, beneath the shadows of the mangroves. It was oddly quiet and I assumed the birds were off hunting food, but now I wonder if the birds knew something I didn't. Maybe they were trying to warn me.

The heat rose quickly. There were a few white clouds scattered across the bright blue sky, but those puny clouds were no match for the blazing sun. Sweat poured across my face and chest. My hands felt slippery against the paddle. If I were out paddling for fun, I'd rest or turn back on such a warm morning, but I pushed through, unwilling to get off schedule so early in the trip. I planned to stop somewhere along Indian Key Pass in the middle of the day to rest and eat something. There were islands there with sandbars and decent shelter, and there were chickee huts scattered through the waters—elevated wooden shelters with thatched roofs in the style of old Seminole houses. During the tourist season the shelters might be occupied by campers, but I suspected most would be empty in the summer. It was hot but clear. I hoped the good weather would hold, but storms came most afternoons no matter what the forecasters said, just as they had in White Forest five years ago, during the summer of Pansy's disappearance.

I kept my strokes low and smooth, like Iggy had taught me, and rowed in the direction of a wide low-slung string of islands in the distance. A pod of dolphins danced ahead of me and I followed in their wake, knowing the water would always be deep enough where they swam. I imagined those dolphins were guiding me toward my father. I made good progress the first morning, traveling farther and faster than I anticipated, but after noon the sky turned gray and the breeze turned to a strong wind. I pulled my boat toward a small island. The water bucked beneath me. I felt very small all of a sudden. I leaned into the paddle and dug hard toward the narrow strip of sand on the edge of the island. When the kayak scraped against the sand, I jumped out and hauled the boat to higher ground. I tethered the kayak to a sturdy root and rested on a large piece of driftwood. I watched the gray sky darken through the thick canopy of silvery-green leaves. I didn't mind getting wet. It was the wind that worried me. I'd read stories of men being swept out to sea and never heard from again. I knew tropical winds could blow in without warning, but it had been a calm storm season. We'd had plenty of rain, but nothing destructive. Still, as I crouched beneath the shelter of the mangroves, I wondered if I should turn back. I ate one of the granola bars and drank a bit of water.

Rain fell through much of the afternoon. I was chilled and tired by the time the storm passed but determined to keep moving. There were still a few hours of daylight left. I launched the kayak and pressed forward. It was rough, but I did as Iggy taught me and kept the nose of my kayak pointing into the chop. It was easy to see how a strong wave hitting the side of my boat might flip me over. The heat rose again. The tides shifted. I set my intentions toward the west, but the tides kept urging me north.

Iggy had taught me to read channel markers and there were a few signs along the water. I consulted my map and turned toward West Pass. Soon I was paddling through a thick grove of trees, my route no wider than a large stream. According to the map, I should have been traveling west through a wide channel, but my compass said I was traveling east. It made no sense. East was exactly the wrong direction. I thought something must be wrong with my compass and I was damn sure going to give Iggy a piece of my mind about his crappy equipment.

After an hour in the pass, though, I realized the sun was dipping behind me and I knew the compass wasn't to blame; the map was wrong or I'd misread the channel markers. I spun around and retraced my path. I found myself back at the same island where I'd sheltered earlier, exhausted and frustrated. I decided to camp for the night and start fresh in the morning. It was getting late and I didn't want to be on the water in the dark. I knew predators were most active at dawn and dusk. Shark attacks were rare, but they happened.

And there were more aggressive predators to worry about. I'd heard the stories. I knew about the mother who fished on the banks of the Allen River, the same place she'd fished for a dozen years, a place where she felt as safe as she felt in her home, until an alligator crawled out of the water and clamped its massive jaws around the torso of her two-year-old son. She didn't have time to scream before the creature dragged the boy beneath the water's surface. I'd met the woman. She told the story to anyone who'd listen, and there always came a point where it seemed it might turn out okay, where you hoped she would tell you the boy got away, or the gator was killed by a passing hunter, or the whole thing was some big misunderstanding, but the story always ended the same way. She never saw the boy again, never saw a splash or a struggle. Her son disappeared into the muddy waters and it was like he'd never lived.

"I couldn't even tell him goodbye," she'd say, as if *that* were the big tragedy.

And I knew the story of the fisherman who'd sliced open his hand with a boning knife and dropped his bloody palm into the Gulf of Mexico for a rinse. The shark must have already been swimming beneath his boat to strike so quickly. He made it to the hospital on his own, though the doctors said he should have been unconscious with the loss of blood. They chopped off his arm above the elbow, leaving a web of purple scars around the stump. The man said he figured it was the worst boning knife injury in the history of mankind.

And I knew about the teenagers who'd sneaked off from a church picnic to make out in a copse of cypress trees alongside a canal. They never saw the nest of water moccasins, but the whole congregation came running when they heard the girl scream. The doctor joked about the effectiveness of the cottonmouth contraception.

There were stories of coral snakes and bears, of crocodiles and panthers, of quicksand and poison plants. I did not want to become one of the stories people told.

I ate a granola bar and doused my neck and ankles with bug juice. The sun set over the water and turned the blue sky yellow before fading to black. I made sure to fix the direction in my mind. When I set out tomorrow, I'd head west no matter what the map said. Even with the bug juice, mosquitoes buzzed against my face and neck. I pulled the tarp tight around me and lay back on the sand. A bird squawked, a frog croaked, and water lapped against the shore. I tried not to think too much about the wild animals all around me. Iggy always said most animals wouldn't bother you if you didn't bother them. I hoped he was right. The night sky filled with stars and I watched a few thin clouds float across the moon. No matter how I turned, I couldn't get comfortable. The sand beneath my back felt like concrete. Between the hard, unforgiving sand and the strange noises, I didn't believe I would ever sleep. I must have dozed, because I woke to a stabbing pain in my right shoulder as the sky was just beginning to take on the first gray light of morning. I massaged my aching shoulder and hoped it was nothing more than a muscle cramp.

Mosquitoes packed my nostrils and ears. I spat on the ground to clear the bugs from my mouth. When I rolled from my tarp, I felt something slither across my calf. The bottle of bug juice I'd brought was half gone already, but I squirted a liberal amount in my hands and rubbed it across my face and neck. My back and legs ached from sleeping on the hard sand, and my shoulders were sore from paddling. My hands were stiff as claws from gripping the paddle and I desperately wished for coffee. But my mood rose with the sun, which seemed to levitate from the water like an orange balloon on a string. It washed the sky with coral and pink, brighter than any neon sign. It was almost enough to make up for my breakfast of warm water and beef jerky. When the sky was fully lit, I launched the kayak. I didn't know what time it was. My watch had quit working.

I paddled through shallow water. Several times I had to climb out and pull the boat to deeper channels. I twisted my ankle stepping across the mangrove roots and coral. Sharp shell fragments tore at my feet. My arms and shoulders ached and the tops of my legs were burned bright red. A few times I thought I heard a motor in the distance, but I didn't come in contact with anyone. By midday, the water level rose and I navigated the channels without getting stuck. I nearly dug my paddle into a manatee, which I mistook for a mottled rock until it opened a lazy eye and scared the bejesus out of me. Most of the islands I passed were small and inaccessible, the roots of the mangroves like a web of hands clasped tight against intruders. Herons marched along the shoreline, watching for signs of prey. Osprey hovered in the sky. A saw-toothed crocodile no longer than my forearm eyed me from its resting spot in a shaded cove. The mosquitoes grew more aggressive. They swarmed around my face in an angry mass and it took every ounce of courage to hang on to my paddle. Iggy said every creature had a divine purpose, but I could see no reason for mosquitoes to live.

By late afternoon, I was a mess of stinging welts and sunburn and frustration. Frankly, I was lost. None of the markers I searched for were where I expected them to be. No matter which direction I turned my kayak everything looked the same. I'd been paddling for so long, it seemed impossible I wasn't there yet, but the landmarks I looked for didn't appear. It's like my map was created for a different Florida, one that no longer existed.

I spotted a dilapidated chickee shelter off the shore of a small island, not much more than a mudflat beneath a hammock of hardwoods. I decided to stop for the day. I didn't know where I was, but the elevated wooden shelter meant I could sleep off the hard sand that night. My feet sank into the mud and I fell to my knees when I disembarked. The kayak felt heavy, as if it were taking on the weight of my worry. I tied it to a wooden piling and climbed the ladder to the chickee. The thatched roof was worn, but it provided some shade from the brutal sun. I slathered my neck and shoulders with the bug juice and tried not to think what would happen when it ran out. My sunburnt skin felt raw and tender. I hadn't eaten in hours, but I wasn't hungry.

It was sometime in the late afternoon, the sun still well above the horizon, when I lay back on the wooden platform and closed my eyes. I woke with a start a few hours later when something crawled across my leg and burrowed beneath the elastic band of my shorts. I ran my hands around my waist and flicked away a large spider. It was only the beginning. Creeping, burrowing, biting, stinging insects seemed to crawl across every inch of my body. I was outnumbered. I cursed and screamed, though no one could hear me. I wished for a tent, something with a zipper and a screen. I used more bug juice, knowing I'd be out come morning. I hauled the tarp up to the chickee platform and wrapped it around me as a defense against the bugs. I tried not to cry. I'd been stupid to make this trip alone. The next day I would turn back. Maybe I could try again with better supplies.

I felt sick, thinking how I'd failed. I'd discovered nothing new about my father and now I was a mess of bug bites and sunburn and I was lost in a place where I might never be found. I hated myself. My brother was starting a family and a new life without me. I hadn't considered my own future. I was too busy chasing the past, chasing the ghosts of Daddy and Pansy.

It was dusk and clouds rolled in to obscure any sunset. Everything seemed gray and wet and filthy. Miserable and full of self-pity, I listened to the buzzing insects and the lapping water and the call of the birds. My T-shirt scraped against my raw skin, the cotton gone crunchy from saltwater and sweat. My palms oozed with blisters. I stank of chemical bug juice and rank body odor. The thought of clean, fresh bathwater filled with sweet-smelling soap nearly made me weep. I was desperate to eat something other than sugary granola bars and too-salty beef jerky. I wanted a beer or a Coke, anything with carbonation. I dreamed of these things when I managed to sleep. It was lovely, and in my dream I knew it wasn't real. *Whatever you do, don't wake up.*

At the first creep of dawn something rustled in the mud below the chickee hut. The scampering sound of small animals, a cackle that rang out like laughter, a vicious hiss; I hoped it was nothing more than a dream. I pulled myself from sleep and rolled out from under the tarp. It was still dark, nothing but soft gray light in the sky. The noise came from the direction of my kayak. I climbed down to investigate. A pair of glowing orange eyes met mine. I crept forward, hoping my movement would be enough to scare the creature away. That's when I saw the second set of eyes. And the third. Raccoons were feasting on my meager stash of food. I clapped my hands and charged forward, shouting. They scampered into the nearby trees, and I surveyed the damage.

One of the raccoons continued to lurk nearby. It staggered sideways a few steps, but kept its eyes on me. The creature seemed odd. It was a small raccoon, nothing like the ones in Mississippi, which could grow large as a dog. This one was no bigger than a small house cat, but even so, I wanted it to go away. I hissed at it, and waved my hands. Instead of leaving, it moved toward me. It *lurched* toward me. It had the gait and mannerisms of a man gone knee-walking drunk. There were rumors of moonshine stills on the islands and barrels of rum left behind from the days of prohibition. Maybe this raccoon had gotten into a stash of liquor. It made an odd noise, a high-pitched bark. It was not a noise I associated with raccoons. I backed away, hoping to keep some distance between us. Mercifully, a cloud moved and exposed the waning moon, giving me more light.

Here I was, in the land of crocodiles and alligators, sharks and stingrays, black bears and panthers, and my biggest threat was a barking drunk raccoon. It would be funny if I weren't lost and exhausted.

I made myself as big and noisy as possible, but this was no ordinary raccoon. Instead of running away, the raccoon charged at me in a flat-out sprint. I screamed and headed toward the chickee platform. The beast latched onto my leg and sank its sharp teeth into the flesh of my calf. I felt and heard something rip below my knee. I fell. I kicked at the creature with my free leg and twisted around to grasp at it with my hands. It sank its teeth and claws deeper into my flesh and hot pain seared through my entire body. I grabbed the creature with both hands, and pulled. It tore from my leg in a snarling fit, thrashing. I flung the devil away from me.

My injured leg squirted blood and I couldn't look at the jagged hole without feeling an urge to vomit. I scooted toward my kayak, keeping the raccoon in sight. It gathered itself to charge again. I reached behind me and grabbed the only weapon I had. When the raccoon ran at me, I swatted it with the flat of my paddle. It flew through the air and landed with a sick thump on the edge of the water. Still, it wasn't done. It came at me with its rodent paws held high. I raised the paddle and slammed it on the creature's small head. It barked and scrambled to escape, but I was too furious to let it go. It took a dozen blows to do the job, but by the time I finished, the raccoon was split nearly in two. Bloody entrails and gray fur stuck to the blade of my paddle.

I crouched in the fading moonlight, covered in mud and blood and sweat, panting and terrified and confused. I'd killed something in a fit of rage, and I had no remorse. I'd kill it again if I could. I'd spend the rest of my life killing that raccoon and not feel I'd wasted a moment. My heart seemed to beat through my whole body, a thrilling, pulsing rage.

I screamed into the sky, shouting with a fury that rose from my gut and rushed through my veins. I was angry with myself and with everyone who'd led me to that watery wilderness on the edge of the world. I was furious with my parents for their carelessness and their absence. Furious with my mother for the way she gave up on living. Furious with my sister for being born only to be lost. Furious with my brother, who should have watched us better. Furious with the woman from Pittsburgh for her dire and accurate predictions. Furious with Granny Clem for all the secrets and lies, and for playing God with the babies she birthed and sold. Furious with Bubba and his stupid aliens and his sad, pathetic life. Furious with Cheryl for getting pregnant. Furious with the dark water of the quarry and the dark water of the Gulf, and furious with the creature in the haunted woods and the beastly raccoon. I gave all my anger to the night sky, screaming until my voice was no more than a whimper. Some wild creature howled back at me, as if we were having a conversation.

Spent, I perched on the edge of the kayak and poured fresh water onto the gaping gash created by the raccoon's teeth and claws. It burned. The morning sky grew light and my terror and fury faded into pain. My food was gone and I had less than a half-gallon of fresh water left. No one knew where I was or had any idea how to search for me. I took off my T-shirt and tied it around the wound on my leg. The loss of blood and the ebb of adrenaline left me weak and shaking.

I pulled the kayak to the water's edge, falling to my knees several times. Pain shot through my body when I put any weight on my wounded leg. I left the tarp and bug juice behind. I couldn't stand the thought of climbing up the chickee platform to retrieve them. It didn't matter. I would either make it home that day or not at all. I pushed the kayak into the water and climbed aboard. Dense fog crept over the water, making it impossible to guess what lay ahead. The slightest breeze made me shiver. My teeth slammed together so hard my jaw ached. I paddled blindly, consulting the compass to keep heading east. If God existed, he was surely laughing at me now. What a mess I'd made of everything. Morning sun rose and burned off the fog across the water, but the ability to see didn't clarify my path. The mangroves were a maze.

I'd gone searching for a dead man and I felt near death myself. Fever overtook me. The chills left me shivering under the hot sun. The exposed skin of my back and shoulders burned and stretched tight. When I dipped my paddle into the water, I feared something would snatch it from my hands. My head ached and my arms felt heavy. I had no idea which direction I traveled. My kayak seemed to spin in circles.

The delusions started midday. Dreams of people I never knew came to me like bedtime stories. The smell of rotting fish filled my nose and I wondered if the waters beneath me were poisoned or if, like the water from the quarry, they were cursed. Maybe the waters weren't cursed at all. Maybe the curse traveled with me. I closed my eyes against the searing sun and waited to die.

I found myself back at the quarry, back at the waters where my sister disappeared. I dreamed of soldiers and slaves, of wealthy men and powerless women, of blues music on a dark night. I dreamed of the Choctaw chief who'd signed over the land where the quarry stood. I dreamed of dark-skinned men, driven by a whip and threatened with guns, digging the quarry with crude tools under sunlight and moonlight. The men dug a thousand pounds of gray rock from the spring bed, which branched out from nearby rivers. The rivers carved rocks from mountains five hundred miles away. The mountains rose up from prehistoric seas. The seas formed from ancient glaciers. By the time the water-washed and ice-smoothed rocks were deposited in the flat land near the woods, they were the size of a man's palm and gray as death. I dreamed of the things they pulled from the rocky earth: fossilized pottery, hard slabs of petrified wood, shards of bone, a fragment of human skull, blood-stained flesh.

I smelled the rotten stink of sulfur and the warm salt-scent of blood. I smelled my mother's cigarettes and buttery lemon cake and the grape aroma of hyacinths in bloom. And I felt my mother's hands, cracked and dry, against my face. I felt Bubba's warm breath against my ear. I felt the warm plop of raindrops on my belly. I felt the rope swing between my fists, my palms blistered and oozing. And I heard my mother's rattling cough. I heard a terrible sad song. I heard men chanting and women screaming and children running for their lives. I heard the Devil whisper and I heard a baby cry. I heard the screech of metal against stone.

And I knew we were all the same—the people of the Delta and the people of the Everglades, the people of the rivers and of the cold, burbling springs and of the warm Gulf waters and of the swamps and of the oceans, the people who lived a hundred years ago and the ones who weren't yet born. My ancestors slept beneath the water, slept beneath the rocks, slept beneath the shell mounds and the mangroves and the cypress strands, slept beneath hardwoods and soft cedar, slept beneath sugarcane and cotton. But Daddy wasn't sleeping. I felt him with me on the surface of the water. There were so many things I wanted to tell him, so many questions to ask.

The rumble of approaching death sounded suspiciously like a boat motor. I opened my eyes. Ghosts and dreams receded. A small skiff towed my kayak through the water.

"Hey!" I shouted.

The man in the skiff didn't hear me, or didn't acknowledge me. We circled the islands. Water sprayed gently across my body. My throat burned. I tried to shout again, but couldn't. The man turned back to me and nodded. He wore a long beard and a fisherman's hat. His skin was the color of leather and his smile was so familiar.

Stop, I thought. *Stop and let me see you.*

But the man kept going. We seemed to be heading out to sea. My leg pulsed with pain. My mouth went dry. I felt around for the bottle of fresh water, but it was gone. The man shifted his boat to just above an idle as we drew near a sandy shore. He tethered his skiff and pulled me toward him, hand-over-hand across the towline. At shore, he lifted me from the kayak and carried me across a narrow path. We came to a wooden structure, not a chickee with an open roof or a loosely woven thatch, but a two-room cabin with a propane stove and a cistern of fresh rainwater.

He placed me on a bed, a single mattress on a stack of wooden crates. He unwrapped my leg, poured something cold and stinging across the wound. Sweat pooled on my exposed belly, yet I shivered. The man covered me with a soft quilt. He placed a copper mug with fresh water against my lips and held my head so I could drink. Cold water slipped across my tongue and chased away the nightmare visions. The man wrapped my leg in clean strips of cloth. He placed his rough palm against my forehead. He slipped a pill into my mouth and brought the water to my lips again. I resisted, because I didn't know what he gave me, until he ran his thumb across my throat and I swallowed without thinking. He told me a story I wouldn't remember, except sometimes in my dreams.

My vision blurred and my eyes grew heavy. I dozed, though I fought to stay awake. I knew this man. He was the creature from the woods, the one I'd seen in the flash of lightning on the day we lost Pansy. He'd found me or I'd found him. And I knew for sure what I'd always suspected, but couldn't admit. The creature from the woods wasn't a monster and he wasn't an apparition either. He wasn't a figment of my dark imagination. He was my father.

SHE LOOKED STRONG. THE muscles of her arms and legs were ropy and thick. Her hair, sun-streaked and tangled, hung past her shoulders. She had a pretty face; not the sort of pretty that would turn any heads, but the kind of face you'd be glad to see over a plate of eggs every morning.

Earl tended her wound and covered her sunburnt skin with one of his shirts. He gave her fresh water. If a wild animal had caused her injury, he knew he didn't have much time. She needed more than a couple of aspirin. It was a shame. He'd like to talk to her for a while. It seemed like years since he had a real conversation with anyone but his sister, and even those visits were rare. Becoming a new person was like printing money. You needed to let the ink dry before circulating. His ink was still wet.

In a large zippered pocket of her cargo shorts he found a plastic bag with a gray stone, the newspaper article about his tours, one of his sister's carvings, a letter in a handwriting he recognized, and a photo he hadn't seen in three decades. He slid the photo inside a book at his bedside. He held the stone in his fist. It was colder than the water of the quarry on the day when he dove and dove and failed to save his sister's baby, failed to save Ora. He tossed the rock as far as he could into the Gulf and hoped the waters would carry it away. He tucked the rest of her treasures back into the plastic bag and added the notebook he'd been writing in for so long. The stories belonged to her as much as they belonged to him. Maybe they would bring her some peace.

On her wrist, she wore a battered silver bracelet. He inspected the charms, looking for information about who she'd become. She'd become an adventurer, he decided. She'd become curious and brave. The hourglass charm had broken and spread its contents on the island. Next year, he'd have Mississippi wildflowers sprouting in the Florida sand.

He carried her to his boat, leaving the kayak on the island. He would think about her whenever he took it out. He delivered her to a spot where he knew someone would find her quickly. He waited off the shore and watched. It took only a few minutes before a man spotted her and called for help. He turned his boat south as the wail of the ambulance filled the air.

He disappeared into the mangroves and checked on the bundles of cash he'd stashed away years earlier. He'd thought dying would put an end to any search for him, but he was wrong. He'd escaped the law. It was tougher to escape your own family. The cash was right where he'd left it. Most of it was real. If he had to, he could start over somewhere else. He hoped it wouldn't come to that.

She'd called him Daddy.

"Your father is dead," he'd told her. And it was true. The man she'd known was gone.

EIGHTEEN

I WOKE TO SUCH whiteness I thought I was in heaven, but it was a hospital room, cold and sterile and bright. My eyes ached and my throat was sore. Someone took my hand and squeezed it. I squeezed back, still unable to see anything beyond the white lights and white ceiling tiles.

Willet spoke. "Bert? Jesus, Bert, are you with us?"

I tried to speak, but couldn't.

A woman came in, a nurse. She slipped a straw in my mouth and told me to sip, not gulp. The lukewarm water dribbled across my chin, but I managed to swallow. I coughed. My eyes focused and I saw the nurse's face, round and doughy and sweet. Her hair was as white as the ceiling. She smiled at me, closed-lipped but kind. "You gave your brother quite a fright."

"I'm sorry," I managed to say.

"I expect he'll forgive you." She moved around the room, writing notes on a clipboard and filling the cup at my bedside with fresh water. She ticked her tongue against the roof of her mouth as she worked, making a wet, clicking noise. "I'll be back," she said. "Rest."

When she left the room, Willet appeared in my field of vision. "Goddamn, Bert," he said. "What the hell were you thinking?"

"How did I get here?" I asked.

Willet said a man found me on a picnic table near the harbor. I was sunburnt and mosquito-chewed. I wore a man's denim work shirt with a note pinned to it. The note displayed one word scrawled in all-caps in a shaky hand: *RABIES?*

The hospital started me on a round of vaccinations. I'd already received the first shot, Willet told me. I'd get the next one in a few days. The doctor said we were lucky they had a supply of the vaccine on-site. I suffered from dehydration and sunburn. A bag of fluid dripped into my veins. The burn would fade. My mosquito-bitten arms and legs, pink and crusty with calamine lotion, would heal.

"I'm hungry," I said.

Willet promised to bring me a basket of hush puppies and fried grouper. I could see how worried he'd been when he thought he might lose me. I was ashamed about how I'd behaved when I found out about Cheryl's pregnancy and I tried to tell him so, but he waved his hand like none of it mattered. I told him about the man on the water, the one who'd cleaned my wound and given me his shirt. I tried to tell him about our father, but Cheryl showed up and fussed over me.

She told me not to talk so much. "You should try to sleep," she said. Already she was becoming maternal.

Cheryl and Willet left me at the hospital. They promised to return with supper and icebox pie. Alone, I sorted through my possessions. The clothes I'd been wearing were gone, replaced by a clean hospital gown, but my plastic sack of treasures lay on a shelf across the room. I asked the nurse to bring the bag to me. The quarry rock was missing as was the photo of Daddy and Chester and the girl, but in their place was a small thick notebook, its pages warped from water damage. The cover was softer than skin and when I opened it there was a note scrawled on the inside of the front cover. *For you*, it said. The writing was smeared in places, but legible. I read the first pages about the birth of the quarry and wondered if it were fact or fable and if it mattered. I wondered which parts of my own adventure were real and which parts were nothing but a dream. I drifted in and out of sleep for the rest of the day, waking briefly when the nurse came to check my vital signs and when someone dropped a tray in the hallway. At one point, Iggy was there. He sat on the hard plastic chair next to my bed and cried.

"It's okay," I told him.

"I knew you were up to something foolish," he said.

The bedside phone rang in the late afternoon. Granny Clem told me she was mighty glad to hear my voice. "Willet said you got yourself into a big mess," she said. "Was it worth it?"

I thought about it. The doctor said I could have died and I knew he wasn't exaggerating, but I'd gone searching for my father and I believed I'd found him. I had the book of stories, which was more than I'd ever had before.

"It was worth it," I said.

Granny Clem asked if I needed her to come for me. I thought about how nice it would be to have Granny Clem serving me hot tea and soup, but I didn't like the idea of her driving so far alone. I heard her cough and the slight wheeze in her breathing. I knew Granny Clem would drop everything for me, but I was grown now and I couldn't ask her to do it.

"I can take care of myself," I said.

As promised, Willet and Cheryl came by in the early evening with supper from the Crab House. They laid out Styrofoam containers filled with fried fish and sliced pickles. Audie came along. I ate from a tray while they pulled chairs around my bed and ate off their laps. The nurse came by. I offered her a hush puppy.

Willet and Cheryl and Audie asked me questions, but they didn't pause long enough for me to answer. I wanted to tell Willet about the man who'd saved me, but I knew Cheryl and Audie would think my story was ridiculous. They would say I'd imagined the whole thing. Our father was supposed to be dead. We'd buried him. How could I say he was alive without sounding foolish or delusional? It was a story for my brother, a family story; I couldn't blurt it out in front of anyone else. So I told them about the raccoon and how I got lost, despite my map and my compass. Audie kept saying he was sorry I'd gotten lost. He apologized for the bad channel markers. It would be months before I understood why he felt responsible.

After I left the hospital, I stayed with Willet and Cheryl for a week. I hated it. Cheryl's father wandered through the house in the middle of the night, opening doors or banging on them if they were locked. He mumbled to himself and shouted at us for no reason. My wound and my sunburn healed bit by bit. I went to the hospital every few days for injection boosters and a checkup, but after five days I insisted on going back to the apartment. I'd gotten used to living alone and I liked it.

When I told the story of the man who'd dressed my wounds and cared for me, people assumed I was rescued by one of the Everglades hermits. And I suppose I was, though I believed I knew the identity of this hermit. Willet, when I told him, was skeptical. I'd been hallucinating and babbling when they brought me to the hospital, and he thought I was imagining things. When I showed him the newspaper photo and article, he went pale. He recognized Daddy.

"It can't be him," Willet said.

"But it is."

"No, he's dead. We buried the sonofabitch."

"Willet—"

"No!" Willet slapped the paper down between us. He seemed angry.

"Look at his eyes, Willet. Look at his smile."

"It ain't possible."

He knew it was possible. If any man could disappear and become someone new, it was our father. I told Willet what I'd been doing on the kayak, how I'd been searching for Daddy. "I was looking for him, but he found me."

"Come on, Bert."

"It's true."

I produced the book of stories as evidence. Willet flipped through the notebook and shook his head. "It can't be," he said.

"He's alive."

"It ain't possible."

Willet fixed me a glass of juice and watched while I took the prescribed painkillers and antibiotics. "I need you to promise me something, Bert." One of the pills had wedged in my throat and I gulped more juice to force it down. "I need you to promise me you won't ever go looking for him again."

"But, Willet!"

"Not on your own," he said. "Not without me. Promise?"

"But you're always so busy. You're always working or with Cheryl. And now you're going to have a baby . . ."

"Goddammit, Bert," he said. "This ain't a negotiation. It's too dangerous. We can go back out sometime, you and me, but not on a fucking kayak and not alone. Understand?"

"Really?"

"Yeah, but I won't go stirring shit up before the baby comes. Cheryl's dad is enough to handle. The last thing this baby needs is two batshit crazy grandfathers. Can you understand that?"

"But the baby won't be here for months," I said.

"I need you to trust me, Bert."

I wanted to trust him. I wanted to believe he'd keep his word. I agreed, but I couldn't trust anyone but myself. Willet wanted to take the book of stories, but I wouldn't let him. At night I read from the book and wondered how much of it was true. Granny Clem had said Daddy loved to hear her stories just as I had. Now I knew how a story could take on new life in the telling and retelling and reimagining. If the stories in the book were true, it meant Granny Clem wasn't my blood relation. It meant Chester wasn't my uncle. It meant I had an aunt out there somewhere, an aunt who was raising my sister. It meant Pansy was alive. If the stories were true, then so many things I'd believed about my life were a lie. Yet I didn't feel deceived. I felt enlightened.

My body healed, though I would always have a jagged scar on my leg. Iggy hired me to lead tourists through the mangrove tunnels. I pointed out the air plants and the turtles and the swamp chickens and the anhinga. I showed them how to use their monkey arms. Sometimes, if I sensed they wanted a tall tale, I told them the story of my kayaking trip and the rabid raccoon and the Everglades hermit. I had become one of the stories of the Everglades. At least I wrote it myself.

In January, Cheryl went into labor in the middle of the night. Willet was on the water with Audie. She'd planned to have her baby at the hospital, but she called me and told me she'd changed her mind. She asked me to stay with her. "Willet says you know how to do this."

"Every woman knows how to do this," I told her.

I wished for Granny Clem's bag with the forceps and the pain-killing herbs, but I made do with what we had. I boiled a pair of kitchen tongs in case I needed them. Thankfully, I didn't. I rubbed Cheryl's lower back as she moaned and breathed her way through the night. She cried out in pain a few times, but once she started pushing, the baby crowned and emerged with very little help from me. A girl, just as she'd suspected.

That baby was you.

She named you Rachel. I asked her if you were named for someone. She said no; it was just a name she liked. She said she didn't want you to feel saddled with someone else's name. Let me tell you, it's a beautiful gesture. Meaningless, probably, because we are all saddled with the baggage of our ancestors, but at least you know your mama never intended for you to carry the sins of others. She wanted you to start fresh. You should be grateful.

You were a fat pink baby and I called you my little piglet until Willet made me stop. He said it sounded insulting. I loved your plump cheeks and the many fat folds across your thighs. You were healthy and strong and beautiful. Cheryl let me hold you whenever I wanted. I carried you around for months. Your milky smell rubbed off on me and anyone who saw us together believed you were mine.

I hated myself for all the times I thought Willet would be better off if Cheryl didn't have a baby. I had no way of knowing that baby would turn out to be you. I had no way of knowing how different you would be from the babies I held at Granny Clem's house. How can I explain it? When you looked at me, even in those first weeks, it was with a fierce sort of love and possessiveness. You grabbed my hair or my shirt with your chubby fists and held tight. Cheryl had to pry you from me, uncurling your tiny fingers one by one to force you to let go. And I never wanted you to let go. Even when you pulled out a hunk of hair from my head, I didn't mind. I wanted you to have anything you needed from me. I wanted to be a part of you.

Willet spoiled you with toys and swings and playpens full of soft blocks. Cheryl dressed you in ruffles and bows, always in some shade of pink. I knew they meant well, but I also knew you didn't need toys or frilly dresses. You needed me. I needed you. When Pansy disappeared, I couldn't understand why anyone would take a child from her mother. Could anything be crueler? But in the first months of your life, there were a dozen times when I fantasized about running away with you. I imagined us living in a small house with a small garden. Maybe we'd have a cat. I could picture you crawling, walking, running through the kitchen while I cooked.

It was an early morning in July, almost a year past my ill-advised kayaking trip, when federal agents arrested your daddy and Uncle Audie for smuggling marijuana. They arrested dozens of men. News reports from that week said they took all the men, which, of course, wasn't true. They didn't arrest Iggy or the man who snapped photos of tourists holding a baby alligator. They didn't arrest Cheryl and Audie's father. They didn't arrest the man who'd pulled me to safety. They seized the sports cars, the four-wheelers, and the speedboats. They seized the stereos and entertainment systems, the Rolexes and the diamonds.

Cheryl called me on the morning of the arrests. She asked me to come sit with you. She said Willet and Audie would be free on bail soon and we could all talk about what to do next. I told her I didn't understand.

"My brother is not a criminal," I said.

"He protected you, Bert." She was annoyed with me. "He didn't want you to know. He always protected you."

I called Granny Clem. She told me to stay calm. "I'll think of something," she said. "There are ways to get him out of this."

Cheryl bailed out Willet and Audie with her father's money. When I said I didn't realize her father had any money, she rolled her eyes and told me to stop being so naive. They'd been banking money under her father's name for months. She said the feds would never take funds from a senile and sick old man. She was wrong. After months of investigations and questioning, they froze the accounts where the money was stashed.

When Cheryl's father died, she said she was glad he never understood what was happening in those final months. "He'd have hated being mixed up in all this."

I moved in with you and your mama in your grandfather's home, which he'd owned outright before any of the smuggling started. The feds took all the cars and we were left with nothing but the old truck from White Forest. They took Audie's fishing boat and they came for the kayaks, as well. It gave me some satisfaction to tell them one of the kayaks was lost in the mangroves.

Your great-grandmother tried to save Willet. She offered to set him up with a new identity, but said he'd have to make a fresh start somewhere. He wouldn't be able to stay in Everglades City or return to White Forest. He said he couldn't leave Cheryl and he couldn't leave you. Granny Clem offered to create a new identity for Cheryl as well.

"Better than witness protection," she promised. "Even the government won't know where you are."

But Willet said he couldn't live the rest of his life pretending to be someone else. He'd always be waiting for someone to recognize him or learn the truth about his past. He pled guilty and got ten years. The lawyer told him he'd be out in seven with good behavior.

Your Uncle Audie got fifteen years. He'd been running drugs longer than Willet and was more deeply entrenched with the Colombians. During the months when the trials took place, I learned about the business of smuggling. It wasn't complicated. The men took their fishing boats out to meet a mother ship in the Atlantic. Or they waited for helicopters to drop floating bales at a designated spot. They fished the bales from the water and stashed them among the mangroves of the Ten Thousand Islands until it was safe to load the bales in the backs of trucks. The same people who delivered fresh fish to grocery stores and seafood restaurants delivered marijuana across the east coast of the United States. The men kept the DEA agents confused by switching out channel markers, altering landmarks, and taking complicated routes to keep outsiders lost. Iggy's map was wrong because men like Audie and Willet made it wrong. They were the reason I got lost among the islands.

Nearly everyone was in on the smuggling. Local sheriff's deputies warned the men when the DEA started asking questions and told them where the agents were searching. The men moved the drugs, always one step ahead of the law. They were dubbed Saltwater Cowboys by the national media. They called their bales of marijuana "square grouper." Everyone knew. Everyone but me. So many secrets and lies. From that point on, I vowed to know the truth and tell the truth, even when it was unpleasant. Especially when it was unpleasant.

Here is the truth: your father is not a bad man. He wanted to take care of us. He took care of me and Mama when Daddy and Pansy disappeared. He took care of you and your mama. I'm not proud of myself for being one of the people who took so much from him. Maybe if he hadn't felt such a strong need to provide for us, he wouldn't have fallen into the business of bringing bales of marijuana across the Gulf of Mexico during the "just say no" years of Reagan's America. But maybe not. Maybe he'd have found his way to a criminal life no matter what. He is, after all, Daddy's son.

With Willet and Audie serving time, your mama and I took care of you. She returned to work at the grocery store. She could no longer afford to be a stay-at-home mom. I worked for Iggy, leading river tours. For the most part, I worked in the mornings and your mother worked the closing shift at the store. In between, we handed you off and traded stories about what you'd done that day, when you'd eaten, whether you'd spit up, or if you were fussy. You were a good baby. You laughed often, slept well, and ate hungrily. The whole town came to love you. It would be a while before we saw any sort of baby boom in the Everglades, what with most of the strong, healthy men behind bars.

While Cheryl worked, I took you for long walks through town. I walked along the path beside the canal and stared into the eyes of the alligators sunning themselves on the banks. I pulled you closer into my chest when I saw the creatures and thought about all the things I would sacrifice to save you if you were ever in danger.

Everything. I would sacrifice everything for you.

During one of those walks, we passed the schoolyard as the final bell rang in the afternoon. I watched children run across the green lawn to a line of waiting buses and cars. I saw her. Long dark curls and bronzed skin. Green almond-shaped eyes, that familiar smile. My breath stopped and you must have sensed it, because you started crying. You never cried on our walks. Your sudden wail drew the attention of the girl and the woman who drove the car, the woman who couldn't be her mother, but who looked so much like her I could hardly believe it. The girl met my eyes and something flickered across her face, recognition or concern. I opened my mouth to speak, but she ducked into the car and looked away. I stood there, dumbfounded, on a sidewalk teeming with children, and you, screaming in my arms. I didn't know what to do next. I walked home.

For the next month, I paced our walks to pass by the schoolyard at the same time each day. Most days, I saw the girl. I believe she saw me. One day I got the nerve to speak to her.

"Are you okay?" I asked. "Are you safe?"

She stroked your cheek. "Pretty baby," she said.

"She doesn't belong to me," I told her. What I meant to say was that I wasn't your mother, but it came out wrong.

"Of course she doesn't," the girl said. "No one belongs to anyone."

She turned and climbed into the waiting car. The woman driving the car gave me a suspicious look as she pulled away. I realized Pansy would be nearly thirteen years old by then, just one year younger than I'd been when she disappeared.

In that moment, I was back in White Forest, back in the old house with Mama and Willet and Pansy. I could smell the cornbread baking and the fresh towels from the laundry basket. I could see Pansy lolling on her back, sucking an ice cube in front of the box fan. I could hear Willet cussing the heat. What if we hadn't gone to the quarry? What if the quarry was never dug at all? Would it have made any difference for us?

I went back to the school the next day and the one after that, but I never saw the girl again. I asked around and was told they'd moved. No one seemed to know where. Most days I believe the girl I saw was Pansy, but then I start thinking it's too much of a coincidence. It couldn't have been my sister. When I first saw her, I considered calling the detectives who'd searched for Pansy years before, but the police never brought us any good news. I didn't believe they would help us now. I called Granny Clem, told her I'd seen a girl who could be Pansy, but I didn't trust my own eyes. So many years had passed.

Granny Clem sounded weaker each time we talked and I called her more often to make sure she was alive. I talked Cheryl into taking a road trip to White Forest during the wet season when you turned a year old. There weren't many tourists then and I knew Iggy could spare me and the grocery store could spare her. We drove for two days, retracing the path Willet and I took three years earlier. You were such a good little traveler. You slept a lot and your mama and I sang silly songs we remembered from our childhood. *Nobody likes me, everybody hates me, guess I'll go eat worms* and *They built the ship Titanic.* Songs of isolation and death and tragedy set to happy tunes and I wondered how we could hand down so much sadness, but you laughed and clapped your hands and asked for more.

Granny Clem was so happy to see you. She said she could tell you'd been pulled into the world by skilled and loving hands. She cradled you in her lap and rocked you until you slept. She whispered stories in your ear, and I strained to hear them. She looked frailer and thinner, but she was very much alive. At night, while you slept beside your mother, Granny Clem and I sat up drinking tea and talking. I showed her the book of stories. She ran her hands across the ink-filled pages and her eyes welled with tears.

"Thank you for sharing this with me," she said. "It's not easy for me to talk about those days, when your father was a boy. We lost so much."

I told her I'd started my own book of stories, a new notebook with my memories from our childhood and the story of the trip to Florida. My memory was like a series of interconnected caves, each one containing something new and surprising. The more I wrote, the more I knew.

"Memory is like that," she said.

I asked her if she thought Fern would make a good mother.

"The best," Granny Clem said. "I have no doubt."

She gave you a stuffed rag doll that smelled of lemons. She said the doll contained a magic heart to keep you safe and happy. She folded the three of us in her arms before we drove away: me, you, your mother.

I now understand why Granny Clem kept so many things from me. She hadn't wanted to admit we weren't related by blood, but I knew it didn't matter. We were family, all of us. For good or for evil, we were bound together.

I saw a curtain move as we drove past Chester's trailer and I saw Chester's face in the grimy window. He put a hand to the glass and I lifted my own hand to wave goodbye, but we didn't slow down for a visit.

We drove past Mama and Daddy's old house before we left town. Your mama wanted to see where your daddy was raised. But I refused to drive her past the spot where Pansy disappeared, past the old quarry. No good has ever come from that plot of land. No good ever came from its water or from its rocks or from the woods surrounding it. It's a place for ghosts and spirits, a place where the past lives on forever, but it's not a place for you.

I tell you all this because I don't want our secrets to drown you.

Your daddy will be released from prison right about the time you start school. You won't know him. Going to visit him once a month won't be anything compared to having him home every day. I suspect you'll be mad at him for missing so much. Try to forgive him. He'll do his best to take good care of you.

You'll have a nice life if you want one. You'll travel. You'll read books. You'll meet people who speak different languages. You'll eat exotic food. You'll have your babies in hospitals where doctors and nurses hover to stamp out infection. You'll believe in God. You'll believe in science. You'll believe in the Devil and monsters and fairy tales. You'll believe in flying saucers and government conspiracies and extra-sensory perception. You'll visit fortune-tellers and preachers and professors. You'll take up baking. You'll write poetry. You'll sing in a band. You'll search for truth and reason when the world makes no sense, when bombs blow up buildings, when tyrants are elected, when friends hang themselves, when babies die because no one bothered to feed them. You'll carry with you the curse of the quarry and the secrets of the swamps and the rivers and the ocean.

I'll teach you how to kayak. You'll welcome the ache of your shoulders after a long day with the paddle. You'll never be lost on the water, because the water is part of you. But someday you might row a far piece and find yourself on the edge of the world, where alligators and crocodiles live, where manatees swim, where sharks circle, where dolphins play, and where dead men walk among the mangroves.

Don't be afraid.

You were born from cotton slaves and plantation owners, from preachers and kitchen help, from healers and murderers, from liars and truth-tellers, from criminals and lawmakers, from bigots and from the oppressed, from monsters and saints. You were born from water and from earth and from blood.

And someday you may feel them watching you; those creatures crouched beyond the trees, hiding in the water, lurking on the horizon, those creatures that live beneath shifting sands, above the dark clouds, or beyond the stars. But I tell you they aren't beasts or ghosts or aliens come to read your dreams. Those eyes you feel watching you are the eyes of your family.

They mean you no harm.

ACKNOWLEDGMENTS

My tales about Florida are pure fiction, but I was inspired by true stories and I'm grateful to the people who let me ask too many questions. These include Lynn McMillan of the Smallwood Store, and Justin and Alli of Shurr Adventures. Thanks to Alli for teaching me to use my "monkey arms." Thanks to Captain Kent of Allure Adventures for the tour of the Ten Thousand Islands and for sharing his memories about life in the Everglades in the 1980s. In addition, I read stories from reporters including Mike Clary and Peter B. Gallagher and I watched Billy Corben's documentary *Square Grouper: The Godfathers of Ganja*. Thanks to all the journalists doing the hard work of recording the truth every day.

To Sandra Bond for her support and for getting this manuscript to Chelsey Emmelhainz, who found a dozen ways to make it better. To Beth Canova for thoughtful notes and steady guidance. To Stella Connell for spreading the word. To Jordon Koluch, Erin Seaward-Hiatt, Sarah Vostock, Kim Lim, Cal Barksdale, and everyone at Skyhorse.

Special thanks to the Mississippi Institute of Arts and Letters, the Mississippi Library Association, the Willie Morris Award for Southern Fiction, and the Janet Heidinger Kafka Prize at the University of Rochester for the recognition of this book. I am so grateful.

Thanks always to Lighthouse Writers Workshop, my literary home. Much gratitude to the Amtrak Residency Program. Shout out to the members of Salon Denver.

Much love to my family, especially my mother. Finally, to my husband, who paddles alongside me in the vast ocean, in frigid mountain lakes, in warm Gulf waters, and in life—come high winds or low tide, I want you on my team.

Reading Group Guide

1. The title of this book is taken from a longer quote by William Faulkner: "The past is never dead. It isn't even past." What does this quote mean in the context of this novel?

2. Bert's search for her sister and her father consumes her life for many years. How does this obsession change Bert? How might Bert have been different if she'd never lost her family members?

3. Granny Clem provides medical help to women who cannot afford or don't have access to ordinary doctors. Some of the help she provides is illegal. Are there situations where breaking the law is morally justified?

4. The book provides glimpses of history or myth surrounding the quarry and Bert's ancestors. What makes these memories and myths important? Do you believe the quarry contains real evil or are the characters projecting evil upon it? How do these sections inform your interpretation of modern events?

5. Race and racism play a key role in shaping the town and people of White Forest. Though the town and the events that shaped it are fictional, there are many places in America with a long history of racial injustice. Can a town or a family ever escape the horrors of the past? If so, how?

6. The book contains a number of references to the supernatural, particularly in the stories surrounding the quarry. Why do the characters cling to stories about ghosts, aliens, curses, and monsters rather than looking for logical explanations when terrible things happen? Is this something particular to the South?

7. In the beginning of the book, Willet criticizes his father for being dishonest and criminal, but later Willet seems to follow in his father's footsteps. Why would he choose to live a life he finds so objectionable? In what ways are his choices different from his father and how are they similar?

8. At its core, the novel is about what makes a family. How does Bert's concept of family evolve throughout the course of the novel? What does she learn from the family members she interacts with and from the ones who have disappeared?

9. Granny Clem is a strong, independent woman who chooses to live outside the traditional feminine expectations of the South. Yet, she is one of the most maternal and nurturing figures in Bert's life. How do Granny Clem's unconventional choices influence Bert? What kind of woman do you think Bert will be when she is older?

10. The book explores the power of storytelling and secret keeping, particularly among family members. How do the stories the characters tell one another change over the years? Why do they keep some things secret? What is the difference between a story and a lie?